THE TALE OF THE SWAMP SONG

Crimson Smoke and the Emerald Flame

K.C. NORTON

RILEY ROOKHOUSE

Copyright ©2023 by Riley Rookhouse. All rights reserved. Published by Story Garden, Columbus. StoryGardenPublishing.com

Cover illustration by Hannah Elizabeth, HannahElizabeth.ca

Cover lettering by James T. Egan, BookflyDesign.com

Managing editor: Diane Callahan, QuotidianWriter.com

Copy editor: Angela Traficante, LambdaEditing.com

Sign up for notifications of upcoming releases by Riley Rookhouse at RileyRookhouse.com

 Created with Vellum

Content Note

This story contains descriptions of untreated mental health, self-harm, and suicidal ideation.

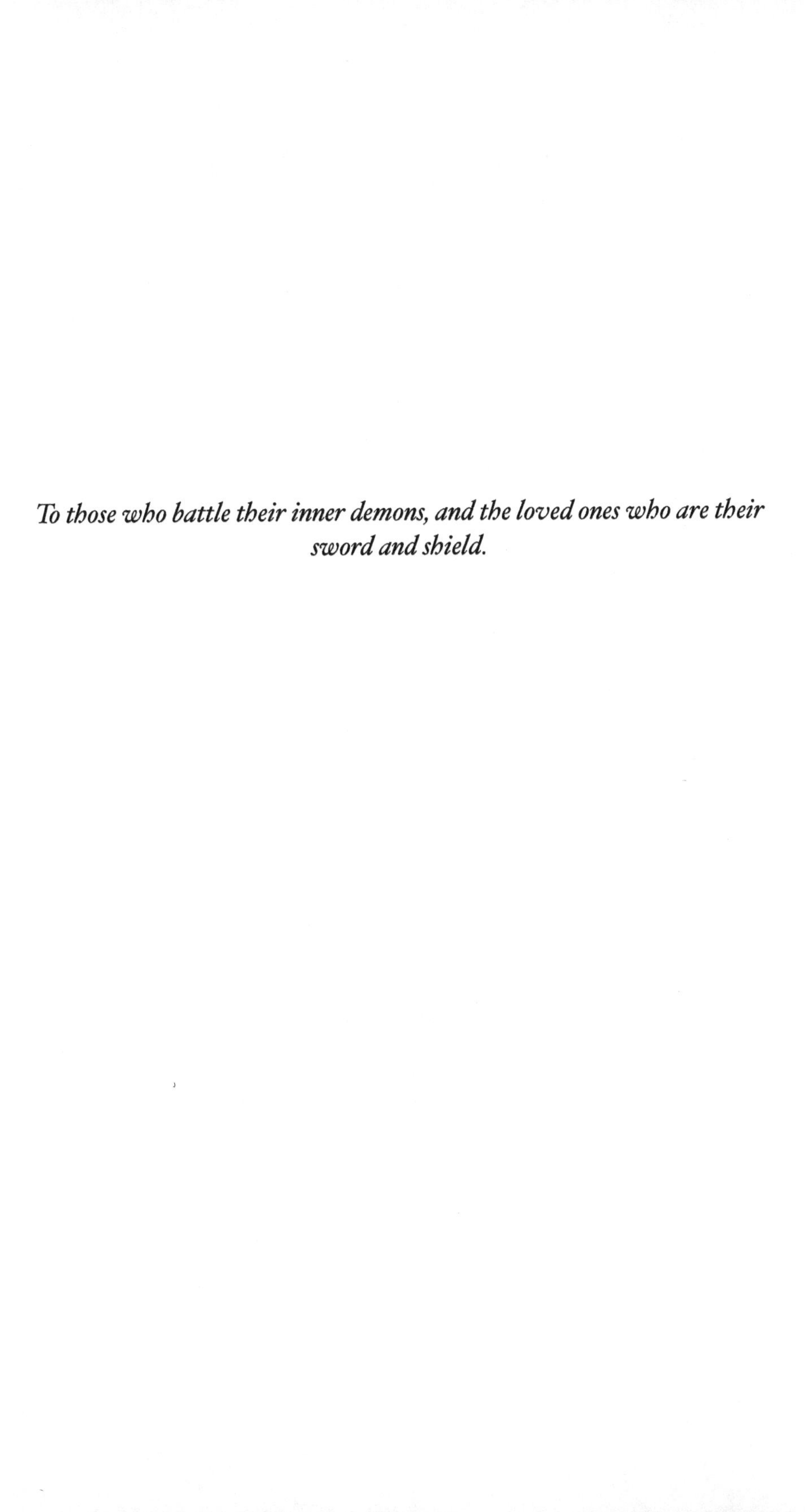

*To those who battle their inner demons, and the loved ones who are their
sword and shield.*

Chapter One

The doctor, the Lightweaver, and I stared down at the babblebird in alarm. I'd encountered the creatures on the second day of my existence, when Lower Bound's resident auger, Amaya, introduced us to the menagerie living in her rafters.

In general, babblebirds were squat and plump avians of middling size, with clever eyes and large banded beaks. Their excellent memories made them useful for sending word-for-word messages across vast distances. Last spring, Aindreas had killed one that was meant to report back to the Conjury. Now, one of its portly cousins sat on Tincrown's kitchen table, scratching its face languidly with a three-toed foot.

Emerald's sturdy, thick-knuckled hands were pressed together, shielding his mouth. I would have been able to tell that he was deep in thought, even if I hadn't had a direct line of connection to his mind.

As it stood, I could hear his thoughts loud and clear. *[No, dammit. Please, don't make us leave.]*

In the time I had known him, Emerald had changed a great deal. His formidable size hadn't altered in the six months since I gained sentience, but he carried himself differently. Instead of walking with his shoulders rolled toward his ears, he carried himself more upright. His eyes were no longer sunken in his face, and I'd seen him smile more in the last few hours than in all the time we'd worked together to solve the mystery of Dyrne. He'd even let his black hair grow out a little, so that it curled around his ears, framing his moss-hued face, and he no longer confined himself to grunting and pointing, as he had done those first days in Lower Bound.

It didn't take a genius to work out the reason for the half-jotunn's change of spirits. As much pleasure as it gave me to taunt him for his obvious affections for Tincrown, the doctor was evidently better at more than healing open wounds or determining the cause of a victim's death. When I had allowed myself to be banished in the spring, Emerald was like a houseplant kept too long in the dark. In Tincrown's company, he had blossomed into a livelier version of himself.

I could not read the doctor's thoughts, but as Tincrown stroked his newly grown beard, I noted that his fingers were shaking. He was not the only one who feared what the babblebird's message would mean for the pair of them. He was a slight fellow, and at first glance was Emerald's opposite in every way, to a near-comical extent. He was only a little taller than I was in my form as Simon, yet he barely reached Emerald's chin. If he ever decided to leave the life of a physician behind, he might easily find work as a beanpole. His black hair had been allowed to grow out in my absence, and his narrow face and prominent nose were, when taken with the rest of his features, extraordinarily pleasing to the eye. Distinctive, even. In what little of the summer sun reached the high village, his already burnished skin had deepened to the color of new copper.

He was not, by any means, as handsome as *I* was, but I was sure that there were some who wondered what drew him to Emerald.

I did not wonder. I knew Emerald enough to understand that he was the rare sort of man whose affections ran deep and true. They were more alike than unalike. If I searched over the whole island and the continent beyond the seas, I was positive that I would never find two people more suited to one another than these two lovestruck fools.

And now this damnable babblebird was threatening to tear them apart.

Since both of my companions were so obviously reluctant to speak, it fell to me to coax the fat, striped creature into speech.

"Could you repeat that?" I asked.

The bird stopped grooming itself and returned both feet to the table before straightening up and speaking in the voice of an older woman. *"Harpax sends greetings. Your employers will be speaking to his good friend as soon as possible. If you are available, come around for tea at your earliest convenience. Reply preferred."*

"Gods." Emerald massaged his forehead. "What does that mean?"

"Simple enough." I crossed my arms and turned to face him, making every appearance of leaning my hip against the kitchen table. In reality, I was little more than a refracted collection of light made to *look* like a person, who—for reasons that confounded and annoyed my creator—had become more than mere illusion some six months before. So I couldn't truly touch the table.

But, as I had discovered over the course of my young life, I could certainly put on a show.

"You remember Harpax. Maximilien's horse?" I waved at the babblebird. "Amaya has been kind enough to inform us that the Conjury—*your employers*—will be questioning Maximilien as soon as possible." I tapped my finger against my lips and stared at the ceiling. "Which will be a trick, given that Maximilien has been dead almost as long as I've been alive."

Emerald leveled a venomous glare at me. "Yes, *thank you*, Crimson. However would we have worked that out without the benefit of your staggering intellect?"

"Play nice," Tincrown said with a chastising tap on Emerald's large hands and a small smile.

"Do they have ways of doing that?" I asked, looking between the two men. "Questioning the dead, I mean?"

"I'm sure they've found one." Emerald lifted one hand and ticked off the possibilities as they occurred to him. "A necromancer, or a spiritualist, or a seer... all of which are rare enough, but the Conjury has the resources to track anything down."

Tincrown flinched, and I couldn't blame him. Fear of the Conjury had sparked the troubles that had plagued his town for the last two years, and we had only *just* worked out a plan to hide Dyrne and its invisible residents from the long, grasping arm of the organization. Kovin Isle stood at the southernmost reaches of Conjury territory, and from what I had gathered, the mainland-based bureaucracy's presence on the island was limited. If it kept expanding, however, Dyrne's future was at stake.

None of which would matter, of course, if the corpse of Maximilien could be questioned. The dead scout had worked out Dyrne's magical secret even before we had. His attempts to contact the Conjury had failed, but if his spirit could be interrogated through manipulation of the *Aidea*, Dyrne would soon fall prey to the Conjury's machinations.

"If there's any danger of Dyrne being discovered, we have to go," Emerald said. "We should meet with Amaya. See what she knows."

"I'm ready as soon as you are," I told him.

"Come on," Emerald told the doctor. "We should pack." He made a move toward the staircase at the back of the little house, but Tincrown caught his arm. A long look passed between them, and for the first time, I had a sense of what it was like to be on the *outside* of a silent conversation.

"Crimson," Tincrown murmured, "would you please give us a moment alone?"

He won't come with us, I realized. *Dyrne needs a doctor, and now that the town has been stricken from the map, there's no way to send for another. Tincrown can't leave, or the town will have to make do without a trained medic.*

And we *have to leave so that we can interfere with the Conjury's plans, or else Dyrne's secret might be discovered.*

Emerald stood frozen with the doctor's hand on his arm, perfectly still except for the rapid expansion and contraction of his chest as he stared at Tincrown.

"I'll be upstairs!" I said loudly, and hurried to the steps. Because I had spent the better part of the last half-year unsummoned and nonexistent, I only had little more than an actual week of life experience. Even so, I knew that not every unfolding drama was meant to be shared with an audience.

※

Dyrne in autumn, as seen through the upstairs room of Tincrown's modest home, was a study in gold and scarlet. The thatched roofs of the little village, which rippled with green when we first arrived, had faded in patches to a warm brown hue. Some of them even bore drooping heads of wheat and amaranth seed. The surrounding forest boasted streaks of yellow and vermilion where the aspens and maples had begun to turn. Instead of the white bottlebrush flowers of spring, even the low-lying shrubbery that backed the houses was now as violently red as my own hair.

I caught sight of my reflection in the warped glass and smirked at the memory of a certain green-clad bard. It annoyed Emerald every time I wore Coirpre's colors, but the blue brocade dress that I wore presently was out of season and didn't match the landscape in the least. I squinted at the windowpane and willed my clothing to adjust to something more appropriate. Within seconds, my deep sapphire dress was replaced by a gold velvet jacket with carmine buttons and black embroidery, layered over loose-fitting black trousers. The outfit would have easily suited Simon, the male counterpart of my current form, but I adjusted the cut of the coat to make the neckline more feminine.

There, I thought. *On the off chance that we encounter someone of good taste along the road, they'll recognize that at least one of us knows our fabrics.* After all, the reason that Emerald had created me in the first place was to draw discerning eyes away from him.

The door behind me opened, and Emerald pushed through. He didn't meet my gaze as he began tossing things into his bag.

"Emerald?" I asked.

"I'll see you downstairs," he said gruffly.

I withdrew, stepping through the open door this time. On my way up, I'd had to pass straight through the polished wood.

Tincrown waited at the bottom of the stairs, nibbling his thumbnail and in obvious distress. The babblebird was no longer sitting on the table.

"Did you send it back?" I asked.

"Mm." Tincrown stared at the blank spot where the bird had been. "We had to let your friend know to expect guests."

I was jealous, at times, of Emerald's affection for the man. The only thing that stopped me from being *properly* annoyed about becoming a third wheel was the fact that the doctor so obviously returned those feelings for my partner in equal measure. Gods and goddesses knew that I was not above a bit of pettiness, but to stoop to disliking someone because he made my friend happier than *I* could was beneath even me.

Emerald emerged from the bedroom, and I took a long look at him. On closer inspection, I realized that he'd left the sleeves of his shirt rolled up to reveal the long-faded marks on his gray-green skin, something rather out of character for him.

"We're leaving," Emerald said. "We have to ask Amaya what she means. It's clear that she kept her message vague to ensure that even if the babblebird was intercepted, its meaning would be unclear. If she's taking such precautions, we should, too."

"Will you be traveling with us even part of the way?" I asked, meeting Tincrown's eyes. Part of me desperately hoped he would change his mind, but I couldn't tell if it was Emerald's wish or my own.

Both, more than likely. Emerald wanted Tincrown with him for his own sake, and I was concerned about what would happen to Emerald's newfound sense of confidence if we struck out on our own.

"I can't." The doctor's wistful expression was enough to make my heart ache. "I belong here. I told you before, this is where Ardus wants me, but Emerald is called in another direction."

"But surely—" I began.

"We've been over it." Emerald spoke in clipped tones, and each word landed like a physical blow. His emotions extended through our link, a bittersweet sadness that overflowed the connection between us. I had gathered from prior interactions that my friend believed himself unlovable. Now he had found someone capable of offering him the very sort of affection he craved, and he could not stay.

"Before you go, there's something else we ought to discuss." Tincrown sat down on the well-worn couch and patted the space beside him. "Don't you think, Em?"

"Do I have to?" Emerald muttered.

Tincrown's dark eyes narrowed. "You promised me that you would. Now, come here."

With a sigh, Emerald swayed over to the little couch and sat down heavily on the empty, faded cushion. The wood frame creaked under his weight. He ran his thumb across one palm, over and over, frowning down at the skin.

"In your own time." Tincrown kissed his cheek.

Emerald made a frustrated sound before lifting his eyes to mine. "I'm *supposed* to tell you about these." He pointed to the little scars ribbing his arms. I had seen them before, and I knew that similar marks covered his legs as well.

"Oh." I sank down to the floor, pulling my knees to my chest and bracing for him to tell me what I had suspected for most of my life.

"I did this." Emerald pressed his palms together to keep his hands from shaking. "Sometimes when I can't stand living in my own skin, I—" His head slumped forward on his shoulders, as if the weight of his words was too great to bear. "I need to do *something*. And I want to punish the person responsible for everything that makes me feel that way. So I do *this*. Did this. And Tincrown thought I should tell you, so now you know."

I wished that I could reach out to comfort him, but fortunately, Tincrown was not as limited on that front as I. He forced the fingers of one hand between Emerald's palms. His other hand traced a few of those marks, as if by touching them, he could force them to heal over, and the memory of all that pain would fade forever.

"That was then," Tincrown reminded him. "You're not there now. And you're not alone, Em. You have Crimson. And me, even if we can't be in the same place right now." He lifted Emerald's chin with his free hand and used his thumb to smear the stream of tears trickling down my friend's cheeks. "You have people who care about you. Remember?"

Emerald nodded, but he didn't speak. Instead, he turned away from the doctor and scrubbed at his face. "Anyway," he grunted. "You told me that I had to talk to someone about it, and Tincrown said *you* should know, partly because people *tell* each other things, and partly... I dunno. In case I ever feel the same way again."

"Do you think you will?" I asked.

He sniffed and refused to meet my eye. "Maybe. Probably. I dunno."

"All right." I rest my chin on my knees. "Thank you for telling me." I had known for some time that Emerald didn't value his life as highly as Tincrown and I did, but I'd never heard him admit it openly before.

"Are we done here?" he demanded, rocketing to his feet.

Emerald had always claimed otherwise, but as I sat there, it occurred to me that there might be some connection between the time I'd conjured myself into Emerald's presence and the time he'd conjured *me* into sentience. He'd been lonely, and from all he'd intimated, he'd never had anyone to rely on but himself. What if I was a wish?

"I suppose we're done here," I agreed. I was unlikely to get more answers today, and Emerald had already pushed himself enough.

"Then hurry up." Emerald hefted a large pack onto his shoulders. It was new, and it seemed to be handmade. Small flowers of all varieties were embroidered into the material. Among them, I recognized the distinctive purple petals of a *panacea forndulata*, the very flower that Tincrown had asked about on our first visit to that very house. White and blue asters bloomed along the straps.

"I'll walk you to the pass," Tincrown said. He got up, too, and took Emerald's hand. "The weather's fine for the moment, but you never know at this time of year. You might change your mind about leaving today and wait until tomorrow instead."

"Maybe," Emerald said.

But I had a window into his mind, and I knew he wouldn't.

Chapter Two

As we made our way along the road that cut through the town of Dyrne, High Priest Nechtan waved to us from the churchyard, where he was tending the graves with Errol the lambkin's assistance. Nechtan still wore his tall, deep purple headdress with its ornate gold stitching, but he no longer bothered with the bandages that had helped disguise the fact that he was invisible. It was rather strange, seeing his robes float around, apparently empty.

But far be it for me, someone made of little more than light, to judge someone's biology for being a bit unconventional.

"Greetings, Master Emerald," he called. While the high priest's back was turned, Errol shoved a fistful of weeds into his mouth before continuing his work.

Emerald returned the greeting with a wave, and he even forced a small smile onto his face. In the early days of our time in Dyrne, we had not been particularly friendly with the high priest of Dathan, but apparently that had changed in the six months Emerald had spent teaching him to cast the illusion that would protect the town from the Conjury's prying eyes.

The high priest approached the gate surrounding the cemetery, wiping his hands together to remove the dirt.

"Where are you going?" he asked.

"We have business near Lower Bound," Emerald said. "We'll be away for a while—just a few loose ends to resolve, to ensure that the Conjury has lost track of Dyrne."

"But you'll return, surely?" the high priest asked.

Emerald's eyes slid toward Tincrown. "If I can manage it. But if Crimson and I make our presence known, it won't be easy to disappear again without arousing suspicion."

[Hold on,] I demanded. **[I assumed we'd go to town, sort out this business with Amaya, and hightail it back here to your boyfriend. Is that not the plan?]**

Aloud, Emerald said, "People in the town know that we'd planned to investigate the deaths of the Conjury scouts. If we disappear entirely after making a brief appearance, it will only draw more suspicion."

"So you're not coming ba-a-ack?" Errol asked. His tufty white ears drooped, and he widened his huge brown eyes.

"Not for a while," Emerald said. "It's... it's what's best for Dyrne."

Silence descended on our little group, and Tincrown laid one hand on Emerald's back.

"Is there no other option?" Nechtan asked.

Emerald shook his head. "Not that I can see. Not if Dyrne is to remain hidden."

Nechtan reached over the gate and took one of Emerald's hands in his. "Thank you," he murmured. "This means more to me than I can say. To all of us. I know that it is not an easy choice, but—"

"But it's the right choice. I know." Emerald pressed his lips into a thin line. "You'll keep them safe, won't you?"

Nechtan's robes swirled as he nodded and clasped his hands before him. "I'll do as much as I can. And as far as Aindreas, I'll continue to do my best, trying to help rehabilitate him, although I don't hold out much hope." Nechtan shook his head. "He seems... broken. That's the only way I can explain it."

Having seen inside the man's head firsthand, I could only agree.

"You remember the spell I taught you?" Emerald asked.

"Of course. And I'll teach it to Kristine when the time is right. I expect that she will succeed me, although I wouldn't object to her being a *little* bit wiser before her real training begins." Nechtan withdrew and bowed to the pair of us. "Farewell, Emerald Flame. Farewell, Simone of the Road. Dyrne owes you a great debt, and you are welcome anytime."

"Safe travels!" Errol added, waving to us so vigorously that he nearly overbalanced.

I fell a few paces behind my companions as we walked the cart track through the woods. The turning trees painted the whole world in warm hues. The shadows were different, too. In spring, the land had been waking up. Now, it seemed to be preparing for a long slumber. Emerald and the doctor walked together, sometimes speaking, sometimes still.

All too quickly, we approached the narrow pass where Cassandra of Wishwind had fallen, and where Aindreas had attempted to send me to a similar fate. The space gave every appearance of being buried under a landslide, with the mountain face shearing away into the gully below. The path was entirely obscured.

"Here we are." Tincrown waved me over, then pointed out the inscription on the wall that danced with brilliant energy, much like his gloves or the Dawyd-goggles. It was cut into the stone alongside Cassandra's memorial. A reminder, perhaps, of what failing to renew the enchantment could cost.

The doctor caught Emerald's wrist and pulled him back. My companion made no attempt to pull away, but for a moment, he simply stared at Tincrown, as if frozen by some sort of spell. Slowly, almost fearfully, he lifted one hand to Tincrown's jaw, letting the pad of his thumb scrape over the peppering of stubble there. I clasped my hands behind my back, pretending to admire the view of the little river gorge running below us and the distant plane of the gray seas. Even so, I felt the rush of hope and fear that surged through Emerald as he pulled Tincrown into a lingering kiss.

[Mind your own business,] Emerald thought.

I kept my eyes averted. **[I didn't say a word.]**

Emerald released Tincrown and swayed back a pace toward the illusion of rockfall. "Let's go," he said. He hoisted his pack higher and stepped into the landslide, disappearing instantly.

"Stubborn," I murmured. "He's not even going to say goodbye?"

"We've said all that we had to say already," Tincrown assured me, still watching the place where Emerald had disappeared as if he might change his mind and return. "But before you go, I wanted to... to give you something, I suppose. If you don't mind." He extended his hand between us, palm up, as if hoping to take mine.

"It won't work like that," I told him. "I can't—" I mimed shaking his hand.

"I know. That's not what this is for. I want to show you something." He wiggled his fingers.

"Nothing private?" I asked, still wary.

"Private?" He chuckled. "Yes, I suppose it is. But it's mine, and I want you to have it."

Reluctantly, I lowered my palm to his, and I was met with an instant barrage of emotion. Kindness, affection, and adoration for my friend; a desire to protect and to heal, accompanied by the knowledge that such ministrations were beyond his skill; fear of what could happen if Emerald was left to himself; acceptance that loving someone whose hurt ran as deep as Emerald's meant that the pain might one day win.

I shivered, and my lip wobbled, but I did not pull away.

"Do you understand?" Tincrown asked. "I wanted you to know, because no matter how many times I've told him, I don't think he believes me."

I understood exactly what he meant. When I finally broke our connection, many of those exact emotions lingered, because they belonged to me, too.

"I'll watch out for him," I promised. "He's stubborn and difficult and sometimes completely impossible, but I'll be there for him."

"That's all anyone can do. Safe travels, Crimson." Tincrown waved one last time before turning back to the hidden village and beginning his trek down the path.

"Crimson! Are you coming?" Emerald's voice echoed back through the scree. "Stop dawdling!"

"I'm right behind you," I promised. With that, I stepped into the mass of conjured stones, passing through them as easily as open air, treading in darkness through the thick of the illusion.

If he already found a way to make the summoning automatic, he could have brought me back sooner than he did, I thought, but again, I kept the observation to myself. I knew exactly why he'd waited, and I didn't need our psychic connection to put the pieces together.

At last, I stepped back into the late morning sunlight and stared down at a remote and ragged landscape drenched in autumn gold. Emerald was a few dozen paces ahead of me.

We did not speak again for quite some time as we left the town of Dyrne and its inhabitants behind.

◈

Time was a slippery thing for me. Just like the natural world, I moved through it freely, but not always in the same way that others did. The seasons had changed while Emerald had been in Dyrne, and the landscape was new to me all over again.

"It's beautiful here," I said aloud.

"Mm," Emerald said. He was still in a sullen mood, and I could hardly blame him. I left him to his own devices and focused my attention on the scenery instead.

The rock wall to our right soon fell away, giving me an unobstructed view of the western part of the island. It was more rugged than the eastern coast, thick with evergreens and rocky outcroppings between this mountain range and the next. To our left, the land was marshy and low, cut through by waterways that ran eastward to the sea, which could be reached in less than two days on foot. Even from our high point, I could only see two settlements: a widespread patchwork of small farms in the valley below, surrounding what looked like a castle on the edge of the river, and the small port town at the mouth of the estuary. That was my birthplace, Lower Bound.

"Do you want to talk about Tincrown?" I asked.

Emerald snorted. "With you? No."

I pursed my lips in irritation, and he glanced back over his shoulder.

"You can read my mind," he explained. "And I'm not interested in having my private affairs unpacked for your entertainment."

"Affairs?" I waggled my eyebrows at him. "Is that *so*?"

He raised one finger toward the sky and shook it. "*This* is exactly why I'm not going to discuss him with you."

Fair enough. I mulled over a few other points over conversation, but they were all equally unpromising. *Do you think Aindreas will ever be rehabilitated? Will Dyrne be safe? Will Tincrown wait for you until you can find a way to get back to him, or is it over between you? What has the Conjury planned for Maximilien, and how are we going to stop it?* Every question that came to my mind was, I felt sure, also a question in Emerald's.

He was right. I *could* read his mind, more or less, and at the moment, what he craved was silence. As the reality of our present troubles sank in, I found myself happy to oblige him.

⁂

The scarlets and brasses of the leaves were lovelier from beneath the branches than they had seemed from the window. Even when the sky began to darken, I could not stop admiring the way the slanted autumn light gilded their edges.

Toward noon, a sheet of rain rolled in off the water, and the lower road became thick with mud. Emerald's bare feet were soon spattered with soil and flecks of shale, and his clothing was soaked through. The new leather bag he wore, however, remained perfectly dry. I wondered if it was enchanted with some sort of *Aidea*. It would be just like Tincrown to give Emerald something that would help protect him in small ways that he had never thought to care for himself.

In the afternoon, we sought refuge in the small cave where we had camped on the way in. The rain wasn't heavy enough to be a true obstacle, and it would be light for a few more hours. If we pressed on, we might make it to Lower Bound before nightfall, but I understood that Emerald was not quite ready to be back among people just yet.

He lit a small fire with a mixture of flint in the enchanted Ignius stone he'd used months ago on our ascent, crouched down beside it, shucking off his wet vest and shirt. He seemed more at ease with his own body than I remembered, but I kept the thought to myself.

From a pocket of his vest, he produced a small glass bottle of brilliant blue liquid that glimmered between his fingers as he removed the stopper. I recognized it as Errol's contraband brew, Shine of the Moon.

"Is that your supper?" I asked, lifting one eyebrow as I broke the silence that had lingered between us for hours.

"Gotta finish it before we're back in civilization," he said. He took a deep draught of it and sighed in contentment. "Gods, I'm going to miss this stuff. Tincrown and I—" He cut off abruptly and downed another swig. When he spoke again, his tone was deliberately casual. "How many of my thoughts can you read, exactly?"

"Too many," I deadpanned. Then a thought occurred to me. "I would assume that it's as many of *my* thoughts as *you* can read. Which is far from all of them, I hope?"

"Hard to say." Emerald smirked into his drink. "For all I know, your head's as empty as a beggar's safe."

I puffed up indignantly, although in truth, I was pleased that we seemed to have found our way back to normal conversation.

"So, when I don't summon you, you're not just... floating around in my head, spying on me?" he pressed.

"No, thank goodness."

Emerald nodded and let out a relieved puff of breath. He stared into the fire for a long moment.

"You know it's the solstice again?" he asked. "Back home, we used to celebrate the solstice with a festival. The brothers didn't all approve of us going, but Harmony convinced them that there was no harm in it."

"Harmony?" I asked. Emerald had never spoken to me of his childhood, and I didn't want to ask too many questions in case he changed his mind about telling me more now, but the way he said the name reminded me of how he spoke about Tincrown, with the same kind of gentle reverence.

"Brother Harmony. My—one of the monks." Emerald waved my questions away. "Just let me tell the story. The festival was one of my favorites." He closed his eyes, conjuring something in his memory. "According to the old story, there were two lovers: Regis of Glacial Walk and Ianna of the Oases. They had next to nothing in common, but the moment that they laid eyes on each other, they were bound by..." He stopped, sniffed once, and drank again. "Love, I suppose. Destiny. Fate. Whatever you want to call it."

"Just like that?" I asked.

Emerald shrugged. "According to the stories. They lived together for a few years, until one day Regis was killed. Ianna was heartbroken, but she was a powerful student of the *Aidea*. She prayed to the gods, and a priest of Driaweep told her that if she completed a ritual, she would be able to bring Regis back from the dead, and she, too, would be able to slip death's noose."

"Ooh." I leaned closer, watching his face intently. "Wait, who's Driaweep?"

Emerald rolled his eyes. "Aster's sake, Crimson, he's only one of the most powerful gods in the whole pantheon. So Ianna completed the ritual..."

"Any idea what it was?"

My friend puffed out his cheeks and glared at me. "Don't you *ever* stop talking?"

"I'm paying attention, I'm just curious!"

Emerald grumbled. "Stop asking questions, or I'm not going to finish."

"I'll be quiet as a mouse." I mimed locking my lips and throwing away the key.

"Fine. So Ianna completed the ritual, and she and Regis escaped death together. But instead of spending their days together for as long as the world turns, they each lived a half-life. In the winters, Regis ruled their estate; in the summer, Ianna returned from a deathlike sleep to take his place. They only met on the solstice. Twice a year, they were together. The rest of the time, they were alone."

I cocked my head and pondered his little tale.

"What?" he asked.

I shook my head and pointed to my lips.

"Oh, for *Aster's*... You can talk *now*, Crimson." He gripped the bottle of liquor in his hands, as if fantasizing about wringing my neck. Under his breath, he muttered, "*Impossible.*"

"So are they still alive?" I asked. "Trading places?"

"It's just a story." Emerald propped his chin against his palm. "It's an allegory about the seasons, and the holiday is an excuse to dance in public and eat too many cakes. If there were *really* rituals for cheating death, the Conjury would know about them by now, and they'd have elevated themselves to godhood. My point was that just because two people are drawn to each other doesn't mean that it always works out, not even in the stories. I'm lucky to have met Tincrown. That's all." He drained the last of his drink and stuffed the empty bottle in his pack. "And now, I'm going to sleep."

He settled down on his dry bedroll next to the flames and closed his eyes. Soon enough, he was snoring, lulled to sleep by a bellyful of Shine of the Moon and not much else.

I sat, staring out at the rain, wondering what Amaya would be able to tell us. I was worried, too, about what would happen to me now that we were going out into the world. The Conjury wouldn't approve of me any more than they would approve of a townful of invisible citizens roaming around the island unchecked. I hadn't been able to hide my identity in Dyrne. How could I hope to hide it in a more crowded city?

You can worry about that later, I decided. *After all, Emerald was summoning you long before you became sentient. He must have a plan for how to get through this, too.*

This was the first time that I'd been left truly alone since I was summoned back into the world after my six-month absence, and I found myself more restless than anyone without a body had a right to be. It wasn't fair that Emerald got to have a life of his own that didn't involve me, while I couldn't so much as wake up without him getting involved.

He made you, I reminded myself, but that didn't go far toward calming me. Just because he'd created me didn't mean that he should have total control over me.

Outside, a distant boom of thunder echoed down off the mountains, and Emerald stirred in his sleep.

How did Regis feel, when he found out that Ianna had given him half a life? I wondered. *Was he grateful? Or did he resent that he was bound to her forever because she wasn't sure how to live without him?*

The rain fell harder, and the night offered no reply.

Chapter Three

Amaya's house sat within an easy stroll of Lower Bound, which was why both Emerald and I were surprised to find her standing in the road even before the bridge that connected this side of the river with the other. She was sitting on a rock, smoking a long pipe from which drifted a plume of white smoke.

"Took you long enough," she said with a lopsided smile. One side of her face drooped in a blank expression, and she held her limbs awkwardly, as if the whole left half of her body struggled to obey her.

"We could have come to you," I told her as we approached.

She shook her head. "I was planning to gather fresh herbs today. The open sky was calling me. Besides, there are fewer prying ears out here in the countryside." She puffed on her pipe again. "You're looking well, Simon, although given that you were a man when last we met, I'm rather surprised to see you appear so... feminine." She raised her right eyebrow.

Amaya had already worked out what I was—at least in part—on our first meeting, so I didn't try to explain the change in my appearance. Instead, I simply squeezed my eyes shut and shifted to my masculine form, the one I had worn on that first night, clothes and all.

"Goodness, that's a clever trick." Amaya nodded in approval. "Did the two of you find what you were looking for in the mountains?" Her eyes slid to Emerald.

"Indeed we did," Emerald said.

"Hmm." Amaya nodded shrewdly. "Interesting, very interesting. Because from what I've heard, that little town on the mountainside was crushed in a rockfall, and this time, the new scouts came back alive."

"Such a shame about the village," Emerald murmured.

"Quite." Amaya snuffed her pipe and tucked it into some secret fold of her cape. "It's funny, though... I don't recall feeling the mountain shift. The stones never complained of a disturbance, and nothing below the peak was damaged. The gods work in mysterious ways, don't they? It's as if they conspired to wipe Dyrne off the map."

Emerald nodded. "Almost."

Amaya reached out to take Emerald's arm. "Well, we mustn't question the will of the divine, don't you agree? Unless I'm very much mistaken, you follow the teachings of Aster, who is mistress over the wild places. In the meantime, walk with me, and I'll tell you the news *I've* heard." She glanced at me, including me in the conversation, for which I felt an unexpected stab of gratitude. "The body of that last scout, Maximilien, has been held by the sisters of the Cronemire ever since his death. Now, most of the time, when a person from the mainland dies, they send the mortal remains back to the continent. However, some enterprising representative of the Conjury has elected to utilize a quirk of the local geography to get to the bottom of the matter. Was his death an accident? Or was he murdered in cold blood?" Amaya scratched her chin. "Who can say? Very likely, nobody could answer the question with more certainty than Maximilien himself."

"A *quirk of the geography?*" Emerald repeated skeptically.

Amaya nodded. "Have you heard of the Cronemire?"

"Only just now," I said. "When you mentioned the Sisters." I vividly remembered the members of the black-clad Sisterhood who had come to collect Maximilien's body on the night of his murder.

"I haven't, either," Emerald added.

We were approaching the bridge, a wide structure that appeared to be built in two distinct halves which met seamlessly above the middle of the flowing water. Tall structures on either bank anchored it to land, and contained winches and enchanted cables meant, I suspected, to allow the two halves of the bridge to be lifted and allow for the passage of cargo ships up the river.

Amaya led us onto the bridge and pointed upriver, toward where the slate-gray seawater mingled with the river's flow. The current of the latter was stained with what looked like dirt and debris, and where they met, the water swirled and eddied, creating streaks of color below the surface.

"See how the water looks almost red?" she asked. "That's where the Gossamer Ocean meets the Bounder. If you were to take a ship up past the castle, you would find yourself in the midst of a bog. *That* is the Cronemire." She released Emerald's arm. "The bog is a strange place. For as long as anyone can remember, the locals have buried their dead there, and the water preserves the bodies. The bones decay, but the flesh toughens into leather and can be preserved for centuries or more."

Emerald gripped the railing of the bridge and peered down into the water. "I've heard tales of similar rituals on the mainland."

"It's not an uncommon practice, when the environment allows for such things. People hate to let go of what they've lost." Amaya leaned against the railing beside him, glaring at the castle. "But the Cronemire is different. In *our* bog, the dead return."

I made a soft noise of surprise. "Like Regis and Ianna?"

Amaya chuckled. "No, they don't come back to life. Every few nights, the Cronemire comes alive, and the dead rise from the bog. They cannot speak properly, not in full sentences or in any approximation of a conversation, but they seem to remember who they were, and when their loved ones come to visit them, the dead appear to remember them." She shrugged one shoulder. "It doesn't last forever, of course. Once the calcium in their bones is consumed by the bog, they have no way to stand or even swim to the edges of the water. And only people who have passed through the Cronemire before are able to return...and not all of them manage it, either. But, fortunately for the Conjury, Maximilien stopped in Upper Bound to inspect a cargo shipment before he began his circuit of the island last spring."

"So the scouts plan to put his body in the bog and question him when he returns?" I asked.

Amaya nodded. "Such as they can. As I said, the dead have no voices, given the water in their lungs and their lack of breath, but they can respond."

"Any idea how long until the dead rise again?" Emerald asked.

"A few days at most. No one knows what causes them to return, so there's no way to predict when it will happen again."

"So we'll need to act fast," Emerald murmured.

As much as I appreciated Amaya's warning, the fact that she'd reached out to us in the first place made me wonder who else had seen through our attempts to hide Dyrne from the Conjury's prying eyes.

"Why are you telling us all this?" I asked. When Amaya turned to examine me, I added, "Why not let the scouts question Maximilien? Surely it would be safer not to meddle."

The right half of Amaya's face twisted into a wicked grin. "A woman who isn't meddling with the status quo isn't doing her job properly," she observed. "And I know what happens when a distant power tries to control people they neither care about nor understand. The Conjury has never had much of a presence on Kovin Isle, and if that ever changes, very few of us will benefit from their involvement here."

"You should be careful what you say in front of a Conjury man," Emerald murmured. "It could get you in trouble."

"*Are* you the Conjury's man, Emerald Flame?" Amaya straightened her cloak. "I thought better of you than that." She patted his elbow, then pointed to a wide path that began on our side of the bridge. "That will take you up the bank of the Bounder right to the town. The Fenguards rule the keep." She wrinkled her nose, and the right half of her lip curled up. "Never met another man of Fenguard's age who acts so like a wayward child, but for all their foolishness, they're good to the locals."

"And the Cronemire itself?" I asked. "Is there any point in trying to understand why and how it raises the dead?"

Amaya lifted a stiff hand to the left side of her face and nodded toward the bog. "I think answering that question may be harder than you suppose. The Cronemire itself presents its own dangers. Although..." She sized me up speculatively. "Some might find it less difficult to navigate than others."

I squinted at her. "If you told us everything you know, it might make things a bit easier on us."

Amaya chuckled to herself. "And do you intend to tell me everything *you* know?" she asked. "About Maximilien, and Dyrne, and what you are?"

I cut my eyes away from her. Emerald was still staring down into the rippling water of the Bounder with all the intensity of a man who had seen a ghost.

Probably caught sight of his own reflection, I mused. *When was the last time he shaved?* I resolved not to mention it to him; two days ago, he'd been in the throes of new love, and now he was mourning its absence. Given my current finery and his ragamuffin demeanor, nobody would think that we were traveling together. That might serve our purposes, on reflection. Perhaps we could do a bit of dividing and conquering in our time in the city.

"That's what I thought," Amaya said. "You know as much as I'm willing to tell you. The rest you'll have to figure out for yourself. Good luck, lads." With a curt wave, Amaya turned and limped away along the bridge in the direction of her home.

"Stubborn, isn't she?" I asked, with more than a little admiration.

Emerald remained silent.

"Emerald?" When he still did not respond, I used our connection instead. **[Em?]**

He jumped and stood upright. "We should get going," he said, much louder than was really necessary. "For all we know, we only have until tonight to interfere with Maximilien's interrogation." He turned sharply toward the towpath.

Don't take his attitude personally. He's having a hard day. I was doing my best to be understanding of his feelings, although a little niggle of annoyance flared up as I did so. After all, I had never once complained about being banished for half a year, and that really *was* his fault. It was one thing for him to be sad, another for him to take it out on me.

Then again, I had seen for myself how deep Emerald's self-loathing ran, and his recent confession about the source of those little scars gave me a bit more insight into the deeper recesses of his mind that I had never explored. According to everything he'd told me, he'd summoned me—or something like me—hundreds of times before I gained sentience. Which begged the question: in all that time, had Emerald been utterly alone?

That was a sad thought, and if it were true, he might need more time to adjust to the company of others. How old was he, anyway? I had never thought to ask.

Looks like Emerald isn't the only one too self-absorbed to notice the feelings of those around him, I thought wryly as I followed him along the riverbank. Maybe once this trouble with Maximilien was settled, I would get around to asking him.

◈

From afar, Upper Bound had appeared to be a thriving little town. Up close, however, we discovered that it was, in essence, a small city.

The keep that Amaya had pointed out to us rose over the

port on a high stone outcropping that overlooked the river. Its venerable buildings were only just visible from the waterside, but the road that followed the slope of the land down to the main city boasted no fortifications. Evidently, whoever lived there wasn't worried about an incursion from the locals.

The lower portion of the city spread out from the docks. Parts of it had been built out over the water on stone foundations set directly into the Bounder, or on heavy wooden pilings that raised the houses well above the water line. New buildings stood alongside older stone structures, some of which came together above street level, in catwalks that connected the upper floors. In the streets around us, a lively assortment of residents went about their daily tasks, dressed in bright silks, burnished plate armor, well-loved leather, and materials I had never seen before. After the rigid uniformity of Dyrne's traditional garb, my head was soon spinning with the sheer variety Upper Bound had to offer.

"Inspiring," I murmured, imagining the wide array of outfits I could conjure for myself using these heretofore unknown articles. I could not *feel* texture, but I could almost imagine how a shining silk scarf would compare to a rucked cotton blouse based on appearance alone. To feel both at once, however, taxed the powers of my admittedly vivid imagination. "Have you ever seen anything like it?"

Emerald shrugged. *[This isn't much compared to Venta Bulgarum. The Conjury capital is easily a dozen times as large.]*

My mouth fell open as I tried to picture a place that would dwarf even this one, and all the people who would live there.

[You look quite the country bumpkin right now,] Emerald informed me.

[Bold words, coming from a man who only owns one set of clothes,] I retorted. All the same, I snapped my mouth shut and stopped gawking quite so openly.

[That would be your mark of civility—] he began.

Someone slammed into Emerald's shoulder, and he stumbled,

very nearly bumping into me—not that he would have actually done so, of course. He would have passed through me, and then everyone on the street would have seen that I was not what I appeared to be.

"Watch it, half-breed," the man snarled. "Clumsy, gods-cursed oaf..."

Emerald's hands balled into fists, and I bristled with righteous indignation.

"Watch your tone," I warned.

"*My* tone?" the man snarled. "Tell your filthy pet to watch where he's going." The man glared up at Emerald, losing interest in me at once. "Tainted bilge rats, getting their stink all over our city..." He flexed his arms, curled his lip up to reveal stained teeth, and thumped his fist against his palm twice.

[Don't start anything,] Emerald warned.

[Start it? He started it! Are you really going to let him talk like that?]

[You've got no way to back up any threats you might make. You can't touch him, which means that if this comes to blows, it'll be up to me to settle things... which will only prove his point.] The weary resignation in Emerald's tone irritated me, not because he was so complacent, but because it implied how common an experience this was for him.

Before either of us could speak again, a woman appeared from a nearby cross street.

"I better not have heard that right, Wilcox," she purred, sauntering in our general direction. The people around us parted like the current around a ship, averting their eyes and pulling their hoods and caps lower to avoid getting involved.

Immediately, the man who had singled Emerald out backed away. "He started it, Marsha."

"Oh, Willie. Don't lie to me." The woman swayed her hips as she walked in an undulating rhythm that would have seemed sultry if it hadn't been so reminiscent of a predator stalking its prey. Her long skirt was slit up both sides, revealing not only her tall boots, but a great deal of pale thigh as well. She only came up to Wilcox's shoulder, but the man trembled before her and seemed to shrink. His posture gave me the impression that he was terrified she'd toss him to the cobbles and grind the tall heel of her boot into his collarbone, but that he would not protest overmuch if she did.

"I'm not lyin', Marsha, honest," he whined. "This big lunk..."

Her hand whipped out and stuck him across the face so abruptly and with such force that he staggered.

"Now, Willie," she said, in the honey-sweet tones of a woman who was *extremely* put out and wanted everyone to know it, "you remember how I feel when you do that. Just 'cause a fella's on the larger side and not the prettiest face of the bunch doesn't mean we get to call him names. And we *certainly* don't imply that his brains have a damn thing to do with his appearance." She stepped forward until Wilcox's back was pressed against the wall and jabbed one slim finger into the center of his chest. "*Do we*, Willie? 'Cause if word should get back to Boo, imagine how he'd feel? We don't wanna hurt *Boo's* feelings, do we?"

"N-no, Miss Marsha." Wilcox pressed his fingers to his cheek, where the imprint of her hand burned like a brand.

"I didn't think so." Marsha turned to Emerald with a syrupy smile. "Now, Willie, why don't you apologize for the mean things you said, and you can get back to work?"

Wilcox cowered behind her, while Emerald and I both gaped like the country bumpkins we truly were.

"S-sorry," Wilcox mumbled. "Didn't mean no harm, sir."

Emerald blinked a few times. "Apology accepted."

Marsha snapped her fingers. "Now, off you pop, Willie, love. And mind your manners like Miss Marsha hears every word you say. 'Cause sooner or later, she *does*."

"Y-yes, ma'am." Willie nodded to us once and scurried away, disappearing down a street that seemed suddenly empty, as if the citizens of Upper Bound had known instinctively to avoid our little altercation.

[I think I'm in love,] I told Emerald.

He choked on a laugh and bowed his head in Marsha's direction. "Thank you."

Marsha waved a hand dismissively. Now that she was facing us, I could see that she was young, perhaps in her early twenties. She wore a great deal of jewelry, most of which seemed quite expensive, assuming that the stones and metals were real. "I can't abide a rude fella," she told us, examining her fingernails. "I don't expect you to forgive him, but don't hold his bad manners against the rest of us. Some of these local boys haven't seen much of the world, and it makes 'em small minded." She smiled at the pair of us, and her eyes widened when she took in my attire. "Say, you boys aren't from the docks, are ya?"

I bowed deeply to her. "Not at all, madame. We're travelers from the mainland. We have an urgent matter to discuss with the Fenguards."

Her smile faded. "Government lads, are you, then?"

Emerald cleared his throat. "Hardly. Although I hear there *are* a couple of Conjury scouts in town."

"Up at the keep," Marsha said, gesturing toward the remote castle above us. "Guests of the laird, they are. Well, I'm sure you know your business, but if you don't find what you need up *there,* you come to me. Me'n'Boo know this town better than anyone else, and we can help you with anything you might need. And if anyone gives you trouble, you let Miss Marsha handle them." She blew us a kiss as she ambled away down the cobbles in the opposite direction Wilcox had taken.

"Well, that was... unexpected." I craned my neck to watch her go.

"Yes," Emerald agreed. *[And I'm glad you didn't mention that we work for the Conjury. I'm not convinced that Marsha's role in this town is entirely aboveboard.]*

[I'm not a complete *idiot.]*

Emerald grunted. *[If you say so.]* "Come on. We should go up to the castle and talk to the Conjury scouts."

We made our way toward the road. The streets widened as we passed a main square that boasted dozens of shops, bakeries, tailors, and even an open-air eatery. In the middle of the square, a skinny, gray-skinned man dressed in moss-stained clothes held a wooden sign that read, *BEWARE OF THE BOG.*

"...the dead should not come back to life after their time has come! The Cronemire is an abomination against both natural order and divine will..." His voice was high-pitched and reedy, and his rounded vowels sounded strange to my ear.

[Swamper elf,] Emerald thought. *[I'm surprised to see one here on the island. Kovin Isle has always been somewhat of a holdout against the Conjury's particular brand of 'progress' and trade...]*

As we passed through the square, a squat creature the rough height of a lambkin wandered over to the babbling elf. At first, I thought it little more than an enormous frog; it walked on two legs, but it wore no clothes at all. In my experience, everyone who was a *person* wore clothes, but to my surprise, it braced its three-toed hands against its damp hips and frowned up at the elf.

"Lafayette," the frog-man said in a deep, burbling voice, "we've been over this. The bog is a thing of beauty."

"Heathen!" bellowed the elf, waving his sign all the more frantically. "You've been taken in by its charms, but the bog is unnatural, filled with dark magic that defies the will of Driaweep!"

*[What in Aster's name is **that?**]* I asked Emerald.

Emerald cast the frog-man a glance. *[A krub,]* he thought, with an air of open distaste.

[Hey, now. No need to be rude, he can't help what he is, and I would think that you'd know better than to judge for what they are.]

[I don't mind krubs,] Emerald assured me. He was still squinting at the small green fellow as if he was trying to remember something but couldn't. *[Funny, I... hm.]* He shook his head and turned his back on the pair. *[Never mind. Doesn't matter.]*

[What doesn't?]

Emerald did not elaborate as we left the square behind and started up the slope to the high castle. There were fewer people here, but plenty of wagons loaded with barrels and crates of every imaginable size came and went alongside us.

[Emerald,] I thought, *[about what Wilcox said…]*

Emerald shook his head and kept his eyes on the cobbles. *[Don't worry about it, Crim. It's nothing I haven't heard before.]*

Somehow, he failed to register that the regularity of such behavior was precisely the source of my concern.

❧

We were greeted at the castle by a ruddy-faced guard who demanded to see Emerald's papers before showing us to a sitting room just inside the keep's entrance.

As we waited for our audience with Laird Fenguard, I stared up at the portrait of our host with growing concern.

"Doesn't look very friendly, does he?" I murmured.

Emerald snorted. *[Cross your fingers and say a prayer to Aster that he's one-fifth as welcoming as Miss Marsha.]*

Even if I'd had lungs, I wouldn't have held my breath. The man in the portrait wore a bitter scowl. His heavy brows were pulled low, and his mouth was pinched into a narrow and remorseless line. An array of medals and gold braiding decorated his rather modern attire, which was partly covered with an old-fashioned blue velvet cape lined with ermine and ribbed with elaborate gold embroidery.

[He looks like an ass,] I thought.

Emerald got up and crossed the little sitting room to where I stood. *[His eyes are somewhat alarming,]* he admitted. *[But that's the style of these formal portraits. He might not be so cold in person.]*

[Look who's being optimistic now!]

Emerald shrugged one shoulder. *[Well, if he walks into this*

room looking like he's just eaten a double helping of Vano-ra's hagbraggh, we'll know for certain.]

Next to his portrait hung another, which looked as though it had been painted by the same artist. A woman, just as frigid as her male counterpart, stared out at us with icy eyes. Her dress was formal, featuring a mixture of modern and archaic styles.

Modern rulers who pay homage to the island's history, I thought. *I wonder what they would think if they found out about what we'd done in Dyrne. Would they side with the Conjury, or would they think as Amaya does, that the residents of the island deserve to live their lives in peace?*

The door opened, and a man bounded through. "Welcome, welcome!" he exclaimed. He wore simpler clothes in the same color as the portraits, mostly blue and gold, although he had the same reddish hair as the fellow in the painting. "I hear you're new arrivals in Upper Bound. What can I do for you gentlemen?" He clapped Emerald on the back, and I managed to duck away before his palm could pass clean through me.

I pointed to the portraits. "We were just admiring these likenesses of your... parents?" I hazarded.

The man burst out laughing and grabbed Emerald's shoulder, shaking it merrily. "Your friend is quite funny."

"Uh." Emerald glanced at me, just as taken aback by this exuberant man as I was. "Is he?"

"Come now." The newcomer hurried over to the portrait and faced us. He folded his hands awkwardly in front of him, lowered his brow, and pressed his lips together. The grim attitude aged him ten years at least, and I realized to my chagrin that the dour gentleman in the portrait and the cheerful fellow in our company were one and the same.

In an instant, he sprang to life again, laughing heartily at our expressions. "Terrible, isn't it?" he asked. "Really, it *does* make me look old enough to be my own father. I blame the outfit—it was *damn* uncomfortable." He leaned toward Emerald, cupping one hand around his mouth as if sharing a secret, although he didn't bother to lower his voice. "All my bits were sticking to my other bits, if you follow. And I expect you can tell why we keep it down here rather than in our private quarters." He squinted at the likeness and shuddered theatrically. "My own eyes would give me nightmares. So! Now you know who *I* am... Laird Edur Fenguard, master of the keep. And you, I'm told, are Crimson Smoke and the Emerald Flame!"

I was poised to fall into my usual role as the distraction, but Emerald dipped into a deep and rather formal bow. "It is a pleasure to meet you, Laird. Am I to understand that you've heard of us?"

[It's not a name,] Emerald told me. **[It's a title.]**

[Oh, blast, did I use it wrong?]

[No. But I could hear you thinking it.]

"More than you might expect," Laird Edur said, ignorant of our quiet back and forth. "In fact, a friend of yours is staying in the keep as a guest."

[You have friends?] I asked, without thinking.

[It's news to me, too,] Emerald replied.

"What brings you here?" the laird asked, dropping into one of the upholstered chairs along the wall and lifting one ankle to the opposite knee. "Is there some sort of trouble? A mystery to be solved?" He rubbed his palms together. "Oh, I do *love* a good mystery."

"As a matter of fact, there is." I shot Emerald a sidelong glance before continuing. "As you may know, we work in conjunction with the Conjury, and last spring, we became involved in the investigation surrounding the deaths of a few local scouts."

Laird Edur shuddered. "Oh, terrible business. Nothing more than a gruesome accident, I hope. Two scouts are here now, in fact. Guests of mine. They're looking into Maximilien of Leviathan Loch's untimely demise."

"We hope to assist them," Emerald said. "Since we've been investigating the matter independently."

"Of course! I'll introduce you." Edur snapped his fingers. "I'll tell you what, you two simply *must* come to the party tonight. A large ship will be docking this afternoon, and I'll be hosting a feast in honor of the occasion. I'll introduce you to the scouts, and you can make arrangements with them to be there at the questioning. How does that sound?"

"Excellent," Emerald said.

I nodded. "We would be delighted to attend."

"In the meantime, Laird Edur, may I ask you one thing? Maximilien's body... where is it now?" Emerald clasped his hands behind his back.

"In the bonehouse near the docks," Edur said. "We had an Arctician enchant a small building to keep it freezing year round. I'm afraid that as our city grows, and more ships come into harbor, we've had to account for a growing number of deaths. Forgive me for saying so, but some of these sailors can be rough sorts, both on the sea and here in our humble city." Edur shook his head sadly. "It's not uncommon for unfortunates who find themselves in debtor's prison on the mainland to be hired on as deckhands to work off their dues. Often as not, they fall to drinking, and between brawls and drunken foreigners who don't know the streets, we've had more and more deaths of mainlanders on our shores in recent years. The Sisters see to their mortal remains, and they're then kept in the bonehouse until they can be transported back to the mainland and returned to their families. Unfortunately, once this poor lad is placed in the bog, he won't be able to make that journey."

The note of pity in Laird Edur's voice sounded sincere. I would not have thought the man in the portrait much given to, or even capable of, empathy. I could see why his theatrical nature rubbed Amaya the wrong way, but I felt that I had found a kindred spirit: kind by nature, fastidious in his grooming, and generous with his time.

Emerald, apparently, felt the same. He bowed to Laird Edur again. "Thank you for your assistance, Laird Fenguard. We'll see you this evening."

Laird Edur waved his hand. "Enough with the rigamarole. You're an honored guest. No need for formalities, Emerald

Flame. And I hope you won't mind me mentioning it, but if you *should* find yourself at a tailor's, give them this." He slipped a brass token out of an inner pocket of his coat and flicked it off his thumb. Emerald caught it in his palm. "That's my seal. Any place of business in the city will accept it in lieu of payment. Wherever you wish to stay and anything you wish to buy while you're here will be added to my accounts."

Emerald turned the token over in his palm, frowning thoughtfully down at it. "That's very generous."

"We're a growing city," Edur said, spreading his arms. "I prefer not to think of us as Upper Bound so much as *Upward* Bound. Clever, eh?" He winked at me. "If we're going to continue to expand our markets on the mainland, we'll need the full support of the Conjury, and by extension, yourselves. I don't want the stain of this incident to tarnish our reputation. I, as much as anyone, want the matter settled." He rose to his feet. "I'll see you this evening, gentlemen. It has been a pleasure." He clasped his hands behind him and bowed slightly at the waist before ushering us back out the door and into the courtyard. While we made our way to the outer gate, he strode deeper in the castle, walking with a spring in his step.

[I must say, Upper Bound is nothing like what I expected,] I mused.

[No,] Emerald agreed, *[it's not.]* He was still eyeing the laird's token, running the pad of his huge thumb over the face, which was embossed with three daggers and a five-pointed star.

When he didn't comment, further, I slid closer to his side, in part to avoid a horse-and-cart that was passing in the opposite direction. *[So, what do we do now?]*

[We're going to secure a room,] he thought. *[I'm going to get some new clothes, and then we're going to go to the party, where you will be incredibly charming, distracting, and everyone's best friend.]*

[Per usual,] I agreed. *[And in the meantime, what will you be doing?]*

[Isn't it obvious?] He flipped the token off his thumb,

Chapter Four

"I want you to know that I hate this plan." I lounged a hair's breadth above the edge of the blankets covering the smaller of the two beds in our newly rented room. Even at his most attentive, Emerald often missed when I was having a good sulk, so I had decided to go all out for his benefit.

Emerald examined himself in the mirror. "The outfit, or the plan?"

"The plan!" I exclaimed, then sat upright. "Although, the outfit isn't what it could be. All black? Really? Not even a single pop of color?"

Emerald scowled at my reflection. "Is it just me, or have you gotten more annoying since you were away?"

"No, you've somehow managed to become even *less* tasteful, which is the problem. We're not in Dyrne anymore, we're guests of the local Laird, *and* we have to impress the Conjury scouts!" I exclaimed, leaping to my feet. "I *know* that you don't care as much about appearances as I do, Emerald, but it isn't just vanity, I assure you."

"Although vanity is certainly involved," he said. "Besides, I don't want to stand out tonight. I'll be stealing a *body,* remember?"

"And doing what with it?" I demanded.

Emerald adjusted the collar of his black shirt. At the very least, it matched his hair, and it complimented his moss-colored skin. It wasn't a *total* loss, but I wished he'd let me have more of a say when selecting his clothes. At the very least, he could have selected a nice brocade. For once, he could have worn whatever he liked, and he had chosen *linen,* of all things. How had a man of such unerringly simple tastes ever succeeded in conjuring someone of my refinement? I had changed my outfit to that of a scarlet-and-gold doublet ribbed with citrine buttons, which was *much* more the thing.

I was so lost in my dismay over his choices—he had, after all, been given *carte blanche* at the modiste's—that I had almost forgotten my question.

"Ideally, I'll only be trading it," he said as he ran one hand over the front of his shirt. "I don't need to dispose of Maximilien's body. I only need to replace it with one that looks sufficiently like him that the Conjury scouts won't notice the difference. According to Edur, there are multiple bodies in the icehouse. All I have to do is a simple switch, and the problem will be solved. When questioned, the corpse will indicate that it got too drunk and died by accident, or some such thing. At the very least, it will throw them off the scent."

I crossed my legs and tucked my arms behind my head, wagging one boot midair in thought. "Very well. Let's say you accomplish this, and the replacement corpse tells the scouts that it... drowned, for instance."

Emerald grimaced. "I'll try to pick a person that looks as though he died in a similar manner."

"And if someone in the city is accused? Yes, you will have caught a murderer, but they'll know that they didn't kill Maximilien."

"Good luck taking that argument to the Conjury. *No, I didn't kill the scout, I only strangled one of the sailors to death with my bare hands.*"

I puffed out my cheeks and glared at him.

My companion rolled his eyes at me extravagantly. "*Now what?*"

"At the very least, you'll ensure that Maximilien doesn't get a proper burial with his kin, and you'll doom a stranger to the same fate."

Emerald let out a growl and bared his teeth at me. "They're dead, Crimson. *Dead.* Who cares what becomes of them? If it means that Parian and Kristine and Nechtan and all the residents of Dyrne can live in peace without paying for Aindreas's crimes, I won't lose a wink of sleep over two men being buried in the wrong graves."

He had a point, of course. I had yet to see any indication that the gods people so often spoke of were more than stories. The citizens of Dyrne, however, were real people in danger of being exposed to an uncaring government who would happily conscript them into unwilling service if their powers of invisibility became common knowledge. The safety of the living, I supposed, mattered more than the identities of the dead.

All the same, I disliked the idea that Maximilien, who had already suffered so terribly at Aindreas's hands, would now be forced to endure the indignity of being buried in the wrong grave. Moreover, we had relied on evidence provided by the dead in order to solve our last case. If Throop of Dunmore had been buried in the wrong grave, our investigation in Dyrne might have taken longer and cost more lives before it was laid to rest.

Then again, speaking of lives... "What would happen to Tincrown if the Conjury found out about Dyrne?"

Emerald turned his back on me. "Let's not even speak of it."

[Very well. What would happen to Tincrown if—]

"He could be arrested," Emerald snapped. "Deported back to Venta Bulgarum for questioning. His medical license would surely be revoked by the Conjury at the least, never mind what would become of us if our part in the cover-up came to light. So can we *please* stop talking about it and just accept that we need to do *something?*"

I sat up. "I can see that. But we don't even know how the

dead communicate with the living during these events. Just because they can't speak doesn't mean that they won't be able do, I don't know, *mime* some sort of response. What if they ask the fellow's name, and he tells them he's not Maximilien right from the beginning?"

"In that case, we'll have to come up with a new plan." Emerald scrubbed his hands over his face. "At the very least, there will be some sort of inquiry into the Sisterhood's records that will buy us a few days' time. And if that happens, we'll send a babblebird to Dyrne and warn them that the Conjury is closing in."

And our attempts to protect Kristine and Nechtan and the others will have been for nothing. That being the case, I had to agree with Emerald. This plan wasn't perfect, but for want of a better one, it was necessary.

"Very well," I told him. "Let us attend the party for which you are so woefully underdressed. While you're out completing your bit of amoral skulduggery, I'll keep an eye on the scouts and let you know if anything is amiss. In the meantime, we shall pray to Aster and Dathan and Ardus and everyone else that your plan succeeds, and then we can head back to Dyrne and inform everyone that they are perfectly safe and sound."

"Mm." Emerald checked his reflection in the mirror one more time before waving to the window, through which we could make out a sliver of rose-tinted sky over the bay. "Come along, then. Let's get this over with."

I followed him through the door, filled with confidence that we'd be back in Dyrne in a matter of days, and this frantic little expedition to Upper Bound would be nothing more than an unhappy memory.

⁂

By day, Fenguard Keep had been a lively and bustling place. In the gathering dusk, however, it was transformed into a lordly haven filled with light and sound. Glass-paneled oil lamps hung along the inner walls, bathing the courtyard in a cheery golden glow that gilded every person who passed through the gates. It was early yet, but the supplies from the newly docked ship were already being unloaded. Crates of fresh fruit and casks of beer were being inspected by the guards as we passed through the pedestrian entrance.

"No wonder they throw such a fuss when the ships arrive," I murmured.

[Upper Bound has a bit of a reputation on the mainland,] Emerald thought. He was watching both the guards and sailors warily. Whether he was preoccupied regarding the fate of Dyrne, or whether he was simply hoping to avoid a repeat of our encounter with Wilcox, I could only speculate. *[The wine of this region is said to be surpassingly good.]*

[You'll have to let me know your opinion,] I replied. I couldn't taste any more than I could touch. For all I knew, Emerald's palette was as rudimentary as his fashion sense. *[When you say that the town has a reputation, what exactly does that mean?]*

Emerald's mouth curled into a half-smile as he slouched up the steps to the garlanded doors of the castle proper. *[That the parties are so extravagant, even folks on the mainland have heard of them.]* With that, he led me into the high hall.

We were instantly immersed in a maelstrom of festivity. Hundreds of voices combined with the clink of cutlery against porcelain, the dull thump of metal on wood, and a layer of merry music engulfed us. Ahead of me, Emerald's spine stiffened, no doubt the result of his usual reception at such gatherings, but I was instantly enchanted. I could now see how plain and unremarkable the small gathering at McLachlan's inn in Lower Bound had been. Lambkins and teguans, elves and dwarves, and even the krub we had spotted in the main square this morning sat side by side at the long, low tables, or held each other close as they danced to the music being spilling forth from a dais at the back of the glittering room.

"Oh!" I covered my mouth to stifle a laugh when I realized

who was playing for the assembled crowd. "I think I know who Laird Fenguard was talking about when he said he knew a friend of ours."

Emerald followed my line of sight and let out a low groan. "Oh, Aster's bloody *menses,* you have got to be *kidding me.*"

A green-clad figure with golden hair and youthful features was tapping the leather toe of his boot against the wooden floor of the stage. At this distance, I couldn't make out the lyrics, which might very well have been for the best. I had encountered Coirpre of Kessingtown on my very first night of consciousness, and I had known even then that his lyrics were more grandiose than substantive.

"Nice to see a friendly face, isn't it?" I chirped.

I anticipated the answering glare Emerald shot at me, and while there was enough sourness in his expression to curdle a whole *lake* of cream, my smile remained fixed in place. In our travels, Coirpre was the person we'd encountered who was most like me: swashbuckling, performative, and blessed with impeccable panache. At the moment, he sported a handsome damask doublet studded with pearls, which I envied immensely.

He didn't appear to have noticed us in the crowd, and I had no way of knowing if the laird had informed him of our presence. Besides, the bard was lost in an up-tempo ballad recounting some great battle.

"She thrashed and she coiled beneath the vast dunes
   And burrowed her way 'twixt the caves.
   There was never a brute
   Of such great ill-repute
   Born to either the stones or the waves.
   Yes, the foul granite shark spread terror and fear,
   Leaving folks in the Springs so depressed.
   But she never did hear
   Her end drawing near...
   For granite sharks, like all rocks, are born deaf!"

. . .

He continued on, recounting a nonsensical but catchy adventure in which he apparently defeated a deaf subterranean beast using only the power of song.

[I thought you told me that granite sharks weren't deaf?] I mused.

"As if we haven't got enough trouble on our hands," Emerald grumbled, ignoring my question. "Let's just figure out where the scouts are and—*blast it.*" He nodded toward the table closest to the music, where Edur Fenguard was deep in conversation with two men in matching violet uniforms. *[Oh, lovely. They would be within spitting distance of that wretched bard.]*

If Tincrown had not been in immediate danger, I would have ribbed Emerald mercilessly about Coirpre's presence, and the fact that he had modeled my appearance as Simon so closely on the bard—save my brilliant red hair, ruby to Coirpre's gold. I exercised restraint, however, and followed him to the far end of the room in silence.

As we wove past the other tables, I noted with interest that there seemed to be no divide between the wealthy upper class, the poorer craftspeople, and the rough and ragged crews of the ships. The latter were easy to identify, since their jackets were emblazoned with embroidered logos. They depicted a three-masted sailing vessel over the letters *TG*.

I tried to speak aloud, but my words were lost in the din, so I resorted to the use of our connection. *[What is that symbol for? With the ship?]*

[The Trader's Guild,] Emerald replied. *[Of the Kingdom of Feynlish, specifically. Over the last few years, they've been edging out the shipping competition in this region. Now they're something of a monopoly.]*

[Are they owned by the Conjury?]

[No. But their interests align.] Emerald glanced over his shoulder with a bitter smile. *[And I have no doubt that more than a few agreements have been made behind closed doors.]*

I would have loved to delve deeper into that political intrigue, but I was distracted by some rowdy laughter from a particular group of sailors. The moment I spotted them, I stopped in my tracks. *[Emerald!]*

Other than my companion, I had never met another person of jotunn ancestry before, at least not since I had become sentient. In the company of humans, it was easy to note all the ways in which Emerald differed from those around us. These three sailors, however, were something else again. At a guess, they were full-blooded jotunn; they were of a similar height and build to my friend, but their granite-colored skin was covered in patches of thick fur, and their eyes burned like embers in the dark shadows beneath their heavy brows. There was a weight to their presence that seemed to throw everyone in their immediate vicinity out of orbit, and a wildness in their appearance that both thrilled and frightened me.

No, not *me*. Emerald. He had stopped, too, and was staring at them, torn between approaching them and tripping over his own feet in his haste to quit their presence.

[Should we greet them?] I asked.

He shook himself slightly, the way the goats of Dyrne did when they got wet. *[No. I have nothing to say to any jotunn.]* He resumed walking without further explanation, but as he did so, one of the jotunn sailors met my gaze and lifted her tankard in greeting. I met her blazing eyes and offered her a small smile, raising my hand in return.

Do they think as poorly of people like him as Aindreas and Parian did, or does he revile them? I wished that Emerald would speak to me more openly about such matters, but as he was already on edge about the predicament with Maximilien, so I held my tongue this time.

We approached the table where Laird Fenguard sat in conversation with his other noteworthy guests.

"The Emerald Flame!" he called as he waved us over. "And Master Crimson, of course."

"Simon will do, My Laird," I said, as I bowed first to him and then to the scouts. "There's no need to lean on prominence titles. And who do I have the honor of addressing?"

Edur waved to the first of the scouts, whose long, thin face boasted high cheekbones and a widow's peak. "This, my friends, is Benedite of Crystal Springs." He indicated the second man, whose flattened nose and unsmiling features suggested he'd walked face first into a stone wall on at least a dozen occasions over the course of his life. "And this is Dirkus of Kinmore."

"It's a pleasure to meet you," I said, dipping my chin in greeting. Aster help me, I was *not* going to bow to these men. "May we join you?"

"As long as this one doesn't drink all the wine." Dirkus eyed Emerald up and down. "You're a big fellow, aren't you?"

"How astute," Emerald drawled as he slid onto the bench. "Nobody's ever noticed before."

Dirkus frowned, but judging by his ruddy cheeks, he was already well into his cups. By the time he decided that he *should* be offended by Emerald's sarcasm, I had already maneuvered into my place on the bench.

"There's plenty of wine for everyone," Laird Edur assured us. "I'm curious to know your theories regarding the death of the prior scouts."

"Yes." Benedite leaned forward on his elbows. There was little mirth in his features, and unlike his companion, he gave no hint of inebriation. He struck me at once as the sort of man who never smiled. "I'm also curious, since I'm given to understand that you spent the last six months investigating the matter."

Emerald reached for an empty cup without comment and filled it from the carafe. ***[You're the chatty one, Crimson. So... chat.]***

I smiled at Benedite. "Six months? Hardly. We looked into it for a week, at most. At first, we thought there might be some correlation between the deaths of the other scouts and poor Maximilien, but that's clearly not the case."

Benedite raised one dark eyebrow. I didn't like the way he

looked at me, which was a first. "Clearly?" he repeated. "And how do you figure that?"

"Why, by getting the lay of the land, of course." I spread my hands wide. "Now that we've seen the locations of the accidents, the whole picture becomes clearer. The old scout, Dawyd, knew the island inside and out, while his successors were much less fortunate." I shook my head sadly and sighed. "Will you be completing a circuit of the island soon?"

"We've already returned from our loop," Dirkus said.

[Nice misdirection,] Emerald observed as he handed me a cup. It was, of course, only an illusion, one that he must have conjured on the sly while the laird and the scouts were focused on me.

[Thank you for noticing.] I accepted the phantom cup and set it on the table before me. I would experiment with my control over it later, when the conversation shifted to something less delicate. "Then you've seen how rugged the countryside can be. Griffins, rockslides, treacherous paths..."

Laird Edur nodded along with my list. "I adore this wild country, but there's a reason it has never been settled or developed to the same extent as the mainland. We've done quite well for ourselves, but you're right, Simon. Outside of the settlements, Kovin Isle is hardly the safest place for travelers."

I raised my cup in an informal toast before pretending to drink.

"So now you've come back to see the matter finished?" Benedite asked. He narrowed his beady eyes at me.

"Of course. Maximilien is the only loose end, and that will be resolved soon enough." I offered him my most winning smile. *[I've settled it all pretty neatly, don't you think?]*

Emerald scowled into his cup. *[Not sure this Benedite fellow buys your version of things.]*

[Then you'd better hope that whatever replacement corpse you choose for Maximilien corroborates my story.] I turned to Edur. "I must say, Laird, this wine is *excellent*. Is it imported, or...?"

[As if you can taste a damned thing.] Emerald slurped from his cup. *[Although it is quite good.]*

"It's a local brew." Edur swirled his cup and winked at me. "Extremely potent, and very highly sought after on the mainland."

"Goes down easy," Dirkus agreed.

Benedite cast a slantwise glare at his traveling companion. "And is too potent for some."

"Indeed." Dirkus failed to take the hint, and immediately reached for the carafe again. "But not for men of the world like us, eh?"

Emerald turned suddenly, as though he'd heard someone call his name. "Forgive me, gentlemen," he said. "I'll be back in a moment." He left his half-full cup of wine sitting on the table and got up. *[Keep an eye on them. The sooner we get this over with, the better.]*

[Good luck.] I waved him off and feigned taking another deep draught.

The second Emerald was out of earshot, Dirkus leaned across the table. "Gods, how do you stand it?" he slurred. "Traveling with an ugly bastard like that? Even ten minutes in his company turns my stomach."

I froze with my cup lifted to my lips, wondering how in Aster's name I was going to respond to that without starting a row. Before I could, Edur brought his palm down on Dirkus's shoulder. His usual smile was gone. *This* was the look of the man in that unflattering portrait we'd encountered on our first visit to the keep.

"You're an honored guest in my home," Edur said, with only a fraction of his prior warmth. "As is the Emerald Flame. I invite you to remember that before you speak ill of him in my presence, *Master* Dirkus."

Dirkus blinked several times as he stared down at Edur's hand. "Er, right. Sorry, m'laird, my mistake...?" He tried to meet Benedite's eye, but the other scout only hid behind his wine as he sipped.

"I understand that the jotunn and their kin are looked down upon by some," I said, grateful twice over that the laird had interceded—for Emerald's sake as well as my own. "What I fail to understand is *why*. My friend is one of the best men I have ever had the good fortune to meet. As for his appearance, the only thing I can fault is his wardrobe." I pretended to finish my drink, hoping that would settle the matter.

A muscle jumped in Dirkus's jaw, and I suspected that he would have argued with me, had Laird Edur not been present or his feeling on the subject not so abundantly clear.

I was so focused on the brooding scout that I had not registered the sudden lack of music. It came as quite a shock, therefore, when a familiar lilting voice sounded behind me. "I can fault more than his wardrobe." Coirpre's green-clad figure slid into the spot that Emerald had just vacated. The bard flashed me a saccharine smile. "The Emerald Flame is also annoyingly stubborn, painfully self-righteous, and aggressively vindictive. I also think he might be the tiniest bit obsessed with me, because the pair of you seem to pop up everywhere I go."

I was not often rendered speechless, but the appearance of the bard left me slightly giddy and starstruck. As ferociously as I had maligned his musical talent on our first meeting, there was no denying the charismatic pull of his presence.

Laird Edur saved me from my tongue-tied silence by applauding. "Another excellent performance tonight, Coirpre. My delight in your talents has not even begun to fade. I take it that your presence at our table means that my wife has arrived?"

Coirpre swept an arm toward the stage, where a gray-eyed woman in a pearl-studded cream gown was looking out over the crowd. When she saw Edur, she beckoned to him with one slender hand.

"Pardon me, gentlemen, I must confer with my lady." Edur rose to his feet and hurried away, leaving the four of us in awkward silence.

When no one spoke up, Coirpre shrugged and reached for Emerald's cup.

"That's the mutt's cup," Dirkus said with a sneer.

Coirpre arched one golden eyebrow at him. "Don't worry," he said in the flattest voice imaginable. "I hear alcohol kills the fleas." He drank the cup dry without breaking eye contact with Dirkus.

The scout shuddered.

Benedite, apparently, had reached the limits of his patience. "Dirkus, we are at the laird's party. If you're going to drink his wine, you're going to follow his rules, or you may well undermine our position on the island. Leave the jotunn alone."

"Fine," Dirkus grumbled, shoving his empty cup aside and glaring at me and Coirpre in turn. "But I'm getting something to eat." He got up abruptly, only to trip over his own feet. With a beleaguered sigh, Benedite followed him.

Coirpre made a rude gesture at their retreating backs before turning to me. "I don't know what he's thinking, leaving you all on your own. Emerald Flame, if you can hear me, I want a word. We have unfinished business."

"I don't think he *can* hear you," I said. The two scouts approached the table of food. I hoped they wouldn't wander too far; I didn't relish the idea of following them around, given Dirkus's attitude.

Coirpre snorted and peered around at the crowd. "You're not fooling me, Emerald Flame. I know exactly what your little puppet is, and that you're the one putting words in his mouth. Did you come all this way just to torment me again? Because I'm warning you—"

"If you want to talk to him, you'll have to wait until he gets back," I snapped.

Coirpre refocused on me. "I know what you are. No need to pretend."

I crossed my arms and glared at him. So much for the awe of meeting one's sartorial heroes. "I've already had to convince Emerald that I'm real. I had hoped that *you* would be less tedious, but it seems I was wrong." How long had my friend been gone? It felt like an age.

The bard snorted and cocked his head. Gradually the smile slipped from his face. "Wait a moment." He leaned closer to examine me, until I was forced to bend backward or else subject everyone around us to the alarming sight of his face passing clean through mine.

"Stop it," I hissed. "What are you hoping to see, anyway? I don't *look* different..."

Coirpre pointed to me. His fingertip hovered so close to my chest that he nearly brushed against me—or through me, as the case may be.

"I have never," he said in clipped tones, "in my life, worn buttons like this." He sat back abruptly. "And you make a valid point about his taste in garments. Which means that either he's copying someone *else* for once, or something unusual is going on." He peered into my cup. "Your glass is empty, Crimson Smoke. I should fill it for you."

I tried to stop him as he reached for the illusion that was my cup, and sucked in a breath of astonishment when he lifted it off the table without any trouble at all.

"What?" he asked, waggling the cup at me. "Did you think I couldn't touch it? Your master isn't the only Lightweaver around, you know." He made every appearance of filling my cup from the carafe, although only a moment before the container had been almost empty, and not a drop spilled onto the table.

"He isn't my master," I said, accepting the cup back. "I prefer to think of him as a mentor."

Coirpre poured real wine into his own cup. "Interesting. And what exactly is your *mentor* doing as we speak?"

My mouth snapped shut.

"That's what I thought." He smirked at me as he lifted the goblet to his lips.

I had not missed the accompaniment of the music until that moment, when a thin, sad melody punctuated the atmosphere of the party. On the wooden stage, Lady Fenguard sat on a stool with her lips pressed to the mouthpiece of a winding, sinuous trumpet. Her fingers were positioned upon its many silver keys, and the tune that emerged was both melancholy and haunting.

"I've never heard anything like that before," I murmured. "Have you? I've never heard music that sounded quite so... I don't know, *lonely*."

Coirpre chuckled. "I'm not quite sure what to make of you."

"I could say the same." I returned my attention to his youthful face. "You have the same powers as Emerald, and yet from what I can tell, you only use them to make yourself look younger. Yes, I've noticed, so don't deny it. I would infer that you only care about appearances, and yet you didn't chime in on insulting Emerald's when the opportunity presented itself. Why not? It might have won you a bit of favor with those... gentlemen." I checked in on Dirkus and Benedite again. Fortunately, they had followed Edur to a spot only two tables away, where they were still in plain view.

Hurry up, Em, I can't be left alone in public for this long or I'm going to start a row with one of the many self-absorbed people among whom I've been abandoned. I wanted nothing more than to reach out to him through our connection, but barring a real emergency, I thought it best to avoid creating any distractions.

I didn't expect Coirpre to answer my question, and certainly not with any real sincerity. To my surprise, however, he slumped against the table and sized me up.

"The Emerald Flame is a thorn in my side," he admitted. "And he's the reason I'm trapped here for two years. Two years! All because he stirred up trouble for me in Lower Bound! Those merchants would have skinned me alive if they'd had their druthers. If Edur hadn't loaned me the money to pay them back, I might not be here now. But he did, and I am, and it'll take me another *eighteen months* to work off my debt, so thanks for that." He took a gulp of his wine, and his frown softened. "It's different, though, isn't it, having a personal grudge against someone, and saying hateful things behind his back just because you have nasty, small-minded opinions about his parentage?"

I stared at the bard, waiting for him to make some additional joke or snide comment.

"Oh, don't look at me like that," he grumbled. "I'm not just a pretty face. Emerald and I have more in common than you might think. And he's so *sad* all the time. Brings the whole mood down." Coirpre drank again as he slouched over the table. "If I'm going to have a nemesis, he could at least try to be a bit more entertaining."

I leaned sideways over the table in an attempt to better read the bard's expression. "I can't tell if you're being painfully shallow or relatably sarcastic."

"Yes, well." Coirpre flapped a hand at me. "I can't tell if you're *real,* so I suppose that makes us even."

The last notes of Lady Fenguard's mournful tune faded, and the audience—who seemed rather more subdued now—broke out in a smattering of applause.

Across the room, a red-faced Dirkus lurched to his feet and staggered away from his seat.

[Emerald,] I thought hastily, *[one of the scouts is either about to storm off in a huff or be sick with drink, and either way, I'm not sure how to follow him without attracting unwanted attention.]*

[My money's on sick,] Emerald replied. *[I just got back inside, and... Crimson. Why are you talking to Coirpre?]*

I rotated on the spot until I found Emerald's hunched form. He stood out above the milling guests much in the same way that Fenguard Keep loomed above the main city, so he was not hard to locate.

[Wait there, I'll come to you.] If Coirpre hadn't been sitting with me, I would have gone limp with relief. Instead, I turned to the bard, who was engaged in sipping his drink with a theatrically morose expression.

"My handler has returned," I said drily. "And like any well-trained dog, I must go to him. I'm sure I'll see you another night."

Coirpre snorted. "Very well. I have a favor to ask, though. If you're capable of keeping secrets from your maker, you can leave out anything even *moderately* flattering I said about him."

I rolled my eyes and backed away from him. "Gods forbid anyone mistake you for a decent person."

His blue eyes flashed. "I have a reputation to maintain."

I scooped up the illusion of my cup on the off chance that anyone should try to touch it later. "Goodnight, Coirpre."

As I wove through the crowd toward Emerald, I pondered the bard's odd behavior. Perhaps I shouldn't have told him my secret, but I didn't want him to think that I was still some luminary puppet without a mind of my own. Emerald had never revealed to me the full nature of their history, and the bard's reaction to our presence only confused me further.

That was not the most important matter at hand, however. Even before I reached Emerald, I asked, *[Is it done?]*

[It is.] Emerald sought out Benedite, who hadn't followed Dirkus on his flight from the hall. *[And as soon as the bog gives up its dead again, we'll know how effective our efforts were.]*

[I hope we won't have to wait long,] I told him. *[The company here leaves a lot to be desired.]*

Perhaps the gods were listening, because that particular wish came true far sooner than I would have believed.

Chapter Five

I no longer disappeared when Emerald slept, so instead, I remained in our rented room, fretting over all the things that could go wrong. The fate of a whole town lay in our hands, and a hundred things could go awry. It had been easier when the only fate I cared about, outside my own, was Emerald's.

I was imagining a series of increasingly dire outcomes when the gleam outside the window faded. Even in the dead of night, lights burned in Upper Bound: candles and lamps in our neighbor's windows, enchanted lanterns held by those who walked the streets even at these late hours, and a constant illumination from the direction of the port itself. As I watched, they did not go out, but they became muted, as if a shadow had passed between our room and the world beyond.

I hurried to the casement and peered through the warped glass. A heavy mist had descended over the whole town, rendering the outside world ghostly and opaque.

"Emerald?" I said aloud, but he was too deep asleep to hear me.

I was on the verge of stepping through the wall to investigate when a bell rang out. Its deep toll sent Emerald shooting upright in bed.

"Whassat?" he demanded, almost toppling off the edge of the mattress in his haste to rise.

"I'm not sure." I pointed outside. "But I think we'd better find out."

Emerald rubbed one eye with his palm as he reached for his shirt. "Remember when you thought we ought to flee Lower Bound because you heard someone was dead?"

"That was a lifetime ago." I shooed him to the door. "Go on. We don't want to miss whatever's happening."

"I'm just saying, you've come a long way since then." He yanked the door open and we stepped out into the hall together.

By the time we reached the streets, dozens of sleepy towns-folk were already outside. They were all headed in the same direction, some eagerly, others with a bit of reticence. None of them seemed alarmed, however.

"Excuse me!" I waved to a woman in her nightshift, who was leading her small child with one hand and carrying a lantern in the other. "What's happening?"

"Well, the dead're rising, ain't they?" The women peered at me as if I was being thick. "Only lasts an hour or so, but if we're lucky, we'll be able to have a chat with my nan before the Crone-mire takes her dead back."

I widened my eyes at Emerald. *[Already! Do you think the scouts will be ready to question Maximilien?]*

[I can't imagine otherwise.] Emerald dipped his head to the woman. "May we follow you, ma'am?"

"Only if you keep up." She hurried along, almost dragging her daughter, who was preoccupied with staring open mouthed at Emerald. "Step lively, Nell, or we'll miss it."

As we walked, more and more people streamed from their doors into the foggy night, joining the crowd as it wound its way inland, away from the port. Soon, the buildings thinned, and the cobblestones were replaced with wooden tracks wide enough to allow two carriages to pass abreast. Below us, solid earth gave way to black mud, and then to water so dark red in the lantern light that it could have been mistaken for blood.

[We're in the Cronemire now,] Emerald thought. There was an undercurrent to this comment that I could not parse, more akin to despair than fear.

I shifted closer to him, wishing that I could take his hand to reassure him. ***[We'll make sure that the Conjury doesn't find Dyrne. One way or another, we'll keep him—them—safe.]***

[Right.] Emerald slouched even further. Maximilien wasn't the only thing on his mind, but his secondary concern was such a faint tickle in the back of his brain that I couldn't unravel its source.

All around us, lantern light spilled through the mist, suffusing the bog in an eldritch glow. Eventually, the wooden trailways turned to follow the edges of the bog. The crowd stopped to stare out over the bog, toward the deepest parts of the water.

The mist was even thicker there, so deep that I could barely see beyond the planks that lined the walk. The crowd stilled, which was as unsettling as the mist itself. I had never heard so many people fall so perfectly silent.

And then a voice cried, "There! Do you see them?"

That first cry gave rise to many others, and soon everyone was pointing and moving about. As the crowd closed in, Emerald had to extend his arms and brace against the railing on either side of me to keep anyone from accidentally passing through my incorporeal form.

[Can you see anything?] I asked, squinting into the gloam.

Emerald shivered. ***[Yes.]***

And then I saw them, too. I had been looking up and out, as if the figures in the bog would be walking toward us. Only when a ripple caught my eye did I understand that they were not walking.

They were swimming.

And there were *hundreds* of them.

I peered down into the dark water as the first of the

approaching dead broke the surface only a few feet away from us. I could not tell if it was a man or a woman, on account of the carmine-tinted leather of its skin. Its posture was hunched and twisted, and its eyes were sunken in its face. The mouth was slumped to one side, as if the jawbone had been eaten away, and its hair was as stiff and brittle as old straw.

I shrank away from it on instinct. I had been able to face Kristine, the girl from Dyrne with invisible skin, but it was not the body's appearance that disturbed me so much as its jerky and erratic movements.

"Who are ye?" asked a man—one of the living ones—standing along the railing.

The figure gaped like a fish, struggling to move its slack mouth. I could not make out its reply. Whatever it said was little more than an exhalation from waterlogged lungs.

"Roland?" the man repeated.

The figure rasped again.

"Roland, I think he said!" The man at the railing turned to the crowd. "Anyone know a Roland?"

"I think tha's me granpap!" a young woman exclaimed.

The water rippled again, and another head emerged. The shrunken and shriveled form was more reminiscent of a lump of melted wax than a woman, but judging by the remains of hair and jewelry still clinging to the distorted revenant, she had been wealthy in life. I wondered if she had ever been lovely—if she had prided herself on the cut of her dress and the color of her capelet.

Someday, I will stop existing. And I will leave nothing behind, not even hair. Not even jewels. It will be as if I never was at all. The realization struck me like a blow.

I glanced back at Emerald, wondering if my sudden sense of mortality had come in part from him, but his expression was inscrutable.

Dozens of bodies were emerging from the bog, and the living scrambled along the walkway, pushing one way and then another in order to get close to their dead loved ones. The atmosphere had shifted from one of eerie quiet to that of a festival day. Emerald stood along the railing, blocking me with his bulk as he stared down at the dark bog below us.

"Come to see the show, have you?" a burbling voice from roughly the height of my hip asked.

I nearly passed through Emerald in my alarm as I spun to see the frog-man we had passed in town earlier that morning. He beamed up at us, with one gold eye fixed on me and the other rolled upward to examine Emerald.

"I... I suppose we have." I couldn't bring myself to look away from the frog-man's single eye. His pupil was slit slantwise, like a goat's.

"Mm." A bulbous, pink tongue slipped between his green lips in thought. "Don't think we've met."

"I'm Crimson. Er, Simon. And this is the Emerald Flame." My own tongue seemed to be playing tricks on me. There wasn't enough room for me to bow without passing through Emerald's arm, and from the corner of my eye, I could tell that he was staring down at the green creature with open skepticism.

"Ah!" Our new acquaintance flicked his other eye toward me and spread his hands wide. "A prominence title! At last, I am among equals! I am known as the King of the Black Hollow, but my given name is—" He blew out the pouch at his neck to an alarming size and let out a noise like the call of a bullfrog.

"Oh, that's... that's lovely." I glanced sideways at Emerald, whose eye had begun to twitch. I pointed to my own neck. "The thing is, I can't, um... inflate?"

"Of course not. None of the dry people can." The frog-man placed a sticky hand to his own bare chest. "You can call me Burp, or address me by my title, whichever suits you."

Emerald cleared his throat. "A pleasure, I'm sure. Are you familiar with the bog, Your Highness?"

[Don't make fun,] I chided.

Burp took no offense at Emerald's tone. Instead, he waved a four-fingered hand toward the depths of the bog. "Of course,

Emerald Flame! I know it well. If you'd like a tour when the dead are at rest, I would be happy to show you my kingdom."

"At the moment, we're rather more interested in your subjects." Emerald nodded to the dead.

"They aren't mine, poor things." Burp crouched down in a squat and peered through the wooden slats of the railing. "The Cronemire brings them back. Doesn't like letting go of the past, you see. Anyone who's met the bog, even in passing, can find another life here." His tone was solemn and respectful as he bowed his head to the living remains. "They come back until she finishes with the bones, and then they end up in the Black Hollow. Nights like these, I leave her be. The water gets... *prickly.*"

[I don't know what you have against him,] I told my companion. *[He's a bit funny to look at, but he's got a flair for poetry. I like him a great deal more than Dirkus.]*

[I don't dislike krubs, Crimson, they just unsettle me. And speaking of Dirkus...] "The Conjury is returning one of its dead to the bog tonight for questioning," Emerald said aloud. "Where might we find them?"

Burp's golden eyes glinted in the misty light surrounding us. "Here," he said darkly.

Sure enough, the rumble of wagon wheels reverberated through the wooden walk. A moment later, Dirkus's voice echoed out above the crowd. "Make way, coming through, Conjury business! Stir your stumps, lads!"

The crowd parted, and a wagon came into view, drawn by a plodding horse. Dirkus and Benedite sat at the front. A black lacquered box the size of a man lay in the wagon bed behind them.

[Is that the right coffin?] I asked nervously.

[I think so. Or rather, it's the one I wanted them to bring.] Emerald's throat bobbed. *[Let's hope this works out as intended.]*

Benedite drew up next to us and glared down his long nose.

"How fortunate that we should find you here, Emerald Flame," he said in a dry tone.

Dirkus glared at Burp, who straightened up to his full height. "Keeping appropriate company, I see," the scout muttered.

Emerald didn't take the bait. "Will Edur Fenguard be joining us?" he asked.

At the mention of the Laird's name, the locals closest to us shifted and bristled.

"Does he knew ye lot are down here?" a woman asked.

"Don't like Conjury folk desecrating our sacred lands," a man added.

"Shove off." Dirkus swung down off the wagon. He grimaced when his feet met the boards and clutched his head. Evidently, the effects of his drinking hadn't entirely worn off yet. "We have your Laird's approval, not that we need it. Lucky bastard is snug at home in bed. Wish I was, too..."

"Dirkus." Benedite's warning tone snapped his companion back into silence.

There was enough space around me that I was no longer in danger of being accidentally stumbled into. Even the bodies in the bog below us had pulled back, with their eyeless faces turned upward and their leathery jaws agape. Emerald left me to help the scouts lift the coffin down from the back of the wagon.

"Ain't right," someone murmured, "feeding their dead to the Cronemire. How do they intend to take him back?"

"They don't," another voice added. "That's the Conjury for you. They take what they want and leave others to clean up their mess."

Burp shuffled out of the way, but he kept his back straight, overseeing the proceedings with the air of a foreman. I couldn't help but notice that though the locals had no compunction about mingling with krubs and jotunn, they hung back from the Conjury men with open distaste. It made me like the townsfolk all the more for it.

Emerald and the two men laid the coffin upon the planks of

the wooden road, and Dirkus lifted the lid. He grimaced when he saw the man inside.

[It's the right one,] Emerald thought with relief. *[It isn't Maximilien.]*

[Well, we appear to have gotten lucky. Apparently, neither of these two idiots knew Maximilien personally, or this would've fallen apart here and now.] I struggled to muster enthusiasm for this turn of events. I was still of two minds about the morality of our undertaking, but I had done little enough to talk Emerald out of his plan. *I might as well celebrate our small victories.*

Burp and I stepped aside to watch as the dead man was hoisted out of his coffin and lowered into the water off the edge of the walkway.

"Ain't doin' it right," one of the onlookers muttered. "Ain't doin' the ritual or sayin' the words or payin' homage or *nothin'*."

"I hope she swallows 'im," an old woman added, waving her gnarled wooden cane at Dirkus's back.

[I'm surprised the scouts tolerate this open dissent,] I thought. Dirkus struck me as the sort of man who would be happy to lay into naysayers.

[They wouldn't if we were back on the mainland. The Conjury's grasp is tenuous on Kovin Isle, though. They're here as Fenguard's guests, remember? For once, they can't do as they please. I'm sure that rankles.] Emerald knelt down to watch a few stray bubbles ripple to the surface as the body of "Maximilien" drifted into the depths.

"She doesn't bring them all back," Burp said. He crossed his arms over his bare, plump belly and watched the bog with interest. "Only those she knew." He rolled one eye up toward me and lowered his voice, although the movement of his lips couldn't have been less subtle. "Would serve these dry folk right if she swallowed him whole and gave nothing back, you know. No offense, Master Crimson-Simon, but I get a bit territorial." He inflated his neck-pouch again and let it empty in a slow, flatulent exhalation.

"None taken." Given the general animosity toward the Conjury, it sometimes slipped my mind that people thought we were with them. Of course, if the truth about Dyrne came to light, our loose association with the Conjury wouldn't help us in the least.

If I'd had lungs, I would have held my breath as the three men crouched at the edge of the bog. Those around us, both the living and the dead, had fallen silent. A final huge bubble worked its way to the surface and burst.

"Well," Dirkus said after a long pause, "I suppose that's that. Bleeding waste of time, could have been asleep, dunno why we bother with these local—"

"Hush." Benedite lifted a long finger toward the misty sky, then turned it like the hands of a clock down toward the water. A pale face, not yet stained red by the peat of the bog, stared up at them.

Dirkus yelped and scrambled back, but Emerald leaned closer. He seemed almost enchanted by that face in the depths. Gradually, the man's scalp rose from the water as he got to his feet. He kept his back toward us, staring deep into the heart of the bog.

"Goes to show how unpredictable she can be," Burp whispered to me with more than a hint of pride.

"Maximilien of Leviathan Loch!" Benedite's voice boomed over the water.

The corpse didn't stir, although the others around it did. They drew back from him just as the living had drawn back from us.

"Maximilien," Benedite repeated.

[He's not going to answer to that,] I pointed out.

[I know.] Emerald stood upright and lifted himself over the wooden railing of the walk before dropping into the bog with a mighty splash. The water, which reached well over the waists of the dead, only reached mid-thigh on his old trousers.

He placed one hand on each of the dead man's shoulders and turned the corpse to face him. "How did you die?" he asked.

The corpse reached a trembling hand to his own neck and clawed at its throat, scratching furrows in the pale, decaying skin.

"Suffocation?" Emerald asked. His relief didn't show on his face, but I could feel it through our connection. *[That's another lucky turn of events, don't you think? Maybe the gods are smiling on us after all.]*

The corpse nodded and stopped its clawing motion.

"Was it an accident?" Emerald asked him. *[Thank the gods they can't talk properly, or we'd be in trouble.]*

Emerald's attempts to steer the conversation, however, had failed. The corpse shook his head once, sharply, with such violence that its neck emitted a crack and lolled to one side.

"*No-o-o-o-o.*" The rasping sound of the dead man's voice made even Burp flinch. As Amaya had told us, it wasn't *speech* so much as a wet and breathless shudder, reminiscent of the bubble that had swollen and burst when he was first deposited beneath the water. "*S-s-s-stol-e-e-e-nnn...*"

"Stolen?" Benedite shifted toward the edge of the walkway and hung onto the railing as he leaned out. "You were killed, you mean? Murdered?"

The corpse let his head roll toward the scout, independent of its neck and shoulders. His eyes were sunken so far into his sockets that they were barely a gleam beneath his brows. "*S-s-stol-e-e-n,*" he repeated, and clawed at his throat again.

Dirkus had finally rallied and returned to his coworker's side. "Who killed you?"

The corpse shrugged off Emerald's hands and turned laboriously toward town. It seemed to take him a hundred years to raise his arm, and I wondered what would happen if he pointed toward the mountain peaks, where Dyrne was nestled away from prying eyes.

Instead, his accusatory finger pointed in the direction of Upper Bound; Lower Bound lay somewhere beyond it around the curve of the river. "*S-s-stole... m-m-m-my...*" Nothing more than a wet gurgle followed.

His voice trailed off, and he turned to the bog. The mist was receding. As one, the bodies turned and lurched away, slipping below the water once more. Bubbles and ripples marked their passing, until those, too, faded from sight. In less than a minute, they were gone, and the bog was back to its usual self.

The citizens followed suit, and Dirkus rolled his eyes. "What a waste of time. Didn't learn anything. If the cursed stick of jerky won't even respond to his name, what good is he? We can't very well pick up our questioning where we left off."

"Guess we'll have to do things the old-fashioned way," Benedite griped.

They headed back to the wagon. Neither of them stopped to offer Emerald a hand up out of the mire.

The scouts might not have learned anything, but we had. Evidently, Maximilien's was not the only murder in the region that had gone officially unsolved.

[What did you say,] I asked my companion, ***[about the gods smiling on us?]***

Chapter Six

Emerald lay on his bed in our rented room and stared up at the ceiling.

"When are we going to talk about this?" I asked.

He snatched up his pillow and pressed it to his face with a groan. "Which part?" he asked, his voice muffled by the goose-down batting. "The one where we've only succeeded in drawing attention to another murder? Or the fact that we have to solve it and delay the Conjury scouts at the same time?"

"You know, it *could* work in our favor." I sat down just above the covers on the side of the bed and crossed my legs beneath me. "Aindreas is almost certainly not responsible for this man's death. Perhaps we can still salvage this."

Emerald shoved the pillow aside. "By pinning Maximilien's murder on someone else, you mean? The Conjury are going to be chasing their tails in search of someone to blame for a death they believe to be Maximilien's. All the clues in his care are going to point straight back to Dyrne, and even if we get lucky enough to solve the murder of a total stranger whose very *name* we don't know, what happens when it turns out that his ship-mate flung him off a dock after a drunken brawl? How are we going to resolve the matter of Maximilien's death when it will be obvious that a sailor didn't do it? The timelines won't match up, much less the perpetrator!"

"Hmm." I ran my hand over my shoulder, wiping an imaginary speck of dust from my pristine jacket.

Emerald's head whipped toward me, and he pointed a blunt finger at my face. "Don't say it."

"Say what?" I batted my eyelashes innocently at him.

"I can hear you thinking it, Crim. *Don't. Say. It.*"

"I wasn't going to say anything."

My friend crossed his arms. "Hmph."

I allowed silence to descend upon us before I added, "Although I *did* tell you that I hated this plan right from the start—"

"*I know!*" Emerald pressed his palms to his ears and made a horrible face. "It's my fault. I acknowledge it. This was a terrible idea, and I should have listened to you. Is that what you want to hear?"

"It'll do." I allowed myself a smug smile. "But we're here now, and it occurs to me that it might be possible to find out the name of our victim, at the very least. Wouldn't the Sisterhood have records of the dead?"

Emerald lowered his hands. "I suppose they would. Although I doubt that they'd take kindly to being questioned by the Conjury, and we can hardly interrogate them at the same time as the scouts."

"Then we will have to find another avenue of investigation. If only you knew someone who could infiltrate the Sisterhood. Someone who could play the part of a woman as easily as that of a man, who could walk through walls if anyone tried to abscond with her, who is clever and charming enough to win others over to her cause..." I stared at the wall and pretended to think it over.

Emerald groaned and reached for the pillow again. "I believe I'd rather smother myself than hear you sing your own praises any longer. You're right, though. The Sisterhood is a good place to start. I can't very well accompany you there, however."

"You shouldn't be with me anyway. *You* should stick close to the scouts and see what they find out."

"Wonderful. There's nothing I'd love more than a whole day spent in the company of *Dirkus*," Emerald whined.

"I'm glad to hear it. Now get some sleep. I'll go to the Sisterhood tomorrow. Between the two of us, we're smart enough to resolve this." I spoke with all the confidence I could scrape together. After all, in the course of my memory, we'd never failed to solve a mystery.

I could only hope that our luck would hold a second time.

⚜

Early the next morning, I stood before the door of the Sisterhood's convent, running my palms over the coarse material of my new dress. It was reassuring to feel real, even if only to myself.

When I slipped into the shape of Simone that morning, I had forced myself to abandon my usual finery. The costume I wore was even drearier than the one Emerald had summoned for me in Dyrne when he'd had the *gall* to place my bodice over the outer layer of my dress. In rough cotton and wool and—*gods help me*—an intentional smudge of mud across my cheek, I had never in my life looked so poor and sorry. I had even gone to the trouble of hiding my scarlet hair under a shapeless linen coif.

Modesty did not suit me, but desperate times called for desperate trappings, and though it pained me, I had risen to the challenge.

The Sisterhood's convent stood outside the confines of the city, encircled by a high wall that blocked all but one side of the entry building from the eyes of those outside.

While it would have been possible for me to slip inside the wall directly, there was very little I could do once I was inside. I could not turn myself invisible, try as I might, and I couldn't sift through the records without the assistance of someone with real hands. I would need to win the sisters over by other means.

I knelt on the steps before the convent, folded my hands before me, and bowed my head in an attitude of prayer. I could no more knock on the door than I could force my way through it, so I had already determined to make my presence known through other means.

I did not have to wait long. Only a few minutes passed before the door opened and a figure emerged, swathed in flowing black robes that reached the top of the stones steps beneath her feet.

"Welcome, child," she intoned in an accent which differed yet again from that of the locals. "What can ah do for ye?"

I pressed my palms together and affected a shakiness to my tone, pitching my voice higher than I usually did when in my feminine form. "I have come to join the convent, if you'll have me."

The figure glanced down the road first one way, then the other, as if she suspected someone of lurking nearby. When she saw no one, she beckoned to me. "Come inside, child. We'll discuss yer circumstances in private."

I dipped my head in a show of false modesty, although my real intention was to hide my smile. *Excellent. I've still got it.*

She waved me through into a small office, where a heavy einwood desk dominated the room. It was not a richly appointed room, like the one where Laird Edur had greeted us, but it had a cozy feel to it—mismatched glass lamps dangled from the rafters, and the wall space that wasn't dedicated to bookshelves and trailing potted plants was taken up with an enormous tapestry depicting a woman in black with bird wings where arms should be. All around her, a riot of flora and fauna decorated the fabric in exquisite detail.

The sister caught me staring and nodded to the enormous work of art. "Remarkable, isn't it? 'Twas made by one o' the Ladies Fenguard centuries ago to depict the Crone, our goddess."

"It's lovely." I was more interested in my host, however. I was quite certain that I had seen her in Lower Bound when the sisters first came to collect Maximilien's remains. She was nearly as tall as Emerald, and almost as broad shouldered, although her movements were more graceful. I wondered idly if she was half-jotunn, too—not that it mattered particularly, although it would be nice to meet someone else like Emerald. I glanced more closely at her robes. Sure enough, a red-and-gold brooch flashed amid the black linen of her modest attire. I recognized the emblem as the same one she had worn in McLachlan's inn, although I still did not know its meaning.

The sister ushered me into one chair, and settled down on the far side of the desk in the other. "Now, tell me, what brings ye here?"

Time to play my part, I thought, and forced my face into a pitiable frown. "I have nowhere else to go," I said in that same quaking voice. "I heard that there was a Sisterhood here, and I thought of how I'd never had sisters before, and that it might be nice to belong somewhere..."

"Child." The sister folded her hands in front of her and spoke to me in a gentle tone. "That is not enough reason tae give your life over tae the service of a goddess. Ye are young. Better tae go out into the world at yer age than to retreat from it entirely. We are always willing tae provide funds tae young women such as yerself. Have ye considered venturing tae the mainlands of Dregandresal? Leviathan Loch has many opportunities for gainful employment, an' the Sisterhood has connections overseas."

I sank back in my chair with every word. It had not occurred to me that the Sisters would turn me away, much less offer me help of another kind. My first impression of them was that they were standoffish and cold.

"I can't—" I said weakly. "That is, um..."

"Ah." She knitted her fingers together, and there was a smile in her voice, although I could not see her face behind her black veil. "There's a man, isn't there? There is *always* a man. Who is he? What sway does he hold over ye?"

I blinked at her several times, at a loss for words. *Think of something believable. Anything. The closer to the truth, the better.*

"Ye're in a safe place," she assured me. "He has no power here. Ye can trust me, ah promise.

"It's, um…" I licked my lips. "I've been having some trouble with my, uh, father?" Gods, I could only imagine what Emerald would say if he heard me referring to him as such.

"Ah." The Sister nodded, as if this was a story she heard often. "Ye are at odds wi' him?"

"Constantly," I said. "And I would love to get away from him, so if there's a way I can sign up or, ah, conscript myself into Cronely service—"

The sister lowered her voice to a whisper. "Does he hurt ye, child?"

"No! No, never." I shrank away from her. The very thought sickened me; *that* was not something I would lie about as a means to an end. "But he doesn't see me as my own person. He seems to think that I'm an extension of him."

"Ah understand, perhaps better than ye know." The sister raised her hands to her veil.

Dyrne had taught me that people were not always what I assumed them to be. The villagers had used their robes to hide their invisibility, but when the sister removed her veil, my hand flew to my mouth in surprise. I forgot my role completely as I took in the contours of her face. Her head was shaved bare, and her copper skin stretched taut over proud cheekbones and blunt but decidedly human features. She wasn't like Emerald at all.

She was like *me*.

The sister smiled faintly. "What is yer name, child?"

"Simone," I said, still gawking at her.

"Ye may call me Aster."

My eyes snapped from her jawline to her eyes. "Aster?" I repeated. "Like the goddess?"

"That is the name ah gave myself, yes. It was not the name ah was born with." As I stared at her, the smile faded from her lips. I wondered if there were people in her life like Dirkus, who said unkind things just to make her feel small.

I leaned over the desk toward her. "Can I tell you a secret, Aster?" I cupped my hand around my mouth and whispered, "I am not always a woman."

The sister's smile returned, gentler now. "Well, *ah* always have been, although it took me a long time tae realize it. My father... did not see eye tae eye on the subject when ah told him the truth. The story he told himself about me warred with my own experience. Does yers feel the same? Is that why ye want tae join the Sisterhood?"

I had lost the thread of the conversation entirely, and I could not see how to salvage it. I was rather glad that Emerald was not here to see how much of a mess I'd made of this interrogation, although I comforted myself with the knowledge that it was no worse than the one he'd made of switching the bodies.

"That isn't the trouble," I told her. "He doesn't treat me any differently whether I'm one version of myself or the other. The trouble is that I can't seem to get away from him. Sometimes I worry that he could erase me entirely. Not with violence!" I hastened to add. "Just with his indifference."

"Is there any hope o'repairing this relationship?" Aster asked.

"Maybe." *Although when he finds out how badly I've flubbed this, it might make things a bit rocky.*

"If ye feel safe doing so, ah encourage you to go home. Talk to him. Ye might be surprised at how much progress ye can make with words. If ye like, ah can teach ye something that may help ye stay grounded in the future."

I twisted my fingers together in my lap. If I wasn't going to gather anything useful about the dead man we'd thrown into the swamp, I might as well learn *something*. "Would you, please?"

"Close yer eyes."

I did as Aster suggested.

"Take a deep breath."

I couldn't follow this instruction, but I pretended to.

"Very good, Simone. Now imagine that ye are elsewhere. It doesn't have to be a real place. It only has tae be a *safe* place. Can ye picture it?"

I tried to imagine the safest place that I could think of. The first place that sprang to mind was Tincrown's house, with its plethora of books and plush, worn furniture and some experiment or other laid out on the kitchen table.

"In this place," Aster said, "ye can be yer true self."

That shifted my imagined room slightly. All at once, I envisioned that I was in Tincrown's sitting room, but I could *touch* things.

"Try spending a little time in this safe place whenever ye like. This is yer palace, Simone. Ye are the queen—or king—of this particular castle. Whenever anyone tries tae control ye, remember this."

"I'll do my best," I said gamely. I wasn't sure that a palace would be right for me, but a cottage of my own, like the ones I'd grown used to in Dyrne, sounded lovely. Pushing the thought aside, I opened my eyes, determined to make one last go of my original purpose. "Would it be possible for me to enter the convent, Aster? Just to get a sense of what it's like?"

She shook her head and offered a regretful smile. "Ah'm afraid not. Those who have given their lives over tae the Crone have done so in the hopes of finding respite from the larger troubles of the world. Ah will nae let those troubles walk through the open door." Aster rose to her feet. "But ah hope ye know ye will feel free tae return tae us at any time. Ah would like to know what becomes o'ye, and if ye ever feel unsafe, we are always glad tae help our sisters... or our brothers." She winked one gray eye at me.

"Thank you." I let her lead me out, wracking my incorporeal brains with every step in an attempt to work out another way to stay. Nothing occurred to me, and soon enough, I was deposited on the step outside once more, with no more information to show for my efforts than when I began.

Chapter Seven

❦

With one avenue of information cut off, I was in no hurry to return to Emerald and confess that my plan, which I had been so smug about the night before, had produced only a dead end. Instead, I wandered out onto the wooden walkway where we had watched the dead come in, and I had a good long think.

Even if I had been able to get into the ledgers of the Sisterhood, there was no guarantee that I would be able to tell who the man in the bog had been. All we knew about him was that he had been strangled, and that something had been stolen from him. That wasn't much to go on.

No, that's not true. Emerald taught you better than that. If he found the man's body in the ice house, we also know that the man was a foreigner scheduled to be shipped back to the mainland. There might be records of who else was there... and in that case, Em might be able to help identify which coffin Maximilien ended up in. Then we would at least have a name to work with.

The moment that the idea occurred to me, I reached out to Emerald. **[Have you got a moment?]**

[Not now,] he told me. **[I'm in the midst of a scintil-**

lating conversation with Dirkus. He has opinions about lambkin women that'd make your hair curl.]

Better not ask what *that* meant. Instead, I dangled my feet over the edge of the boardwalk and stared out into the bog.

In some ways, the landscape reminded me of Dyrne. It had been ominous at night, with all that fog rolling in and the shadows playing thick over the hummocks of peat protruding from its surface. Now I could see that there was more to it: white tufts of what looked like cotton blooming out of the marshlands, the meandering skeletal forms of trees whose greenery only thrived on the topmost branches, and a constant trill of music from unseen songbirds. Lower, more modest vegetation grew from the land and water alike. A pair of redwing blackbirds dipped out of the sky and perched on the tops of two cattails, until their weight bowed them toward the still surface of the bog, before taking flight again.

The sight of the birds sparked an idea. I had become the same sort of bird back in Dyrne and tried to follow Oidche in disguise. Perhaps I could become a bird again and investigate the bog itself? It might be worth the attempt...

Movement beneath my feet caught my attention as two golden mounds rose from the water below me. I let out a shriek of alarm, and a wet squeal echoed my surprise. The outline of a triangular, green-tinged head emerged a moment later.

"Oh, Burp! You startled me, Your Highness." I pressed my hand to my chest as if to soothe the pounding of my imagined heart.

"Master Crimson-Simon!" Burp exclaimed as he pulled himself up onto the boardwalk and shook off a sheen of peat-laden mud. "What happened to you? You're a *woman*."

"Er." I grimaced and glanced down at myself. I had never switched back and forth between manhood and womanhood in Dyrne, and so I had never needed to keep my story straight. That made two miscalculations in one morning. I was happier than ever that Emerald and I had parted ways for the day.

Burp offered me a sympathetic smile. "Did you and Master Emerald fight?" he asked.

"We... did?" I interlaced my hands and tried to mirror his expression. "We did."

"No shame in that, Master Crimson-Simon."

"It's just Simon," I said as he crouched down beside me. "Or, rather, Simone now." Evidently, my explanation had satisfied him, because he did not press any further. Sadly, Emerald's knowledge of krubs was limited, so rather than dig myself any deeper into trouble by asking awkward questions, I let the matter go. Instead, I crossed my ankles. "Lord Burp, I take it you know a great deal about the, ah, neighboring kingdom? The city of Upper Bound, I mean."

"Not as well as I know the Black Hollow, but yes." Rather than sitting as I did, Burp placed all four feet on the ground and lowered himself onto his belly. He blinked each eye in turn, so that one was always open. "Do you need a guide, Master Simone?"

"I'm wondering about the other local powers. There's you, of course. And Laird Fenguard." I ticked the names off on my hands. "The Sisterhood. Who else?"

"The Trader's Guild," he said.

"Oh, of course." I'd already forgotten that they were distinct from the Conjury. Given that our mystery corpse was from out of town, he might very well be one of the sailors. "Is that all?"

Burp sat frozen with his eyes half open. I waited for him to respond, assuming that he was thinking. I was quite taken aback, therefore, when his mouth hinged open impossibly wide and his long pink tongue flicked out to catch a passing mayfly.

"Aaaah," he sighed, smacking his lips in appreciation. "Delicious. Besides the guild, there's also Miss Marsha."

"Marsha?" I repeated as I tried to place the name. "*Oh!* We met her yesterday. She seemed an all-right sort."

"Can't speak to that, Master Simone. I keep to myself, and the dry people mostly don't bother with me. As for local powers, the last and greatest of all is the Cronemire herself."

"I'm not sure I count the Cronemire as a *power*," I said skeptically.

Burp spun one eye to examine me. "She turns the dry dead wet and living," he pointed out. "Surely that counts for something?"

"I suppose it does," I admitted. "Thank you for your help, Lord Burp. And, um, if you see me around in the future…"

"Don't talk to you in front of the other drylings?" he asked sadly.

"Oh, that's not what I was going to say at all!" I shifted around on the walkway, tucking my knees beneath myself. "I was only going to ask that you call me either Simon or Simone depending on how I look at the time."

He perked up again. "Ah, of course! I understand, but as I said, there's no shame in it. Still, a promise is a promise. I won't reveal your secrets, *Simone*." A lacey third eyelid fluttered shut as he winked at me, then pushed himself back to his feet. "A pleasure seeing you. I've got business in the Black Hollow to attend to now."

"The other krubs will be missing their king," I agreed.

"Other krubs?" He let out a croaking laugh and slapped his belly. "Goodness, no! It's only me. Being the head of state is so much easier when you have no one else to answer to!" With that, he hopped over the railing and splashed down into the water below. For a while, I watched his golden eyes skimming just above the surface of the water until they, too, disappeared from view.

I briefly considered finding some private spot in which to rearrange myself into a bird and follow him, but I decided against it. If I tested the limits of my tether to Emerald, I could be snapped back to wherever he was, giving Dirkus and Benedite that much more reason to be suspicious of us. It would be better to head back into town and find information the old-fashioned way.

I longed for the old days, when our lives were the only things at stake, rather than the lives of everyone under our care—including the man my best friend loved.

❧

By the time I found Emerald again, I had taken the liberty of rearranging myself back into Simon. I had even shown a moderate level of restraint when it came to my outfit, opting for the red-and-black garments that Emerald had summoned me in on the night I was born. My fashion sense might be free, but Fenguard might question our modest tab at the tailor's if I showed up in a different kingly outfit every night.

[Where are you?] I asked as I navigated the narrow, criss-crossing streets of the city.

[Out by the docks.] Emerald's tone was flat. *[There's another one.]*

[Another what?]

[Another body.]

I moved faster, weaving between the crowd of onlookers who were gathering along the bay. It was difficult to move without accidentally passing through people, and by the time I reached Emerald's side, I was in a foul mood.

"What happened?" I asked. "What did I miss? Who is—*oh*."

A crew of sailors had taken out a rowboat to fish up the corpse floating face down in the water. Even without seeing his features, I recognized him.

It was one of the jotunn sailors that we had seen in Fenguard Keep the night before.

"Oh, *Em*." I reached out to pat his arm before thinking better of it. He would not want me prying on his thoughts just now, and truth be told, I didn't want to see them, either.

Dirkus and Benedite were watching with glee and indifference, respectively, as a man I'd never met before strutted back and forth along the end of the pier.

"That's right, men, heave to. A big bugger like that ain't gonna haul himself aboard, now is he?" The man in question was dressed in striped trousers and a matching tailcoat in shades of olive and goldenrod, but such was my distress over Emerald's state that I didn't stop to consider whether he might be color-blind—although it *did* seem to be the only explanation for his attire.

[*Are you all right?*] I asked.

Emerald shuddered. "It's nothing to do with me, Crimson. They aren't my people." All the same, he could not tear his eyes away from the dead jotunn.

It took five of them to haul the corpse aboard using an old fishing net. There was no sign of the other two jotunn.

Dirkus seemed to be thinking along the same lines as I was. "Bet his pals did him in last night. Brutes like that can't hold their drink without things getting ugly."

[*Says the man who ran off to be sick in the latrines,*] I thought bitterly.

"Leave it alone, Crimson," Emerald murmured.

[*But...*]

"Leave. It." A muscle jumped in his jaw. He didn't often shut me out of our mental connection, but at the moment, the door to his mind was closed, bolted, and barred.

The man in the questionable suit turned to us as the rowboat pulled back toward the pier. "Now, as I understand it, you fellas are from the Conjury." He adjusted the gold frame of a monocle that he wore over one eye. As far as I could tell, the eyepiece was only for show, as there didn't appear to be any glass in it. "Will you be wanting a closer look at this bloke, or...?"

"I don't think that'll be necessary." Dirkus smirked down at the boat. "We don't bother with dead animals." He spat over the side of the pier.

"Watch it, now." The olive-clad gentleman braced his hands on his hips. "These lot may be bilge rats, but they're *my* bilge rats. Mind your tongue."

Dirkus let out a bellow of laughter, and a moment later, the olive-clad man joined in. They slapped each other on the back as they let out peals of mirth.

"Bilge rats!" Dirkus cackled.

"Bastards and convicts, the lot of 'em," the other man hooted.

Benedite rolled his eyes before turning to them. "My *associate* is right, Hudson. Your folk answer to you, but if you get a whiff of foul play, make sure we know. We're investigating a scout's death, see."

"Aye, aye, that fella from a few months ago." Hudson dashed a tear out of his unmonocled eye. "I'll keep my ear to the ground, gents, but I assure you, this blackguard's death is unrelated. This lot go in and out with the tides, and there aren't many that'll stay in the same port six months on. The Trader's Guild doesn't allow time for idle bedevilment. We keep their hands busy, don't we, lads?"

A lackluster chorus of voices replied, "Aye, sir." Evidently, the sailors of the Trader's Guild didn't like Hudson any more than the locals liked the Conjury. Judging by the sailor's careless handling of the body, though, they didn't much care for jotunn either. They heaved the waterlogged remains onto the deck face-up.

Emerald took one look at the dead man and turned his back.

"Hard to look at an ugly bugger like that, isn't it?" Dirkus asked, socking my friend in the shoulder.

"Mm," was Emerald's only reply.

"Master Hudson?" I spoke up for the first time, addressing the man who was evidently in charge of the docks. "What was this man's name?"

"Him?" Hudson nodded to the dead jotunn. "Neek, we called him. Out of the Infested Mountains, as his kind usually are."

I knelt beside the body of the jotunn. The light had gone out of his deep-set eyes, and his tusked mouth hung open to reveal a blackened tongue. What interested me more, however, were the scratch marks on his thick neck. Almost as if he had clawed at his throat—as the corpse in the water had the night before.

In Dyrne, Tincrown had used enchanted gloves to help determine the cause of a man's death. I didn't have the help of the Aidea, but I'd been able to read people's minds before. Perhaps I could do the same with Neek.

I lowered my fingers gingerly to his throat, prepared to be drawn into the horror of his final moment, or into whatever deep and lightless place the dead inhabited.

As my fingertips brushed his throat, however, I felt nothing. No pain, no terror, no all-consuming darkness. Neek was as empty as a lump of dead wood. Whatever had made him a man had been stripped away with his death.

Stolen, as the life of the stranger in the bog had been.

Chapter Eight

"**I** hope you aren't offended by all this talk of beasts." Dirkus walked so close to Emerald that his shoulder bumped that of my friend as we made our way uphill toward Fenguard Keep. "With you, it's all in jest. You're one of the good ones. One of *our* beasts, you see?" He elbowed Emerald jovially in the ribs. "Like a tame dog."

"Oh, shut up, Dirkus," Benedite spat.

"What?" Dirkus spun so that he was walking backward, lifting his hands wide. "Everyone loves dogs. I had a dog when I was a boy." His gaze slid sideways toward Emerald, and a wicked sneer curled his lips. "She took up with a feyhound, though. Whelped a litter of the ugliest puppies you've ever seen." He leered at Emerald.

"*Dirkus.*" Benedite lunged forward and caught his associate by the collar. "I don't know what's gotten into you, but that's enough. Remember what Fenguard said, if you need help holding your tongue."

My hands were balled into fists at my side. If I could have struck Dirkus a blow, he'd be sitting on his arse in the dust. *[Has he been like this all day?]*

[No. He was hungover in the morning, thank the gods,

and he kept his mouth closed.] Emerald kept his eyes fixed on the keep as we climbed the hill. *[Don't start anything with him, all right? I have to put up with him as long as we're here, and the last thing we need is him to stop being* awful *and start being* suspicious.*]*

I understood my friend's point, but every time I looked at Dirkus, I remembered the violent mix of rage and love that had spilled through me when I crossed paths with Aindreas. I was beginning to see how affection and fury could become commingled, and why a person might be driven to harm someone out of a need to safeguard those under their protection.

[Just remember, we're only doing this until Tincrown and the others are safe again. Then we can go back, all right?] I wished that I could think of something Tincrown might say to take the sting out of Dirkus's cruelty, but since I couldn't, I would have to rely on the man himself to find the right words once all this was behind us.

At the mention of the doctor's name, Emerald's shoulders relaxed slightly. *[True.]*

At least he was letting me into his head again. That was a relief.

It was only midafternoon, but evidently the festivities in Fenguard Keep were already beginning again.

"I thought they had a party yesterday to celebrate the arrival of the new ship," I said.

"His Lairdship finds excuses for parties *every* night," Benedite said. "Last night, it was the ship. Today, it'll likely be a low holy day of a minor god they don't recognize on the island. Tomorrow, he'll find some other reason to celebrate."

"Oh, stop moaning." Dirkus threw one arm around his associate's shoulders and shook him a few times. "You like wine and feasting as much as anyone else."

Benedite's lip curled back. He had the look of a man who would happily elbow his colleague in the throat, and I was disappointed when he exercised restraint. "There are those who like the wine better than I do," he snapped.

[I don't think I can take another night of this,] I thought wearily.

[Then don't. We'll part ways again. I can keep an eye on these two and watch out for anyone acting suspicious, and you can see if there's anything worth examining in the castle.] There was a shifty note in Emerald's thoughts, and I got the impression that he was trying to conceal something from me.

[Are you sure?] I didn't like the idea of leaving him with the Conjury scouts any more than necessary.

[Fenguard Keep is the hub of the city. Everyone comes and goes here, and we know for a fact that the dead jotunn was here last night.] He managed the ghost of a smile in my direction. *[If only one of us was capable of moving silently and slipping through walls if they heard anyone coming, and astute enough to make sense of any evidence they encountered...]*

[I accept your flattery.] I was glad that Emerald sounded a bit more like his usual self. Whenever Dirkus was awful to him, I thought of those little scars that notched his arms and legs, and his confession about their origin.

At least he had me to keep an eye on him now. He was no longer utterly alone.

I drew up short just before we reached the walls of the keep. "Pardon me, gentlemen," I said, "but I will catch up with you later. I have other business to attend to."

Dirkus snorted and tapped one side of his nose. "Other business, indeed. A woman, I expect?"

I managed not to roll my eyes. "You might say that." Given that I would *be* a woman in two minutes' time, he wasn't entirely wrong. I had already made up my mind to conduct my sneaking about as Simone; if I was unlucky enough to be spotted, it would be that much harder for anyone to identify me.

"Or a man?" Dirkus suggested. "Pretty boys like you, they always go for men."

Emerald cut his eyes away, and I wondered what that meant.

Rather than give any more weight to Dirkus's nastiness, I settled for batting my eyelashes and blowing the scout a kiss before turning on my heel. If the gods had any taste at all, they'd smite him where he stood. I liked the man even less than Aindreas, and that was saying something.

It took me longer than I'd anticipated to find a quiet room in which to rearrange myself. Once I did, I was faced with the question of how to dress. My initial instinct had been to dress as a maid so that it wouldn't matter so much if I was spotted—but a maid flying about the keep would draw plenty of attention, and if anyone tried to hand me something, I would be found out. It would be better to be stealthy.

Unfortunately, when he'd first conjured me, stealth hadn't been Emerald's top priority. My purpose, as he'd told me from the beginning, was to see and be seen. He'd made me vain and beautiful because those traits served his purpose. To my chagrin, they also made it difficult to disguise myself.

In the end, and with more than a little irritation, I was forced to do something that pained me deeply.

I had to dress like *Emerald*.

Using his plain black garments as inspiration, I rearranged myself into my second styleless outfit of the day. There wasn't much I could do about my brilliant red curls, so I added a black hood that covered most of my face as well as my hair.

If Emerald was going to be forced to suffer Dirkus for a few days, I could endure this for mere hours.

I slipped out of the small room where I had sought refuge and kept to the shadows, avoiding the influx of guests and guards alike. Most of the activity was centered around the main hall, so I slunk toward one private wing of the keep, made sure that I was alone, and pushed off. In an instant, I was soaring up toward the topmost rooms as the ground fell away below me.

When I reached the roof, I paused for a moment, crouched against the old hand-formed tiles. From this height, I could see everything: the sea, the bog, the city below us, the distant port of Lower Bound, even the bridge where we had met Amaya. The road was hidden by trees, but I knew where it led, and I followed its route with my eyes until I was staring in the rough direction of Dyrne. The landscape was lovely, and the late after-noon sunlight bathed the autumn countryside in a soft pink glow.

It occurred to me for the first time that, although I had never known anyplace but Kovin Isle, I did not think of the island as *home*. What would it take, I wondered, for me to feel any true connection to a place? Emerald was a wanderer, but I had never belonged anywhere. Perhaps I would always be an intruder, an outsider looking in.

If that's what you are, you might as well embrace it, I thought, and I dropped through the roof of the keep.

The rooms in which I found myself were as sumptuous as all the others, but some quality of the appointments made it feel older and out-of-date. I didn't recognize the dark wood from which the hand-turned furniture was crafted, and the upholstery of the couches and chairs was slightly worn.

This must be the Fenguard's private rooms, I mused, padding silently through the uninhabited space. *The keep is hundreds of years old. Some of this furniture must have been here for all that time.*

Along the walls hung luxurious tapestries depicting the keep, the view of the ocean, and other aspects of life in Upper Bound. I was reminded of what Sister Aster had told me at the convent that morning, that several generations back, one of the Fenguards had been a master of the art. I could only imagine that they'd passed it down through the years. It would take a dozen lifetimes for even the most skilled craftswoman to weave all of these.

I examined the room thoroughly, peering into every drawer and hidden panel I could find, although I found nothing out of the ordinary. When my curiosity was satisfied, I peeked through the door into the hallway beyond to make sure that there was no one around. When I wandered into the corridor, I found that it, too, was lined with portraits and tapestries intermittently. Lairds and Ladies Fenguard from the last five hundred years frowned down at me from gilded frames. The style of portraiture had changed significantly throughout the years, but the austerity in their eyes remained the same.

I paused beneath the oldest of them, an image of a young couple with raven-black hair in a flat, old-fashioned style, painted on wood paneling. The Fenguard line had ruled over the land for centuries, and while they had allowed the Conjury and the Trader's Guild to establish business on their shores, they had managed to maintain independence. I would rather bow before Edur Fenguard than *Dirkus* any day.

My thoughts were interrupted by the sound of voices down the hall, and I slunk closer to an open door from which three female voices emanated.

"Will you not be joining the party?" one of them asked.

"In a little while," a second replied. "I am so tired of it all, Odette. A night alone with my husband wouldn't go amiss, but he has been so busy of late..."

I crouched down and passed inside a large chest in the hallway full of clean linens. From there, my body would not be visible to anyone coming and going, and I could press my face into the wall of the room from which the voices came.

Lady Fenguard sat inside, weaving on an enormous loom, while two of her ladies sat beside her with their embroidery. I had been right, then, about how many generations of ladies must have learned the skill. Her current work depicted the bog, but not as I had ever seen it. In Lady Fenguard's eye, the Cronemire was bristling with greenery and wildlife. It reminded me of the tapestry that Aster had shown me in the convent.

The lady herself was engrossed in her task, and my hidden position made it possible for me to get a better look at her than I had the night before. Her russet hair was pinned up to expose her long neck, and once again, her gown and jewels were beyond anything I might have dared imagine for myself. Even so, there was sadness in her expression. I wondered how often Edur left her to her own devices.

"It's not his fault, Lady Dionara," one of the maids said. "The needs of the kingdom—"

"I know that, of course." Dionara Fenguard's hand clenched on her comb as she pressed the topmost row of her weaving into place. "And I will play my part. Only, give me another hour. I will go down then."

They went back to their work, and I withdrew. I felt almost sorry for the lady, whose private life was dictated by the needs of the kingdom.

Once again, I had found very little, but as I wandered the vast and silent halls of the keep, one thing became clear to me: whatever the Fenguards lacked in personal happiness, they did not want for material possessions. I found it difficult to imagine what a stranger from the mainland could possess that they would desire desperately enough to kill for it.

By the time I returned to the party in the form of Simon, the festivities were well underway. Coirpre was finishing his last song as I stepped through the door, and he narrowed his eyes when he saw me. He hastened to bow deeply to the audience before descending the steps two at a time and practically running over to cut me off.

"Where have you been?" the bard hissed.

I turned up my nose at him. "None of your business." I ducked past him, but he retreated to bar my way again.

"He's been a mess all night." Coirpre hooked his thumb over his shoulder at the table where Emerald sat in conversation with the scouts. My spirits sank as I took in my friend, whose cheeks were flushed dark. His eyes were glassy as he stared down at the table while Dirkus prattled on about gods only knew what.

I bit my lip and hurried forward, while Coirpre followed on my heels. *[Em? Is everything all right?]*

[Why wouldn't it be?] Before I could reach him, he picked

up the decanter and splashed another serving of wine into his cup. *[I've been listening to this bastard carry on for hours and praying to the gods you'll find something, because if you don't then Tincrown... Tincrown...]* He grunted and threw back a mouthful of wine. *[I shouldn't have left Dyrne.]*

I had seen Emerald drink before, but the unsteadiness of his movements was new to me. Coirpre seemed just as worried as I was as he took a seat on the bench opposite Emerald, while I settled in at my friend's side.

"Oh good, you're here." Dirkus offered me a vapid smile. "You're friend's bein' all pissy. No fun at all."

"I wonder why," I said drily. On the stage that Coirpre had just vacated, Lady Fenguard was settling onto her stool with her horn, prepared to do her part to add to the festivities. She looked nearly as miserable as Emerald did.

"Probably because he has to put up with this idiot," Benedite grumbled as the first notes of the lady's song wafted over the audience.

Dirkus made a rude gesture without breaking eye contact with me. "What's his problem, anyway?"

Emerald leaned across the table and narrowed his eyes. "You want to know why I'm not being *fun* tonight, Dirkus?"

I forced an awkward laugh. *[Careful, Em. Don't mention Tincrown in front of them.]* I wasn't sure how drunk he was, precisely, but judging by the sloppy hum of emotion roiling on his end of our connection, it wasn't impossible that he'd say something about Dyrne without considering the consequences.

[Not gonna,] he thought, before saying, "You want to know why it bothers me to—*hic!*—see one of them dead in the water? A jotunn? One of those *animals* you hate so much?"

"Do tell," Dirkus sneered. "I'd love to know, since it didn't bother me in the least."

Coirpre's eye twitched, and I briefly fantasized about him breaking the decanter over the scout's head.

"Because it should've been me," Emerald said.

Every eye at the table turned toward him.

"How do you reckon that?" Dirkus asked.

Emerald lifted one shoulder in a halfhearted, drunken shrug. "The first night I came through. In the spring. See, I was chasing you." He pointed to the bard.

Coirpre smiled out of one side of his mouth and made a frantic shushing gesture with the hand that the scouts couldn't see. "Chasing me?" he asked too loudly. "Because he couldn't stand to be away from this handsome face a moment more?"

Before I could intervene, Emerald nodded. "Mostly. Yes, I had proper reasons for it, but I find excuses to go looking for you. Hadn't you noticed?"

Coirpre's smile froze, and the Conjury men let out an unkind burst of laughter. To my surprise, the bard didn't mock Emerald. Instead, he leaned across the table and wrenched the half-full cup of wine from his hand. "I think you've had enough, my friend."

"I agree," I murmured, wondering how in every hell I was going to get Emerald back to the inn in this state.

To my annoyance, both Dirkus and Benedite interceded.

"Let him talk," Dirkus sneered. "He was telling us about the bridge, remember?"

"I smell a confession." Benedite's long, narrow nose wrinkled in anticipation. When he was sober, he struck me as more reserved than his fellow investigator, but his mean streak emerged as he drank. Now, he fixed Emerald with a smile that did little to hide the cruelty glittering in his eyes. "Out with it, jotunn! What happened on the bridge?"

[Emerald, you don't have to answer him,] I said, but it was too late.

"I threw myself off it. In the spring." Emerald grabbed his cup back from Coirpre, slopping a bit of the wine over the rim so that it stained his sleeve vermilion. "Tried to drown myself, but it didn't take. The tide was coming in, and it washed me up toward the edges of the bog—"

"Stop," Coirpre said.

[Em, please.]

My companion rounded on me with a sneer. "Oh, you don't want to hear it now? Because you've never stopped pestering me about it." He pitched his voice high in a poor imitation of me. *"What happened on the equinox, Emerald? Why don't you tell me what happened, Emerald? I want to know what happened that night!* Well, now you do." He waved his cup of wine in the direction of my stricken face. "Who would have cared, anyway? My *family?*" He let out a snarl of what was meant to be laughter that made me flinch away. Before I could protest, he turned back to Dirkus. "When that dog of yours *took up with a feyhound,* what did you do with the pups?"

Dirkus had sat frozen throughout Emerald's confession, but now that he'd been called upon, he leaned forward. His eyes danced with a wicked light. "Put 'em in a sack. They weren't cute, and they didn't take commands. Couldn't hunt worth a damn. What do you do with useless beasts like that?" He leaned across the table and grinned ferally at Emerald. "You've got the right idea. Toss 'em in the river."

Coirpre rounded on the scout as Benedite let out a snort of laughter. "Shut your damned mouth, you absolute—"

"He's not wrong." Emerald set his cup down sharply and turned his attention to the bard.

"Of course he is." I glared at the scout. **[Please, Em, don't say anything else. We should talk about this back in our room. Just the two of us, where it's safe.]**

"Nowhere's safe," Emerald snapped. He pointed an accusing finger at Coirpre. "Would you really notice if I'd disappeared? Would you have given a rip?"

"Yes," Coirpre said at once.

"Dragonshite. You wouldn't. Nobody would've, because there's only one person who does, other than maybe *you.*" He tipped his chin toward me with a mocking smile. "And you'd just as soon be free of me. You've said so more than once."

[You can call me any names you like, you can accuse me of whatever you want, but please **don't mention** him *here.*

Not in front of the scouts.] I wished I could shake some sense into him. ***[You'll never forgive yourself if you do.]***

Emerald paused. "Only one person who'd care," he slurred, although a little of the fight had gone out of him. "And now I'm here with you, instead of *there* with *him*, and I hate it. It shouldn't have been that jotunn sailor. It should have been me." With that, he upended the cup and swallowed it down.

Coirpre got up from the table.

"Leaving?" Dirkus sneered. "You're gonna miss the fun."

"Yes, I'm leaving, and I'm taking him with me." Out of all of them, the bard was the only one who seemed the least bit sober.

"Wanna know what I think?" Benedite snickered into his cup. He seemed to have stooped to Dirkus's level, now that he was inebriated. "I think you already knew that he followed you. I think you liked it. I'm not surprised a fop like you is interested in men, but the fact that you'll entertain the attentions of a—"

I leaned across the table until my face was only inches from the scout's. "Finish that sentence," I snarled through gritted teeth, "and I will make you regret it in ways you can't begin to imagine." I thought of Aindreas, and how on our last meeting, I had stepped into his mind, wielding his body like a weapon against him, if only for a few seconds.

If you could find a way to take control of him, you could use him to kill Dirkus. Throw them both into the sea, and all your problems would go away. Maximilien's death would go unsolved.

Even if I was capable of doing such a thing, the thought sickened me, but I held Benedite's gaze all the same. Let him test me. I would find a way to repay him if he uttered so much as another syllable.

To my great relief, he fell silent, although his bitter smile remained.

Coirpre had made his way around the table, and just as Lady Fenguard's song ended, he reached for my friend.

Emerald slapped his hand away. "Don't touch me," he slurred.

"For the love of Rilus, stop being obstinate." Coirpre adjusted the strap of his lute on his shoulder, then grabbed

Emerald's wrist. He pulled my friend's arm over his shoulder and hauled him to his feet.

"Have fun, boys," Dirkus said with a smirk.

Coirpre paused long enough to make a rude gesture at Dirkus, then he set out for the door, all but dragging Emerald with him.

[Em? Emerald?] I hovered behind them, painfully aware of how many eyes were on us. Our connection was silent.

The two of them hadn't gotten far when Edur Fenguard hurried over.

"What's the matter?" he asked.

"I'm afraid my friend has had a bit too much to drink," I said with as much charm as I could muster.

"Ah, poor fellow." Edur chuckled to himself, blissfully unaware of what had just transpired. "It happens to the best of us. We could make up a room for him here. He's my guest, after all..."

Coirpre opened his mouth, but Emerald roused himself from his stupor just long enough to say, "No. Goin' home. Shouldn't be here." He pulled away from the bard and staggered toward the door.

I bowed curtly. "Pardon me, Laird Edur, I should go with him." I hurried after my companion, who managed to reach the door of the hall before slumping against the frame for a moment.

[Em? Are you all right?]

"Do I bleeding *look* all right?" he hissed. "Stop it, Crimson. Would you all just stop *gawking* at me." He stumbled out of the doorway and in the rough direction of the road.

I emerged into the darkness before I was aware of footsteps behind me. I turned, braced for another fight with the scouts, and found Coirpre on my heels.

"I'm coming with you," he said in a low voice as Emerald's huge silhouette swayed across the courtyard. "Drunk as he is, he might fall in the water again, and you wouldn't be able to do a damned thing to stop him."

"*Fall*," I echoed. We followed the road, staying far back enough to avoid Emerald snapping at us again but never losing sight of him. "That's not what he said." Now that I had a moment to think, I remembered the way Emerald had stared down into the waters of the Bounder when we crossed the bridge the morning prior. Gods, the *bridge*. That very bridge, and he hadn't told me.

"I know." Coirpre looped his thumb through the silk strap of his lute. There was enough light along the walkway for me to make out his expression, although I couldn't tell what he was thinking. "Is it true?"

"I don't know." I lifted my hands and thought of the little marks that marred Emerald's skin from wrist to elbow and all along his legs. *Probably. I suspect he told Tincrown.* Coirpre didn't need to know about that, though. It was bad enough that Emerald had spouted one secret in his inebriated state. I wasn't going to share any more of them.

"So he's drunk off his arse." Coirpre nodded to me. "And you're still sober. Seems like you were telling the truth last night."

I shot a sidelong glance at him. "Why are you here? Really?"

"I told you, the contract—"

"Not in Upper Bound. Here. *Now.*" I gestured sharply to Emerald.

Coirpre wrinkled his nose. Ahead of us, my friend stumbled and only barely managed to remain upright. After a pause, he carried on again.

"A confession like that ruins the mood of the party," Coirpre said at last, in a dismissive voice. "And I've got eighteen more months to go in this city. How could I put on a decent show with the weight of his death on my conscience? Tomorrow, you'd better tell him what a cursed inconvenience this all was. Ruined my night, he has. I'm not going to let him ruin my job as well."

"You're an ass," I said. After a pause I added, "Thank you. For looking out for him, I mean, whatever your reasons."

Coirpre waved a hand. "Don't mention it. Literally. There's no need to tell him about this."

A suspicion stole over me as I glanced sideways at the bard. "Is this the first time you've done something like this?"

"Haven't we had enough confessions for one night, Crimson?" Coirpre arched an eyebrow at me.

We did not speak again until Emerald staggered up the steps at the front of the inn where we were staying and clumsily unlocked the door of our room. Coirpre lifted his hand in farewell and jogged back toward the road to the keep. I had more questions for him, but the more pressing matter was the figure of the half-jotunn who fell through the door and locked it behind him.

I drifted through the wood. "Emerald?" I asked.

"Piss off, Crim." He collapsed into the bed face first and burrowed beneath the blankets. "Told you to leave me alone."

And how am I supposed to do that, when you made me? I sank down into the chair in the corner of the room and watched him until a deep, rumbling snore emerged from the pile of bed linens. *How am I supposed to help you when you can't even help yourself?*

With nothing better to do, I tried to practice the exercise that Aster had taught me, but I couldn't summon the memory of Tincrown's house any longer. Every time I closed my eyes, I imagined Emerald toppling forward off of the bridge over the Bounder, and the dark water closing over his head.

If I'd been anything more than a figment of his imagination and a breath of magic, it would have left me in tears.

Chapter Nine

Sunrise came and went, and Emerald didn't so much as stir. Eventually, his snoring stopped, and he thrashed around beneath the coverlet a bit, but he made no move to get up.

"Are you awake?" I asked.

Emerald grunted.

"Can we talk about—?"

[Go away.]

I sidled closer to the bedside. "Em, what you said last night..."

He pulled the blanket over his head and went completely still.

Unkind words spoken in the heat of an old fight of ours echoed through my mind, and I recalled the expression Tincrown had worn during Emerald's confession that last morning in Dyrne. I had known for some time that my friend didn't value his health as much as I did, and I had felt for myself the depths of his self-loathing on more than one occasion. Even so, I had not understood the extremes to which it affected his mind.

I wished once again that Tincrown could be here to say

precisely the right thing, but since I was the only one present, I would have to do.

"You don't have to talk to me," I said. "But I need you to listen for a moment. I promised Tincrown that I would look after you, and I promised *you* that I would help protect *him*, and the only way that I can see to do either of those things properly is to solve this mystery and get you back—" I stopped short of saying *home*. Dyrne wasn't his home any more than it was mine, although perhaps wherever Tincrown was counted as much as anyplace could. "—back where you belong."

Emerald shuffled under the blankets.

"To that end, I'm going to continue our investigation, on one condition. I need you to *promise* me that if I leave you here, you aren't going to do anything... rash." When he didn't respond at once, I spoke a bit more forcefully. "I need to hear it from you, Em. Promise."

[*I promise.*]

That would have to suffice for the moment. "I'll be back as soon as I have anything to report." I got up and checked myself in the old mirror. Flakes of silver were peeling away in rough patches near the edges from age and wear. Trying to decide on my best course of action, I contemplated another change of identity. Who should I be today? Who would be best qualified to help safeguard the country doctor in the mountains, or my heartsick friend on the bed behind me? In the end, I decided to stay Simon. I wanted to talk to that Hudson fellow, and I would be better served approaching him as a recognizable version of Crimson Smoke rather than under some other guise.

"See you later!" I said with as much cheer as I could fake before ducking through the door.

I had already left the room when it occurred to me that part of my distress regarding Emerald might be selfish. After all, if his plan to topple into the Bounder had gone as intended, I would never have existed.

To my surprise, the notion didn't bother me as much as I might have expected. The idea of being snuffed out now was much more distressing, since now I would know what I was missing. Still, I was more concerned for Emerald's well-being on that front than my own. I would much rather be reliant on a man like him than free to live my own life in a world where he did not exist.

I wondered whether it would have made a difference if I'd told him that.

❧

It was late morning by the time I stepped into the street. Emerald had slept late thanks to his overindulgence the night before, and midday was not far off.

As I made my way through the main square, a bedraggled figure flagged me down, waving his sign in my face. *BEWARE OF THE BOG,* it read, and I realized that I'd seen the same gray-skinned man in conversation with Burp on the morning of our arrival.

"Sir, you seem like a fine gentleman! An upstanding citizen! Hear me, the Cronemire is a wicked place full of cursed spirits. The dead are unquiet, and the living dwell in fear!" He rolled his eyes back in his head and waved his sign in the air. "It is a wicked place, I tell you! *Wicked!*"

"Is that so?" I paused to look him over, then rubbed my chin. "And what do you propose we do about it?"

The man's eyes widened. His posture gave me the impression that no one had ever asked this question before, and that people who took him seriously were few and far between.

"We pray to the gods, young man! We pray to Hharda and Oryx for the cleansing might of the seas, that they may rise up and... and, um... do you have another question?"

I had raised one of my hands to attract his attention. "It can wait until you're done."

"No, go on." He let go of the sign with one hand and scratched his nose.

"I was told that you are a swamper elf?" I asked as I lowered my hand.

The old man's eyes sparkled as he nodded eagerly. "Yes, young man! Lafayette of the Leechless Swamp. The only swamper elf on Kovin Isle, to my knowledge. The only one brave enough to withstand the scourge that is the Cronemire!"

"So you're a swamper elf," I repeated slowly, "who hates... swamps?"

Lafayette drew himself up to his full height. In an instant, he transformed from a hunched old man to a kingly presence, straight backed and regal, with proud features and defiant eyes. "A *swamp*? The Cronemire is no *swamp*! You think all palustrine wetlands are the same, boy? You think acidity levels are of no consequence? Think of the *sphagnum*. Think of the *mineral compounds*. Think of the *curse*. Swamps have been vilified, but you won't catch a self-respecting swamp *raising the dead*!"

"Sorry." I pressed my palms together and fell back a pace. "My apologies, Master Lafayette, I meant no disrespect."

The elf thumped his fist against his sunken chest and coughed a few times. "I should expect no better from a human, I suppose. And one of the great evils of the Cronemire is that it blurs the lines not only between the realms of the living and the dead, but between that of bogs and swamplands. That is what makes it a true abomination!"

"And praying to Oryx and Hharda will somehow resolve that?" I asked.

"Of course, boy!" Lafayette set his sign aside as his enthusiasm returned. "If the sea levels rise, that'll change the salinity of the Cronemire. See, a bog is formed when dead plant matter retains an overabundance of rainwater, but with the introduction of a tidal backwash up the Bounder—"

"Oh, I'm terribly sorry, I've just realized the time." I had hoped that the elf might be able to help me understand the workings of the Cronemire a bit better, but he was clearly not going to be of much use in my investigation.

"No, wait!" He beckoned me back and lowered his voice, glancing shiftily around the square. Plenty of people were coming and going around us, but they kept their eyes averted, presumably to avoid being drawn into conversation with the elf. When he was satisfied that nobody was paying attention, he opened one flap of his shabby, mildewed vest to reveal an assortment of glittering charms. "Would you like to buy an amulet? To keep you safe from the Crone and the gaze of her merciless eye?"

"Oh, no, but thank you." I grimaced at the thought of how badly the cheap, *Aidea*-infused charms would clash with my accoutrements. "Sorry, I don't want to be late."

"Watch yourself, young man!" Lafayette called after me. "The Cronemire feeds on the wicked! She slakes her thirst on the unworthy!"

Maybe we'll get lucky, I thought with a bitter smile, *and she'll slake her thirst on Dirkus.*

I left Lafayette to his ranting and hurried down the street toward the docks, where my first useful inquiries of the day could finally begin.

❧

Hudson of Hardwick Home was, by his own admission, a self-made man.

"First of my family to work for a proper business like the Trader's Guild," he announced proudly as he swept one arm out to encompass the port. It was swathed in a horrid, lemon-hued shirt with a clashing pair of orange breeches that suggested he'd dressed in the dark. "My father made his living as a shipwright, repairing the fishing boats of his neighbors and the fleets of his betters. Well, you don't see *me* bending the knee to any man, do you, Master Crimson?" He bared his teeth at me in a ruthless smile. "Today, I oversee the docks of Upper Bound, but mark my words, I'll be sailing for the mainland before long to work for the main office."

"I have no doubt that a man of your capabilities would flourish on Conjury-ruled lands," I assured him.

As Hudson and I strolled along the pier toward where the

jotunn had been found floating the day before, I tried to take his measure. He was not quite as instantly dislikeable as Dirkus, and although his attitude toward the men and women under his command had rubbed me the wrong way the day before, I could not immediately write him off as a villain. There was something hungry and scrappy about him that his poorly tailored clothes, unevenly-trimmed muttonchops, and ornamental monocle failed to disguise. He had not spent his life looking down on the people around him; rather, he had clawed his way up from the bottom rung to the top of the local heap. I respected his fortitude and yet didn't care for his company in the slightest.

"Thank you." Hudson dipped his head in acknowledgment of my words. He was more reserved with me than he had been with Dirkus the prior afternoon, perhaps because he found me more difficult to read. "This is the place, sir. We found him floating out there. Thought he was a bit of old driftwood at first."

"Had anyone reported him missing?" I asked. While I knew there was no connection between Maximilien's death and Neek's, it was possible that the body we'd switched out for the bog belonged to one of the jotunn's peers.

Hudson smirked. "I know you're used to finer ways of doing things, Master Crimson, but dockside, we don't *miss* each other much. The traffic we see here rivals that of many major cities on the mainland. And the jotunn keep to their own. Our crews don't know each other well. His few friends might have missed him, but nobody reported him absent, and even if they had, we wouldn't have wasted much time searching for him."

I tried to keep my expression impassive as I asked, "Why not?"

Hudson folded his hands behind his back. "I take it you don't spend much time with sailors, sir?"

"Not as a rule," I admitted.

"Then let me be the first to tell you, there are all sorts of reasons a fellow might go missing from his post. Some of them fall in with unsavory characters on leave. Some desert their posts if they get a better offer of employment. And some of those are non-voluntary offers, if you catch my drift. We aren't their jailors, you know. They can do what they like. And if I may speak plainly, it's not uncommon for them to disappear and turn up dead a few days later."

I wrinkled my brow. "And that isn't cause for concern?"

Hudson's humorless smile widened. "Why do you think most of our men sign on with us?"

"For a bit of adventure?" I hazarded. "A chance to see the world?"

"I suppose some of them might, sir, but by and large, their intentions aren't so starry-eyed. Many of them would be convicts otherwise. They turn to the sea to avoid arrest by leaving the area. You throw enough criminals on a ship together, let 'em stew on the open sea for a bit, and... Well..." Hudson shrugged one shoulder blithely. "Tensions boil over. Conflicts brew."

"The members of your crews *kill* one another?" I asked.

"Come now." Hudson waved a hand dismissively at the open water. "You've seen how they drink. In their cups, men will say and do things that they wouldn't dare while sober."

Emerald's drunken confession of the night before was, I supposed, proof of that. Knowing how it affected people, I wondered what the appeal of drinking was in the first place. It must produce a wonderful feeling in anyone with a physical body to be worth all the trouble it caused.

"I take it that Neek isn't the first sailor to die like that?" I turned back toward the water, remembering the way the dead jotunn had floated there. When I closed my eyes, Emerald filled my vision in the corpse's stead, and I had to bite back a small cry of distress. Of course that was what my friend had pictured as we'd stood here, watching the sailors dredge up their dead companion.

I wish he'd told me the truth sooner, although I wasn't sure what I could have done to help even if he had.

"Nah, there are plenty of others who've met similar ends." Hudson folded his hands behind his back, the haphazardly stitched lines of his jerkin bunching in awkward waves, and nodded toward the large shipping vessel. A crew of sailors was busy loading it down with cargo, presumably exports from the island. "I run the docks, but I leave management of the crew to the captains. As I've said, we're a very important port. We've got ships coming and going every few days, never mind the local ships. That keeps me busy."

"And Neek's remains will be sent home on this ship?" I asked.

"Or the next. We'll be loading the rest of the remains tomorrow just before she sets sail."

That meant I only had a few more hours to see who Emerald had swapped with Maximilien before my chance would slip away. "I'd like to review your records before then," I said. "To check for any... discrepancies."

Hudson stared at me for a moment before letting out a bark of laughter. "Ah, there we have it, *Master Crimson*. The real question you've been waiting to ask."

His change in tone caught me off guard. "I'm sorry?"

The dockmaster stepped closer and leered at me. I was suddenly aware of his height, and the strong lines of his shoulders beneath his colorful attire. If I'd been a man of flesh and blood, I might have found him intimidating.

It made me wonder what he would be capable of if a sailor had something he wanted.

Something worth stealing, for example.

"I know you're not who you say you are," Hudson sneered. "And I've been playing along because I was curious to see what you were after, but your game has failed."

I pressed one hand to my chest. "I assure, I am Crimson Smoke, partner of the great Emerald Flame..."

"Where is he, then?" Hudson demanded.

"He's, erm, preoccupied." I wilted a little under the dockmaster's glare.

"Have you got papers, then?"

Back in Lower Bound, McLachlan had asked for our papers, but Emerald had them. Even if I could summon some now, I had no idea what they would look like, and I couldn't very well hand over intangible papers anyway. "Emerald has them."

"Of course he does." Hudson jabbed one tanned, calloused finger at my chest, and I flinched away before he could touch me. "And pray explain then, *Crimson Flame,* why haven't you drawn a single breath in all the time we've been standing here?"

"Well, I—"

"I know exactly what you are." Hudson loomed over me, and I took another step away, so that the heel of my boot was only inches from the edge of the pier. It was a pity that Emerald wasn't here to loom back. What would happen if he backed me right off the edge? I didn't dare let him touch me, as it would only confirm his suspicions and open us up to a whole new set of troublesome inquiry with the Conjury scouts, but if I *did* take another step backward, I would either hover over the whitecaps unharmed or fall into the water without a ripple or a splash. No matter what, it would be terribly suspicious.

I lifted my chin in a Coirpre-worthy show of defiant bravado. "And what am I, then, Mister Hudson?"

"You're a Lightweaver."

That brought me up short. "Pardon?"

"There's no point in denying it." Hudson flapped one hand in my direction. "All the signs are there. You don't breathe, you don't cough, and you haven't wrinkled your nose once despite the reek of low tide. You're clearly casting an illusion over your true form to make yourself look like one of those Conjury detective fellows. I don't know what your game is, but it doesn't take a genius to figure out who you work for, so why don't you pack off and tell that conniving wench to stop sticking her nose where it isn't wanted." Hudson retreated a step and glared at me.

Conniving wench? I struggled to piece together who he might mean, until I recalled another of the names Burp had provided the day before. "You mean Marsha?"

"You know bleeding well who I mean." Hudson's upper lip twitched. "She can carry on with that witless lowlife all she wants and I won't have a thing to say about it, so long as she keeps her business in town. These are my docks, Lightweaver. And I keep what's mine. Are we clear?"

I nodded. "Perfectly."

"Very well." Hudson stepped aside and bowed sardonically, with one arm extended back toward town. "You may see yourself out. And tell her to pray that I don't inform the *real* Crimson that you tried to pass as him. I imagine his jotunn partner would rip your leg off and feed it to you."

I went obediently, but my mind was already churning. Hudson watched me as I beat a hasty retreat back to shore. On the deck of the trading vessel, a few dozen sailors moved crates of cargo to and fro, busy as a line of ants. Several of them sang as they moved, marking their pace with a measured basso melody.

"The sea goes on forever, and her belly's never full.
When a storm drives from the weather, she'll be glad to eat you whole.
Her boundless blue is bottomless, with fishes in her depths
That will tear a crew to pieces and will turn our ships to wrecks.
Look away, sailors, hey, look away..."

I didn't dare glance back until I'd passed the stone wall that separated the city from the harbor. Once I was out of Hudson's line of sight, I dipped to one side out of the flow of foot traffic to consider my next move.

I had learned a few things, but I hadn't come across a single shred of proof regarding the identity of our nameless corpse. On the other hand, Hudson was the most threatening figure I had encountered in town, and the first one to strike me as a probable killer.

I could do better than that. Given the sorry state in which I had left my friend, I was resolved not to return to him until I had, at the very least, a name.

Diplomacy had failed. It was time to try my hand at skulduggery instead.

◈

The docks were lively that time of day, and Hudson had made it clear that the bodies from the icehouse wouldn't be taken aboard until the following day. That gave me a few hours to figure out a plan.

Unfortunately, I wasn't even sure what I was looking for. Dozens of small buildings could be found all over the docks, and I didn't relish the idea of peeking into every one of them, especially not in such a crowded location. After some consideration, I retired to a quieter corner of the city and rearranged myself into someone a little less conspicuous.

I had not yet figured out the rules of my appearance. I could not, for example, give myself brown hair or a more impressive build. After several attempts, I *was* able to give myself a tattoo on my bicep, and a sailor's tan on top of that. I wished myself a ragged cap, reminiscent of the jaunty one sported by Hudson but far more weathered, and tucked my hair beneath it. For good measure, I added a shabby and worn Trader's Guild emblem to my equally shabby and worn coat. A man as attentive as the dockmaster might notice me, but if a jotunn could be missing overnight without comment, I could only hope that the other sailors wouldn't take note of my presence. Wearing my new disguise, I stepped back into the flow of foot traffic and slouched along the quay.

I hadn't made it to the next pier before a sunburnt dwarf stepped into my path.

"Where're *ye* headed empty handed?" he demanded.

You are a consummate actor. You were made for the stage. Keep calm. I took the appearance of a breath—just in case this fellow was as attentive as Hudson had been—and crossed my arms.

"Who's askin'?" I demanded, trying my hand at the local accent.

The dwarf's face turned purple, and a vein throbbed in his temple. "Yer *first mate* is askin', tha's who."

"Not *my* first mate," I shot back. "I'm with the other ship. The better one. So, erm, piss off."

"Ours is the only guild ship in port, brigand!" The dwarf lunged for me, and I danced away.

I should never have been left to solve things on my own.

The first mate swiped at my heels. "Get back here! Ah'll have yer guts for garters, ye ignorant tosser! Talk te th' mate like tha' again and see where it gets ye! Righ' out te sea, boots-first, wi' an anchor round yer ankles, tha's where!"

In the future, I told myself as I ducked beneath a chest carried between two sailors, *I am going to be choosier in regard to my character roles. Politeness suits me better than surliness. Emerald would have been much better at this sailor bit than I am.*

The dwarf was still bellowing obscenities at me, and other people were turning to stare. In an attempt to avoid further trouble, I darted sideways and found myself at a dead end facing a rough-hewn stone wall. The first mate's footsteps were still pounding after me—another giveaway that he was real and I was not. For want of a better option, I pushed through the wall into a storage building filled with crates of packed cargo.

Only to find myself face-to-face with a jotunn.

"Where is he? Where's tha' sharp-tongued ra' bastard?" A fist pounded on the wall behind me, and I lifted one finger to my lips, offering the jotunn what I hoped was a charming smile. He grunted, but he didn't hail the dwarf. Instead, he turned to his companion and grunted, nodding his head in my direction as if to say, *Can you believe this imbecile?*

One day. That was all it had taken for me to ruin Emerald's plan to cover Aindreas's crime and secure the future of Dyrne. When he sobered up, he was going to be furious with me.

Eventually, the pounding on the wall stopped, and the dwarf's voice faded into the distance. I pressed my palms together and bowed to my wary hosts.

"I'm so *terribly* sorry for barging in like that," I said. "I assure you, there's a very simple explanation..." *Which I had better think of in the next ten seconds, because if word gets out that a miscreant redhead is sneaking through walls all over the city, someone is going to ask questions.*

Before I could dig myself an even deeper verbal hole, the second jotunn crossed her arms and squinted at me. "You. Know you. From party."

"Ah, yes." I ran my hands over my unrumpled vestments, more to calm my nerves than anything. "I saw you there two nights ago. At the keep." Curse my unforgettably handsome face and my inability to be covert in public. She'd not only seen me walk through a wall, she'd *recognized* me.

The jotunn nodded. "You have friend. Jotunn. Like us."

"Yes. Well, sort of. I have a friend who's *half*-jotunn, and he assures me that there is a difference." I grimaced. "And you had another friend, too. I'm sorry to hear about Neek..."

The man growled, and the woman made a sharp, dismissive gesture with one huge hand. "Not Neek. *Nweke.*"

The way she said her friend's name struck a chord with me. I had initially written off her broken speech as a sign of her ignorance and subconsciously praised myself for thinking that it didn't impact my opinion of her. The lilting tone of her voice when she said his name properly made me realize that she was speaking another language. Their native tongue, most likely.

In some ways, I was as ignorant as Dirkus, and I hadn't even realized it.

My shame banished all thoughts of escape. "I'm sorry," I repeated. "About Nweke."

Her lips twitched into a momentary smile. "Your trade tongue pretty, but your spirit tongue very bad."

The other jotunn said something to the woman in their language, and she nodded once. It occurred to me that if I couldn't understand what they were saying, that probably meant that Emerald wouldn't, either. Or would we have both understood if he'd been here to hear them? Like my own abilities to transform, there were so many things I didn't understand about our connection.

"You make small-boss angry," she said. "Why?"

I bit my tongue before replying. Diplomacy had failed. Skul-duggery had been a disaster. I decided it best to attempt honesty this time. "I'm trying to get into the icehouse," I said. "Where they keep the bodies of the dead sailors. My friend and I are trying to solve a murder."

The woman's heavy brows knit. "Murder. Like Nweke?"

I nodded.

Someone pounded on the door at the far side of the room. "Are you lot bringing them crates or nae?"

I hunkered down beside the nearest stack of cargo and pressed my hands together again in supplication.

The male jotunn lurched into motion, while the woman I'd been speaking to crouched beside me to whisper. "Hide now. Meet at sunfall. You help find Nweke-slayer?"

"If I can," I whispered back.

She nodded to me. "Then we help you, jotunn-friend."

And just like that, I added another murder for us to solve.

Chapter Ten

I waited on the roof of the little building until the first of the moons rose over the water and tried to imagine the mainland where the ship would soon return. Hudson's earlier words bothered me, not because I had failed to play my part correctly—although in truth that rankled—but because he had pointed out more ways in which I did not fit. What did the stink of low tide smell like? What would it feel like to have the breeze that stirred the bundled sails of the ship rustle my hair? How could I fake every aspect of living when I did not fully understand the sensations that everyone else in the world took for granted?

I would like to drink wine in excess, or strum my fingers over the strings of a lute. Just once, I would like to live freely, without having to worry about my tether or the state of my creator.

I would like to know what I am missing.

"*Hsst!*" From below me, a voice hissed into the dusk. "Jotunn-friend! You here?"

I peered over the edge of the roof to find the two jotunn standing below me. When the woman saw me, she raised one huge hand to beckon me down.

I held up one finger, then hurried to the other side of the

building and drifted down to the cobbles where she wouldn't see me. There was no point in letting her know *all* my secrets.

I returned on foot to meet them. In the dark, their eyes burned like miniature moons, illuminated with a glow that reminded me of the *Aidea*-inscribed artifacts I'd encountered over the last few months.

"Thank you for meeting me," I whispered.

She waved her hand toward the keep. "Is nothing. Everyone else gone to castle."

"To celebrate the ship's departure?" I asked wryly, thinking of what Benedite had told us about the Fenguards' endless parties. I hoped that Emerald had not gone tonight.

She nodded. "Easier for us. Everyone drinking or drunk already. We stay. Help you." She rubbed one temple. "Forgive. Trade tongue not..." She growled as she trailed off.

"Your Osmarian is better than my spirit tongue," I pointed out. "What are your names?" I crossed my toes inside my boots and prayed that she wouldn't make the sort of noise Burp had when introducing himself.

"This Asha. No trade tongue, so he stay quiet. Me?" She placed one hand to her chest. "Yoyoh."

"A pleasure to meet you, Yoyoh," I repeated. "I'm Crimson."

"This way, Crim-sin." Yoyoh gestured to me.

Asha eyed me suspiciously and said something in their tongue as I followed Yoyoh along the pier.

Left to my own devices, I would never have found where the remains of the sailors were kept. The building the two jotunn led me to had nothing special to recommend it, although when Yoyoh pointed us toward the right door, I could make out a small line of frost just beneath the jamb.

"Locked," Yoyoh said, rapping her knuckles against the door. "Secure. But no trouble for you?"

My gaze bounced between the door and the jotunn.

Yoyoh winked. "No trouble for me, neither." She planted her feet and reeled back, then brought her mighty fist crashing into the edge of the door just beside the lock. The door shuddered in its frame and then swung open.

She pushed the door wide and waved me through, then spoke to Asha. They exchanged a few words before she slid in after me. "He wait. Stand guard. In case small-boss come back and yell again."

Yoyoh closed the door behind her, plunging us into darkness. The only thing I could see on the black of the windowless room were the two golden pinpricks of her eyes.

"Did you bring a light?" I whispered.

Yoyoh grunted. "No need. I see."

Her night vision might be excellent, but if I was going to learn anything, I needed to be able to see.

Emerald was able to create a flame when he took control of me in Dyrne. I wonder... I held out my palm in the darkness and glared at it, willing a flame to come to life.

Nothing happened.

"Crimson?" Yoyoh asked. "You need fire?"

"Give me a moment." I closed my eyes, trying to think my way out of the problem. When I had first tried to fly, it hadn't worked until I tricked myself into believing that it would. Emerald could conjure flame at will—not flame that would *burn*, but flame that would give light. If I couldn't imagine a light source into being the same way that I could change my shoes or my coat, there must be another way to go about it. I needed something that I could interact with even though it didn't exist in the real world.

If I couldn't conjure the illusion of fire, perhaps I could find another way to make it.

I reached into the pocket of my battered Trader's Guild jacket and fished around for a moment before my fingers met something solid. I picked up the stones and clutched one in each hand. Ignius and flint, just like Emerald had shown me on our walk through the mountains. With a rising sense of self-satisfaction, I knelt down and struck the two of them together until sparks leapt from my fingers.

A flame came to life on the floorboards beneath me, bright as any real fire but requiring no fuel. I tucked the stones back into my pocket and scooped the flame up in my palm. It was nothing but light and did little more than prickle my palm with an idea of what warmth might be, although I couldn't say for certain.

Yoyoh watched me with interest, then nodded toward the stack of plain wooden boxes. "What now, firestarter?"

I rose to my feet and took in the space. Unlike the coffin meant for Maximilien, these were fashioned from unpainted wood. There were only a handful of them, with handwritten labels applied to the outside. The contents of the largest box were easy enough to guess, and Yoyoh went to it, laying her palm against the lid. She murmured something in her tongue as I bent over to read the label.

Neek, it said in tidy handwriting. *Deliver to Leviathan Loch and contact recorded claimant.*

Excitement thrummed through me. All I had to do now was determine which coffin held Maximilien's body and see who it was supposed to belong to.

"Can you lift the lids?" I whispered.

Yoyoh glanced up at me with a frown. "To look?"

"It would help me a great deal," I said. When she hesitated, I added, "It might help me find Nweke's killer, too."

I hated using manipulation to coerce her, but it was certainly effective. Yoyoh got to her feet and reached for the lid of one of the other boxes. She tugged it once, but it didn't come off.

"Nails," she whispered. "Should I pull?"

"Not necessary," I told her. "We're looking for a coffin that's had the lid removed once before, one that someone has already disturbed."

She shuddered. "Who disturbs dead? Already bad enough."

We do, I thought with another surge of guilt, but I was hardly going to share that tidbit. "Someone desperate." *Desperate to save the people who are counting on us.* I wondered how long that logic would serve us, and what lengths we would go to in the name of protection.

It had served Aindreas well enough for a long time, after all.

She heaved one box aside as though it was nothing more than an illusion and tried the lid of another. It took her four tries to find the one with the loose lid, and when the lid slid free with minimal effort, I relaxed a little.

"That's him." I bent over the body in the casket. Six months had changed Maximilien greatly. Whatever the sisters had done to preserve him had kept his flesh relatively intact, but his closed eyes had sunk to hollows in his face. When he'd switched the bodies, Emerald had switched his clothes as well. Whoever had gone into the bog had worn the Conjury scout's outfit, while the scout himself now wore a shabby jacket much like my own. One corpse looked much like another after enough time had passed, but Maximilien's was the first body I had ever seen, and his image was forever seared into my memory. This was him, I was sure of it.

"Thank you," I sighed. "What does the lid say?"

Yoyoh turned the lid of the coffin toward me so that I could read the note. The words written there made my eye twitch.

Unknown. Deliver to Lev. Loch for mass burial.

"Blast it," I muttered. I wondered if my harping over the ethics of our plan had driven him to choose this particular coffin, or if our bad luck was simply that consistent.

"What?" Yoyoh asked, kneeling beside me.

"They don't know who he was." I stared down at the dead man in consternation. "That's no use at all."

The jotunn pointed down at the corpse. "This man important?"

"To my case? Yes."

"And to know him... this helps Nweke?"

I could only give her so much false hope. "Perhaps," I said. "I'm doing my best, but I'm afraid that doesn't mean much lately." I detested the thought of going back to Emerald and admitting that I'd wasted another day, while Dirkus and Benedite were off doing gods-know-what.

Yoyoh uttered something that sounded like a prayer before lowering her massive hand to Maximilien's chest. "Some men keep... personal gods. Not all, but sailors believe. Big sky, big ocean, they need big gods. Little man needs little god for himself." She dug her fingers into a secret pocket within his coat, much as I had searched for the stones in mine. When her fingers reappeared, she was clutching a tarnished silver coin.

"What you calling this?" she asked, holding it up.

"An amulet," I murmured. Lafayette had tried to sell me one that very morning, although this one was much more valuable. The face was etched with the profile of a woman and the name *LEMDA* inscribed beneath it.

"Goddess of protection," Yoyoh said. "Not strong enough for him."

If the man could afford such a fine amulet, what else might he have carried that someone would want to take from him?

"It's beautiful," I admitted. "But how does that tell me who he is?"

Yoyoh turned the amulet over in her palm, and I let out a hiss of triumph. Carved into the silver were the words that made our whole venture worthwhile.

Goddess protect ye, Kessel of Kinmore.

At last, I had found the name of the man in the bog.

❦

Midnight had come and gone by the time I returned to our room. Kessel's amulet was now back in Maximilien's pocket, where it might serve to identify the dead man so that his family might get a sort of closure, even if they couldn't bury the right body.

I was brimming with excitement as I slipped through the door. "Emerald!" I hissed. "You'll never believe it. I learned a new trick, and I made friends with the jotunn, and I've learned the name of—"

The moonslight sifting through the window revealed my friend's form in silhouette. He lay splayed on the bed, face down and arms outstretched. A half-eaten meal and two empty bottles of wine stood on the side table.

I paused for a moment, unsure of what to do. On one hand, he was still here, alive and unharmed as far as I could see. On the other, he didn't budge even when I stood there for a moment, staring at his back. I had been afraid for him before on more than one occasion, but I had never had to fear what he would do to himself without someone to watch over him. It would be wrong to pry into his thoughts, but if he was hurt and I failed to summon help in time, the outcome could be disastrous. Loyalty and fear weighed on me in equal measure.

My whole day had been steeped in shades of guilt. Before I could change my mind, I bent forward and brushed my hand against his outstretched arm and got no information at all. When I tried again, I had to reach deeper, only to feel—

I lay in the bed, one side pressed into the sheets, breathing in the slightly sour odor of my own exhalations. Against my cheek, the pillowcase was sticky with sweat. I was so *heavy*. Not only in terms of the weight of my body contouring to the sagging mattress, but from everything that pushed down on me from above. My heart beat irregularly in my chest, and it took an incredible force of will to open one eye. The room was dim and smudged, the edges of things not as sharp as I was used to, and I was too cold and too hot at once—

I reeled back and the world resolved, leaving me at Emerald's side once more. I wrapped my arms around myself tightly. I was used to what I thought of as *feeling*. I could rearrange my coat or my skirt without issue, but I had been *Emerald* just now, and it was nothing like the same. It had been so much more, and so much worse.

I wished I had never touched him. Worrying for him was bad enough. *Being* him was worse.

The physical sensations were only the start of it. In my heart, I had felt nothing when I was him, but not the nothingness from Nweke's body when it was pulled from the bay. Emerald appeared to be in the same place I went when I was dispelled, an empty weightless place in which there was no sense of time.

That's what he's doing when he drinks, I thought miserably. *He's erasing himself for a moment so that he won't have to live in his own head.*

I was still debating what to do when Emerald gave a tremendous snore and rolled over on his back. He shivered fretfully and muttered something unintelligible before lapsing back into silence.

I collapsed onto the chair in the corner and watched him for a while. His loud breathing made the whole room feel smaller, but at least it was better than that awful silence.

Closing my eyes, I tried to will myself back into the mind-cottage Aster had taught me to inhabit. Instead of Tincrown's house, I imagined myself in the cave in the mountains where I had first realized that I cast a shadow. In the silence of that private place, I struck my stones together to make a blazing bonfire whose flames climbed so high they scorched the stone roof above me.

This time, when I passed my hands through the flames, they burned me right down to the bone.

Chapter Eleven

Emerald was still snoring when the sun rose, and I didn't bother to wait for him. After what had happened the night before, I didn't want to face him, and he could always reach out through our connection if he wanted to talk. In the meantime, I was intent on paying a visit to the infamous Miss Marsha.

I had only reached the bottom of the stairs, however, when the landlady flagged me down.

"*There* you are, Master Crimson. There's a fella here who's been bothering the staff all morning tryin' ta have a word with ye." She indicated the front desk, where a familiar figure in a handsome green coat was arguing with the clerk. The man behind the desk pointed to me, and Coirpre turned.

"Oh! Crimson!" He hurried toward us.

The landlady snorted. "He's your problem now," she muttered, before beating a hasty retreat.

"Are you heading out?" Coirpre asked. "Meeting Emerald somewhere?"

I held my hands out between us. Technically, the bard had done nothing wrong, but I was already disturbed by my interaction with Emerald, and any reminder of that awful night in the keep was unwelcome. I was anxious to put a little distance between me and anyone who might ask inconvenient questions. "I'm busy, so if you'll excuse me..."

"I just wanted to ask how he is. Dirkus and what's-his-nose were saying awful things last night, and—*oh*! I'll get the door." Coirpre pushed it open to allow me through, then followed at my heels like a blond puppy. "And I wanted to see how he's doing, you know."

I stopped in the street outside the inn and turned to him. The roads weren't busy yet and most of the passersby were tradespeople going about their morning deliveries.

"I do not, in fact, *know*. Aren't the two of you enemies?"

"Enemies?" Coirpre scoffed and fanned himself. "Hardly. More like nemesis...es. Nemesi? Nemeses? *Rivals*. Archrivals, in fact."

I stared at him.

"Listen, it's quite simple." He pressed his hands together, palms apart, resting his fingertips against his chest. "*I am the infamous bard, the Lightweaver extraordinaire, capable of slipping every trap that has ever been laid for me.*" He lifted his hands toward the second floor of the building, indicating a window at random. "*He is the noble Emerald Flame, my only match in the art of illusion, capable of catching everyone who crosses his path. All but one. He is the one relentless bloodhound this wily musical fox cannot shake, and I am the one mysterious rogue he can never quite catch. That's our thing.*"

"Oh, good *gods,* you are insufferable." I turned my back on him and headed off down the street.

"Hear me out!" Coirpre bolted around me to cut off my path. "He made you in my image, didn't he?" He waved at my hair. "With a few tweaks here and there, I admit, but the likeness is uncanny."

"You call them tweaks. I call them improvements." I glared at him. "Let us agree to disagree." I turned around and set off in the opposite direction.

Once again, he barred my way. "All I want to know is that he's safe."

I crossed my arms and tried not to roll my eyes. "Why?"

Coirpre spluttered for a moment. "Well, because... because... because if he isn't, I shall have to reinvent myself."

"You were doing just fine before we arrived," I observed.

"Because I knew he'd show up eventually. He always does."

Under other circumstances, I might have enjoyed this conversation, especially if Emerald had been suffering through it at my side. Given that I was now working essentially alone, my patience was wearing thin. "Tell me the truth, or leave us alone."

"That *is* the truth!" he insisted.

"Bollocks." I held out my hand. "Tell me, or *show* me, or go."

The bard examined my outstretched palm. "Show you?"

"Let me see what's really going on under all the style. If Emerald really did design me after you, then there must be substance under there, buried somewhere *very* deep down." I took a step forward, and the bard fell back a pace.

"It's the truth," he said, although there was less conviction in his voice this time.

"Then show me." I lifted my chin. "Let me see what you're *really* thinking, or find someone else to bother."

"Can't you just tell me?" he whined.

"For all I know, you're sniffing around in the hopes of stirring up more trouble for him. We have *enough* trouble, thank you." I advanced again, until we stood nearly toe-to-toe. "So either show me your intentions, or go back to the keep and play songbird for all the lords and ladies."

"I'm not trying to—" Coirpre began. He glowered at me like a spoiled child who was unaccustomed to being told "no." When I didn't flinch, he knotted his fingers together and glared down at the knuckles. "When you see something, does he see it, too?"

"What, are you worried that he'll find out how shallow and petty you really are, despite being archrivals?" I demanded. "No, he doesn't see what I see, even when he's sober."

Coirpre's knuckles tightened, and he stood there for a long moment before thrusting one hand out toward me. "Fine, but make it quick. And no poking around in there, all right?"

I hadn't expected him to take me up on the offer, but curiosity alone would have been enough to convince me. Before he could change his mind, I settled my palm over his, then *into* his, accepting access to the foremost of his thoughts.

They were not as clear as Tincrown's had been, and nowhere near as unwavering. If I'd had to guess what I'd find rattling around in Coirpre's brain, I'd have said *not much,* but I was wrong. At first, I was met with a barrage of emotion. Prominent among them was genuine concern. Below that was a sort of sickness, but not disgust. Heartsickness, I might have called it. Grudging admiration for Emerald as a Lightweaver mingled with the confidence that Coirpre was better, and the simultaneous fear that he was not. His mindscape was a study in contradiction, and just below the *conscious* thoughts lay a few fragmented memories of a small, flaxen-haired boy crying on a dirty floor; a boot connecting with a skinny ribcage; and an old but still-visceral desire to shrink down into a single point of light and then wink out, if only to escape the misery of *being* for one moment more.

I hastily pulled my hand away, and the man before me resolved into the same old Coirpre, just as I had always known him, a man who had built a career on shallow vapidity. He pouted, but despite the immaturity of his expression, I could now catch a flash of wariness in his eyes. He was frightened of me.

"You said that you wouldn't poke around," he said softly.

"I didn't." I clasped my hands together as I had the night before after my brief glimpse into Emerald's nothingness. "Or rather, I didn't mean to."

Coirpre stared at his own palm as if it had betrayed him.

"He's not all right," I blurted. "I mean, he's still up there, breathing, not bleeding or anything. But he isn't whole. He's barely spoken to me since the other night." I remembered how Coirpre had walked us back to the inn. Was I never going to have my fill of guilt? I shouldn't have bullied him into revealing things I wasn't meant to see. That was how this whole sorry business with Emerald had started in the first place.

"Mm." Coirpre clenched his hand into a fist. "Drinking, is he?"

"Evidently."

"It's not the worst thing he could be doing," Coirpre said. "I didn't know it was that bad. If it gets any worse, let me know, will you?" He flashed a grin that wasn't the least bit convincing.

"Why, so that you can rob some new merchants and convince him to start chasing you again?"

"Or slip some baneberry elixir into a certain scout's cup," Coirpre suggested.

I cracked a forced smile. "Oh, would you, please?"

Coirpre shook his head and backed away. "I'm serious, Crimson. Without him, a decade of artistry falls to pieces." Something silver flashed at his throat, a small pendant bearing the face of a god I could not make out. It reminded me of the amulet we'd found on Maximilien's body the night before, and I held up my hand.

"Wait, Coirpre! One more thing." I hurried back to his side. "What do you know about Lemda? When he's in this state, it's been hard for me to..." I tapped my temple, hoping that he would understand.

"Lemda, the Shield of Faith," he said. "The goddess?"

I nodded.

"Nothing much. She's the goddess of protection, restitution, and revenge. She has a temple in Venta Bulgarum, if I recall. Why?" He gave me a shrewd look. "Is this part of whatever case the two of you are working on?"

"I'm not sure. Someone mentioned her yesterday, and I didn't know much about her."

Coirpre lifted on blond eyebrow. "Now who's keeping secrets?"

I backed away. "Ask your archrival about it the next time you two cross paths," I taunted, before taking my leave of the bard.

The silver amulet of Lemda might have failed to ward off

Kessel's demise, but it might yet be the means by which his death was avenged. Now that I knew his identity, I was going to find out who had killed him, pin Maximilien's death on the one who deserved punishment, and reunite my friend with the only person on Kovin Isle who knew how to lead him out of the darkness.

No matter the cost.

Chapter Twelve

I did not have to go far to find someone who was familiar with Marsha.

"Marsha of Midtown?" The baker's apprentice I had flagged down outside the inn smirked at me. "'Course I've heard of her. Everyone knows Marsha. You got business with her?"

"I do."

The curly-haired lad did a wary scan of the street and lowered his voice. "Well, if I was you, I wouldn't be so open about it, huh? Her sort of business isn't the type you shout from the rooftops, is it? Don't know how things are where *you're* from, mister, but 'round here, we've got this thing called subtlety." He nodded to my outfit. "Doubt *you've* heard of it, though."

I bit back an acerbic reply and forced a smile. "Hypothetically, if I was hoping to make contact with her, how might I go about it?"

The baker-boy sized me up. "You got coin?"

"No." I glared at him. "What I've *got* is the authority of the Conjury at my back and a few questions about a dead government agent."

To his credit, the baker-boy hardly batted an eyelash. "Fat lot of good that'll do ya."

I could never quite tell how much the name of the Conjury would move the locals to action. Evidently the leadership of Upper Bound carried enough clout that they didn't have to fear the central government to the same extent small towns like Dyrne did.

A grubby urchin ran past us, and the baker-boy snapped his fingers. "Oy, Tala, this ponce wants a word with the *headmistress.* He's bein' a real prick about it, too. Mind showing him the way?"

The child stared up at me with wide, curious eyes, pushing matted brown hair out of its eyes. Beneath all the dirt, I could only speculate how old the child was—I could not, in fact, say with any certainty whether or not it was human.

"You got coin?" Tala asked. The child's deep voice made me jump. Evidently, she was a dwarf, and she sounded fully grown, although she would have barely come up to Carthan Deepvein's waist.

"Nah, he might dress like a cockscomb, but he's happy to snudge us common folk." The baker-boy smirked at me. "Have fun in school. Don't get your ears boxed." He chortled to himself as he pushed his cart back into motion and went about his errands.

The young dwarf stared up at me with unrestrained disgust. "You really ain't got no coin at all?"

"I'm here on official business," I told the child. "No bribes." I would have been happy to hand out coins to all comers if it got me what I wanted, but I was hampered by my inability to touch anything, much less carry a purse.

The girl curled her lip at me. "Mingy hedgepig," she muttered. "Come on, then."

I felt a bit silly in my finery as I followed the squalid dwarfess into the lower parts of the city. Accepting directions from a child a third my height was embarrassing enough, but as we left the more well-to-do areas, I became increasingly aware of the attention I received from those we passed. They were not looking at me with adoration; rather, they eyed me with the sort of malice that I felt toward men like Dirkus.

You aren't just out of place here, I realized. *They resent you. It might cost you nothing to dress in the specter of silk, but for them to wear the same might cost more than they'll earn in a year.* I had considered my role in the world to be twofold, one self-serving and one the highest calling of all. I was meant to be seen, and I was meant to advance the cause of justice. Beauty was good, and lies were bad. It was a simple equation that allowed me to quantify the world around me.

Only, Emerald and I had been perfectly content to tell lies lately, and external beauty was neither cheap to manufacture nor a guarantee of good intent. Coirpre's childhood memories flashed through my mind unbidden. What kind of lies, I wondered, would a girl like Tala be willing to tell if it meant she could live in comfort? Was Coirpre's plan to trick wealthy merchants out of their money really any worse than the measures Emerald and I had taken to protect Dyrne?

The more time I spent in the world, the more I realized that I knew almost nothing about it.

Tala stopped abruptly at the mouth of a long alleyway. "Tha' way, Sir Snudge. Knock three times on the door." She gestured furtively until I bent down to her level. "When they ask who ya are, 'tis code. Password's *I'm a fribble.* Tell 'im that an' he'll let you right in." She winked at me, her expression dead serious, before scampering back the way she'd come.

I stood there for a moment, mulling over my plan of attack. Mostly, I needed to know about Kessel. Judging by what Hudson had told me the day before, there was some contention between Miss Marsha's people and the folks on the docks. Hopefully, my conversation with her would help move things along. I still hadn't mastered the art of appearing to breathe, but my options were few, and I couldn't wait for Emerald to pull himself together. Gods only knew how long I'd be standing around if I did that.

Only when I reached the wooden door did it occur to me that I could not, as Tala has suggested, knock three times. I stood outside the door and pursed my lips in thought as the distant strains of a harp thrummed through the wood.

My incorporeality had not deterred me thus far. I would not let a mere *door* defeat me.

"Knock knock knock!" I called, pitching my voice to jovial heights. Already, the tone of the interview was taking shape in my head. For this performance, I would be cheerful, airheaded, and—ideally—utterly charming. "Hello, is Miss Marsha in there?"

Something thudded heavily on the other side of the door, and a gruff, masculine voice called, "Who's there?"

I smiled at the door on the off chance that someone was able to see me through a hidden keyhole or suchlike. "I'm a fribble."

A riotous burst of laughter emerged from beyond the door. "Are you, now?" a familiar voice asked. "That's too funny, Boo. Let him in."

The door opened inward, revealing a room totally at odds with the rest of the area. My mouth fell open as I stepped inside. "Goodness," I murmured.

If Hudson of Hardwick Home was transformed into a room, this would be it. Where the rooms of Fenguard Keep had brimmed with antique elegance, Miss Marsha's office could not have been less refined. Throw pillows and wall hangings in a variety of colors vied for my attention; glass oil lamps of every shape and hue dangled from the rafters; dozens of paintings in every imaginable style cluttered the walls; rugs and animal skins littered the floor; and among the handful of couches, chairs, and side tables, no two articles of furniture matched. Hudson's mode of dress might have been charitably deemed *poor man's fancy,* but this room was *blind man's chic.*

I could not help falling just the teeniest bit in love with the place.

"You are indeed a fribble," Marsha said, eyeing me with the same intensity that I took in her room. She was reclining on a green velvet chaise with all the regal indifference of a queen in repose. Beside her stood an immense harp, evidently the source of the soothing music, despite the fact that it appeared to be playing itself. "We've met before, haven't we?"

"Only in passing," I told her, dragging my eyes away from the chaotic finery of the room. "A few days ago, one of your men insulted my friend. You put a stop to it."

"I remember." Marsha's dark eyes twinkled. Her black dress had fallen open along one side to reveal her calf, and a fair bit of thigh as well. "He reminded me a little of my honey-bun."

The man who had opened the door for me grunted. "You were lookin'?" he asked.

"Trust me, Boo, it's hard to miss a man of his size, but he wasn't half so pretty as you." Marsha pursed her lips and blew the man a kiss. "Fribble, allow me to introduce you to Boudreaux. Close the door, baby, and come here. Our guest won't make trouble, will you?"

I shook my head as the door closed, and Boo stepped into the lamplight.

As petite as Marsha was, Boudreaux was the opposite. Where she was lean and long-limbed, he was bulky and square. He boasted short and stocky legs, arms as muscular as Emerald's, a heavy brow, small and rather beady eyes, and cauliflower ears that made him appear to have been struck about the head as a child and perhaps well into adulthood.

On top of it all, he had commissioned some inferior artist to tattoo nearly every visible inch of flesh. These dermal etchings were neither elegant nor functional; among them were no magical symbols meant for channeling the *Aidea*. On one huge bicep stood a portrait of a woman, whose features reminded me more than a little of a krub, over a banner bearing the word *Mother*. On the other was an equally unflattering portrait over the word *Marsha*. It was impossible to say, given the quality of the portraiture, whether Boudreaux's mother and Burp could have passed as twins, or if she was the handsomest woman on the mainland. Marsha's likeness could not in good conscience be called such.

"A pleasure to meet you, Boudreaux," I said with a bow.

He kept his beady eyes narrowed as he circled around behind

Marsha's chaise and stood behind her, glaring down his crooked nose at me.

"So, honey, do you have a name?" Marsha waved a manicured hand at me, and her eyes glimmered. "Or will I have to call you Fribble all night?"

"It's Simon," I told her.

"*Simon.*" She repeated my name low and carefully, as if she was sucking on a sweet. "I approve. And you're here, which means you lads didn't find what you were looking for at the keep." She licked her lower lip and sat up slowly. "Why don't you sit down, Simon, and tell us what brings you here?"

I did as she suggested, perching on a red brocade armchair. The legs and finials had been gilded in cheap gold paint which was flaking away from the wood. "I have a few questions for you," I said, mimicking her easy posture. Boudreaux narrowed his eyes and made a great show of cracking his knuckles.

Could I learn to do that? I wondered. I didn't have knuckles, but technically, I didn't have a tongue either. I had only ever made an effort to *speak*, but if I could scoff or click my nonexistent tongue, why couldn't I make a sound like knuckles popping, or silk rustling, or imitate the wet splash boots in a soggy patch of fen?

Evidently, when the bodyguard cracked his knuckles, most people didn't stare at him thoughtfully. He bristled beneath my indifferent gaze and curled his lip back in a vicious snarl.

"Down, boy," Marsha said with some amusement, reaching back to pat the big man's arm. "This little fellow is Miss Marsha's guest, so let's play nice for now, all right?" She returned her attention to me. "Don't mind Boo. He's just protective. An' I *did* tell you to come visit if you got bored in the keep. It's nice to know you remembered me."

I inclined my head slightly toward her. "I thought it prudent to visit. Wherever I go in Upper Bound, your name seems to come up. You have quite the sphere of influence."

Marsha threw her head back and let out a musical laugh. "Ooh, Boo, I like this one. He's a charmer."

Evidently, Boudreaux did not share her sentiment. Judging by the nasty look he sent my way, it seemed he didn't approve of *charmers*.

"Who have you spoken to?" Marsha preened. "Who's mentioned my name?"

"The King of the Black Hollow," I said. "And Hudson, down at the docks."

"*Pssht.*" Marsha waved a dismissive hand. "They're hardly on par with Laird Fenguard."

I considered her before speaking again. "Fenguard has money, and he has clout with the Conjury, but it seems to me that he doesn't have a finger on the real pulse of this city. He's not in the mix. Not like you."

"Oh, *honey.*" Marsha's winning smile fell away and was replaced with a shrewd stare. "You lied to me, Simon. You're not a fribble at all. Evidently, you're smarter than most of those government lads."

"I understand the difference between a figurehead and those with true power," I replied.

Marsha got up from her chaise. As she passed, she dragged one finger over a sigil carved into the wood of the harp, which fell instantly silent. She crossed the room to a painted fragment of what I recognized as a map, although I did not know it well enough to recognize where this area stood in relation to the larger continent.

"That's what separates folks like you and me from the rest of 'em, Simon. I grew up in Upper Bound with hardly a coin to my name. I was plain. Ordinary. Boring. But then I went to the mainland, and I learned a thing or two." She tapped one fingertip against the map, indicating a miniature town along the coastline. "One year in Leviathan Loch was as good as a lifetime in Upper Bound. I met all sortsa folk from all over the world. I met some of the best fellas I've ever encountered... and some of the worst. I came back different. Smarter." She spun back to me, and her dark eyes blazed in her face.

She was as consummate a performer as I was, and she was

playing the same part that I had settled upon when I arrived: a charming fool. Now, with that artifice fallen away, I saw her as she was. Like Coirpre, she had come from nothing, and she had secured her own power, dragging her dreams from fantasy into the real world.

"I already know who you are, Crimson Smoke," she said coolly. "I know about your friend, the Emerald Flame, and that bard the laird is keeping as a pet up in the keep. I know everything that goes on in this town, because you're right. I'm the real power in Midtown."

Boo let out a dreamy sigh, gazing at Marsha with the sort of besotted admiration that Emerald had so often lavished on Tincrown.

"Then you know," I asked her, "about Kessel?"

A wrinkle of confusion appeared between Marsha's eyebrows. Boo wasn't as subtle. "Who?" he asked.

"You tell me." I leaned back in my seat, still smiling, although I was careful not to sink into the plush velvet. "I know almost nothing about the matter, which is why I came to the expert."

Marsha and Boo exchanged a look, and she shrugged one shoulder. "Sorry, love, never heard of him. Is he local?"

"No," I said, examining my nails. "A sailor, born in Kinmore."

"A *sailor?*" Marsha sashayed back over to her chaise and poured herself into the seat. "That's none of my business. I keep my men in line. If you want to know about those seaward-bound hooligans, talk to Hudson. I don't have nothin' to do with them, and I'm happier for it."

"Hudson seemed to think otherwise," I said. "In fact, he mentioned you specifically. He seemed to think you were paying me to stir up trouble of some kind."

She laughed again and twirled a long lock of midnight hair around one marble finger. "As if. He's nothing more than a housecat who thinks himself a weirling. I work for myself. Isn't that right, Boo?"

"That's right, Marsha," Boudreaux echoed from behind her.

"Once his cargo leaves the port? That's another matter."

Marsha winked. "But I don't bother with his men. No point. They come and go so fast, they might as well have never been here at all."

"And die just as quickly," I added.

Marsha sat up straight. "Did this Kessel fellow hop the twig?"

It was my turn to be brought up short. "Sorry?"

"Did he shoot his star?" When I continued to stare, Marsha rolled her eyes a little. "Did he *become a landowner?*"

I glanced at Boudreaux for assistance.

"Did he," the big man intoned, "*go to the bog?*"

His choice of words unsettled me, but at least I understood the thrust of the question. "He didn't *go to the bog.* Someone put him there." Us, technically, but that was beside the point.

"Ooh, gods-ha'-mercy." Marsha fanned herself with one hand and crossed her legs demurely at the knee. "An' you think one of my fellas had something to do with it?"

"How *dare* you." Boudreaux advanced on me, his ire rekindled. "You think my Marsha would let something like that happen? We ain't *like* that. You take it back."

"I didn't accuse you of anything," I said coolly.

Marsha hiccupped and dashed away what I was certain was a fake tear.

"An' look, you made her cry!" Boudreaux seemed to double in height as his anger intensified. He loomed over me, cracking his knuckles for all he was worth. "Tell her you're sorry, or I'll rearrange your face!"

I stared up at him, utterly nonplussed. "If I wanted my face to be rearranged, I would happily do it myself, thank you very much. I'm not impressed by your posturing, and I doubt Miss Marsha is, either."

A vein pulsed in Boudreaux's temple, and his face turned red, then purple. "How dare you," he panted. "How—dare—you..." He fell back a pace and clutched at his chest.

In an instant, Marsha was at his side, pressing her hands to either side of his face. "Boo, baby, are you all right? Breathe, baby. It's just one of your episodes."

"Nobody talks to me like that. *Nobody.*" He glared daggers at me.

And then, quite unexpectedly, he burst into tears.

Marsha wrapped her arms around his shoulders and glared back at me as I looked on in positive bewilderment. "I hope you're happy. Poor Boo, did the bad man make you cry? It's all right, baby, it's all right." She rubbed circles on his back with one hand as he sobbed against her shoulder.

"W-what good am I if I c-c-can't even intimidate folks for you?" Boo wailed. "I'm n-n-not smart, Marsha, you know th-that."

"It's okay, baby," she murmured. "If I wanted a smart fella, I'd have found one. I want you, pigeon. Only you."

The scene had gone from unhinged to uncomfortably intimate, and at any rate, I wasn't going to learn anything more here. With some misgivings, I backed away toward the door and slipped through with no one the wiser.

Miss Marsha was a dead end. In Dyrne, I had been faced with an overabundance of likely suspects. Now, when the fate of a whole village rested on my shoulders and my associate was lying useless in a drunken stupor, I was left with none at all.

❦

After making sure that I was quite alone, I adjusted back into my ragged sailor's attire, minus the Trader's Guild emblem, and set off through the streets of Midtown.

Dyrne had been small, little more than a hamlet centered along one main street. Upper Bound, by contrast, was so large that there were whole distinct communities within its walls, all within the distance my tether to Emerald would allow. The people of Dyrne didn't have much, but they never struck me as *lacking*. Their lives were simple, and they were content with that.

The lives of the people of Midtown, however, were more... *narrow*. Unlike the beleaguered sailors in the harbor, they were not downtrodden and stone faced. Even so, it was possible to tell that there was something lacking in their comportment. Something akin to dissatisfaction. Certainly, they did not dress like the pedestrians in the wealthier parts of the city, although very few of them were as soot-smudged Tala had been, and I saw no signs of rampant illness or hunger in their midst. That struck me as odd, although I could not have said why. It did not match what Emerald would have expected, but I could hardly ask him about it now.

No one paid me any mind as I approached a square much like the one where Lafayette preached about the differences between swamps and bogs. Even the structure of Midtown was a shabbier counterpart of its neighbor. I was about to cross the square and head into the next alley when one of the other pedestrians grabbed her friend's arm and hissed, *"Look, Brigid!"* She pointed to a cross street. *"It's her!"*

I turned to see who she was looking at and was startled to recognize a familiar wan face, framed in russet curls.

"Lady Fenguard?" I murmured.

It was indeed the lady, although she was dressed much more modestly than I had seen at any feast. She strode across the cobbles with her two handmaids in tow. *Odette*, she'd called one. I hadn't heard the other's name.

A small crowd of people collected in the square, barring her way.

"Is that you, m'lady?" asked a woman carrying a small baby at her side. A little girl with black curls stood beside her, clutching the woman's hand.

I expected the lady to keep moving, but she paused to see who had spoken. When her eyes lit on the baby, her expression softened.

"It is indeed me," she said in her sweet, sad voice. "And who is this?"

The woman who'd spoken bounced the baby on her hip. "'Tis Caleb, m'lady, an' I'm Clara. An' this here is Columbine."

"Columbine." The lady's smile widened, and the sadness lifted from her for a moment. She lowered herself to a crouch on the

cobbles so that she and the little girl were eye to eye. "Like the flower. Aren't you lovely, darling?" She held out a hand.

The girl hid behind her mother's skirts, eyeing the lady with wide, dark eyes.

"Come here, Columbine, and show me your best curtsy. If you do, I'll grant you a wish."

The girl glanced up at her mother.

"Show 'er, lovey," Clara urged.

The child stepped forward, lifted her drab brown skirts, and ducked into a clumsy show of deference.

"Wonderful!" The lady clapped in delight, and her laughter was like music echoing from the venerable stones around us. "And what will you have for a wish?" The rest of the crowd, myself included, watched as if enchanted. There was something in Lady Fenguard's face that reminded me of Emerald, a sorrow that lingered even when she smiled.

The little girl bit her thumbnail. "I want a pearl," the girl said in a high, clear voice. "Just like the one on your necklace."

"*Collie,*" her mother hissed, then she dipped her head to Lady Fenguard. "Sorry, m'lady, she don't mean nothin' by it."

"She shall have it, of course. I made a promise." Lady Fenguard undid the silver clasp at the back of her necklace and took the strand between her hands. They were thick, almost blue pearls, each of them as long as the pad of her thumb.

"My lady," one of the maids said in a warning tone.

Lady Fenguard shook her head, as if to ward off an old argument. "It is only jewelry, Rose." She twisted the strand of pearls between her hands until it broke, then held out her hands to Columbine. "Take one," she said. "And another for your brother."

The little girl's eyes widened, and she scrambled forward to retrieve her prize before rushing back to her mother's side.

"Who else wants one?" The lady's eyes alit on every child in the crowd in turn. "Come now, don't be shy."

One by one, the children emerged from the assembly, bowing and curtseying to earn the rewards.

"Poor thing." The woman who'd first pointed out the lady's

approach shook her head sadly. "They say she can't have children herself."

"She's still young," the other replied. "And they can afford to find someone with *Aidea* to help them get with child, gods know."

Something I had not quite understood before came into sharper focus. Lady Fenguard, alone in her rooms, passing away the hours. Her constant sadness. To want something that one could not have was a terrible fate. Was being at odds with oneself a necessary aspect of being corporeal?

And what would happen if the Fenguards *had* no child to take over ruling their ancestral keep? Who would stand between the people of Upper Bound and Conjury's greedy grasp?

In the center of the courtyard, Lady Fenguard dispersed fat pearls the size of hummingbird's eggs to her diminutive admirers until she was left with empty palms.

Chapter Thirteen

The ship on which Yoyoh and Asha were to set sail was scheduled to depart that afternoon. A crowd gathered on the docks to see them off, and I—still dressed in my grungy sailor's garb—retreated to the roof of the building where I had met the jotunn duo to wave farewell. We were too far away to speak, but as the lines were hauled in and the sails unfurled, I caught sight of the two huge figures on the decks. Asha happened to glance my way, and I waved to him. The jotunn waved back, then said something to his companion. Yoyoh looked up and placed one hand on her broad chest, over her heart. I repeated the gesture, assuming that it signified a promise to her... and to Nweke.

The dwarven first mate looked quizzically at Yoyoh, then at me. A scowl of recognition crossed his face, and I ducked to safety before he could draw attention to me. Hudson couldn't arrest me, but he *could* make my life more difficult. Since my present level of difficulty was all I could stand, I beat a hasty retreat.

I was much less handsome as a ruffian, but also far less conspicuous. As I strolled along the streets of Upper Bound, I contemplated my next move.

Nothing came to mind on our case. Every thread I had followed turned up nothing. Knowing Kessel's name didn't help me if I had no idea who to ask about his demise.

Unless I ask him, I mused. *When the bog gives up its dead again, perhaps I will be able to ask him. Dirkus and Benedite will be looking for Maximilien, but Kessel won't answer to that name. Perhaps I can find a way to question him.* Of course, it would be infinitely easier if Emerald joined me in my endeavors, but there was little enough I could do on that front. I dreaded returning to the room to watch him drink himself into a stupor—and then lie in said stupor throughout the duration of the night. Truth be told, I suspected that having someone to talk to would be good for him, but I was also uncertain how to broach the subject of our last conversation.

I didn't realize where I was headed until I was almost at the door of the sisterhood's convent. I hastily ducked behind a low wall and rearranged myself back into the appearance I had worn during my last visit, when I had crossed paths with Aster for the first time. When I was done, I got up again and headed for the steps.

"Hello?" I called, wringing my hands together. "Aster? Are you there?"

"What can ah do for ye?" a voice asked behind me.

I jumped and turned to find two figures standing behind me. They were dressed in the concealing black robes of the Sisterhood, but judging by their proportions, neither of them was Aster. One appeared to be a human woman of middling height, while the other was, at a guess, a lambkin.

"Sorry." I smiled nervously at them. "I was here the other day and spoke to Aster. She gave me some advice, and I was hoping I might be able to speak to her again."

"Ah see." The human woman nodded. Her accent was like Aster's, at least as far as my ear could discern. "Aster is very good at giving advice, isn't she?"

The lambkin nodded as well. "You may accompany us in, child, and wait in the receiving room. Sister Gemma will fetch

Sister Aster for you." She took a step onto the first stair and swayed precariously.

The woman, evidently Sister Gemma, bent forward to catch her, even as I reached for her—no doubt a residual instinct layered into my connection to Emerald. Fortunately, I was far enough away that I didn't touch anyone, and Gemma was able to right the smaller woman before any harm was done.

"Tha-a-ank you, dear," the lambkin bleated wearily. "After such a long day, my grasp on the *Aidea* is taxed beyond measure."

I wondered why the *Aidea* would be necessary for her to walk, but I followed the two women up the steps without comment. Gemma let us into the cozy receiving room where Aster had spoken to me before, then motioned for me to sit before passing through the locked door at the back of the room.

Left to my own devices, I stared intently at the door. Would there be any record of Kessel in their books? The coffin had indicated that Kessel's identity was unknown, but the sisters were supposed to handle the dead before they were placed in the icehouse. Had they somehow missed the emblem?

Could the *sisters* be involved in the deaths? The idea struck me like a blow. Who would have an easier time covering up murders than the people tasked with processing the evidence? It would be devious, certainly, but also brilliant.

I stared at the back of the door, chewing my bottom lip. The sisters went about in all black. If I conjured myself a similar outfit and slipped through the door, I might be able to gain access to the inner sanctum and move about freely. It was tempting, but I would encounter the same problem: even in the robes, I wouldn't be able to handle the records. And what if the sisters *didn't* keep their veils on in private?

For an awful moment, I envied Aindreas and the people of Dyrne.

The door opened, and I started guiltily as Aster stepped through. She hadn't bothered with her veil this time, and she smiled when she saw me.

"Ye're back," she said softly. "How did it go?"

"Um." I cut my eyes away from her. "Not ideally, to be honest. My father's... not well lately."

"Sit with me." Aster padded over to the far side of the desk. "Would ye like some tea? Or something stronger, mayhap?"

"No." The word came out more sharply than I had intended.

Aster's eyebrows rose. "Ah take it ye don't approve of alcohol?"

I sank down in the chair I'd occupied before. It was turned at a slight angle away from Aster's, but since I couldn't move the chair, I made do with twisting to one side and trying to make my posture look natural. "The night after we last spoke, my father got very drunk. Drunker than I've ever seen him." I picked at my fingernails. "He said some terrible things, and we haven't spoken since."

Aster winced and closed her eyes. "Can ye tell me what he said?"

I considered this. My newfound suspicions regarding the Sisterhood made me leery of revealing too much, and I was in no hurry to spread the secrets that Emerald had let spill at the Fenguards' table. On the other hand, Aster didn't know my friend, and I had no one else to turn to for advice, since the only person in my usual confidence was the source of my current discomfort.

"Sometimes," I said slowly, "he... hurts himself. He gets sad, but it's more than sadness. I'm not sure how to explain it. He doesn't like to talk about it, but, um..." I looked up to meet her gray eyes. "People can be cruel to him."

"Ah." Aster interlaced her fingers. "That's a heavy burden for anyone tae bear, an' it can be difficult tae see the ones we love in pain."

"There are only a few of us in his life who care about him, but the thing is, he doesn't listen to us. It's as if any kind word we have for him doesn't matter half as much as the awful things strangers say."

It was Aster's turn to hesitate. Without her veil, her face was easy to read, and I could tell that she was remembering some dark part of her own history.

"Ah think ah understand yer father," she said at length. "The people in our lives tell us stories about ourselves. The story ye tell yer father, from what ah can understand, is that he's flawed but deserving of love."

I nodded slowly. "Very much so."

"But other people in his life have told him another story." Aster waved one hand in the air as if plucking hateful examples from the ether at random. "That he's ugly or stupid or unlovable. When ye hear the same story often enough, ye start to believe it."

I thought of all the unkind things that Dirkus had said to Emerald in the last few days alone. Then I imagined a hundred Dirkuses, a thousand Dirkuses, a *lifetime* of Dirkuses speaking to baby Emerald in the same manner, with no Tincrown—or even me—around to counteract them.

"Oh." I wiped a stray tear from my cheek. "*Oh.*"

Aster nodded sympathetically. "Ah don't wish tae pry into family matters, but are ye able tae speak with yer mother about this?"

I was about to reply that it was just me and Emerald, but according to Coirpre, I was fashioned after him. Did that make him, to some degree, a parent? Or merely a muse? The silence stretched a beat too long before I said, "It's complicated. But my father *did* start seeing someone recently."

"Ah'm glad that yer father has other people in his life," Aster said. "But ah wasn't asking for his sake. Ah was asking for yers. Yer father needs people in his life tar support him, but so do ye."

"I'm perfectly fine," I assured her.

The sister lifted one shrewd eyebrow. "Are ye aware," she asked, "that it is not your job tae save his life?"

I shook my head. "What? No. Of course it is. Who else would do it?"

"Yer father." Aster smiled, and it softened the square planes of her face. "Ye can help him, certainly. But he's an adult. Ye're his *child*. It isn't yer job tae save him."

My smile felt wooden on my face. Of course, what she was saying was true for other children. *Real* children. But I was not and never would be one of them.

Aster sighed as she studied my features, then ran one hand over her shaved head. "Remember what ah was saying about stories? If ye've been told yer whole life that yer father is yer responsibility, ye're bound tae believe it. Just consider what ah've said, all right?"

"I'll think about it," I told her.

"That's all ah ask. In the meantime, have ye been practicing that exercise we tried last time?"

"I've managed it more than once." I leaned forward in my slanted chair. "Is it all right if the, er, palace looks different each time I go?"

Aster nodded. "Of course. It's yer mind—and it's not as if ye're going to a real place. The purpose o'the exercise is simply tae make ye feel safe and in control, no matter what yer environ-ment. Ye might find refuge in a childhood memory one day and require a fairytale the next. Shall we try it?"

I sat up a little straighter and closed my eyes.

"Imagine," she said, "that ye are walking down a long tunnel. At the end of that tunnel is a door tae the thing that ye most need right now. Do ye see it?"

"I think so," I said. I did my best to imagine it, anyway.

"Open it."

I did as I was told and almost laughed aloud. I had envi-sioned Marsha's cluttered sitting room, with all of its knick-knacks and mismatched furniture and gaudy paintings.

"Why has yer mind taken ye here?" Aster asked. "Ye don't have tae answer aloud. Just ask yerself what ye need that ye believe can be found here."

Order, I thought at once. *A system. To me, it looks like chaos, but Marsha understands where everything belongs. There's a story to all of it. There's a through-line.*

Right now, Nweke and Kessel's deaths don't make any sense to me. But they make sense to someone, and I need to figure out the through-line.

I wandered through the room, touching everything, picking objects up and putting them down. I found an inlaid jewelry box and opened it, but it was empty except for a velvet lining. Of course, I wasn't really *in* Marsha's room, so it wasn't as if I could search for clues. I could only remember the things I'd seen.

Things, in fact, that I had taken special interest in.

I turned sharply to the wall where Marsha had laid one finger on the map. *One year in Leviathan Loch was as good as a lifetime in Upper Bound*, she'd said.

My eyes snapped open, fixing at once on Aster's face. "You sent Marsha of Midtown to the mainland."

Aster's brows pulled together. "Ah beg yer pardon?"

"My first day here, you offered to help me leave Upper Bound." I tapped one finger to the end of my nose, then pointed at her. "You must have made Marsha the same offer. That's how she was able to travel in the first place."

"Ah'm afraid that ah can't speak about anyone else's personal business," Aster said, but the smile tugging at her lips told me that I was right.

I got to my feet. "Thank you for the help," I said. "I should be going." It was difficult to think straight as I examined this new tidbit of information from every possible angle. What did it mean?

How many other connections had I failed to uncover?

Aster walked to the door and opened it, ushering me out into the twilight. "Ah'm glad that ye reached out for help. If ye need anything more, come again and we can speak. And remember what ah said about yer father. We don't fall into habits overnight, and they can be difficult tae break, but unless we try, nothing will ever change."

"Thank you," I murmured, hurrying away down the walk. I wished that I could lay the pieces out before Emerald and ask him to show me the full picture.

But when I returned to the room that night, he was already

dead to the world. One glimpse of his form on the bed was enough for me. I retreated through the back wall and wafted back down to street level, then found a spot along the quayside. If I was lucky, the dead would rise again that evening, and I would find some opportunity to question Kessel.

Luck, however, had not been on my side in quite some time.

Chapter Fourteen

"Master Simone?" a worried voice asked from my left.

I opened one eye. It was morning, and a slimy green monarch stood beside me, reaching one hand in my direction.

I yelped and pushed back from him in my haste to get away. Burp's face fell as he took in my expression.

"Sorry, Master Simone, I didn't know it would bother you if I —" He frowned down at his hand. "I find the dry people somewhat strange to the touch myself. I meant no offense."

"What?" I blinked rapidly. I'd been wandering through my memories of Fenguard Keep, hoping to spot some new clue. I'd spent the night doing the same exercise Aster had led me through, but I'd found nothing new in any of my other memories. "You startled me, that's all."

"Oh." Burp smiled sadly, as if he could not quite believe it.

I glanced around us. This early, there was no one else on the boardwalk over the bog; the sky was bathed in amber and saffron tones as the sun climbed over the lip of the horizon, fractured on the whitecaps of the Gossamer Ocean, and gilded every ripple in the Bounder.

"Listen," I said, "I'll tell you a secret, but you must keep it to yourself." I held one hand out to Burp. "Only two other people in this miserable town know the truth about me, but I'd rather share this secret than have you think... whatever you're thinking now."

Burp squinted at me as he reached out to lay his palm on mine. His hand barely passed through mine before he jumped straight up in the air. I only got the barest glimpse into his mind, and what little I saw was benign.

"Ooh." He clapped his sticky hands together. "That's a neat trick, Master Simone."

"Miss Simone," I corrected.

Burp shrugged. "You win some, you lose some. No need to dwell on it. But I don't understand what happened just now."

"I'm different?" I offered him a weak smile. "It's somewhat complicated, but I'm a little less tangible than most other people. You mustn't tell anyone."

Burp saluted with one hand, pressed the other to his heart, and squatted down so that his rump touched his heels and his knees stuck out in opposite directions. "I"—he made that bull-frog noise again—"King of the Black Hollow do solemnly swear to you, Master Crimson-Simon, that I will not betray your confidence."

I covered my mouth to hide my smile. "I'm moved by your loyalty to a friend," I told him.

The krub's eyes had already been enormously wide, but at my words, they all but bulged from their sockets. "*Friends?*" he croaked. "Are we really friends?"

"I consider us so. Don't you?"

"Master Crimson-Simon, I have never had a true friend in all my life." Burp clasped his hands together in utter rapture. "If it weren't for your disability, I'd offer you a krub-bath at this very moment, that's how much this means to me."

"A *what?*" I asked.

"A krub-bath." Burp batted his inner eyelids at me. "Have you never heard of it? Among my people, it is customary to offer a bath to your kin and closest friends. It makes the skin supple and improves your, hmm..." His pink tongue darted over his lips. "I don't know the Osmarian word for it. I'm not sure you have one, come to think of it. Anyway, it does a body good. And I hear that it has a particular effect on the dry people that some people like very much."

I glanced sidelong at my new friend. "What *exactly* does a krub-bath entail, Master Burp?"

"Well, it starts like this." Burp thew his head back, opened his mouth wide, and inflated his neck-pouch. He emitted a deep gargling noise from the depths of his throat, which started abruptly and never stopped. Within seconds, a sudsy foam spilled over his lips and dripped down from the corners of his mouth. It only lasted a moment, but even when he stopped, the shining pearlescent bubbles slid down his neck and chest to gather on the wood below us. Not one of them popped.

He closed his mouth, bubbles rolling out as he did so, and wiped the residue from his lips.

"So we do that for a bit," he said, "until you've got enough for everybody—"

"But I don't have a body," I said hurriedly. "So that's beside the point."

"Quite right. We shall have to find another way to celebrate our friendship." Burp flicked a bit of foam off his belly.

I nodded toward the bog. "Perhaps you'd be willing to take me on a tour of your kingdom instead?"

Burp swooned. "Master Crimson-Simon, I thought you'd never ask."

All of my investigation had left me with far too little to show for my efforts. Lafayette the swamper elf's injunction to *BEWARE OF THE BOG* was as good a lead as any other.

I walked along the surface of the bog, while Burp paddled along with his head above water, utterly content in his element. When the water grew too shallow along the peat hummocks, he rose up and walked. His bowlegged stride across the peat mounds was so at odds with his graceful swimming that I suspected the latter was came more naturally to him.

"What are your homelands like?" I asked.

Burp shrugged. "Don't know. Or rather, don't remember. I was taken from them when I was just a krubibie."

"I'm sorry, I didn't mean to pry." I should know better than to assume that everyone I met had a happy childhood among loving kin. As a matter of fact, I had met very few people in Upper Bound who had.

"Oh, it's not like that," Burp explained. "It's not a sad story. Krubibies don't need their parents as much as the dry people do. We manage pretty well on our own. And I don't mind being the king of a lovely place like this. I'm not sure I'd have become king if there were other krubs around to fight me for the title. Someone brought me here as a gift for the Fenguards, thinking they'd never met a krub before, and they were right. That Fenguard's a decent fellow—he put me out here and wished me luck, and here I am."

"You don't get lonely?" I asked.

Burp rolled his eyes. "I remember just enough about my family to know the traditions. One krub alone is better than two together, especially when you're a skinny fellow like me."

I glanced down at Burp's pot-belly as he trotted along a peat patch. What was a normal krub built like, if he was considered svelte? "And you don't get lonely."

"It's just how I like it." Burp stopped in his tracks and cupped one hand around the hole in the side of his head where I supposed one ear must be. "Be quiet for a moment and just listen to that."

I came to a stop, although my passage had been silent apart from my voice. A few distant bird calls sounded in sweet harmony, accompanied by the bass thrum of an insect. Animals moved about in the branches above, and with each shifting breeze, the leaves above us rustled together with a sound like silver coins.

"Isn't that the sweetest song you've ever heard?" Burp whispered.

There was a sort of melody to it, and I could have stood there listening for quite a long time longer. After a while, Burp continued on his way, and I went with him.

In the distance, a cloudy miasma gathered among the trees. "What is that?" I asked as we approached.

"It's the outer ring of the Black Hollow," Burp explained. "Most people can't go there. The air's a bit... stagnant, I suppose? It gets rather murky. It doesn't bother me. I just swim under it and try not to poke the skins."

I stopped where I stood. "*Skins?*"

"I told you, when the Cronemire's done with the bones, the dead wash up in the Black Hollow. They don't seem to *mind* when I poke 'em, but it feels rude."

If I'd had a stomach, no doubt it would have lurched. I liked the idea of swimming around with leathery skin-sacks left by the deceased almost as much as Emerald would have undoubtedly enjoyed the promise of a krub-bath. I might not be able to touch them, but simply knowing that they were lurking down there disturbed me. No wonder Lafayette had been so opposed to the bog when we spoke.

"Most folks can't withstand the smell," Burp said agreeably. "Someone tried to visit me once—well, not *me*, but my kingdom —and she nearly died. I expect she would have, if I hadn't turned her boat around and dragged her back to town. Poor lass was never the same. But it won't bother you, friend!" He beamed at me. "You can be my very first guest!"

"I'm looking forward to it." Never mind the skin-sacks. I would simply walk through the murk to whatever lay beyond.

I had only gone a few more paces when a familiar knot pulled at the middle of my chest, just below where my ribcage ought to have been.

"Dammit," I muttered.

Burp blinked up at me. "What is it?"

"I can't go too far away from Emerald," I complained. "I'm

bound to him, and when I get too far, I get pulled back to him." It was annoying enough at the best of times, but my irritation at this particular setback was anything but mild. He'd left me on my own for days, drinking endlessly and not contributing a damned thing. Now he was not only failing to help, but actively hindering our work.

I took another step, and the tug grew more insistent.

"Are you hurt?" Burp asked, watching my face.

"No," I said through gritted teeth. "But I might vanish." It wasn't fair that *I* should be pulled back to Em. Why couldn't he be pulled to me? He wouldn't even have to *do* anything, only lie here on this lump of peat with a bottle of wine and carry on feeling sorry for himself.

You don't mean it, I thought. *You want him to get better.*

Better than what, though? Because at the moment, the only person Emerald had to blame for his state was himself. The sadness I could forgive. The endless river of wine was another matter.

I took one more step and pressed my hand to the middle of my traitorous chest. "This might be as far as I go," I panted. "I'm sorry, Burp, I'd love to see it. Perhaps another time. I'm sorry if this is a bit startling, but—"

Emerald must have moved, because I did not. One instant, I was standing next to a deeply concerned krub in the depths of the Cronemire, and the next, I was silently falling onto my arse in our rented room.

"Blast it all to every hell!" I cried, wishing I could punch something.

Emerald stood over me with his jaw slack. His face was covered in a thick layer of bristly stubble, and his green eyes were bloodshot.

"Why did you have to do that?" I demanded as I sat up.

"Sorry," he whispered in a hoarse, shy voice. "I only meant to shave. Where have you been?"

Confronted with his miserable expression, I couldn't maintain my anger. He seemed diminished and thinned out, as if his skin and the bones beneath it were no longer quite the same size.

"Aster's sake, Em." I got unsteadily to my feet. "Have you been wearing those same clothes for the last three days?"

He snorted and turned away from me. "You *would* worry about the clothes."

"I'm worried about *you!*" I hurried around the front of him again. I might not be able to block his path, but I *could* make it so that he had to walk through me to escape, and I very much doubted that he would have any interest in giving me that much access to his innermost thoughts. "You won't talk to me, you haven't gone out, and every time I come in, you're..." I trailed off, trying to find some way to phrase my concerns without sounding accusatory. "I don't know how to help you," I said at last.

"You've been gone all the time," he muttered, staring down at his feet. "Figured you were better off without me."

I threw my hands in the air. "Em, I've been an absolute *mess* without you! I got chased by a dwarf, I've made a grown man cry, I've been offered a krub-bath, and I've managed to make enemies of nearly everyone of importance in the city. I've been called a snudge and a fribble and a *hedgepig*, whatever that is! Worst of all, I've only managed to find a handful of clues, none of which have led anywhere. And I've had to do it all on my own, because as bad as all that has been, it's better than sitting here and watching you fall to bits and not having the slightest clue what to do about it!"

Emerald lifted his eyes to my face, and the ghost of a smile tugged at his lips. "All while dressed as a peasant, apparently."

I waved both hands at my clothes. "This is what I've come to. You should see Simon's outfit!" I rearranged myself into my sailor disguise, just to prove my point.

"Aster's sake, you must be at your wits end," Emerald teased, but there was a hollowness to his attempt at humor.

I flung myself down into my chair in the corner. "This isn't funny, Emerald. You talked about k—" I choked on the word.

"Offing myself?" Em asked in a deceptively light voice. "Yeah, I did. At a party. In front of *Coirpre*." He lifted his hand to his face and shuddered. "What a mess."

"Out of everyone in Upper Bound, Coirpre should be the least of your worries."

Emerald lifted an eyebrow. "Did he say something to you?"

"We talked," I said as I glared up at him. "Which is more than I can say for the two of *us*."

"We should fix that," Emerald said. He sounded wearier than ever.

I tucked my legs up beneath me. "Why don't you start shaving, and I'll tell you everything I know."

Chapter Fifteen

It took me quite a long time to explain everything that had happened in Emerald's absence. I left out a few personal points, mostly involving Coirpre. I also revised my description of my conversations with Aster to avoid any mention of seeking advice or the exercise she'd taught me. Coirpre had asked me not to tell Emerald about our interactions; as for Aster, I wanted to keep a few things for myself, including her insights into Emerald's behavior.

Partway through our conversation, a maid came up to deliver lunch. She seemed surprised to find me there.

"Do you want a meal brought up?" she asked, nodding toward the tray. "I've only got the one."

"I'm perfectly content," I assured her.

She turned to Emerald as she sat the tray down and took the old one. "Will you be wanting any more wine brought up, sir?" she asked.

Emerald glanced at me. "No, thank you."

She nodded and withdrew.

Emerald picked up his spoon, but he didn't begin to eat right away. "Well, it seems that you've learned a few things. That's interesting, about the jotunn." He tapped the crust of his vegetable pie with this spoon, staring down at it, lost in thought. "It's a pity you didn't get to learn anything more about the Black Hollow, though."

"Emerald." I took off my ragged cap and ran my hands through my hair. "I have been trying to protect you *and* Dyrne *and* your boyfriend. Could you please not do that?"

He scooped up a spoonful of steaming pie. "Do what?"

"Criticize me for not having done enough."

Emerald paused with his spoon to his lips. "I wasn't criticizing. You've done remarkably well on your own."

"Oh." Emerald's praise for my investigatory efforts was usually lukewarm at best. Outright compliments left me somewhat off my footing, especially since I'd learned so little. "Are you sure? It doesn't feel like it."

"I'm sure." He took a bite at last and chewed carefully, watching me all the while. When he swallowed, he added, "You didn't do things *exactly* the way I'd have done..."

"Of course not," I laughed. "Here it comes."

"...but you thought on your feet. You found a name, and you managed to learn a bit about everyone on your list of subjects."

I crossed my arms, trying not to feel too pleased with myself. "And I suppose this is the part where you ask me some vague and esoteric questions designed to lead me toward a particular conclusion?"

"That hardly seems fair. You've done the legwork on your own, so why don't I try my hand at the reasoning?" He took another bite and stared up at the ceiling as he chewed, lost in thought. "Given that you've managed to speak to everyone you suspect might be involved, we can infer that one of three things is true from a purely rational perspective. Either you have spoken to the murderer or to someone who knows more about the killings than they've divulged, *or* the person we're looking for is someone else entirely who we haven't yet considered. Who exactly is on your list again?"

I held up one hand and ticked off people on my fingers. "There's the Sisterhood. I don't know much about them, but they wouldn't let me into the convent, and they *do* handle all of the dead, so that's two points against them. We know that Kessel had something stolen from him, and we do know that Nweke was at his party the night before we died. So maybe someone else from the castle? Hudson oversees the sailors, and he was secretive enough that I don't trust him. He has the most access to the bodies, so he could have changed the label on Kessel's coffin to *Unknown* to hide his identity—but he also seems to have the most to lose if he's uncovered?"

"But you also know from experience that people will take risks if they think they stand to gain enough by it," Emerald observed.

"I certainly haven't ruled him out. Marsha and Boudreaux were adamant about not being involved with sailors, but there's no reason to believe them." I rubbed my temples. "Would you look at that? In one fell swoop, I've managed to rule them all both in *and* out."

"What about Burp?" Emerald asked through a mouthful of pie.

I snorted. "Burp?"

Emerald shrugged one shoulder. "Technically, he was on your list to begin with."

"Yes, but he's..." I held my hand to krub-height. "He's no bigger than a lambkin, and we're looking for someone who killed a *jotunn.* They're huge, Em. How would a little fellow like Burp overpower someone that large?"

"I can't picture *any* of the people you named overpowering a jotunn fairly. But keep in mind, Nweke was drinking that night." Emerald scraped the last of his pie out of the dish and didn't meet my eye.

"Hmm." I pondered this. "What effect do krub-bubbles have on people?"

"No idea," Emerald said.

I waited for more explanation, but none was forthcoming... which was passing strange, because I thought Emerald knew just about everything.

I thought of Burp's smiling face when he told me that we were friends and offered to draw me a krub-bath. How sinister, to imagine him saying the same to his victims before drowning them in bubbles and picking their pockets, adding their trinkets to some hoard in the heart of the Black Hollow. I didn't want to believe it, but Emerald was right. I couldn't rule him out just because we'd agreed to be friends.

Emerald set his tray aside. "We also might be looking at someone who's made use of the *Aidea*. Of course, without examining the bodies more closely, it will be hard to tell for sure. Given that the real Kessel is in the bog, and Nweke's remains are on the way back to the mainland, there's no way to know for sure what kind of *Aidea*, if any, might be involved."

I clapped my hand to my forehead. "It didn't even occur to me. I've never met anyone but you and Coirpre who use it much, at least not in my presence. The people in Dyrne don't count, they weren't *using* it—" I sat up straighter. "Oh! When I was at the convent, one of the sisters said that her *Aidea* was overtaxed! You don't suppose it was related, do you?"

"I can't say for certain, but that does point to one person who might be involved."

I got up and began to pace. "But even when I tried to disguise myself and begged to join the convent, they wouldn't let me in."

"We have other ways of getting inside," Emerald reminded me.

"Right. You could kick in the door, and I could waft through it... I'm sure that will go over well." I lashed one foot out toward a wine bottle, wishing I could kick it instead.

"We could ask Laird Fenguard to help us," Emerald said.

I stopped in my tracks. "We *could*. Do you think he'd take our side? Put in a good word for us with the Sisterhood? Insist on looking at their records?"

"He's been nothing but obliging so far." Emerald got up. "But there's only one way to find out."

I held up a warning hand. "I will go with you to Fenguard Keep on one condition," I warned.

"Let me guess." Emerald plucked at his shirt. "Change my clothes?"

"We have murders so solve, but we *do* still have standards." I flapped one hand in his direction. "I don't need a working nose to tell that you stink."

"Predictable," Emerald muttered, but he smiled when he said it. For a moment, he looked like his old self.

I could only hope it would last.

⁂

It was midafternoon by the time we set out for the keep. Emerald, to my relief, looked almost presentable. His haggard demeanor had not been much improved by the shave, but he was no longer quite so down in the mouth.

As we climbed the hill, I glanced down at the port below us. "Another ship came in," I observed. "It must have arrived while we were in the room."

"Something to celebrate," Emerald said neutrally.

I bit my tongue. He was right. A new ship meant a new party, which meant more drinking, which meant—

"Dirkus," Emerald muttered.

I glanced up. "What?"

Sure enough, Dirkus was strutting down the hill toward us with Benedite on his heels, beleaguered as always.

"Well, look who it is!" Dirkus crowed. "The Emerald Flame. Haven't seen you in ages. Where have you been? We took bets on whether or not you decided to finish what you'd started!"

Emerald stiffened, and I wondered how our killer had chosen their victims. More importantly, I wondered how we could steer them toward the Conjury scouts. Both of them, ideally, but I wasn't picky.

"Only joking, only joking, you know I don't mean it." Dirkus slapped Emerald heartily on the shoulder.

"Right," my friend grunted. "Excuse us, we're on our way to see the laird."

"Have fun," Benedite drawled. "Say hi to your boyfriend while you're there. Evidently you gave him the cold shoulder the other night, and he hasn't been the same since."

Emerald's eye twitched. *[Is there a reason they think Coirpre and I—?]*

I pretended to be very interested in a passing cart. *[You may have confessed to more than one thing the other night. I thought you remembered.]*

Emerald sighed and nodded to Benedite. "I'll keep an eye on my boyfriend if you keep yours in line." He nodded to Dirkus.

Benedite coughed and spluttered. "He's not—*never.* Gods, don't even joke about that, it's disgusting."

"What?" Dirkus singsonged as he walked backward along the trail. I would have given anything for a cobble to come loose beneath his boot and send him tumbling down the hill. "Got something against men, Bennie?"

"I've got nothing against men in general. I've got everything in the world against *you*," Benedite snapped. "A face so ugly not even a mother could love it."

Dirkus sneered and caught Emerald's eye.

My friend winced. *[Driaweep's bleeding bunghole, please tell me I didn't mention my family the other night.]*

[Only once or twice.]

Emerald uttered something foul as we left the scouts to their excursion and finished our ascent to the main gate.

Laird Edur Fenguard was standing in the courtyard, deep in conversation with a merchant driving a cartful of wine. As we approached, his face lit up, and he hastily disengaged from his conversation to join us.

"Emerald Flame!" He held out both hands in greeting. "It's been days since I saw you. Where have you been? Have you made any progress in your investigation? Lady Dionara was dismayed that she didn't get a chance to meet you properly the other night, but I told her, *Don't you worry! If this fellow is half as bright as the bard insists, he's out there right now putting the matter to rest.* I tell you, the fate of that poor scout leaves a pall hanging above our city. But we've got the right men for the job on it, eh?"

I held my tongue and examined the buttons on my coat. It was nice to be back in my usual standard of dress, and admiring my outfit gave me something to do *other* than glare accusingly at my friend. He was here now. That was what mattered.

"Actually," Emerald admitted, "I haven't been... feeling well. But you're right that you've picked the correct person for the job. Crimson has been all over the city, and he's learned a great deal."

I started at this unexpected praise. **[You didn't need to tell him that. Unless you're worried that I've cocked it all up and want to shift the blame onto me?]**

[If anyone's made mistakes, it's me. I'm giving you proper credit, Crim. Accept the compliment.]

Edur laid a hand on his chest. "I'm sorry to hear that you haven't been well. Does this have anything to do with the reason you left the party so abruptly the other night?"

Emerald cleared his throat and shifted from one foot to the other.

Immediately, the laird lifted his hands. "Say no more. I know how it goes, when you've had a bit too much wine and celebrated too late into the night. Forget I asked. I'm only glad that we have Master Crimson with us to continue the search."

"To that end, we wanted to ask for your assistance," I cut in. Emerald's discomfort radiated through our mental connection with such vivid intensity that I felt as if it was *my* stomach that roiled with anxiety. An impressive trick, given that I didn't possess a stomach and never had. "We were hoping to gain access to some of the Sisterhood's records, specifically regarding the bodies they've processed to send back to the mainland."

Edur cocked his head. "*Bodies,* you say. Not just Maximilien's records?"

"I had hoped to examine their records more generally," I admitted. If nothing else, I wanted to learn all I could about

Kessel and Nweke, but Emerald had also made it clear that part of our job was to look for patterns. What if there was something else going on in Upper Bound? Something more sinister than a single murder and a run of random bad luck? Most of the deaths centered around Dyrne had been written off as accidents, and people seemed to treat the deaths of the sailors the same way.

Edur stroked his russet beard and stared off in the general direction of the bog. His warm manner had cooled somewhat, and for the first time, I saw that there was more to him than a man who liked to throw lavish parties.

"I understand that your work is important," he said slowly. "And I wouldn't speak my mind so plainly if the other two asked this of me. However, I am given to understand that you two are less, ah, *enthusiastically devoted* to the expansion of the Conjury." He hesitated another moment, then he waved to us. "Come with me."

We followed him across the courtyard and back out of the gates. Instead of descending the path to the city, however, he turned right along a narrow footpath that followed the outer curve of the wall. We walked in single file until we reached a small paved area beneath a portico that overlooked the city. A black, wrought iron bench sat upon the heavy stone slabs. From that vantage point, it was possible to see every place I had ventured in the last few days: Midtown, the port, the wooden walkway, the convent of the sisterhood, and over the Cronemire itself.

Edur dropped down heavily on the bench and spread his arms over the back. He looked very nearly as tired as Emerald had when I returned to our room that morning.

"Dionara and I come here sometimes," he said. "We've taken different approaches to how we serve the region. My wife is more interested in preserving our history, while I am more preoccupied with its future. We don't always see eye to eye, but when we come here, we *both* see the purpose of all our life's work. We have given ourselves completely to the city." He turned his head to meet Emerald's eyes, and then mine. "Consider all the moving parts that are at stake." He pointed first toward the channel of the Bounder, where a newly arrived Trader's Guild ship sat in the port. "Commerce and expansion will be our path to the future. I was more than happy to make arrangements with the guild and the Conjury to secure our long-term survival." His finger traced a path inland. "Then there is the matter of the locals. I have done my best to ensure that my people are able to thrive and grow. It's a balancing act, and I don't always get it right, but I've done my best."

Emerald shuffled over to sit beside the laird. "You've managed better than most cities I've visited on the mainland," he said.

"There's always room for improvement." Edur waved to the Cronemire. "And on top of all that, I have tried to make sure that we don't strip the land clear of resources. If we export too much or grow too fast, we won't survive. We can't stay rooted in the past, but I'm not about to throw away my people's future with both hands in exchange for a few years of prosperity."

I pretended to lean on the bench at Emerald's side. "So all the people I've spoken to answer to you? Hudson, and Marsha, and the sisters?"

"Hardly," Edur said. "If anything, I answer to *them*. It is my duty to represent and pursue their best interests. Sometimes, that means courting the Trader's Guild or complying with Conjury demands." He glanced down at his lap, where he'd folded one leg over the other and was letting his heel bounce against the stone. "Other times, it means pushing back. I understand that you would benefit from skimming the Sisterhood's records, but if I demanded that they answer all your questions, it would also mean putting the private records of my kingdom in the hands of two Conjury representatives. We are allies, not vassals."

The last time that a local leader had refused to show us records, it had been in an attempt to keep a secret that might have destroyed the town. I could not blame Edur for his caution any more than I could blame Nechtan for wanting to keep Dyrne's secrets.

Selfishly, I was reluctant to demand more information, too. If we had never learned Dyrne's secret, we would never have had to *hide* it. Our present difficulties might have been avoided entirely.

"I understand the difficulty of your situation," Emerald said slowly. "Especially the need to do whatever is necessary to protect those who are counting on you."

Edur relaxed and let out a relieved burst of laughter. "Well, thank the gods for that." He placed one hand on Emerald's shoulder and squeezed. "You know, Emerald Flame, we're not so different. I think we might have been friends, under other circumstances."

"If our alliances didn't put us at odds, you mean?" Emerald asked wryly.

"Precisely. But never forget, a government is just a collection of people. Perhaps we'll be able to change the course of the future if we act from a place of mutual respect. Let me think about your request, Crimson Smoke. Perhaps there's some compromise we can reach that will allow us both to get what we want." Edur shook my friend's shoulder gently, then got to his feet. The sun was inching toward the horizon, and the thin sliver of the first moon was already climbing over the sea. "My guests will be arriving soon. Perhaps we can talk about it over a carafe of wine?"

"No, I don't think—" I began.

"Gladly," Emerald said. "I could use a drink."

"Excellent." Edur set out on the path again, and Emerald followed, but I stood rooted to the spot.

[Are you really going to drink again?] I demanded. *[We can come back tomorrow. Discuss it with him then.]*

[I can handle this,] Emerald assured me.

His words said one thing, but I could feel the truth through our connection. At the mention of wine, a sort of hunger had flared within him. It reminded me of the way he'd sometimes felt when watching Tincrown, but a twisted version of the irresistible pull that had bound him to the doctor. He didn't *long* for a drink. He *needed* one.

[Very well,] I said at last. ***[You go with Fenguard, and I'll see to another matter. Divide and conquer.]***

[Precisely,] Emerald agreed.

The trouble was that the divide between us had deepened to a gulf, and I was no longer sure whether it was us or the wine that was doing the conquering.

Chapter Sixteen

I had no intention of going to the keep, but I also had no plan for a better way to spend my time, so I wandered away toward town with the vague notion of putting some distance between myself and Emerald.

You should have gone with him, I thought. *Maybe if you stayed by his side, you could persuade him not to drink so much.* Thinking that made me feel less guilt than anger, however. I didn't blame Emerald for the other night, but he'd had three days to sober up, and he'd spent most of that time in the bottle instead. Aster had told me that it wasn't my job to save him—but what would happen to me if Emerald did something foolish? He could harm me, too.

Even if he didn't overindulge, the thought of spending another few hours in Dirkus and Benedite's company didn't leave me particularly enthused.

I was mired in my own thoughts when I passed a large group of sailors. Most of them were human, but one straggler at the back caught my eye. He was a krub—or at least, I presumed he was. Unlike Burp with his smooth, bright green skin, this fellow was mottled dark green and brown with a white underbelly. His eyes were silver, and a hornlike protrusion of flesh projected above each eye. He was a great deal heavier about the middle than my friend, and easily half again his size.

He caught me staring and flexed his disproportionately short and scrawny arms. "Never seen a krub before?" he asked in a deep, booming voice. "Get an eyeful, dryboy." He flexed again, striking a pose. The rest of the sailors laughed amongst themselves as they hurried ahead.

"Actually, I *do* know another krub. He lives here, in the Cronemire." I dimly recalled that Burp had said something about meeting other krubs, but a sailor was unlikely to stay. Perhaps it would be good for my friend to meet one of his kinsmen.

"*Is* there, now?" My new acquaintance stopped short. "Well, well, well. I look forward to meeting her."

"He's a gentleman, actually." I thought that I'd said so already, but I was getting the impression that this new arrival wasn't the brightest will-o'-the-wisp in the bog.

"Big fellow, is he? Muscular?"

I shook my head. "I wouldn't say so."

He rubbed his hands together gleefully. "If you see him around, you tell him Squelch is in town. I'll look him up in the morning." The massive krub followed his crewmates toward the keep with a new spring in his step.

I wondered if I'd made a mistake in mentioning my friend, but there was nothing I could do about it at that point. Instead, I made my way out the wooden ramp around the Cronemire.

As night settled over Upper Bound, I headed out into the bog again. I didn't go far this time. Instead, I settled on a peat mound under a tree and sat down with my legs folded beneath me. Just as I had done that morning when Burp first escorted me out into the fen, I closed my eyes.

Back in Dyrne, Emerald had solved key elements of the mystery right from the beginning. I had not been able to see the connections between things. As the soft rustling of reeds and the trill of crickets echoed around me, I closed my eyes and stepped into the space that Aster had taught me to inhabit.

This time, the appearance of my mind-cottage was reminiscent of Laird and Lady Fenguard's private rooms. I was surrounded by imagined paintings of every suspect that I had named. What I needed was to find a connection between them. Portraits of Marsha, Hudson, the sisters, the Fenguards, Burp, and even Dirkus and Benedite stood along one wall. I walked down the line, looking at them all, but I saw nothing new.

Maybe I'm coming at it from the wrong angle.

I turned around to face the opposite side of the corridor. A series of mismatched images hung there, and I walked along, peering at them intently. The first was of Lafayette, holding his sign that read, *BEWARE OF THE BOG.* Next came Kessel's body, standing upright in the water, looking just as he had when he tried to tell us why he had been killed. Then Nweke, as I had seen him that night at the feast, seated beside Yoyoh at the long table.

The fourth picture did not make sense at first. The canvas was nearly black, with only a dash of silver at the topmost corner, like a full moon seen from deep underwater. I leaned closer, trying to make sense of it, and the darkness seemed to ripple across the canvas. Without thinking, I lifted my hand to the oils and let my finger caress the uneven surface. The instant I touched it, I jerked away, startled by the force of a memory.

This painting wasn't something I'd experienced. It was drawn from Emerald's memory, from when he'd dropped like a stone through the surface of the Bounder and let the current carry him deep.

Oh, Em. The longer I stared at that picture, the more it sickened me. How could my friend think so little of himself that he would do such a thing?

When ye hear the same story often enough, Aster had said, *ye start to believe it.*

I forced myself to step away and proceed to the last image. This one was not a painting, and when I realized what I was seeing, my jaw dropped. It was the tapestry from the convent, which had hung behind Aster when we spoke. It showed the winged Crone in her black robes, standing amid the riot of life that comprised the swamp.

"Wait." I snapped my fingers. In my imagined world, they even made a sound. "There *is* a connection here." I retreated to the prior painting, the one lifted from Emerald's memory. Lafayette's parting words rang in my memory.

The Cronemire feeds on the wicked! She slakes her thirst on the unworthy!

My friend had made it clear on more than one occasion that he did not believe his life to have the same value as everyone else's. He had confessed to me in Tincrown's sitting room that he'd tried to harm himself before... but as far as I know, he had only taken it to such extremes on one occasion, when he was just downriver from the Cronemire.

Nweke's body had been found in the water not far from the Cronemire, too. When I returned to Kessel's portrait, another connection occurred to me. "Nweke died the same night that the bodies rose from the bog," I murmured.

Beware of the bog. Even Burp had said that the Cronemire could be dangerous. He'd saved some woman's life by helping her escape the poisonous fumes of the Black Hollow.

"It all comes back to the Cronemire," I said aloud. I began to pace the hallway between the two rows of the paintings. "I should have thought of it sooner. There must be some connection between whatever magic allows the dead to return and the thing that stole—" I stopped dead as my own phrasing struck home. "The thing that stole Kessel's life." I struck my palm to my forehead with a satisfying slap. "His *life*! I thought Kessel was trying to tell us that he'd been *robbed*."

Something tugged at my chest. At first, I thought it was some imagined sensation. That wasn't unusual in my mind-cottage. The pull grew stronger, however, until it yanked at me with the same urgency as my tether. I stumbled and had to catch myself against the wall. My wonder at being able to feel the cool stone beneath my palm was immediately overshadowed by the sense of being pulled in several directions at once.

This wasn't just the tether at work. This was something else.

Oh, no, I thought desperately. *Something must have happened to Emerald.* Fear clawed at me, although I was not sure whether I should fear the lure of the Cronemire or of Emerald's own hand more greatly.

The tether yanked again. I tried to yield to it in the hopes of going to Emerald's side and finding some way to help him.

Instead, I fractured like a windowpane, and bits of me went spinning in every direction. Rather than disappearing entirely, as I did when Emerald's spell lost its grip on me, I was scattered to the winds.

۞

It was dark, and I stood on the edge of the bog while a strange mist hovered around us.

"Good," Emerald said. He stood to my left, swaying from one foot to the other like a cattail in the night breeze. "You came. Wasn't sure that was gonna work."

I did not move.

"Figured I'd try to make you look a lil' different," he slurred. "Cuz you've gotta try to find the body, right? And I'll have to pretend to be, you know, bothered about Maximilien and all."

I was deep underwater, crushed by the pressure of the rippling whitecaps above me.

"You're not mad just because I drank a little, are you? I had to. For T —for him. Gotta keep up appearances. You don't know what it's like, having to sit there and take it while Dirkus runs his mouth forever." Emerald scraped one hand over his face, hiding his bloodshot eyes. "Say something, Crim. Please."

A voice that sounded like mine but did not belong to me said, "Something."

Emerald snorted. "Smartass."

From a long way away, I saw my friend standing in front of a dark-haired woman with a button nose and silvery eyes. She was staring straight ahead, never blinking. I could see out of her eyes as well, but it was like pressing my face to a sooty window and trying to make out what was happening in the street beyond.

Or like trying to make out the light of the crescent moons from under the surface of the river.

"Fine, be that way. While I'm dealing with the scouts, you can go out into the bog and look for... look for... what's-his-name. The sailor. Kimmel? You know, the one we switched."

The figure that was not me stood there, staring.

My fragmented consciousness took a long time to understand what had happened. I hadn't felt the pull of my tether. Emerald had been trying to summon me, but instead of calling me back to the physical world, he'd created an empty illusion. He thought she was me, but she wasn't. She was as empty as I'd been before my birth in the woods.

[That isn't me, Em!] I tried to reach out to him. I was certain that it must have been an accident on his part. He'd promised that he'd never trap me in my own mind again, and I was certain that he hadn't done this intentionally. It was an error. He'd figure out the truth soon enough. In the meantime, I had to fight to keep from being swept away in pieces, like ashes scattered on the waves of the open sea.

Emerald gestured at the Not-Crimson. "I know you understand. You can be mad at me all you like. I deserve it. I should stop. I will stop. But we have to..." He rested his palm on his forehead. "Just help me, all right? Please? Just let me fix the mess I made, and then we can do things your way."

The Not-Crimson nodded. "Yes, Emerald."

"Thank the gods. I'll meet you back at the inn when this is over, yeah?"

"Yeah," the empty illusion replied.

Emerald waved and lumbered off. He didn't seem quite as drunk as he had the night Coirpre and I had followed him home, but it was obvious that he was fighting to maintain his focus.

"It's not me, Em," I tried to say, but I was only shards of myself, with no teeth and no tongue and no voice at all—not even the illusion of them.

The Not-Crimson stepped off the empty stretch of boardwalk and into the water. When I had followed Burp toward the Black Hollow, I had walked along its surface. She stepped into the fen and walked along the bottom. In doing so, she let the water pass through her—through me —through the illusion that Emerald had cast in my place. Usually when I interacted with an object, I could not feel anything. A stone or a wall or a chest of drawers didn't have emotion or desires or even memories.

The Cronemire was different. As the Not-Crimson traversed the bog, we felt its desires. The water seemed to be full of consciousness, each of them only a piece of the whole. They were not entirely unified, but there was a common thread that bound the whole together: a desire to preserve the past in order to feed the future. The bones of the dead fed the roots of the trees, which provided shelter for the birds, which helped the berries go to seed, which fed the insects, which fed the frogs, which fed the snakes, and so on in an endless cycle of regeneration.

Every death allowed something else to thrive.

I wished that I could pull away. The voice of the Cronemire was too loud. It was too hungry. What should have been a natural cycle was thrown out of order, and its need to consume outstripped its ability to replenish.

The Not-Crimson stood in the water for a long time. Emerald had only told her to look, and he had not even remembered the name of the man she was looking for. With no thoughts of her own and no clearer instructions, there was little she could do.

At last, the mist receded, and the next order Emerald had given the Not-Crimson took effect. She walked back to the land and returned to Upper Bound, weaving mutely between the locals as they headed home for the night. She found her way to the inn, then waited outside its closed door for Emerald to return.

It was a relief to be rid of the Cronemire's hunger, but when I was no longer being assaulted by its tangle of voices, I was still helpless. I tried to climb back into the Not-Crimson's body, but I could not find a way to reach her. It was as if I was trapped on another plane, a ghost haunting my empty body, which in turn was nothing more than a tapestry of light.

Emerald returned at last, and he pushed the door open, allowing the

Not-Crimson to step through before leading her up the stairs. Only when they were locked in their room did he address her.

"Well, good news. They tried to find Maximilien again when the dead returned, but nobody would answer to that name. Dirkus threw a tantrum, n' Benedite threatened to throw him in the bog next. They've written it off as a, uh... You know." He snapped his fingers a few times. "A loss. A mistake. Some bollocksed-up trick of the Aidea."

The Not-Crimson retreated to the corner and stood there with her hands folded in front of her.

"Still not talking?" Emerald flopped down on the end of the bed. "That's not like you."

It was a relief to hear those words. I had been wondering how long it would take him to realize that something was wrong. I could forgive a mistake. I'd tried to rearrange myself into entirely different people, so I didn't blame Emerald for trying to do the same. He could finally put me back together.

"Did you at least learn anything from the sailor? Did you find him?"

Silence.

"Crim, this is stupid. You're being petty." Emerald squinted his blood-shot eyes at the figure in the corner.

She didn't stir.

With a sudden burst of anger, he lurched unsteadily to his feet and snatched an empty bottle off the side table before throwing it at the far wall. It shattered against the plaster.

"I know you've got something to say to me!" he bellowed. "So say it and get it over with!"

I had never seen Emerald react like that. In my experience, he'd always been gentle and kind, even when his words were surly.

But he wasn't kind with himself, was he?

I felt a distant nudge, and the Not-Crimson lifted her silvery eyes to his face without lifting her chin. She glowered at him, and her lip curled back in disgust. I was certain that I had never worn that expression, not even with Dirkus. Even with Aindreas. And I had never, never, looked at Emerald like that.

"Nobody wants you here," she said. "Nobody can stand you. You're impossible. You're a liar. You don't keep your promises."

Emerald fell back a step, his momentary anger replaced with dismay. "What?"

"You're a disappointment." She took a step forward. "The only mistake Tincrown has ever made was in loving you. You've failed him. He trusted you, and you can't control yourself for one night?"

"Stop it," Emerald said. He took a step back toward the wall, shrinking in on himself.

[It isn't me!] I thought, but my words echoed back unheard. **[It isn't me saying those things, Em. I don't believe them.]**

But when you heard the same story often enough, it started to feel true. Especially when the person telling that story was you.

"Dirkus was right about you," the Not-Crimson said. "Parian was right about you. Tincrown only pretends to like you because he's nice, but if he could see you right now, he would be disgusted."

"Stop." Em retreated another step, and his foot landed among the shards of the broken bottle. With a wordless cry of pain, he collapsed against the wall and pressed his hands over his ears. "Stop talking, Crim."

[It isn't me, Em.] I wished that I could fend her off. **[You're making her say those things. She can't stop because you won't stop.]** I might not be able to touch anything else, but at least the illusions that Emerald and Coirpre cast were real to me. If I could have pulled myself back together, I was sure that I could have overpowered her. This was the first enemy we'd ever faced that I could theoretically have vanquished on my own, and yet in my current state, I couldn't do a damned thing to help.

The Not-Crimson knelt down beside Emerald so that her face was only inches from his. "Nobody cares about you. Nobody likes you. Nobody loves you, not really. The world would be better without you in it. It should have been you in the bay, not Nweke. It should have been you. It should have been—"

Emerald made a sharp gesture with one hand, and the world went dark.

Chapter Seventeen

When I did not exist, I was nowhere. I was lifted out of time. There was no space between when Emerald banished me and when he summoned me again, no time for me to worry that he wouldn't. In the blink of an eye, I went from being scattered to being whole again. Only the light from the window gave me any sense of how much time had passed. It was late morning.

Emerald sat on the edge of the bed with his injured foot on his thigh. He was picking at the bits of glass still lodged in his skin. He didn't acknowledge me, even when I knelt down to meet his eyes.

"How," I asked softly, "could you ever think that of me?"

His hand stilled, but he kept staring blankly at the cuts on his heel. "What?" he rasped.

"It wasn't me," I said, and this time, at least, he could hear me. "You summoned something else, and I couldn't talk, and I couldn't make her stop. I couldn't do *anything*." My voice rose an octave, and I clawed at my chest. He had summoned me as Simone this morning. Only when I clutched at the material did I realize that I was wearing blue. I was wearing my apology dress, the one he'd given me in Dyrne after our first fight.

I wondered which one of us had chosen this particular outfit.

"Crim." He lowered his foot to the floor and leaned forward. There was a new pain in his red-rimmed eyes. "Are you serious?"

"Of *course* I'm serious!" I shot to my feet. "I want to help you, Em, I really do, but nothing I say when I'm *me* seems to help, and I can't control you like you control me." I dug my fingers into my scalp and tugged at my hair. "You tried to rearrange me and failed, you made the thing you *did* summon say things that I would *never* say, and then you erased me." My eyes filled with tears that were real enough to blur my vision, even if I couldn't blot them on the sheets.

"Aster's sake, Crim. I'm so sorry. I didn't mean to." Em scooted closer to me.

I backed away. "Did you mean to throw that?" The broken bottle glittered in the sunlight. "Or spend days up here drinking alone? Did you *mean* to stay at the keep? Gods, how long did you wait to summon me back? I don't even know."

"It's only been a few hours," he said.

"But it didn't have to be." I retreated toward the door. "You could have waited weeks. Months. I'm sorry that you believe all those awful things deeply enough to make something that looks a little like me parrot them back to you, but I'm afraid of you right now. And the worst part is, you didn't *realize* it wasn't me." I wiped a tear off my cheek. "It's like you don't even know me. And right now, I don't feel as though I know you, either."

His features crumpled, and he pulled his thick legs up to his chest, hiding his face in his hands just as he had hidden from the Not-Crimson the night before. I hurt for him. I wanted to help him, but what could I do for a person who had absolute power over me? Whose self-loathing was woven into every warp and weft of my being? I couldn't think of anything.

I knew that I shouldn't leave him alone.

And I left anyway.

Burp was sitting in what I had come to think of as our mutual spot on the boardwalk over the Cronemire.

"Hello," he said sadly. He dabbled his toes in the water below. "I was hoping you'd come. Were you in a fight again?"

"Yes," I said as I settled beside him. "A real one, this time."

"And you lost?"

I rubbed my forehead, wishing for relief from my headache. Only then did I realize that it wasn't mine, but rather an extension of Emerald's hangover. Of *course*.

"I don't think either of us won," I said.

"Ah." Burp nodded. "The worst kind of fight. Speaking of fights, Master Simone, I'm to be in one as well."

The sheer misery in his voice startled me. "You're *what*?"

"There's a new krub in town," Burp explained. "When there's one krub, he's king, but when there's a second, we have to fight. It's the law of our people. And the loser..." He trailed off with a sigh. "Well, let's just say that there's only ever one king."

"Oh, *no*. You have to fight Squelch?" My hand flew to my mouth. "Burp, I'm the one who told him about you!"

"You've met him, then?" Burp swallowed hard. "Big fellow, isn't he. *Fit*." His lips wobbled.

"Do you have to fight even though he's here with the Trader's Guild? Won't he be gone in a few days?" All of my friends seemed destined for trouble.

"He was asked to leave the crew. Krubs aren't always popular with the dry folk." Burp pulled his feet back up onto the boardwalk and tucked all four of his limbs beneath him. "He's here for good. He came by this morning to ask for a tour of the Black Hollow. He kept saying how much he liked it here and giving me the most awful smile." Burp squeezed both sets of eyelids shut.

"Is there anything I can do?" I asked. "I can't help but feel that this is all my fault."

"He would have found out about me eventually. But it means a great deal to me that you asked, a *great* deal. You're a true friend, Master Simone. I can't tell you how nice it is to know that someone cares what becomes of me."

How was it, I wondered, that some of the best people I knew doubted their value at every turn, while the likes of Dirkus strutted through the world without a care? The unfairness of it all beggared belief.

"Will you come to the fight?" Burp asked. "I have no doubt that I'll be, ah, *deposed*, but it would be nice to have someone rooting for me. A bit of local support, you know."

"Of course I'll support you," I said at once, glad to know that there was something I could do for at least one person I cared about.

Burp rolled one eye toward the heavens. "The battle will take place two days from now, at high noon. If you like, I can try to show you around my kingdom one last time before..." He cleared his throat.

"I would like nothing better." The mention of the Black Hollow reminded me of my revelation from the day before. If the magic of the Cronemire and its ravenous hunger had somehow led to Nweke's death, then it would not be long before another body turned up in the river.

I got to my feet and straightened my skirt. "I'm sorry, Burp, I have to go. But I'll be here two days from now at sunrise. I'll find a way to go with you this time."

"I shall be glad of the company in my last hours as king." Burp stood up, too. "Until then, Master Simone." He stood there on the edge of the dock as I hurried away. Before I reached a curve in the walkway, I heard a splash behind me, and when I glanced over my shoulder, he was gone.

Chapter Eighteen

there was a body floating in the bay of the Bounder. He was face-up this time, with his empty eyes staring at the sky.

In my scruffy sailor's uniform, I was able to sidle through the crowd to watch as he was fished out of the waves. Hudson was overseeing the recovery efforts again.

I wanted to return to the room and find Emerald to tell him what I'd worked out. If the Cronemire was indeed magic, then it was unlikely that I would have any experience with the *Aidea* that drove it. His vast store of magical knowledge would come in handy, but it wasn't the sort of information that lingered at the forefront of his mind where it would be easy for me to glean from afar.

Going back would mean apologizing, though, and I wasn't yet prepared to do so.

Let him stew a bit longer, I thought. *You've confronted him enough times to know that words won't make a difference. Let him sit in that small, dark room at the inn and think about what he did. He knows better. He* should *know better.*

My resolve lasted until the sisters lifted the pallet bearing the swollen, empty form of the dead man onto their shoulders. They made no move to hide him as they carried him away toward the convent in a solemn little procession. Their countenances were hidden by their robes, but the dead man's were on full display for the world to see. I wasn't sure what events had led to him floating face-up in the brackish water of the bay, but I knew what had brought Emerald there.

How can you expect him to recognize you when he can't even see himself clearly? I crossed my arms and bit the inside of my cheek, turning my face away from the dead man and staring down into the water that lapped gently at the weathered and sun-bleached dock pilings. My own reflection scowled back at me, as Emerald's reflection must have frowned at him when he stepped over the edge of the bridge on the night of the spring equinox. *How can I expect him to understand how much his actions hurt me, when he is so lost in the deeply worn ruts of his own pain?*

On one hand, it was quite clear to me that I could not excuse him entirely—but if I turned my back on him now, he would have no one.

And whose fault is that? He's isolated himself from everyone, and then he cries to the laird that he has no friends. My irritation warred with my compassion.

In the end, compassion won. With more than a few misgivings, I retraced my old steps, keeping the door to my mind-cottage firmly shut as I did so.

I will not let him in. I will not let his bitterness and self-pity cloud my judgment. I will speak to him plainly, and only let him take as much of me as I am willing to give.

To avoid any sort of confrontation with the inn staff, I took the back entrance. Which is to say, I approached from the alley at the back of the inn and leapt like a wight-cat from the ground behind the inn to the height of the second floor. I stood in midair for a moment and closed my eyes, trying my best to exert the self-control that Aster had taught me.

With one last effort of will, I strode through the wall, speaking before I laid eyes on him. "Listen, Emerald, I'm still angry at you. I haven't *forgiven* you. But I heard about the sailor, and I wanted to make sure that you're all right. Emerald?" I stood in the middle of the empty room. The bed was unmade, and the empty and broken bottles were still strewn about, but I was alone in the small space.

As far as I could tell, there was no sign of a struggle, though who could have said one way or another with any certainty? Emerald had, more or less, lived the last several days in squalor. Nevertheless, the door was closed, and none of the furniture was overturned. There was no reason to think that anyone had come into his room with the intent to do him harm.

In that moment, I worried less about whatever menace stalked the streets of Upper Bound, and more about what damage Emerald might have done himself in my absence.

Don't panic, Crimson, I thought, and then proceeded to do exactly that. The only place he'd shown any inclination to go was the castle—although after our fight that morning, I doubted it would be his first destination. I had no idea where to look for him, and I had reason to believe that time was precious. Rather than scrambling about like a fool, I closed my eyes and willed myself to his side.

Although my tether had pulled him to me against my will several times, I had only attempted the reverse once before, in Dyrne, when I had seen Kristine and Parian in the hot spring. Back then, my fear and horror and desire for comfort had pulled me back to him. Fear drove me again, but this time it was of a completely different variety.

[Please be safe. Please don't have done anything irreversible. Emerald. Emerald. EMERALD.]

"Crimson?" His voice was so small, I could not imagine it emerging from a man of Emerald's size. A frisson of relief passed through me as I opened my eyes, only to be dashed by the tableau in which I found myself.

I did not recognize the area precisely, although some parts of the landscape were familiar. I stood in a lonely place along the waterside, on a rocky slope midway between Upper Bound and the bridge over the river. Fenguard Keep rose to our left; to the right, the mouth of the Bounder opened out into the sea. The ruddy fresh water of the peat bog mixed with the seawater there, swirling together as the waterways collided.

Emerald sat on the bank with his legs drawn up to his chest and his arms resting on his knees. His hands were still extended before him, palms up, as if they'd been supporting his head. He must have looked up when I appeared. His eyes were puffy and swollen, his jaw tight, his lips parted. His boots were missing. Two empty bottles sat beside him, although one had been shattered so that the sharp fragments lay scattered among the river stones. I could not tell if he had dropped it, or broken it on purpose again, and the uncertainty of that frightened me. I wasn't sure what he had used to harm himself in the past, but broken glass seemed as plausible a weapon as any.

"Crimson?" he repeated. "Is 'at really you?" His speech was thick to the point of being unintelligible.

"Emerald?" I sank into a crouch beside him, trying to meet his eyes. "What happened? How did you get here?"

He turned his head away so that I could not see his expression at all, and his whole body shuddered. Once it began, the trembling didn't stop.

"Emerald? Please say something? You're frightening me." I inched closer.

"I can'... I can'... words're hard." His voice wavered and broke. "'N I tried t' talk through, y'know..." He knocked one knuckle against his temple with such force that I flinched, even though I'd managed to hold the wall between us firm. "But y'shut me out, n'I get it, I'd shut me out, too. Tried to. Didn't take." His hand moved to his face, so his next words were even harder to understand. "Didn't try hard enough."

I looked down at my boots, which appeared to rest against the stones. "Can you tell me now?"

"Can't. Not with... I can't with... can't *say* it, even to you. Not now that you hate me."

Of course I don't hate you, I almost snapped, but I stopped myself. We were on treacherous ground, and this was different even than the night before. Instead of being a harried mess, Emerald seemed almost calm. Still. It was his stillness that worried me, because for once I could not read beneath that surface.

I waited for a moment as I chose my words carefully as I repeated my earlier mantra. *I will only let him take as much of me as I am willing to give. Am I willing to offer this now?*

My anger over Emerald's actions would keep, but I was not sure that this conversation, such as it was, could be delayed. The broken bottle and our remote location by the water left me uneasy.

"If I let you use our connection, do you think you could tell me?"

"Mm." He cleared his throat. "Dunno. Could try."

Steeling myself for the flood of his emotions, I followed Aster's instructions and opened the door of the wall I had built between us. In an instant, I was swept away in the tide of his self-loathing and despair.

[...hate me, of course you hate me. Who wouldn't? It's bad enough that people hate me for what I am, but if people were smart, they'd know enough to hate me for who I am. I'm the wrong person. I've always been the wrong person. I'm too selfish to deserve you, too broken to deserve Tincrown, too sour to be proper friends with Coirpre, and I want too much to fit in at home. I can't keep my mouth shut even at a gods-cursed party. I'm too clumsy when I'm numb, and I ache when I'm not. I try and I tried and I've been trying, and I'm never good enough, I'll never be good enough, I'm not what I'm supposed to be. I look wrong and I feel wrong and I talk wrong and I act wrong and I'm the wrong. Damn. Person. Can't get anything right, can't save anyone, and even when I lock myself up in my room so that I can't hurt anything else, I find ways to hurt you.]

"Emerald," I said aloud, in a vain attempt to fight the relentless undertow of his thoughts.

[I just want to stop being wrong, Crim, but I can't make

myself smaller, and I can't make myself kinder, and I can't stop thinking about him and missing him and wanting him, and I just want it all to be quiet. I want it all to go away. I want to make it go away.]

"Emerald," I said again, louder this time. "Stop. Just for a moment, stop. Look at me."

He did as I asked, and it nearly broke me to see the wreck of his face, with any trace of bravado or artifice stripped away. His mouth pulled so far down at the corners and his brow was so deeply furrowed that I seemed to be looking at a stranger's face, wet with tears and contorted by misery.

"I need help," he said aloud. *[I need help, Crim, but I don't have anyone else to ask but you, and I don't have any right to ask you.]*

If I'd had any hope of rationalizing with him, I would have pushed back and told him that he was being a fool, but he was so deep in his cups that I didn't think that this would be a fruitful avenue of conversation.

"I know someone who might be able to help us," I told him. "But I'll need you to come with me. Do you think you can?"

He nodded and tried to push himself to his feet, but even before he was upright, he swayed and staggered and fell back to the river stones with a thump. When he did, he let out a sob. *[Can't even walk, Crim. Can't even do that right.]*

I stood upright without any such issues. *[Then I'll go get help, all right?]*

"No," he said before I could take so much as a step, and he reached up toward me as if he could grab me and hold on. *[No, don't leave me. Please, don't leave me. I don't know what I'll do if I'm alone, Crim. I'm not... not safe. Can't be trusted. Please, please, don't leave me.]* His eyes shifted to the water, to that rust-colored eddy where the bog met the sea. I remembered the form of Nweke floating face down among the pilings.

"All right," I said. "There's another way. I can try it, but I need your permission. Do you trust me, Em?"

[More than anyone. More than myself.] Tears streaked his cheeks, and he sobbed again. *[As long as you don't leave me, you can do whatever you like.]*

"You shouldn't say things like that," I murmured, but even so, I reached out to take his hand.

I had read people's minds a few times, but I had only ever managed this particular trick once, and that had been by accident. I wasn't sure that it would suit my current purposes, but I couldn't think of anything else to try.

The moment our fingers met, everything Emerald was feeling flowed into me, battering me from the inside. All of that hate and reproach and judgment and disgust became not *his*, but *ours*.

The sensation of it all was so awful that I was tempted to pull away, but I was stopped first by guilt and then by shame. I could barely face the full force of what Emerald felt for himself, and I knew that he didn't deserve it. How much more wretched must *he* feel, when he believed all that loathing was well earned?

Instead of jerking away, I clung to him and tried to follow Aster's advice. Rather than grapple with Emerald's feelings, I accepted them. The thoughts themselves might not be true, but the *feeling* they evoked in Emerald was real. I acknowledge them as fact, as inarguable yet immaterial as the cry of the gulls wheeling overhead, or the stirring of wind among the evergreens, or the whisper of waves in the bay. They were only noise. They could not hurt us.

In Dyrne, Emerald had only used his mind to control me, but being what I was, I could not do things by halves. One instant, I was outside of Emerald, hoping to make some form of contact with him. The next, I *was* Emerald.

The instant I slipped into him, his voice went silent, and all that raging worriment was stifled. I took a breath, and then another, marveling at the myriad sensations available to him that I had never been privy to before. The cool, smooth texture of the stone beneath his palms, the kiss of the wind against his skin, and the tang of the salt breeze was entirely unfamiliar to me. I would have reveled in them, and might have considered exploring my sense of taste as well, but I knew exactly how unpleasant such a possession could be. I had no intention of adding to his distress if it could be avoided.

"Emerald?" I asked, in Emerald's voice.

He did not answer, but I hadn't expected him to. When he controlled *me,* I had been able to hear him, but I hadn't been able to reply. If this worked the way that I assumed it did, he was still in here somewhere, crushed into the back of his own consciousness.

In case my theory was correct, I told him, "I'm sorry if this is uncomfortable. It's only temporary, I promise. I'm going to get you where you need to go, and then I'll go again, all right?"

I tried to get to my feet and toppled at once, just as he had. "How drunk are you, precisely?" I asked in a teasing tone. He was a large man, but all the same, standing up struck me as being harder than it should have. It was as if he was weighted down.

On a whim, I dipped Emerald's hand into his pockets. When I did, his blunt fingers were met with some resistance. I pulled out a fistful of the hard, smooth objects inside, and felt my borrowed stomach clench as I realized what I was holding.

Stones. The pockets of his vest were weighted down with stones. When I explored the pockets of his trousers, I found more, and I let them tumble through his fingers back onto the riverbed.

"Oh, Emerald," I murmured. "Em. Would you really have found *this* easier than asking for help?"

I turned his pockets inside out, and the flood of pebbles answered the question on Emerald's behalf.

With his myriad pockets empty—his clothing was lined with more pockets than I would have believed, which would have fascinated me under any other circumstance—I was finally able to heave him upright and stumble away upstream in the rough direction of the bog. Without shoes, it was slow going, and several times I glanced over my shoulder to where those two bottles lay, with the broken fragments bright as stars and sharp as daggers glittering in the autumn sunlight.

Even without the stones, distinct from the aching fog in Emerald's mind, I was aware of a terrific weight upon him, bowing him, *crushing* him, a physical extension of his emotional burden. Fighting against that weight, I guided Emerald upstream, past the walls of Fenguard Keep and the settlement of Upper Bound, toward the welcoming solitude of the Convent of the Crone, the only place in that part of the world that had offered either of us succor rather than a window into another world of vice run rampant—or the promise of oblivion.

Aster will help him. She has to help him.

And if she tries to turn us back or refuse us, I'll simply have to find a way to change her mind.

Chapter Nineteen

It took an interminable stretch of time for us to reach the convent, since I had no experience piloting a body and Emerald, in his current state, was no use whatsoever. The walk gave me plenty of opportunity to question the wisdom of my trajectory. If the Cronemire was the source of Upper Bound's troubles, the convent might be one of the most dangerous places on the island.

On the other hand, I could only think of two people in the city who had shown any inclination to help us with our personal troubles. One was Coirpre, and he was up in Fenguard Keep, which to my mind was the *last* place Emerald should go. The other was Aster.

I wasn't sure that I believed in portents, but the sister had taken the name of Emerald's patron goddess. It was the only good omen available to me, so I latched on to it and did not let go.

When we finally collapsed on the steps of the convent, we were gasping for breath.

"We're here," I told Emerald. "Don't worry, I've got a friend here who I think can help you."

It also occurred to me that this might be our chance to investigate the convent. Emerald hadn't indicated that Laird Fenguard intended to help pressure the Sisterhood into showing us their records.

Although, to be perfectly frank, I wasn't worried about records at the moment. All I wanted was someone to speak kindly to Emerald and ensure that he was not alone.

With my mind made up, I dragged us both up the steps and knocked Emerald's fist against the door three times. The wood was reassuringly solid beneath his fist.

It seemed to take an eternity for anyone to answer, but to my relief, the door opened at last to reveal a familiar black-shrouded figure.

"Thank the gods," I sighed in Emerald's voice. "We need your help."

"Ah'm sorry," Aster said, "the Sisterhood only opens its doors tae followers of the Crone."

"That isn't true," I said, lowering Emerald's voice sufficiently so that any passersby on the street would not overhear us. His body had begun to tremble uncontrollably, although I was not sure if this was a result of my possession, his drunkenness, or simply his state of mind. "I know it isn't true, Aster. You've told me as much yourself."

The sister shivered and recoiled from me. "How did ye...?"

"I know how this *looks*," I said, "and I don't have time to explain, but you're talking to Crimson—or rather, to Simone. Remember when you told me to work on my boundaries? I've been building my mind-cottage, just liked you asked, but I had to make an exception. My, um, *father* is in trouble."

Since leaving Dyrne, I had grown accustomed to seeing the faces of the people I was speaking to, and the fact that I could not see Aster's troubled me. I had no way to know what she was thinking.

"Please," I whispered, in Emerald's hoarse voice. "I know you have secrets, Aster, and I respect that. But if you help him, I'll tell you all of ours, and I swear by every god or goddess that neither of us will do any harm to you and yours. *Please.*" As I spoke, I turned Emerald's arm over, so that the tidy raised scars along his wrist were visible.

Aster let out a soft cry and bent down to take his hand, tracing the marks with her fingertips. At the same moment she did so, I backed out of Emerald's body, slipping free until I was my own self again. The relief of being released from Emerald's tormented mindscape was absolute, and although I longed to be able to touch and smell and taste in a form of my own, I didn't envy Emerald everything that came with it.

The sister squeaked in alarm as I appeared from thin air in the form I'd used when visiting her before. Emerald collapsed in on himself again, sobbing as he clung to Aster's hand like a lifeline. The sister reached up to push her veil back, revealing her face. To my great relief, she did not let go of Emerald's hand.

"How is this possible?" she asked in a voice full of wonder.

"I'm not real in the traditional sense," I told her. "I'm, erm, *corporeally challenged*. I needed to get him help, but I could hardly prop him up, so I..." I made a convoluted hand gesture to imply stepping into him, because I was not entirely sure how to describe it. "I promise I'll explain everything, but I need to know that he's safe first."

Aster's pale eyes bounced between Emerald and me. My friend presented a piteous sight, and I wished that I could find some more direct way to comfort him, just as he had done his best to comfort me after Aindreas attacked me on the mountainside. For the moment, it was enough that Aster could hold his hand in my stead.

"It's plain that he is troubled, but ah can't risk harm tae the women and girls who have sought asylum here. If he were tae lay a hand on any of them, ah would never forgive myself."

I shook my head. "Even if Emerald had the temperament, he wouldn't have the inclination. Trust me, his devotion to his boyfriend borders on the sycophantic."

A whisper of a smile passed over Aster's face. "Is that so?"

"I know him well enough to make that oath. I've been in his head." I crouched down beside Emerald. "I swear to you on whatever you like that if you take him in, he will not harm a soul, other than perhaps himself."

Aster pressed her palm over Emerald's wrist. After a moment of quiet contemplation, she addressed my companion. "Ah'll take ye in long enough tae treat ye. Tonight and tomorrow, perhaps. After that, there's a guesthouse on the grounds where ye may stay as long as necessary. Come along." She got to her feet and pulled Emerald up after her. Before I could warn her about Emerald's weight, she already had him braced against her shoulder and was guiding him up the steps through the door of the convent.

"You're stronger than you look," I murmured.

Aster glanced over her shoulder and offered me a small smile. "Most of us are."

☙❧

As Aster led us through the door that separated the receiving room from the convent itself, I felt no sense of triumph. If this was what it took to enter the inner sanctum, I would rather have gone the rest of my life without knowing.

The moment we stepped through the building and into a wide courtyard, a cluster of women descended upon us. They were not wearing their veils, and while their garments were still a uniform black, they had put aside their shapeless robes as well. Foremost among them was a human woman with long red hair tied back in a thick plait.

"Help me, Gemma," Aster said. She turned to me and fixed me with a stern frown. "Ye will wait here until ah return. If anyone approaches ye, tell them that ah will take responsibility for ye... for now. We will have tae speak in greater detail with Shepherdess Linsee."

"No." I balled my hands into fists. "I'm not leaving him."

Aster gazed at me. I was certain that she was going to refuse my request, but I was not going to let Emerald be carried away into the depths of a convent so closely tied to the bog.

"I know that you said it's not my job to save him," I murmured. "But I can't leave him. I'm all he has." I risked a glance at my friend and realized that was not the full truth. In a voice so small I was not sure she would hear it, I added, "He's all *I* have."

Sister Gemma hovered between us. She looked a great deal like Aster, although I did not think they were sisters.

"Very well," Aster said. "But only if ye swear that ye will not stray from his side until we have consulted the Shepherdess Superior. Swear it on something that matters tae ye."

I chose the thing that was, in that moment, the most important to me. "I swear it on his life."

"Very well." Aster nodded to Gemma. The other woman ducked beneath Emerald's free shoulder, and the two of them heaved him upright. He was still weeping, and I followed the three of them along the inner wall of the convent, past an orchard filled with uniform rows of carefully pruned bushes heavy with ripe red fruits.

The Convent of the Crone was laid out in a giant square. Other than the entrance I had come through, the outer wall was solid. Two stories of rooms faced inward around the courtyard, which contained shrubs, a tidy garden, and a pond surrounded my stonework and covered with a wooden pavilion. From the outside, the place seemed forbidding, but I did not feel the least bit threatened, although a handful of sisters watched our progress with wary eyes.

As we walked, I found that I could not quite bring myself to look at my companion. This was not the Emerald I knew. *My* Emerald was stodgy and irritable and often sad, but he wasn't *helpless*.

The sisters carried him into a small, private room and helped him into the bed. Emerald immediately curled up in a ball beneath the sheets. It was remarkable how small he could make himself when he put his mind to it.

Gemma left and returned with a pitcher of water and a cup. She set them on the table beside the bed without speaking and ran her hand across Aster's shoulders as she prepared to leave a second time. "Ah'll fetch Linsee," she murmured.

I wondered what lay between them, but I didn't care enough to ask at the moment. Instead, I sat down beside the bed and pulled my knees up to my chest.

To my surprise, Aster sat beside me, although her posture was more open than mine. She leaned back against the side of the bed and sighed.

"Ah'm going tae need an explanation of some kind. Ye've lied tae me, and yet..." She frowned up and over her shoulder to where Emerald lay. "And yet, there seems tae have been a grain of truth in it."

"I didn't lie." I sighed and rested my forehead on my knees. I wasn't sure how it was possible when I didn't have a body, but all the same, I felt weary and stretched thin. "He's my father, my mentor, and my friend all rolled into one. And we *have* been fighting. I might have elided certain details, but most of what I said is true."

Aster nodded slowly. "And what are you, exactly?"

"I wish I could tell you." I closed my eyes. "I started as a lightweaving, but then I became... more. He never meant to make me, well, *me*, and he still isn't sure how he did it."

Aster lifted one hand to the brightly-colored emblem on her chest and ran her thumb over it. "Can ye tell me more about tha'?"

"I only know that it happened near the spring equinox, in the woods at the edge of Lower Bound, the night after he—" I stopped short of revealing the full details. "After he fell in the Bounder," I said instead.

"Hm." Aster considered me carefully. "A being made o' light and thought, born when night and day hold equal sway over the world, in a place that is neither wild nor tame." She nodded knowingly. "Ah think ah might be able tae help ye understand yerself a little better."

Something scraped against the stones outside the door, and Aster got to her feet.

"Ah will leave you here tonight, Simone." She paused. "Is that really your name?"

"It's one of them." I watched her from the corner of my eye.

"What do yer *friends* call ye?" she pressed.

I tugged off my cap, so that my brilliant red hair spilled over my shoulders. "Crimson."

She smiled. "Ah can see why. In that case, Crimson, ah will ask ye tae stay within the walls of this room tonight. Ah will speak on yer behalf and do a little research of my own. Ah know that the walls can't hold you, but ah hope that your promise will."

I nodded solemnly. "So long as he's safe, I'll stay here until someone comes for us. If something happens to him, though..."

"In that case, ah will gladly release ye from your bond." Aster went to the door, but she stopped to smile back at us. The unguarded kindness of her smile reminded me a little of Tincrown. I still did not trust the Sisterhood as a whole, but I trusted her. "Good night, Crimson," she said.

"Good night, Aster."

For a long time after she closed the door, I sat on the floor, feeling utterly sorry for myself. I had managed to help Emerald, but I knew that what I had done was only temporary. What was to stop him from filling his pockets with stones again, or finding his way back to the riverside? If I hadn't pulled myself to his side in time, what would have happened?

Outside, it began to rain. At first, the hiss of raindrops against the stones was barely a whisper, but it grew louder as a storm blew in from the Gossamer Ocean.

Eventually, I got up and sat on the edge of the bed. Emerald was still shaking, although I was not sure if he was awake or asleep.

You do not get to pick and choose which parts of him to care about, I thought. *Telling yourself that he is not* your *Emerald just because you don't like acknowledging his flaws is no better than him dispelling you when he gets angry.*

"Emerald?" I whispered.

He didn't reply.

Instead of stepping into my mind-cottage that night, I only watched him, braced for something to go wrong. I had left him once when I knew he needed me. I would not make the same mistake twice.

Chapter Twenty

Emerald was still sleeping when the door opened the next morning. It was still drizzling and gray, but Aster's smile made the room a little brighter.

"There's someone here tae see ye," she said. "Ah left him in the entryway."

My first thought was that Burp must have come to look for me, or perhaps Laird Fenguard had come to do as we had asked. Instead, when Aster opened the door for me, I found Coirpre standing by the door, fidgeting with the leather strap of a bag slung over his shoulder.

"Crimson!" he exclaimed. "Is everything all right?"

I opened my mouth to reply before realizing that I wasn't sure how to answer. To buy myself some time, I turned the question back on him. "What are you doing here?"

The bard lifted the bag off of his shoulder, and I realized that he was holding Emerald's embroidered pack, the one Tincrown had given him. "The other night, Emerald was, ah..." He swallowed. "He had quite a lot to drink. And then he wasn't at the keep last night, so I went by the inn this morning, and they said both of you were gone. I was afraid that..." He trailed off.

"That you wouldn't find us anywhere," I finished.

"Precisely." He held the bag out to me, then he seemed to realize what he was doing and set it on the desk instead. "I finally found someone who could tell me that they'd seen someone matching his description come here yesterday."

"He's here," I said.

"Alive?"

I nodded.

Coirpre raised one blond eyebrow. "Your lack of enthusiasm doesn't seem promising."

"I'm not sure what to tell you," I admitted.

He rolled his eyes and reached for the door. "Fine. If I haven't proven myself by now—"

"That's not what I mean." My voice cracked, and he stopped with his hand on the knob. "I don't know what I'm doing. I thought about trying to find you yesterday, but I was afraid to leave him on his own, and..." I hiccupped and bit back a sob. "Oh, *blast it*! How can I be such a mess when I don't even have tear ducts, for Aster's sake!"

Coirpre turned back to me. "Is he safe here?"

"Safer than he'd be at the laird's table downing cask after cask of wine." I rubbed at my face, marveling that I had actual tears running down my cheeks. At least, they felt like tears to me. "Thank you for bringing his bag. He would have missed it."

"Yeah, well." The bard shrugged. "The inn's given away your room. The landlady had some choice words about all the broken glass." He pulled the door open and stepped out into the rain before I could respond.

I couldn't pick up the pack, so I returned through the door that led inward. The instant I passed through, I found myself face-to-face with Aster, Gemma, and a lambkin who glared up at me from a wheeled chair.

"Crimson," Aster said gently, "please allow me to introduce Shepherdess Superior Linsee."

I had seen the Shepherdess Superior several times, always in the gauzy black robes of the sisterhood. Her stature had indicated that she was a lambkin, and if any further clues were needed, the hooves that peeked beneath the hem of her robes would have sufficed. While her race was obvious, she didn't bear much resemblance to Errol. Her wool was shorter and thicker, mottled black and brown rather than white. Her ears were long enough that they flopped down alongside her head, but her left ear had been badly torn at some point in the past. Her right horn curled into a handsome spiral, but the left was broken off almost to the bone, leaving only a jagged nub on her brow. Her left eye was either so badly damaged that she could not open it, or else it was missing entirely. Both limbs on that side of her body were made of wood that fitted against her side. They were jointed like a puppet's and intertwined with what appeared to be living vines.

She lifted her right hand to point accusingly at me. "Who are you?" she demanded. "I've heard Aster's explanation, but I'm not sure that I trust her judgment at this moment. She has already broken the rules by allowing you to be here. According to her, you have promised to tell us everything in exchange for being allowed entry into our domain."

The one thing I was truly good at, the one thing I had been *made* for, was charming those who had no intention of being charmed. My purpose was artifice.

And I had run out of it entirely.

"I owe you," I told her. "More than I can say. If repaying that debt means telling the truth, then I'll do it gladly."

❧

I did not tell them everything. I avoided lying, but there were some things I could not explain without jeopardizing the safety of Dyrne. I left out the matter of Maximilien entirely, focusing instead on Kessel and Nweke, and on the aspects of Emerald's predicament that I could reveal without betraying his confidence. As to my identity, I was as forthcoming as I could be.

Linsee's anger ebbed as I spoke, and by the time I was finished, she was nodding.

"Am I to understand," she asked, "that you have somehow deemed us trustworthy, in spite of your suspicions about the Cronemire?"

"If you wanted us dead, you could have easily dispatched us last night," I pointed out. "I couldn't have stopped you, and I doubt my friend could have, either. I chose to trust Aster, and it seems to me that my trust was well placed. Am I wrong?"

The shepherdess superior gave me a lopsided smile. Like Amaya, her muscles didn't obey her entirely.

"I don't deny the evidence that you have uncovered," she said. "The bog holds many mysteries. Our stories go back generations, and there are many tales of strange and unexplained happenings occurring within it. The founding members of our order were blessed by the bog itself, but as time passed, the Cronemire... festered." She shivered and wrapped her arm around herself. "You have told us what you can, Crimson. Perhaps it is time for us to do the same." She sat upright and began to climb out of her chair.

"Shall I help you?" Gemma asked.

"No, no." Linsee waved her away.

I was afraid that when her wooden hoof hit the ground, the leg would give way beneath her, but it did not. Something crackled through the misty air instead, and the vines entwined with the wooden leg came to life, holding the limb steady. Linsee took a deep breath and waved for me to follow her. As she moved, the vines twisted and pulled, manipulating the wooden constructs so that they moved in the same way her flesh and blood limbs did.

No wonder she complained of being exhausted the other day, I thought. *She must need the* Aidea *to work her replacement limbs.* I'd never seen anything like it, and I couldn't stop myself from staring at the clever invention.

"Why don't you use the chair?" I blurted as she stepped out into the drizzle.

"It sticks in the mud," she said. "And I have something I want to show you."

The three of us followed her out across the courtyard until she arrived at one of the shrubs I'd noted the day before. She reached up to pinch a fat, rosy berry between two fingers.

"According to the records of our order, the Crone once dwelled deep in the bog." Linsee's voice took on the same lilting quality that Emerald's did when he was telling me a story. "Men feared her, for she was ruthless against all those who wished to harm her. Only the sisters knew of her gentler side. While she would ravage anyone who attacked her, she offered succor to anyone fleeing injustice or hardship." Linsee glanced at the two sisters who stood beside us. Evidently, this was a part of the story that resonated deeply with the current members of the little order.

"Whenever women fled to the bog to escape from their troubles, the Crone took them in. She gave them shelter, so that they might survive, and the bog provided for their every need. When their numbers swelled, the Crone even blessed them with the gift of the bogberry bushes. These bushes grow nowhere else on the island except here, within these walls." Linsee chuckled and stepped back. "That is our secret, Crimson. We grow berries that make the sweetest wine in all of Kovin Isle, and we support our convent by selling barrels of it to the mainland. When women in need come to us, we either offer them a place here, or we help them escape their circumstances and establish themselves in the world—using the money we earn from selling one of the finest vintages Dregandresal has to offer."

When she stopped talking, it took me a beat too long to understand that she was finished with her story. I shook my head. "Wait. That's *it*? That's why you don't let people inside?"

"We wish to protect our sisters *and* our secrets," Linsee said.

"B-but what about the bodies?" I demanded. "You keep the dead here, too."

"After the Crone stopped speaking to the members of our order a few centuries ago, the bog changed," Linsee said. "The miasma arose in its center and the dead began to rise again. The Sisterhood took it as a sign, and we became the ones responsible for caring for the dead before they were sent to her. It seemed like a natural extent of the Crone's will." Her expression darkened. "The Conjury scouts saw fit to simply toss an outsider into the sacred waters. When done properly, our rituals honor both the bog and the bodies we offer to her."

"So everything I've told you about the connection between the nights when the dead rise, and the bodies found dead the following morning—?"

"Has seemed like nothing more than coincidence to us before," Linsee finished for me. "We have not thought to question when sailors drown, and they have not been found *in* the bog. I'm sorry, Crimson. I respect your intentions, and if there's anything we can do to help, please tell one of us. Everyone here has done their best to make their lives simpler and more rewarding."

If I hadn't seen the truth of her words reflected in her psyche, I might not have believed her, but she had let me past every one of her defenses. I believed wholeheartedly that the shepherdess superior could tell me nothing more about Kessel's death.

"It seems to me that you have two mysteries to solve," Linsee told me as she headed back across the courtyard to where her chair awaited her. "The murders are one, and the truth of your own nature is the other." She glanced over her shoulder at me, and her one good eye glimmered. "Although I wonder if the two may be more related than you suspect."

We had almost reached the covered walk which surrounded the convent's inner sanctum when Emerald's voice echoed through my head.

[Crimson? Where are you?]

Any promises I had made to Aster about staying close to her flew out of my head in an instant. **[I'm here,]** I told him. **[I'm right here.]** I tugged on our tether, disappearing from the courtyard and rematerializing at his side. It would have taken me less than a minute to run to him without the use of our bond, but even that was too long. I didn't want him to think that he was alone, or that I'd left again.

He was sitting up in bed with one hand held out before him, examining a smooth pebble that seemed insignificant in his broad palm. It was the same size as the ones I had pulled from his pockets by the fistful on the riverbank. In my haste to quit the shores of the Bounder, I must have missed one.

A man of his size would probably not have noticed the weight of a single stone in his clothes, but I imagined every unkind word spoken by the likes of Dirkus as that pebble. One might not be enough to make him take notice, but an avalanche of them would easily drag him under.

Emerald turned the pebble over in his palm before lifting his eyes to mine. "I'm sorry, Crim," he said.

My lower lip wobbled. I had managed to keep my facsimile of a body in check even in the face of Coirpre's unexpected kindness, but the instant I was able to stop worrying that I would never have a chance to speak to *my* Emerald again, the weight of everything he'd put into my head over the last few days came crashing down all at once. I dropped down into a crouch, hiding my face, making myself as small as he'd become when he faced the Not-Crimson in our room the night I'd been blown into pieces. I bawled so loudly that I could barely hear him when he said, "Oh, hell, Crimson," and all but tumbled out of the bed in his haste to reach me.

I was dimly aware of him kneeling on the floor in front of me, just as I was aware of his throbbing headache that pained me through our mental link. For once, all of Emerald's feelings were overshadowed by my own.

"I'm sorry," he said again. "I shouldn't have done that, I should have been more responsible, I should be stronger, I—"

[Stop.] I couldn't bring myself to lift my head or stop sobbing long enough to speak properly, but I could still think for myself. *[You don't need to be sorry, not for this. I just... I just...]* I sniffed a few times and did my best to swallow my

tears. He needed to hear what I had to say, not in his head, but aloud. At last I managed to croak, "I'm just glad you're here."

Emerald crossed his arms over his chest as he stared at me. I thought he was about to push back with some grumpy, dismissive phrase, the way he so often did. When he stayed silent, I realized that he was hugging himself.

I wiped my nose on my thin sleeve before mirroring his gesture. This was the closest we could ever get to embracing one another, and even if it was a bit lonely, there was comfort in it.

"I'm glad you're here, too," he whispered.

Chapter Twenty-One

I hovered protectively over Emerald as he ate the simple breakfast that the sisters had brought him. When he was finished eating, he got up and went to the door of the room.

"Thank you for bringing me here," he said. "We shouldn't impose any further."

I shot upright. "Em, don't be absurd. Where are we going to go?"

Emerald backed out into the walkway. "We still have work to do. And I'm fine, see?" He held out his arms as evidence, indicating his person, evidently unaware of the deflated and rather bedraggled figure he cut.

I lifted one eyebrow.

"Oh, don't do that," Emerald griped. "I know I was a mess yesterday. It won't happen again. I'm done. From here on out, my only focus is on figuring out what happened to the drowned men. I can separate my problems from the case."

"Right." I rested my hands on my hips. "Because you've found that so easy up to this point. Or, here's a thought... instead of insisting that you don't need help, why don't you accept the help that's already being offered?"

"Because yesterday morning, another body turned up in the harbor," he shot back. "The longer we wait, the more likely it is that someone else will end up dead."

My emotions were already rubbed raw, and I was in no mood for his obstinance. "And the longer you pretend that everything's perfectly fine, the more likely it is that the next person to end up in the bay will be *you!*"

He sucked in a deep breath and hunched his shoulders to his ears.

"You must know I'm right," I pressed, advancing on him. "Emerald, please, talk to someone. If not me, then maybe Aster? She's been able to help me. Maybe she could—"

"Emerald."

My friend jumped, and both of us spun toward the open door. The misty rain was still falling in the courtyard, and the voice that wafted in from the open space seemed to have come from another world.

In an instant, we were on the same side again. Emerald caught my eye and nodded once before taking a few cautious steps out from the cover of the walkway.

"Yes?" he called.

"Emerald. Come to me. By the water."

"Well, if that's not the most ominous thing you've ever heard," I muttered.

"Yeah," Emerald said. "Creepy." He took another step forward.

"Right," I hissed. "We're in the midst of investigating a *haunted murder-bog,* and when you hear a voice telling you to go to the water, you don't think twice. I wonder why I'm skeptical of your sense of self-preservation?"

Emerald held up a hand to silence me.

"Emerald?"

"It's not coming from the bog," he whispered. "It's coming from the pond in the courtyard."

"Oh, well if it's only a *pond* talking to us, that's much less disturbing," I muttered.

He ignored me and made his way across the wet grass. The sisters must have found ways to occupy themselves indoors, because the walkways were empty.

Or they know something's wrong, I thought, *and don't want to have to watch for themselves as something terrible happens to us. According to Linsee's story, the Crone didn't much care for men. Maybe she's displeased that one of her followers broke the rules and allowed a man into her sacred space? Is that the sort of thing gods take issue with?*

The pond sat in the middle of a carefully maintained rock garden, and the pavilion above it was decorated with bright murals and little mobiles made of sea glass. A school of ornamental fish swam lazily about its far edge. One more step brought us within view of the pond. Only then did we see the body in the water, floating at the edge of the pond. Its glossy hair floated around its narrow shoulders, and two silver eyes stared up at me.

I yelped and fell back a pace. Emerald, for his part, broke into a grin.

"What's the matter, Crimson?" he asked. "Never met a pearl elf before?"

I stood rooted to the spot as the figure lifted itself up onto the edge of the pool. The woman in the water did not move like the bog bodies did on the nights when they walked the Crone-mire. Rather than the russet-stained corpses, the pearl elf's skin was deep umber with a warm coral undertone. She smiled as she pressed her hands together and bowed her head to me.

"I'm sorry," she said as she fought back an impish smile. "My apologies, Crimson. I didn't mean to startle you. I'm afraid I've been eavesdropping."

Her Osmarian was much better than Yoyoh's, but her accent suggested that the trade tongue wasn't her first language. Now that I looked more closely, I could see that she was not human. Her hair was pale blue, and the pupils of her eyes were a curved line through the silver iris, with no whites at all. When she tucked her hair back, she revealed a blue-tinged ridge of flesh with spines around the lobe that reminded me of a rockfish spine.

"Are you—?" I began.

"A pearl elf, like your friend said, and a member of the Sisterhood." She held out a webbed hand to Emerald. "You may call me Kakura. Please forgive me if I've been too forward, but it's hard to leave my pond. I have to make do with listening to gossip, and the two of you are the most interesting thing to happen here in some time." She slid backward into the water and waved to the cover of the pavilion. "Join me for a little, why don't you? You won't solve your mystery in the rain."

Emerald sighed and ducked beneath the canopy. "Is there a reason you called me?"

Kakura paddled on her back across the pond with her eyes closed and a contented smile on her delicate features. "I thought you might need someone to talk to. Someone you can easily run away from. I'm easy to escape, I promise. I can barely walk on land. If you tell me something and feel the urge to flee in shame, all you have to do is walk through the front gate."

Emerald tapped his fingers against one thigh. *[Talk to someone, you said?]*

[Please. Em, please. I don't care if it's her or someone else. All I know is that I don't want anything like yesterday to happen ever again.]

"Why should I trust a self-proclaimed eavesdropper?" Emerald asked the pearl elf.

Kakura didn't take offense to his tone. She reached the far edge of the pond and laid her hand on the stones, pushing herself upright in the water. "Because I know the sound of a broken heart when I hear one," she said.

Emerald pressed his lips into a thin line. He took a few steps toward the elf and sat down on one of the heavy, flat stones that lined the pond. "Fine. Let's talk."

Kakura folded her arms and rested her elbows on the edge of the pond, propping her chin on her arms so that she could watch my friend. While Emerald sat twiddling his thumbs, I stepped under the awning to join them.

"I've felt awful before," Emerald blurted, looking everywhere but at the two of us. "But this is worse. I never felt that I fit anywhere, but I've tried to be the kind of person who I can at least *respect.* I had an, hrm, moment of weakness last spring." Emerald tugged off his boots and dipped his feet in the pond, presumably so that he'd have something to do other than sit there and be stared at. I waited for her to be offended, since I would have if somebody put their feet into *my* home unasked, but she seemed to expect it. Perhaps his vulnerability bought him an excuse for lack of graciousness. He was never comfortable as the center of attention, which was, presumably, one of the reasons he had invented me in the first place. "I thought that was the lowest point, but then... I met someone. A doctor."

Kakura made a soft noise of encouragement and let her head fall to one side so that she could watch my friend more attentively. "And how has meeting this person changed your perspective?"

"I, ah..." Emerald kicked his feet in the water of Kakura's bathing pool and shot me a sidelong glance. His cheeks darkened. "It's... delicate?"

"Don't you dare." I glared at him, unable to hold my tongue a moment longer. "No keeping secrets from me. Not after yesterday." ***[Not after I had to walk you here from* inside your own skin.** *I want an explanation too, Em.]*

He sucked in a breath and leaned forward, resting his elbows on his knees. "Fair enough. Do you know about the Brotherhood of Guise?"

I shuddered at the words, and Kakura cocked her head at me. Her phosphorescent hair trailed in the water around her shoulders as she drifted over to my side of the pool. "Do you know it, Crimson?"

I hesitated before answering. My reaction had been involuntary, driven by the force of Emerald's memories about his childhood. I reached out through our connection to gather whatever information he would allow me. To my surprise, he made no attempt to shut me out this time.

"They worship Guise the Unifier," I said. "And they run a, um... a school?" That didn't seem quite right, but Emerald nodded.

"The monastery where I was raised was built in Guise's honor. It was... not a happy place." Judging by Emerald's bitter expression and the sharp pang of loneliness that shot through him at the words, this was something of an understatement. "The brotherhood that ran an orphanage for undesirable children." He snorted at the words, but his grimace lacked the barest trace of mirth.

I had not met enough children to have a clear sense of what my friend would have looked like as a child, but I felt a profound mix of pity and anger on behalf of that little boy. *Undesirable.* What a wretched thing to say about anyone.

Even worse, Emerald believed it.

He went on. "Guise's followers believe in homogeneity and unerring civil obedience. They raised children to emulate those principles, and they told us all sorts of things about the right way to live. Cleanly. Without complications."

"And this doctor of yours was a complication?" Kakura asked.

"That's not what I mean." Emerald rubbed one fingertip over the wrinkle between his eyebrows. "The Brotherhood of Guise made it clear that we were born in error, and that only by following their principles could we correct that error."

Kakura made a soft humming noise but did not interrupt.

Emerald fumbled with his words for a long moment before he tried again. "The brothers didn't caution us against love, but against, ah... physical affection." I had never before heard Emerald stumble over his words so clumsily. "My mother didn't want me. Because she didn't want my father." He pressed one hand to his mouth and fell silent, trapped in a truth to which he could barely give voice.

I drew my knees up to my chest, trying to crush the swell of sadness that rippled through me. I wished for something to say, but no words came to mind. What could I possibly say to help him? I didn't know, because *Emerald* didn't know.

Kakura let out a deep sigh and kicked her legs behind her. Several of the glittering fish swam around her in an undulating dance, as if the pearl elf was part of their school.

"Before I came to the Cronemire, I was with a man I didn't want," she said. There was no malice in her voice. "In Venta Bulgarum."

"The Conjury city?" I asked.

She nodded, and her silvery eyes searched my face. "Among certain elites, pearl elves are captured and traded like property. We are beautiful, and outside of the water, we are weak. It is difficult for us to escape captivity once we are taken in. I was traded to a man who wanted an ornament rather than a wife."

Emerald shuddered. "I'm sorry."

"You have no reason to be. It is old history." Kakura smiled as she pushed off from the side of the pond. "But I think I understand a little of your story. When I was imprisoned, I came to believe the same thing you hint at: that violence and love are intertwined."

Emerald nodded, and his face went slack with relief. "Yes. Exactly."

I shook my head. "But that's not true! I mean, I know it *can* be. I felt it with Aindreas, but Tincrown isn't like that. And *you* weren't like that when you were with him."

Kakura nodded as she floated on her back through the water, smiling up at the sky. "This is true, Emerald Flame. There are different types of love. Tomas, the man who kept me as his pet, never loved me. He loved being admired and envied by men who could not afford a living jewel, and he delighted in having power over someone, that was all. Now, this doctor of yours, do you love him?"

Emerald let out a small squeak, and I bit back a smile.

Kakura laughed and rolled over in the water to look at him. "And do you love him for what you can take from him?"

"No." My friend shook his head furiously.

"I cannot speak for Guise and his followers," the elf told him. "But to my mind, the idea that love is a poison only serves the narrative of those who wish to harm us." Kakura's legs rippled the water as she swam back toward Emerald and interlaced her hands. She folded them over one of his knees and let her chin rest on her knuckles, staring up at him. "The Brotherhood of Guise told you that you were a mistake. Would this doctor ever say the same?"

Emerald passed one hand over his eyes. "No. Never."

"Then it sounds as if he values you more than the people who raised you did. I'm sorry for that, Emerald. When people try to convince us that we are small, it can take a long time to undo those lessons. But you are powerful. I can feel it. You are no child, but you have not come into your power yet. By the sounds of it, the Brotherhood of Guise is afraid of what will happen when you do, but those who love you will grow to meet you when you finally arrive."

Emerald stared down at his feet. "I tried to talk to him about this once. He said something similar, but... that makes it all sound so simple. So easy." He pressed his palm to his chest. "It doesn't *feel* easy."

"Change rarely does." Kakura sat up and waved to a figure who approached across the courtyard. "Hello, Aster!"

The nun bowed her head to pass beneath the edge of the pavilion, and she had to push aside one of the sea-glass chimes to avoid walking into it. I'd been right about her height; she was very nearly as tall as Emerald.

"Ah'm sorry to interrupt," she said gravely, "but ah'm glad ye're here. There's something ah need to show ye. Ye remember the body we pulled from the harbor yesterday?"

Emerald and I nodded in unison.

"The shepherdess superior asked me to examine him more closely." Aster rubbed her palms together anxiously. "Ah could tell ye what ah found, but ah think ye'd better see it for yerself."

Chapter Twenty-Two

I had never met Cordell of BelaMontis in life, but when Aster led us into the room where the sisters cared for the dead, I recognized him at once. I had watched him being carried away from the quay just before Emerald—

I closed my eyes and pushed the thought away. My friend was safe. That was all that mattered.

Blissfully unaware of my train of thought, Emerald approached the table where the corpse lay and stood over him. "So he was drowned, like the others?"

Aster shook her head. "It's difficult for me tae see a pattern. When we examine the bodies, we not only prepare them for burial, but also examine them tae make sure that there's nothing strange about 'em. We live on the water. Accidents happen." She laid one hand on Emerald's arm. "Among other things."

My friend swallowed hard. "Of course."

Aster walked around the table so that she stood across from us. A black cloth covered Cordell's body, stopping just shy of his face. She gingerly folded the cloth back to reveal the man's arms and torso. "There are no marks on him that would indicate foul play. He has not been stabbed, there are no unusual marks on his neck or wrists tae suggest that he had been strangled or restrained, and we found no fresh bruises anywhere else on his body. Tae me, this looks like a man who fell in the water and drowned. Whether 'twas by accident or by design, ah can only speculate."

"Right." Emerald's green eyes swept over the corpse.

"*However*." Aster raised one finger, then pointed it down at Cordell's chest. "In the ordinary course of our work, we would stop there. In light of our earlier conversation, ah looked deeper. There are those who use the *Aidea* tae harm others, and while that is outside the scope of anything ah can prove, there is one bit o'tangible evidence that ah could produce." She reached onto the bench behind her to retrieve a phial of what appeared to be murky water.

Emerald took it from her and held it up to the light. "What is this?" he asked, swirling it in a slow circle. As he did, small particles of debris and ruddy sediment were lifted up from the bottom of the glass.

"Water, taken from Cordell's lungs."

My friend's eyes widened. "*Really*."

"I don't understand." I shuffled closer and squinted at the container. Even from a few inches away, I couldn't tell what I was meant to observe. "What *should* water taken from a dead man look like?"

"His body was found in the harbor," Emerald said. "The water there is a bit murky, but it's mostly seawater. If he'd drowned near where he was found, I wouldn't expect to find bits of algae and freshwater plants stuck in his lungs." He shook the phial again. "If Cordell drowned in water like *this*, he likely drowned deep in the bog itself. Given what I've seen of the tides in the Bounder—"

I cut in as the facts fell into place. "He died somewhere else and was moved to the harbor after the fact. And why would someone move him, unless—"

"They were involved with his death," Emerald finished.

"Kessel told us that he was murdered," I added, riding the swell of my mounting excitement. "So we know that at least one person was killed unjustly. He pointed to the bog, so we know that he was killed there. And we know that Cordell was killed there, too." I pressed my hands together in front of me as my mind whirled. "And whoever kills people like this doesn't leave a mark, but almost *certainly* uses the *Aidea,* so assuming that Nweke is one of the victims, we wouldn't have to ask ourselves who could overpower a jotunn, because—"

"They're using the *Aidea* to enchant them in some way," Emerald cut in.

"There's something else that ye should know," Aster interjected. "Ah looked at our records, and Kessel of Kinmore's name is marked in the books. We were able to identify him."

"So someone *did* change the label on his coffin!" I exclaimed. "I knew it!" *[When you switched his body for Maximilien's, you weren't the first person to tamper with evidence surrounding his death.]*

"Which suggests," Emerald said slowly, "that whoever killed him had access to the icehouse where the bodies are kept."

"That might point us back toward Hudson," I said eagerly. "He recognized what I was, so he must know enough about the *Aidea* to notice when someone else is using it."

"Unless Marsha lied about not being in a conflict with Hudson," Emerald added. "Don't forget, he was worried that she might be trying to move in on his territory. Someone might be trying to frame him."

"Or there might be more than one person involved!" I said.

Aster cleared her throat. "Before ye get too far ahead of yourselves, let me tell ye what else ah've learned." She pointed to the phial in Emerald's hand. "Do ye see those largest pieces of plant matter?"

Emerald swirled the jar again, then nodded. "They're quite distinctive."

I squinted again. "Are they, though? They just look like jagged little green bits to me."

My friend rolled his eyes. *[How come you never bother*

with the bits of knowledge that I happen to find the most interesting?]

[Because you think jagged little green bits are interesting!]

Emerald glowered at me and put a whole thought into our connection: not just words, but a shared memory, in which he and Tincrown pored over a book discussing plant identification. *[Yes, Crimson, I do happen to find green bits interesting.]*

I tried and failed to smother a suggestive smile. *[Ah, yes, and our good friend Tincrown shares your fascination with all manner of green bits.]* I wiggled one eyebrow.

Emerald choked. *[Crim...]*

Unaware of our silent conversation, Aster withdrew to a bookshelf in the corner and pulled out a slim, handwritten volume. "The Sisterhood has a long history of taking interest in the local flora. As Linsee told you, the bogberries that grow here are not found anywhere else on the mainland or the island, not even other parts of the bog. The same is true of other plants. In fact, every attempt the swamper elves have made to get anything from the Cronemire to grow in the Leechless Swamp has been met with failure. But I digress." She opened the book and turned to an early page, taking care not to damage the brittle folio. "Look here." She pointed at the illustration set among tidy notes. It was drawn as a circle that connected three illustrations: a tiny, jagged seedpod; a many-mouthed carnivorous plant; and a much taller version of the same, which sported massive upright cups. The artist had taken the liberty of depicting a hapless gudgeon tumbling into its veined maw, where it would presumably land on the small pile of bones drawn at the bottom of the cavity.

"*The Life Cycle of the Hagmouth,*" Aster read. "It's a rare subspecies of pitcher plant."

[How come all of your friends like to look at pictures of unusual flowers?] I asked, wrinkling my nose at the grim illustration.

[Because plants are fascinating,] Emerald retorted.

[Unlike clothes, which aren't nearly as compelling as you seem to think they are.]

Aster tapped her fingertip against the page, underlining a passage that was too scribbled for me to make out clearly. "*The hagmouth is so rare, in fact, that it is only found at the heart of the Cronemire.*"

I held up one hand. "Wait. I thought it wasn't possible to *get* to the heart of the Cronemire."

"For most people, it isn't." Aster closed the book. "The air is so dense and poisonous that no one can safely visit the Crone's most sacred site. It's been like that for generations, evidently, although nobody seems to know why."

"But if the hagmouth seeds are only found in the heart of the Cronemire, and Cordell's lungs are full of hagmouth seeds, that means *someone* must have been able to get there."

"They must have found a way to get him there alive, too. His last breath was taken under the water there," Emerald mused.

"But he didn't have to be conscious at the time," I pointed out.

"True." Emerald's eyes unfocused. "If we're going to solve this mystery, we have to go there."

"I entreat you not to put yourself at risk," Aster said.

"Emerald would be at risk if he went all the way into the swamp," I said, "but I wouldn't." A plan was already taking shape in my mind's eye. "The two of you might not be able to accompany me into the Black Hollow, but I know someone who can."

Chapter Twenty-Three

Burp was waiting for me on the boardwalk when I approached. I had arranged myself as Simon in anticipation of our outing, and dressed myself in blood-red battle armor that glinted scarlet in the morning sun. Black leather trappings stood stark against the metal, and a tooled black half-cape hung from my shoulders. *Much more compelling than plant pictures, if I do say so myself,* I thought, Em's little dig about clothing sticking with me longer than I would have liked. Plus, I had chosen the armor for my new friend, Burp. *A little bit of solidarity to make him feel better. Can a plant do that?* Probably, but I didn't want to mention it to Emerald, lest I get a full inventory of the ones that could.

"Master Crimson-Simon! Look at you!" Burp got to his feet and admired my outfit. "You look ready for battle."

"I wanted to show my support for my friend. If Squelch realizes that you have supporters who may seek vengeance, maybe it will put him on the defensive."

Burp blubbered. "I don't think anything will dissuade him, but it's good to know that you care. If I could give you a krubbath right now, I would."

Seeing the poor fellow so despondent almost made me regret

"

my suspicions. Burp had only ever been kind to me, and I hated to think that he might have had a hand in the deaths of the sailors.

And yet, I'd liked Aindreas well enough before he revealed his true nature. People were capable of lying when it suited them, and no matter how much it troubled me to suspect Burp of wrongdoing, I had to put the facts first. All the same, I hoped that I was wrong.

I gestured toward the mist at the center of the bog. "Shall we try again, Your Highness?" I asked. "You've described your kingdom in such wondrous detail."

"Of course." Burp hopped off the walkway and waved to me. "Come along. We only have a little time left."

[All right, Emerald,] I thought, *[we're leaving. Try to stay out of sight, won't you?]*

[I'll keep my distance,] he promised.

The sisterhood had allowed us to borrow a small skiff. Emerald would not be able to accompany me into the Black Hollow itself, but he could stay close enough to ensure that my tether wouldn't yank me away this time.

We followed the same trail that we had taken the other day, although Burp made more frequent stops to admire the bog, and to sigh wistfully at everything from the way the light spilled through the water to the whisper of the breeze among the rushes.

"I hope that you will be able to hear the beauty of the Hollow," he said. "It's my favorite music in all the world, and I've never been able to share it with anyone before." He offered me a shy smile, adorable on his wide mouth. "I know it's silly, but sometimes I think she's singing it just for me. The bog, I mean. Everyone else gets to hear little snatches of her voice, but I'm... oh, never mind."

"What?" I asked as I walked along the surface of the water. After the other night, I had no intention of sticking my feet in the murk. The sense of merciless hunger had been too powerful and much too unpleasant. "You can tell me, Burp. I promise not to laugh."

"It makes me feel special. As if she chose me. As if she *likes* that I'm her king." He chuckled awkwardly. "I know she's only a bog, of course, but it's nice to pretend."

"Maybe she did," I suggested. "Maybe when Squelch challenges you, the Cronemire will find a way to put him in his place." *Or maybe the bog is intent on murder, and you're a killer who has sent an untold number of men to a watery grave. Who knows!*

"That's a lovely thought," Burp said.

We approached the toxic cloud, and Burp dipped low in the water. "I'll meet you on the other side," he said. The Cronemire rippled as he dropped out of sight and swam deeper.

[Don't get too close,] I told Emerald. **[If I start to feel the pull, I'll let you know, and we'll figure out a new plan.]**

[I'll be here. Let me know what you find.]

With those words, I stepped blindly into the fog.

For the first few paces, I could not see a thing. The mist hung thick and heavy around me, such that I could barely make out my hand when I held it in front of me. My imagination ran rampant. With each pace, I imagined fresh horrors, compounded by the memory of the walking corpses which had risen from the Cronemire's fetid depths.

"Nearly there, Master Crimson-Simon!" Burp's voice called.

I steeled myself to behold a nightmare and took that final step.

The mist gave way around me, and instead of hellscape, I found myself standing in the water at the edge of a grassy island. Sprawling trees whose roots rose from the fen crawled between the water and the land, thick with hanging vines. Epiphytes—a term that I seemed to have pulled from Emerald's mind and his endless botanical interest—had made their homes on the trunks and branches. Hagmouths as tall as a man sent up twisted stems that were capped with delicate pink blooms. Songbirds peered down on us from the trees, and when I turned to get a full view of the island, a jewel-toned water snake undulated away into the roots of the trees.

My jaw dropped in wonder. "Burp. It's *beautiful*." The tapestry in the convent couldn't begin to capture the variety and vibrancy of life here.

"Isn't it?" The krub placed his hands on his narrow hips and admired the view. "There's my throne, if you'd like to see it." Burp nodded his gelatinous little head toward a raised stone dais in the center of the island. Among the carpet of mosses and curled mouths of carnivorous plants, alongside the twining tendrils of ferns and the broad, fat lily pads as big as a wagon wheel, amidst the drooping, birdlike orchids and the plump pink fruits of the bogberry bushes, that was the only thing that looked man-made rather than wild-grown.

"You'll like it even better up there," he said. "That's where the music is the loudest."

I took a step forward, and as I did so, my boot passed through the nearest cluster of plants. In other parts of Kovin Isle, I had done the same thing many times, passing through the heather and low brush common in Dyrne without so much as a thought. In the Cronemire, it was different. There was a spark there, a bit of life, a breath of thought in every reed and flower. Touching them was nothing like touching a gridgeon or a goat, but all the same, I *felt* something, and it bore no resemblance to the relentless hunger I'd experienced before.

"This isn't at all what I imagined," I whispered.

"No need to be so quiet, Master Crimson-Simon. The bog won't mind." To prove his point, Burp strutted up the worn stone stairs on the center of the island, inflated his neck-pouch, and let out an echoing burst of sound that seemed too voluminous to have come from such a small body. "Hello, Hollow!" he boomed. "Today, your king greets you for what may be the final time. I've brought a friend. Would you like to meet him?"

He fell silent, and when the last reverberations of his voice died away, there came a soft sigh from the trees around him, a rustling that might have been the wind but didn't *sound* like wind.

I glanced around me, expecting to find someone there. There were eyes on me, I was sure of it, although I couldn't tell who they belonged to.

"Was that a yes?" I asked.

"Of course, Master Crimson-Simon. You're a friend of the bog." Burp squatted down in a little patch of filtered sunlight and squeezed his third eyelid shut before letting out a happy sigh. "The Cronemire approves. Any friend of mine is a friend of hers, if you take my meaning. And the sisters like you, too. You're safe enough here."

Very slowly, and with a pause between each step, I advanced up the stairs. Either Burp visited even more often than I realized, or something else had come that way not too long ago; the steps were worn smooth, and moss did not grow upon them.

At the top of the steps lay a deep bowl carved into the stone, like a great cauldron filled with the black, peat-soaked water of the bog, with a sturdy rim, wide enough for a man—or a krub—to circumnavigate it easily without setting foot on the mossy greenery.

"Now, I like the sun, Mr. Simon," Burp said without opening his eyes, "but if you want to hear the music best, you'll need to step down in there. Don't worry, the water's warm. I know dry folk get peculiar about the cold."

"Not all of us," I said with a wry smile and descended into the little cavity. At the deepest point, the water reached my waist. Although I could not vouch for the temperature, I could feel that water; not as a physical touch, but a *metaphysical* one. There was life in those waters, an aimless intellect that did not belong to the natural world. As the water rose to my navel, I wondered how the feeling of the Black Hollow could be so different from my last encounter, when the Not-Crimson had stepped into darker waters.

"What happens now?" I asked.

Burp didn't answer me. He didn't need to. The swell of sound that arose around me was enough. A chorus of frogs joined with the alto hum of crickets to form a trilling harmony that dropped back to silence just as quickly as it had begun. At the same time, a prickle of power flowed through the water in which I stood. The sensation reminded me of the slight pull I'd felt when Linsee worked the vines that powered her wooden arm.

"Hello, Hollow?" I glanced up nervously at the branches. "Are you... alive?"

I jumped when the plants around me stirred in unison. *It's only a breeze,* I thought, except the branches weren't moving in the same direction.

Still half-convinced that I was losing my mind, I said, "If you're trying to talk to me, could you let me know by doing something... I don't know, something that *couldn't* just be a trick of the wind?"

Everything around me went completely still for a few seconds. Then, somewhere above me, a bird began to whistle. It was soon joined by a single frog, then a cricket, then a swish of water. No other creature made the slightest sound as the songs joined together in undeniable unison, meeting for a note or two before splitting off into harmonies, wandering, and then meeting again. They stopped abruptly, and the quietude returned for a few seconds before the usual sounds began again.

"Right." I shifted in the stone basin. "Point made."

[Crimson?] Emerald's voice echoed through my head. *[Everything all right?]*

[You won't believe this, but the Black Hollow isn't a graveyard,] I told him. *[It's an amphitheater. And either I've somehow managed to be poisoned by hallucinogenic swamp gas despite my lack of respiratory system, or the place is talking to me. You haven't been poisoned, have you?]*

[I'm well away from the Hollow, if that's what you're asking. What do you mean by calling it an amphitheater?]

[I'll explain when I get back.] For the moment, I was

more intent on trying to make sense of what was happening around me.

I rotated in the little pool, trying to determine whether there was a locus of some kind where the Hollow's power was strongest. "It's nice to meet you," I called up to the canopy.

Burp's head appeared over the lip of the basin. "Who are you shouting at?"

"I'm trying to talk to your... kingdom," I said.

Burp nodded. "I understand. I do it all the time."

"Does she usually answer?" I asked.

The krub licked his eyeball thoughtfully. "I mostly talk, and she mostly listens. Then sometimes she talks, and *I* do the listening. But I've never really asked her questions before. Is she talking to you?"

"I think so." Once again, just when I thought I understood how things worked, the world shifted slightly and I was back at the beginning. Burp hadn't tried to kill me, and the bog hadn't either. Evidently, I'd gotten the whole thing wrong somehow. *Again.*

"Did you kill Kessel of Kinmore?" I asked the bog.

The sounds echoing into the amphitheater didn't change. Of course, the bog might not know people's names. I considered this carefully before trying again.

"Sailors keep turning up dead in the harbor," I said. "We think they might be dying here, in the Black Hollow. Has anyone died here recently?"

Something clattered on the ground near Burp's feet, and we both looked down at a little mound of discarded rubble. I had thought that it was a collection of twigs, half-swallowed by the mossy groundcover of the island. Their dry rattling loosened them from the earth, and I realized that they were not twigs at all.

They were bones. Old bones, partially bleached by the sunlight that fell through the branches.

"Oh my," Burp murmured, standing on one foot and then the other as he hopped backward. "Oh *no*."

"Did you kill those sailors?" I asked.

The bones rattled more loudly, and Burp whimpered.

"Why?" I asked.

The rattling stopped, and a soft gust of wind rustled the leaves above us like a regretful sigh.

I ran my hands across the surface of the water in that little basin, leaving not so much as a ripple in my wake. The sensation I gathered from the water had changed fundamentally from the first time I stepped in. Of course, the Not-Crimson had been the one to experience it before. Maybe experiencing the bog second-hand had tainted my reading.

That wasn't the only difference, though, was it? The Not-Crimson stepped in the water the night that the dead rose. Whatever causes that event might be the thing that caused the natural cycles to feel all out of whack. The bog hungers, the dead walk, and a new corpse shows up the next day...

"Do you *decide* to kill them?" I asked.

Off the shore of the island, a ripe, flatulent noise bubbled to the surface, sending a small geyser of water in its wake.

"Bog gas," Burp observed. "I'd take that as a no. This is remarkable, Master Crimson-Simon, truly remarkable. She's really taken a shine to you. Ask her something else."

"Does someone make you do it?" I asked. "Can you tell me *who?*" Strictly speaking, I wasn't convinced that a bog's testimony could be entered in court, but it could point our investigation in the right direction.

The sounds changed, but it took me a moment to understand what was happening. It began with a single songbird above us, but soon enough the water rippled, a frog let out a basso ribbit, a woodpecker tapped out a staccato beat against a tree trunk, and the noises swelled to form a piecemeal melody.

"Ah, there it is." Burp sighed and settled back onto his belly, letting his golden eyes roll in pleasure. "That's her song. Isn't it beautiful?"

He was right, and I found it astonishing that the bog alone

could produce such a complex and lovely strain of notes. Unfortunately, it didn't answer the question I'd posed.

"Who comes out here?" I asked. Every person I'd previously suspected couldn't have entered the Black Hollow on their own without being choked by the fog of decay that surrounded the island paradise.

The music continued, and Burp swayed to the sound, waving his hands in time as if conducting the refrain.

Even as the song continued, I could feel the power in the water draining away. The bog seemed to be growing tired, and soon the music trickled away to nothing.

"Dammit," I mumbled. "What am I supposed to do with that?"

At least I had no further reason to suspect Burp. As much as I would have liked to get an answer to my question, I was glad to know that my friend wasn't involved. I turned to him, fully intent on apologizing for entertaining the thought to begin with, and found him staring up at the sky.

"It's almost time," he murmured. "Squelch will be waiting for me. We'd better go."

I floated up out of the basin and followed him down to the shoreline. This time, I stepped into the water, just to be sure, but there was no malevolent intent that I could detect. Whoever brought the bog to life in the dead of night was also responsible for disrupting the natural order.

Lafayette had told me, *You won't catch a self-respecting swamp raising the dead!* Perhaps he was right, but evidently, the Cronemire didn't get to decide for herself.

At the edge of the mist, Burp lifted one hand to wave to the Black Hollow. "No matter what happens now, I hope that you will remember my rule fondly." He wiped at his eyes before taking a huge gulp of air and diving beneath the swamp-gasses. I followed him into the mist, wishing that I had more to show for my efforts, with the Cronemire's song still running through my mind.

Emerald's skiff sat low in the water; it had not been designed for a half-jotunn. I made my way across the surface of the water before Burp spotted him.

[Good news. Burp isn't the killer. I was able to speak to the Cronemire, strange as it sounds, and I think someone is using the Aidea to compel it—or her, I suppose? But whoever is killing the sailors is killing them here, that much is certain. Em?]

My friend was leaning over the edge of the boat, staring down into the bog's murky depths.

[Em?] I repeated.

I could not make out what was the matter with him until I stood right at the edge of the boat. Only when I reached him and glanced toward my feet did I realize what held him so enraptured.

Three ghastly faces stared up at us. Their eyes were sunken and shriveled into features turned leathery and stained carmine red by their time in the peat-steeped waters. Their mouths hung open as they drifted against the underside of the boat, with their shriveled hands crossed over their chests. None of the three had any real shape to them. They looked less like corpses and more like clothes that had been removed and cast aside. The bog had consumed their bones, leaving only their skins and russet tufts of hair.

"Emerald," I said aloud.

My friend jumped. When I looked again, the bodies had drifted deeper, and before long, they vanished altogether.

"Gods," Emerald murmured, "what a miserable place."

"I didn't know that *you* were coming, Master Emerald!" Burp paddled up to the boat.

My friend shook himself, and when he opened his eyes again, he managed to appear utterly composed. "I thought I would offer you a ride to the site of battle. Crimson told me about your upcoming fight. You ought to save your strength."

Burp's eyes welled with emotion. "Oh, you are too kind, Master Emerald. You are *far* too kind." He hauled himself up into the boat and settled against the pointed bow. "It feels like one of the old stories, when the great krub-heroes of yore first settled in their swamplands. I don't know you as well as Master Crimson-Simon, but I am glad that you're here to witness the end of an era." Burp slumped against the bow with his hand to his sloped forehead.

"Don't talk like that," I said bracingly. "Defeat isn't inevitable if you keep the right mindset. Isn't that right, Emerald?"

My friend shifted the oars in their locks, but I caught his eyes sliding toward the water where the ghoulish faces had been.

"That's right," he said dully. "Chin up, Burp. You may triumph yet." With that, he sank the oars into the water and sent the boat skimming across the still, dark surface of the Cronemire.

Chapter Twenty-Four

E merald was alarmingly quiet on our journey back to the shore of the bog. Burp's low mood seemed to have infected him, and the sight of the remains floating in the water hadn't helped.

There was another thing which troubled me. The day before, in the shelter of the Convent of the Crone, Emerald's mind had felt more peaceful and balanced than it had in some time. His hangover had faded, and he had slept soundly in his borrowed bed, with the backpack Tincrown had given him tucked under one arm.

As the hours passed, however, his gnawing hunger had returned. It was not the sort which could be sated by a hearty meal and a full belly. He wanted wine, or something stronger, and his need was so fierce that it reached all the way into me.

I did not mention it as we pulled the boat into shore, but I didn't let Emerald out of my sight as he tied off the line, stowed the oars, and pulled on the oilskin cover. If I hadn't been able to read his mind, I wouldn't have been able to tell that anything in particular was troubling him. There was no telltale shake or his hands, no glassy vacancy to his eyes—nothing, in short, that would betray his urges if I could not feel them for myself.

There's nothing wrong with wanting, I told myself. *It's become a habit, and like Kakura told him, change can be painful. So long as he doesn't act on it, there's no harm done.*

When his task was finished, Emerald dusted off his hands and waved one arm to our krub companion. "Lead the way, Master Burp."

We made quite an odd procession as we set off along the boardwalk, but I was glad that Burp didn't have to go alone. He kept his stride stately and proud, and despite his height and his ungainly proportions, he looked every inch a king.

His confidence lasted until we had almost reached town. As we rounded a bend, I became aware of the bawdy laughter of sailors, accompanied by a wet *slap! slap! slap!* that echoed off the houses closest to the bog. Burp stopped in his tracks, and his shoulders began to tremble.

Squelch stood knee deep in the water on the landward side of the boardwalk. He was in the process of erecting a flat-topped mound of peat, roughly as wide across the center as I was tall, and standing nearly waist high to the hefty krub. He whistled to himself as he slapped his broad hands over the top of the mound.

One of the sailors took a pull from his flask and spotted Burp as he lowered the bottle from his lips. "Look, Squelch, your friend's arrived!"

The horned krub looked up from his work, and his already wide mouth widened even further. "Well, well, well. Look who it is. I thought you might not come."

Burp tried to square his rounded shoulders. "I'm not a coward," he said with as much dignity as he could muster. "I know the laws of our people. Where there is one krub, he is king, and where there are two..."

"They fight." Squelch flexed his chest and his meaty thighs. "Are you ready?"

"Not yet. There's one more thing to do." Burp pivoted toward Emerald and clasped his hands in front of him. "I have one favor to ask, Master Emerald. Since I cannot give *Simon* a krub-bath, would you allow me to give you one in his stead?"

Emerald lifted an eyebrow at me. ***[Do I want to know?]***

[Doubtful. It involves spit.]

He shuddered, but Burp's enormous eyes glistened with unshed tears, and like it or not, my friend was too compassionate to deny the krub his last request. "Maybe a small one?" Emerald asked warily.

"Really?" Burp looked so delighted that it would have taken the worst kind of person to tell him no.

[I hope you appreciate this,] Emerald thought at me, while nodding solemnly to Burp.

The krub immediately threw back his head and began to gargle. Squelch nodded his approval, but the sailors collectively gagged. One of them leaned closer to me to whisper, "That's how ol' Squelch got kicked out of the Trader's Guild, you know. They hired him to swab the decks, but he just walked around *foaming* everywhere and mopping his spit around. Claimed it was more sanitary than soap. Nastiest bleedin' thing I ever saw."

Emerald managed not to flinch as Burp sudsed at the mouth. When the krub had amassed a suitable quantity of sputum, he began to gather it up by the handful and rub it onto Emerald's outstretched arms.

"You know what, I take it back," the sailor said as he uncapped his flask again. "This is worse."

When Burp was finished, he bowed to Emerald and then to me. "Thank you both. It has been an honor, gentlemen."

Emerald waited until Burp strode off toward the field of battle before wiping his arms on his trousers. ***[That is by far the foulest thing that I have ever intentionally endured.]***

[It was kind of you to let him,] I replied.

Emerald strode over to the sailors, who were now lounging along the edge of the boardwalk to watch the fight. The one who'd spoken to me held out his flask.

"I'd need a drink after that," he said.

Emerald barely hesitated before he accepted the bottle.

[Emerald.] I glared at his back. ***[What happened to 'I'm
never drinking again'?]***

***[That was before I let a small green man rub his mucus
all over me,]*** Emerald retorted. He glared at me as he took a
defiant gulp of whatever was contained in the sailor's flask. The
moment the liquor met his tongue, he sighed contentedly, then
handed it back.

Short of possessing him again, there was little I could do to
keep him from drinking, but a twofold misgiving settled
over me.

Burp stood before the ring Squelch had constructed and
bowed to his opponent. "I'm ready whenever you are," he said.

"Oh, don't lie." Squelch winked at him. "You get a bit of a
thrill out of all this, don't you? You've done this before, surely?
You must know what it's like to win a battle."

Burp shook his head.

The challenger fell back a step. "You mean to say you've *never*
fought before? You don't have a single win to your name?"

Burp seemed to shrink in the face of this mockery. "No," he
mumbled.

Squelch stared at him for a long moment before bursting into
cruel laughter. He tucked his webbed hands under his ample
belly. He tried to stop it by covering his mouth, but when he
pressed his lips together, his neck-pouch inflated until the air
came rushing out in a snort.

"No wins!" the larger krub wheezed. "King of his whole bog,
and never a single challenger! I tell you what, Burp, I'll go easy
on you. Give you a sporting chance." He squatted down, then
burst upward in a mighty leap that easily carried him to the top
of the mud pile.

If a challenge had to be issued, so be it, but I didn't like
Squelch's attitude. I cupped my hands on either side of my
mouth and shouted, "Go on, Burp! Give him every hell!"

My friend shot me a grateful smile before attempting the
same maneuver as the larger krub. His jump didn't carry him
high enough, and he ended up on his belly, scrambling against

the loosely-packed mud. Squelch watched him fail for a moment before taking pity on him and dragging him to the top and onto his feet.

"You know the rules?" Squelch asked.

Burp nodded and rubbed his hands together. I'd never seen him look so determined. "No spitting, not biting, no kicking, no tricks. Whoever stays on the mound wins."

"And whoever falls off the mound loses," Squelch added with a wicked grin. He hunkered down in a crouch.

Another sailor shook his head. "Say what you will about krubs, they're certainly interesting. Hope your little green friend makes it out all right."

"Can't see how he will," a dwarf put in. "Skinny lad, ain't he?"

Burp cast one last woebegone look toward the bog, then sank down across from Squelch. Both were positioned toward the center of the ring, a good arm's length from the edge. They reached toward each other, interlocking their fingers, with their elbows braced at shoulder height.

"Three," Squelch said.

"Two," Burp whined.

"One." Squelch grinned. "Give me your best shot, Your Highness."

With a whistling, high-pitched battle cry, Burp threw his full weight against his enemy, pushing for all he was worth. Squelch slid back a few inches, but his cocky smile remained in place, and he didn't fight back.

"You can do it, Burp!" I called.

Emerald thrust one fist above his head and pumped his arm. "Cheers, Burp! Push him!"

Every muscle strained beneath the slick green skin, and the King of the Black Hollow cried out again, giving his all to the fight. No matter how much he puffed and panted and inflated his neck-pouch, however, Squelch's feet slid only incrementally.

At last, Burp's grip slackened. He wheezed a few times.

"Is that all you've got for me?" Squelch taunted. "Because it's my turn now."

Burp sobbed.

"Go on, Squelch, show 'im what you got!" The sailors laughed and elbowed one another as they cheered on their ex-crewmember.

Sure enough, and to my great dismay, Squelch's massive thighs flexed again. He dipped low, adjusting his angle, and in an instant, Burp was lifted into the air and thrown backward. He landed with a moist thud, rump-first in the mud.

Alone in the ring, Squelch lifted his arms in the air. "Victory is mine!" he trumped. "Behold, the new King of the Black Hollow!"

I leapt down to Burp's side. My friend was too stunned to move. He sat in the muck, staring up at the usurper.

"I lost," he said vaguely. One of his gold eyes rotated to meet mine, and the second followed a moment later. "I *lost.*" His mouth trembled.

"Is there anything I can do?" I asked. "Emerald could be your second, he could challenge Squelch in your name. We could appeal to the laird..."

"No." Burp swallowed a breathy hiccup. "No, I lost fair and square."

Squelch hopped down beside my friend and leered at him. "Poor, fallen Burp. I hope you've said everything you have to say."

Burp nodded, and before he could get to his feet, Squelch caught him by the wrist and hauled him to his feet.

"You know what happens now?" the victor asked.

Burp bowed his head. "I do. You... you don't need to say it in front of everyone. Do I at least get to decide where you bury me?"

"Loser's choice," Squelch told him.

"I know the place, then." Burp sniffed and waved forlornly. "Goodbye, Master Crimson-Simon."

"Burp—" I whispered.

Squelch led my friend away into the swamp. Several times, Burp looked back at me. I tried to keep a brave face for his sake, but soon enough, the two small figures were swallowed by the fen, and my friend was gone.

[The king is dead,] Emerald thought grimly. *[Long live the king.]*

Chapter Twenty-Five

❧

By the time the sailors gathered themselves, the haze of Emerald's drinking had already seeped into my consciousness.

[How drunk are you, exactly?] I demanded.

Emerald stared down at his hands and blinked a few times. ***[I don't feel well.]***

[It's the wine.]

[It wasn't wine. It was rum or something. And I only had one mouthful. You saw. I don't think this has anything to do with that.] Emerald swayed on his feet. ***[This feels different. It makes things... sharper.]***

The sailors traipsed off toward town, leaving me alone with my intoxicated friend.

I was beginning to wonder if the rest of my life would be like this. I had been genuinely afraid for him only two days before, but I was already mourning Burp, and Emerald's constant drinking was becoming more tiresome than alarming.

[I thought things were going to be different,] I complained. ***[You promised. Whether it was wine or liquor, you chose to swallow it.]***

[I know.] Emerald sighed. *[But I'm telling you, it shouldn't have been enough to make a difference.]*

I turned in the opposite direction. *[Can we please just go back to the convent?]* One of the sisters would have to let us in, and they would see that Emerald had been at the bottle again.

[I'm sorry, Crim.]

No doubt he meant it, but his apologies were getting old. I couldn't accept this one, so I held my tongue.

Our progress was nowhere near as slow as when I'd possessed him, but Emerald kept stopping to examine flowers that hung over the edge of the boardwalk or squint at a particularly interesting beetle that clung to a nearby tree.

"Never seen one of them before," Emerald muttered. "What do you think they're called?"

This behavior was bizarre, even for him, and when I peered at his eyes, I saw that his pupils had grown huge, almost eclipsing the brilliant green of his irises. That was new, and a twinge of guilt shot through me.

"Emerald?" I asked. "Do you think there might have been something in that drink?"

"Maybe." Emerald stopped again to stare down at his hands. "I can't feel my hands."

I hope that his drink wasn't poisoned. But the sailor he took the flask from was drinking it just fine, and he had a great deal more. Unless someone used the Aidea *on Em already?* The possibilities were disconcerting, but even as I watched him, Emerald started giggling.

Perhaps it wasn't poison, after all. He certainly seemed to be in a good mood. Maybe he'd been exposed to something in the bog. Hopefully it wouldn't last, and at least if we made it back to the convent, Sister Aster would be able to keep an eye on him.

As we walked, I began to hum. I wasn't aware that I was doing it until Emerald asked, "What's that?"

"It's the song of the Black Hollow," I explained. "I tried to ask who was responsible for killing the sailors there, and it just started... singing at me."

"Singing?" Emerald repeated.

"I'll explain more when you're, uh, feeling better." We were almost to the convent, and as much as it pained me to admit it, I was desperate to get away from my intoxicated friend. He could be someone else's problem for a while, and I could try to figure out our next move.

The sound of Emerald's footsteps on the boardwalk died.

What now? I wondered irritably. *Another bug? Another plant?* I whipped back to face him.

Emerald stood perfectly still, gazing down at his boots. "Oh," he said. "*Oh.*" His voice came out thick and slow. His thoughts were too muddled to make out clearly. Gradually, as if he were moving through a particularly thick syrup, he raised his head to meet my eyes. "I need," he slurred, "to go to the keep." At the mention of that place, his wine-hunger pulled at me again.

If I'd had the capability, I doubt that I would have been able to resist the urge to shake him. "No, Em," I snapped, "you don't. In fact, I would argue that it's the last place in the world you should be."

He groaned. "Crim, you don't under*stand.*"

"No, I don't." I advanced on him. "And believe me, I'm trying. I can *feel* it up here, Em." I jabbed one finger at my head. "I know it's hard for you, but you promised you'd try."

He scowled at me. "I told you, 'm not drunk."

"Convincing." I crossed my arms over my chest. "The trouble is, you've told me all sorts of things, and you keep breaking those promises. Forgive me if I don't find you reliable lately."

Emerald's lip curled back a little, and his brows pulled in low. He looked like nothing quite so much as a petulant child who had been denied his favorite toy. "I'm going to the Keep."

"You're not." I advanced on him. "I'll stop you if I have to."

"You wouldn't," he hissed.

"You don't think so?" I narrowed my eyes. "Try me. I'm not going to watch you hurt yourself again. I'll stop you as many times as I have to."

His mouth split into an ugly smile. "Oh, I see. I see, Crimson. You want a body so badly that you'd try to take mine. Is that what you want? To replace me?" He shook his head and stumbled to one side. "No. *No.* Trust me. You don't want that. Don't want this." He gestured to himself. "I've been trying to get rid of it for years."

"I know. And I'm trying to protect you from yourself, but you're making it impossible!"

He gripped either side of his head. "You're not listening, Crim. I have to go to the keep. Now. Come with me."

"I'm sorry, Em," I said, and I reached for him.

His eyes widened, and whatever was happening in his mind, he was still clear-headed enough to react before I could reach him. He made a sharp gesture with one hand and hissed something under his breath.

In the same instant he dispelled me, I closed my eyes. Emerald could push me out of the real world, but there was one safe place for me that even he couldn't reach. As I blinked out of existence, I managed to redirect my banishment so that instead of going *nowhere,* I ended up tumbling to the floor of my mind-cottage.

"No!" I howled, pounding my fists against the stones until my bones bruised. This was the one place I could feel anything, but from here, I couldn't affect the real world at all. Emerald could do anything to himself, could go anywhere, could fill his cup with wine or his pockets with stones, and there was nothing I could do about it. "Emerald!" ***[Emerald! Let me out!]***

Silence was my only answer. I might as well have been nowhere, for all the good it did me to have evaded the emptiness of absolute unbeing.

❧

I had never visited the room in which I found myself. It wasn't Marsha's rummage-sale apartment, or Fenguard Keep's halls, or anyplace else familiar.

It wasn't blank space, either. There was a flagstone floor, four plain white walls, and a dark-blue ceiling littered with what looked like hand-painted stars.

When I finally stopped yelling, I sat up on my knees. I was no longer Simon. I hadn't meant to, but I'd somehow changed myself into Simone, wearing the striking black-and-white outfit I'd selected in Dyrne when I stood before the church of Dathan to point out the killer. I'd been wrong about the killer's identity. Apparently, my subconscious was intent on reminding me of my past failures.

I struggled to my feet. I'd managed to bruise my knees on the stone floor, which was a first. The pain that came along with it was a welcome distraction from my sense of betrayal.

"Fine," I snarled at the empty room. "If you're going to send me away, I'm going to find a way to solve this mystery without you! I don't need you!"

I waved one hand around the room to encompass the walls. The portraits I'd created before reappeared, this time including every person I'd encountered in Upper Bound. Burp, Dirkus, Benedite, Coirpre, the sisters—and I had even added Emerald among their number. I walked around the room, frowning at them in turn. Nothing occurred to me, and my anger swelled. I wanted to hit something.

On a whim, I spun back to the center of the room and snapped my fingers. Something like a scarecrow appeared in the middle of the room, propped up on a sturdy stand. The figure was lumpy and misshapen, and its green face was haphazardly painted on over a canvas skin, but it looked enough like Emerald that it would suit my purposes. I strolled around it in a slow circle, then I stopped in front of it. I flexed my hands into fists and fell into a crouch.

I struck the dummy as hard as I could, right in the middle of its broad, padded chest.

"Let's consider the facts," I snarled, and punched it again. "You've left me to do all the work, begged me to save your life, forced me to watch you fall apart again and again, and then *banished me*. But don't worry." My knuckles thumped into its wooden frame, sending a satisfying jolt of pain up my arm. "I won't let that get in the way of the thing we're here to do. After all, I'm a *professional.*"

I spun the dummy around to face the portrait of Burp, pointing over its shoulder. "We know that we can rule him out." I snapped my finger, and the painting disappeared. I rotated the dummy again to face the tapestry of the Cronemire. "And we know that the bog is involved against its will. A fact which you would never have figured out without *me,* if I might remind you." I punched the Dummy-Emerald's shoulder as hard as I could.

The portrait of Hudson drew my attention. "We know the killer was able to change the label on Kessel's coffin in an attempt to make him more difficult to identify." I strode out from behind the dummy and nodded to the picture of Marsha. "He made it clear that Marsha and Boo aren't welcome on the docks, and according to them, they have no interest in the sailors. No evidence points to them, so I believe we can rule them out." I snapped my fingers, and their portraits vanished as well. Each time one of the paintings disappeared, the others grew in size, looming larger over the little room.

"Now, as for Hudson... we know that humans can't breathe the marsh-gasses, but whoever is using the *Aidea* to compel the Black Hollow might be able to make a path through the smog. Hudson knows a thing or two about the *Aidea,* since he was able to realize that I was an illusion." For the time being, I moved on from the dockmaster and approached the sisters. "We've ruled all of the sisters out. The bog favors them, but we've gotten close enough to them to see that they aren't involved." I snapped my fingers again.

For the first time, my private world disobeyed me. The rest of the pictures vanished, but Linsee's stayed, expanding into the space the others left behind.

I crossed my arms over my chest and stared at the painting, wondering what I was missing.

"The shepherdess superior uses the *Aidea,*" I muttered. "She controls her prosthetic limbs using living vines, which I suppose might *parallel* the way some magic user commands the hollow. But I still don't think she's involved."

I snapped again, with less confidence this time, but something in my head wouldn't let go of Linsee. With no idea of what else to do, I moved on, spinning the dummy of my friend—if he could still be called that—to face the final wall.

The portrait of Emerald smiled back at me. For some inexplicable reason, I'd imagined the version of him from the day he summoned me back to Dyrne, the only time I'd ever seen him truly happy. When I squinted at the smudge of oils behind him, I recognized a blue and amber silhouette that must have been Tincrown. Over his other shoulder, a bright red figure hovered among the outlines of the village, dim and blurry.

"You know the worst part?" I asked, turning back to the dummy. "You didn't just tell me the truth. I could forgive anything you did—*anything*—but lying. Even this, even sending me away because you didn't want me to force you into something. But lying?" I crouched again, driving my fist into the scarecrow's gut. "I have a window into your head, you idiot! I know when you're putting me off! I've done nothing but try to help you, even when you didn't want my help." I punctuated every few words with a blow that thumped against the dummy's chest, where Emerald's ribcage would have been if I had been pummeling him and not the padded canvas.

"Do you think I care when you dress like an urchin? No!" *Thump.* "I only want you to take a little pride in yourself. To walk proudly, as you should, instead of hiding!" *Thump.* "I want you to listen when Tincrown and Coirpre and I tell you that you're *worth* something, instead of listening to the likes of him!" I stopped my battery long enough to wave a hand toward the portrait of Dirkus. "He doesn't matter. His opinion doesn't matter. So how come you let his words drag you down like a thousand"—*thump*—"little"—*thump*—"stones?" *Thump.* "How come you couldn't bring yourself to tell me what happened the night before I was born, but you could tell *him* the truth without any prompting—"

I stopped short, my fist only inches from the dummy's chest. The memory of that awful confession was all too clear. Dirkus's laughter, Benedite's taunting, Emerald's relentless flow of words, Coirpre's desperate attempts to stop him, and beneath it all, the tug of a melody. A song I'd heard before.

The same song that the Black Hollow had sung when I stood at the center of the island.

"Oh." I lowered my fist, no longer seeing the room around me. "Oh *no*." My heart thumped in my chest, and my lungs struggled for air as I staggered back from the dummy. "No, Emerald. Please tell me you didn't..."

He was right. I should have listened when he told me that he needed to go to the keep. He'd wanted a drink, but he'd been following me until I sang the snatch of song from the Black Hollow. It was a song I'd heard before, one that Emerald had heard even more often, since he was the one who'd visited the Fenguards at every opportunity.

"No." I turned back to the wall of paintings. Dirkus's wicked grin sickened me, but I dismissed him; he was a temporary evil in Upper Bound. Benedite, likewise, I could remove from our list of suspects. Coirpre was hardly a saint, but he wasn't a killer, and even if I'd believed it of him, my jaunt through his head was enough to prove it. That left three portraits hanging on that particular wall.

I spun back to Hudson. The harbormaster had access to the icehouse, but he wasn't the only one. When I snapped my fingers, his image disappeared. The shepherdess superior still smiled down at me from beside the tapestry of the bog—a tapestry given to the convent by one of the Ladies Fenguard centuries ago.

After the Crone stopped speaking to us a few centuries ago, the bog changed. Linsee had told me that when she revealed the convent's secret.

This time, when I snapped my fingers, the shepherdess superior vanished.

"No," I groaned. Why hadn't I been paying attention? When

I'd walked the private halls of Fenguard Keep, I had seen portraits of the Fenguards across the centuries. The earliest of them had depicted a couple with black hair and smiling eyes. Over the years, the Fenguards' hair had turned ruddy, like those of the bog bodies. It hadn't been a whole family tree. It had been the same two faces, painted over and over. Never a child, never a family, only a laird and lady wearing different clothes, painted in different styles. I had even thought that the tapestries on the wall would have taken lifetimes to complete, but I'd been wrong. It was one lifetime, an impossibly long lifetime, made longer by the *Aidea*—although I did not yet understand how.

We have given ourselves completely to the city, Laird Fenguard had said. A party every night would not only celebrate the expansion of the city, but it would provide a reasonable explanation for a stream of drunken sailors stumbling to their deaths in the harbor. And every night, at every party following Coirpre's performance, childless Lady Dionara sat down to play her horn. Every night, a variation of the same song.

The same song I had heard in the Black Hollow.

I gasped for air, surprised by the ferocity of my need to breathe now that I, evidently, had found a place where my body followed the usual rules. Emerald must have recognized the song and put it all together. Even through the haze of liquor and whatever else was happening to him, he'd been able to piece enough of it together to understand the truth that had eluded me.

I ran my fingers over the gilded edge of his portrait frame, where the outlines of the two figures he relied on to keep him safe and sane were nothing but faded ghosts. He'd told me that he needed to go to the keep. He'd begged me to come with him.

And I hadn't listened.

Which meant that he was going to confront the murderers alone.

"Emerald!" I screamed. **[Emerald! I'm sorry! I understand now!]** "Please, bring me back. I'll help you." **[I'm sorry,**

I should have listened.] "I should have at least heard you out!" ***[I should be there with you. You shouldn't be alone.]***

No matter how much noise I made, there was no reason to think that he could hear me. I drove my shoulder into the wall with the vain hope that I could batter my way out by force. He hadn't been able to dispel me this time. Perhaps I could summon myself back into the world. I tried to pull on my tether, but it didn't exist here. Wherever I was, I was too far away to reach him.

"They're dangerous," I sobbed. "They killed Nweke. If they could overpower him, they can get you, too. Em!"

It was useless, but that didn't stop me from trying. I would not give up on him again, even if it meant battering myself against the confines of the room like a moth at the glass, hoping desperately to reach the flame.

The only thing I managed to do with any success was bruise myself against the cold edges of my private unreality.

Chapter Twenty-Six

I could not say how long I spent in my ineffectual efforts. I screamed until my voice was raw and clawed at the stones until my fingers bled.

Aster was wrong, I thought madly. *It is my job to save him. This time, it is my job. I can't protect him from himself, but I have to protect him from Edur.*

I was scraping the mortar from between the stones with my fingernails when a voice very clearly said, "Crimson."

I sat up and looked around the room. "Emerald?" I asked.

The paintings still hung in place, and the battered dummy stood at the center of the room, grinning its lopsided grin. As far as I could see, nothing else had changed.

I wiped one hand across my brow and let my shoulders slump. *You're going mad,* I told myself.

But the room shifted subtly on its axis, and the voice repeated, "Crimson."

I knew that voice, although it was warped and distorted. I stared at one of the blank walls. Beneath my gaze, it contorted subtly, so that the planes of the plaster bowed and heaved as if something was pushing against them from the other side.

"Crimson."

I went to the wall and laid one palm against it. "Coirpre?" I asked. "Is that you?"

The wall shuddered. It felt thinner than before, more flexible. Moreover, it was warm.

"Coirpre!" I called, falling back a pace. At Edur's table, he'd been able to interact with the illusion of the cup Emerald had summoned. Was it possible for him to do the same with me?

The plaster cracked, and I fell back another pace. If there was any chance of escaping, I would take it. I skidded back against the far wall, took one last breath, and pushed off. I had no experience with running, and it was harder than I'd thought, but the knowledge that Emerald was in danger drove me forward. I hit the wall with a bone-jarring force and lodged in the now-pliant material of its surface. One of my arms groped blindly, trying to make contact with anyone, anything, that would allow me to pull myself the rest of the way through.

"Coirpre!" I bellowed.

"Crimson?" From the space beyond the wall, a hand closed over mine and tugged.

I landed on all fours in the middle of the Sisterhood's entry room. When I tried to gasp for breath, I couldn't. The floor beneath me felt like nothing at all.

I was no longer in my imagined world. I was an illusion again. Somehow, I was *back*.

I sat up to find Coirpre half-collapsed against the floor, panting heavily. His blond hair was plastered to his forehead, slick with sweat. The illusion of youth that he usually cast over himself was conspicuously absent. The bard glanced up at me and shook his head.

"Rilus's blessed knob," he murmured. "I can't believe that *worked.*"

We weren't alone. An elaborate series of sigils and signs had been drawn on the floor around us, centered around loci, at each of which knelt a member of the Sisterhood. Linsee sat ahead of me, Kakura to my right, and to my far left, Aster's hands shook above a sigil that still burned bright. Gemma stood behind her with wide eyes.

"Thank you," I babbled. "I was trying to get back. Em's in trouble. He walked right into danger—he's going to confront them without any help, and it's all my fault. Where is he?"

Coirpre sat back on his heels and pushed his damp hair out of his eyes. "I was hoping you'd be able to tell *us*." He tugged on a chain around his neck, and I realized that he was wearing Emerald's necklace, the one that my friend used to cast his light-weavings, including me. "I found this on the floor of the keep at the party. I recognized it at once, but there was no sign of him." He slipped it back into his shirt, where the cord hung alongside the necklace he usually wore. "I figured that he couldn't cast you without it, but I couldn't do it on my own. It took all of us." He waved to the sisters.

I looked down at the elaborate series of marks on the floor in dismay. "How long did this take you?"

"A few hours." Coirpre's weary face confirmed this assertion.

"*Hours?* They've had him for *hours?*" In that case, Emerald might already be gone. Maybe that was why Coirpre had been able to summon me. Maybe my life wasn't tied to Emerald's, but to the gem itself.

What a miserable thought. I'd rather be tethered to my friend, however flawed he might be, than to some cold and soulless stone.

"*Who's* had him?" Linsee asked.

"The Fenguards." I tried to pull on my tether, but it didn't work. I had been summoned through the gem, and dragging myself back to my source left me right where I already was. "They've been doing something to the sailors at the party, something involving the song Lady Dionara plays on that horn, and then killing them."

Coirpre cocked his head. "Her song? It's just a truth song."

I stared at him, forgetting the urgency of our situation for a moment. "You *knew?*"

"It can't hurt anyone," Coirpre said. Then he grimaced.

"Well, all right, it *can* hurt people if they say things they didn't intend to. That's why Emerald blabbed to Dirkus about throwing himself in the river. I've told people a few, erm, *delicate* tidbits while under the influence. I reckoned they do it to get information out of people to help grow the city and all that." When I continued to gape at him, the bard rolled his eyes. "Oh, come on, Crimson, I'm not an *idiot*. I've had six months to work this out."

"And did you work out that the Fenguards are taking sailors to the Cronemire?" I demanded. "That every time the dead rise, a new body turns up the next day? Because I'm sure that they're on their way to the Black Hollow with Emerald *right now*, and if we don't stop them, the next person to turn up dead will be a half-jotunn investigator with a reputation for wandering around town intoxicated, and I'll bet you anything that the Conjury won't bat an eye."

Coirpre's face went frightfully pale. "What do you need me to do?" he asked.

"I need you to get me closer." I got to my feet. "Whatever the Fenguards do in the Hollow makes it possible for them to pass through the smog. That should allow you to approach as well." I shook my head. "Only, I don't know how they do... whatever they do. Dionara must use the *Aidea* to play her song, and they must use another form of it to control the Hollow. A Lightweaver might not be able to stop them."

"You have more than a Lightweaver on your side," Linsee assured me. "If the Fenguards are misusing the Cronemire, it is our business, too."

"We will help you," Kakura said. Out of the water, her limbs seemed weaker than before, but her silver eyes flashed with anger. "The Crone despises injustice. That evil should occur in the seat of her power is unthinkable."

"We're with you," Aster added, and Gemma nodded along.

It was a relief to know that we had allies, but the sensation was short lived. The members of our little war party had just begun to gather themselves when a bell tolled outside. When I peered through the window, I realized that a shroud of fog was already descending around the convent. Any moment now, the dead would begin their inland march.

I turned back to Coirpre and saw my fear reflected in his eyes. He lunged for the door.

[Hold on, Emerald, we're coming,] I thought, forgetting that I might not even be connected to him anymore.

My terror redoubled when a faint, watery voice echoed back to me, as if from very far away. My illusion might be bound to Emerald's stone, but our mental bond transcended whatever mechanism of the *Aidea* allowed Coirpre to summon me. It was only one word, but it both proved that he was still alive and chilled me to my core.

[Hurry.]

❧

As Coirpre and the sisters set sail into the bog, I did not linger with the boat. Instead, I flew ahead to the very limits of my tether—I was indeed tethered to either the stone in the necklace or to Coirpre. I pulled ahead of the boat, so far in the lead that I could not hear or see them trailing after me. I was determined to reach the island first, even if my ability to help Emerald would be hampered by my incorporeality.

As I passed over the unquiet dead, I found myself looking about in search of a small, green fellow, too freshly buried to have absorbed the reddish water of the bog. I saw no sign of Burp, which both saddened and relieved me. Perhaps the bog's magic didn't work on krubs. Or maybe the Cronemire held her deposed king so dear that she'd pulled him close to her enchanted heart and refused to let him go.

Every second of delay was an agony, and when I reached out to Emerald again, I got no answer. *Please let it be the result of the Fenguards' magic,* I prayed to any god that might be listening. *Please don't let it mean that we're too late.*

There was no miasma left to encircle the island. It had been either dispelled or dispersed by the Fenguards' magic. I only realized how close I was when I heard the first strains of a melody, played in two-part harmony. The sad, lovely trill of Lady Dionara's horn mingled with the Cronemire's rendition of the same, intertwining in a haunting duet.

I drew nearer, now at the very limits of my tether. As close as I was, I could only proceed at the glacial pace of the boat, or else risk getting tugged back to the bard's side all over again.

Emerald knelt on the side of the stone basin, bound in living vines that twined tight around him, holding his arms and legs in place. His head lolled forward on his neck in defeat, with his chin pressed to his chest.

Lady Dionara Fenguard sat to one side. Her lovely gown and glittering jewels had been replaced by rough garments that would have allowed for her to pass through the city unnoticed. Her faded red hair was pulled back in a simple chignon. Only the horn gave away the fact that she was more than an ordinary woman of the city.

Edur was dressed much the same. He knelt on one knee before my friend, with the same charming smile he always wore. Even in the midst of this betrayal, he looked nothing like the harsh man in the portrait we'd first encountered.

"Tell me what you've done," the laird said. "Confess your sins to me."

My friend made a soft noise before speaking. "I've failed everyone," he droned. "I've strayed from the teachings of the only people who care enough to raise me. I disappointed Crimson. I failed Tincrown. I've hurt everyone I love, again and again, and I—" He squeezed his eyes shut before whispering, "*I shouldn't exist.*"

[Emerald!] I thought, but he ignored me. Very likely, Dionara's song disrupted our connection somehow. Either that, or my friend was too far gone to listen.

"I understand." The laird rose to his feet and laid one hand against the crown of Emerald's head. "People make mistakes. I offer you absolution, Emerald Flame. Tonight, I offer you the chance to become something else, something larger than the whole, a single thread in a tapestry as old as the island itself. I offer you a way out. Your legacy will be intertwined with the legacy of Upper Bound." Edur Fenguard bent down to brush a kiss across my friend's forehead. "Thank you," he murmured, "for your sacrifice."

I had finally reached the edge of the island and placed my foot on the moss, just in time to hear my friend cry out in pain. The vines around him yanked and tightened, pulling him backward into the stone basin with a mighty splash before dragging him below the surface.

Chapter Twenty-Seven

Any element of surprise I had was lost when I let out a screech of fear and anger. Edur turned to face me, but he betrayed no concern. If anything, he seemed amused.

"Ah, Crimson Smoke. I was wondering when you'd turn up. What excellent timing. I thought I was going to be the only one to refresh myself tonight, but it looks like we'll both get a chance, my dear."

Lady Dionara lowered the horn from her lips, and the bog's song petered out along with hers. "It would be nice to go a little while longer without having to select another sacrifice," she said wearily. Unlike her husband, she did not strike me as triumphant.

A splash startled both of the Fenguards, and Emerald pushed himself back to the surface, drawing a huge breath the moment his head emerged. *[Crimson?]*

[I'm here! Coirpre and the others are coming to help, but they need a little more time.]

He'd barely been up for a moment when Edur made a sharp gesture with his hand and my friend was dragged down again. "You're distracting me, Crimson," he said, clicking his tongue. "This ritual requires precision and finesse. Dionara, love, will you see to her?"

The Lady of Upper Bound set her horn aside and got to her feet. "Of course, my darling." She took a step toward me.

Behind her, Edur jumped down into the stone basin where Emerald was silently drowning.

"You're a shapeshifter," the lady observed, eyeing me up and down. "A man one minute, a woman the next. I take it that you have some power over the *Aidea*?"

I bared my teeth at her. "Let him go."

"You don't understand. This is necessary. Without your friend and others like him, it all falls apart." She lowered her voice as she padded toward me. "And you've heard how he talks. When he confronted Edur in the keep tonight, he admitted that he doesn't even *want* to live. It's been so long since we had a willing sacrifice. Isn't it better this way? For all of us?"

Coirpre was close enough that my tether had slackened. I could no longer feel its pull. If I charged to the pool right now, I should be able to reach it. Meanwhile, I could feel Emerald's will to fight against the vines that held him underwater slipping away.

"You're a monster," I told Lady Dionara.

"No." She shook her head, smiling at me as though I were an ignorant child. "No, not a monster. I stand on the brink of becoming a goddess. As for you, your life alone is worth nothing, but Edur and I are very nearly there. Perhaps you will be the one who tips the scale."

She grabbed at me, and her hands passed through my arms. We only overlapped for the span of a few seconds, but that was all it took to let me see everything I needed to know in a series of jewel-bright recollections.

Whenever I'd touched anyone but Emerald, I'd gotten on the barest snatches of feeling, and only what was in their head at the time. There, in the Black Hollow, my skill was different. Its power bled into me, allowing me to see deeper. Just as Tincrown had wanted to show me how he felt about Emerald, the Black Hollow *wanted* me to understand everything that drove the

Fenguards to make their terrible choices. Memory overlapped memory, so that they all blurred together.

I saw Edur as he had been when they were young and first in love, sitting by her side on that spit of land that overlooked the city. The Upper Bound of those bygone days had been little more than a jumble of sod-capped huts spread pell-mell around the countryside. The town beneath them grew as their black hair turned gray. Dionara's hand sat against her belly, one that never swelled with the promise of a future for the island, but her head rested against Edur's shoulder all the while.

I saw Edur holding a book, pointing to an open page. I felt Dionara's doubt as she read the description of a ritual that would allow for their youth to be restored. If done right, it would give them a chance to extend their lifespans not just for a few years or even a few decades, but forever. The cost would be high, but the rewards were beyond imagining.

I saw her agree, knowing that it might well cost her soul. To quell her doubts, she spent her time in the act of creation, weaving tapestry after tapestry to tell the story of the bog, mastering the arts of music and painting. Her first portrait showed the pair of them returned to their youth, capturing the brilliance of their smiles. Over the centuries, both love and joy decayed, leaving her cold and alone, trapped in an eternal prison of her own making, but unwilling to let go of her past. She was unhappy, but the city thrived.

I saw that it was enough to keep her going, but only barely.

Not even a full second had passed, but when her hand passed through me, I understood her. She believed that the future of Upper Bound was worth any amount of suffering, because she *had* to believe it. How else could she justify not only killing, but the solitary depths of her own pain?

I fled past her, making straight for Edur Fenguard. His wife's *Aidea* was what pulled the truth from their victims, but it was his command of the natural world that killed them. I flung myself on the laird, hoping to possess him as I had possessed Emerald.

If I could manage that, I could release his control of the vines that still held my friend below the water.

Instead of sliding into Edur's consciousness, however, I only tumbled through his chest. As I did, I beheld the world through his eyes, sinking into the depths of his memories, which swirled up like sediment from the bottom of a glass phial.

I saw Edur bent over a book, pointing to a picture of a man performing a ritual. The figure was caught between the realms of the mortal and the divine, elevated by a confluence of convoluted magic and the sacrifice of some large, winged beast. The laird's thrill was obvious. He knew of just such a beast, one who made its home in the bog below the keep. At his insistence, his wife agreed to help him. It was worth it, they both believed, to ensure the prosperity of their homeland.

I saw the island at the center of the bog, and an enormous, black-winged bird, twice as tall as a man and more bloodthirsty than even the most vicious of the berserkers who populated the highlands on the southern shores of the island. It had once been a terrible beast, but it was brought low by the laird's magic, tangled in the greenery of the bog by the augur *Aidea* that the laird employed. He did not need to be strong enough to fight it hand-to-hand in order to bring it crashing to the ground, so that the keel of its breastbone scraped the island—the island did the work for him. While he held the monster captive, his wife drew a knife across its throat, letting its blood spill out onto the soil of the Black Hollow.

I saw that it was not enough. The ritual didn't fail, but it didn't succeed, either. The Fenguards were granted a second youth, but they still aged. They returned to the island decades later, this time with human sacrifices. With the help of the laird's magic, they stole the last breaths of their victims, again and again and again, down through the centuries. Each new sacrifice bought them less time, and the Cronemire grew stronger. When his wife turned to solitude and creation, Edur turned to drink, drowning his guilt in a series of endless festivities.

I passed through the laird's chest and landed without a splash in the water at my friend's side. Emerald was still struggling, but only feebly. His eyes shot wide beneath the water as he looked up at me, his lips pressed tight together, holding the very last scrap of air in his burning lungs.

"You're an illusion." The laird blinked at me in confusion. "Imagine that. I didn't even think to ask him that. He must be powerful, to keep you here even now."

"Let him go," I growled, crouching low in the bowl. No wonder the swamp's power was strongest here. This wasn't just an amphitheater, or even a throne. It was an altar upon which life after life had been stolen.

"Why should I?" the laird demanded. "You can't stop me. You're powerless here."

Emerald shuddered beside me, and his eyes rolled upward.

"Your kingdom is built on bloodshed!" I insisted.

"So is every kingdom," Edur retorted. "I only take the unworthy and the wicked—those who, by their own confession, have made terrible mistakes."

"That's why you have Dionara play her song?" I asked.

The lady approached the edge of the basin. "Of course. In the old days, we took criminals, but now we can find sacrifices outside the island. The sailors are ruffians, and we only choose the worst of them."

"And what about him?" I pointed to Emerald and glared into Edur's face. "He isn't the worst of them. You treated him like a friend."

The first hint of doubt appeared in the laird's expression. "We might have been friends," he said regretfully. "But to let him live would be to risk the future of the city. I cannot allow that. Not after everything I've given."

Everything you've stolen, I thought. *That was what Kessel wanted to tell us. The Fenguards stole not only his life, but his last breath.*

Where are you, Coirpre?

Emerald's limbs slackened against the vines, and Edur bent toward the water. "Here it is," he whispered, with the same desperate neediness that sometimes entered Emerald's voice when he spoke of wine. "His last breath. Let's not waste it, Crimson." The vines lifted Emerald's limp body toward the surface, and Laird Fenguard bent over him.

[Emerald?] I could still feel a spark through our connection, but it was little more than that. One single, floating spark, where there had once been a bonfire.

I hurled myself at the laird a second time, knowing that I would not have another chance. If I could not possess him now, then Emerald would be lost to me forever.

Stepping into Emerald's consciousness hadn't been all that difficult. For one thing, he'd been drunk—but all I really needed to do was stop being myself and take over for him. I'd taken for granted how easy it was and failed to account for the fact that he'd *created* me. When I tried to touch the laird again, all I could feel was his power; the thrill of bending the world to shape his will; the willful indifference toward my dying friend; the unwavering certainty that he would win. When I tried to take control, I found myself scrabbling fruitlessly against the walls of an ancient fortress. Given a limitless span of time, I might eventually have found a weakness, but *time* was the one thing Emerald didn't have.

With a snarl of frustration, I dove beneath the water, reaching for my friend.

The moment I was submerged, however, my plans changed.

On my first visit to the Black Hollow, I had sensed a collection of disparate consciousnesses, disconnected voices that seemed to cry out to me from every reed and root. When I landed in the water without a splash, I felt the change. Whatever magic the Fenguards had worked to dispel the miasma in the air and disturb the bodies of the long-dead, it had also served to awaken the Hollow itself. The water hummed with energy that matched the frequency of my own existence. I could not touch the real world in any meaningful way, but the *Aidea* was different. I could feel it, hear it, *taste* it, just as inhabiting Emerald's body had allowed me to experience the living world, and the Fenguards' magic was bitter indeed. It was tied to the bog, but it was *not* the bog.

[*Just a little longer, Emerald,*] I pleaded as I plunged my hands into the warp and weft of the Cronemire's *Aidea*.

I blinked out as I had many times before when Emerald dismissed me, only this time, I did not vanish. Instead of disappearing altogether, or even being banished back to my mind-cottage, I was torn a thousand different directions, drawn like water into the capillaries of leaves. It was nothing like when he'd tried to summon me twice over. I sank into the peat and flooded the ancient, boneless scraps of leathery flesh that belonged to the oldest bodies in the Cronemire. I burst free in puffs of spores, only to be breathed in by birds and beasts that lingered on the mossy shores of the Black Hollow. For a moment, I was *everywhere,* and I let myself relax into that new state of being.

And then, when I was everything, I stretched and flexed and became one thing again.

In the stone bowl of the Black Hollow, Edur Fenguard reached both hands into the water to draw up the limp body of a man I barely recognized. Seen through the myriad eyes of the bog, Emerald was just another corpse set adrift. Edur dragged his lifeless body up from the depths and pressed his mouth to Emerald's. A thin thread of *Aidea* bound the two of them together for a moment, hunter and prey, unworthy god and unwilling sacrifice. I saw the intention behind Edur's *Aidea*—to steal Emerald's last breath for himself.

No.

If I'd been myself, I would have screamed the word, but now that I was the Cronemire, it was not a sound. It was a decision. What Edur wanted was not his to take, and this time, I was not powerless to protect my friend.

This time, I had saturated the very world.

With a low groan, one of the heavy branches that climbed the old tree over the dais gave way. Edur looked up just in time to stumble backward as the limb crashed into the pool.

"Edur!" Dionara caught her husband as he stumbled backward. "Are you all right?"

Edur wiped the back of his hand across his mouth. "Something's wrong," he said. He tried to pull on the *Aidea* again, to put the world back in the order of his choosing.

I felt the tug of his power, but it was nowhere near as overpowering as the pull of my tether. The vines he was trying to manipulate barely twitched under his command. When I moved them, however, they went willingly. The Cronemire alone was not strong enough to defy the Fenguards, and neither was I, but together, we had become more than the sum of our parts.

At my urging, the Cronemire reached out to Emerald and lifted him from the water. His eyelids twitched, but I could not tell if he was breathing. How did you make someone breathe? That was the sort of information I would have tried to pull from my friend's mind, but I was thoroughly lodged in the consciousness of the bog.

"Stop it!" Edur tried to compel me again. His mouth was pressed into a thin, tight line, and his eyes had turned cold. "How dare you turn against your master! Everything you are, I made you."

Oh, but I had heard those words a hundred times. Emerald had tried to coax me into doing his will on more than one occasion, but the real anger that arose from his words came not from me, but from the bog itself. For centuries, Edur and Dionara had twisted and pulled the Cronemire in every direction, ruining the bog's natural cycles. *That* was what I had felt the night the Not-Crimson stumbled into the water. That grasping, insatiable desire to expand belonged to the Fenguards. They must have been standing in the basin at that very moment, forcing Cordell below the water until Dionara could bend over him and claim his final breath.

My anger gave me power. It was not enough to exist in every living thing, spread thin throughout the island. The Cronemire gathered herself, pulling inward.

The Fenguards watched in alarm as beasts and bones alike

were drawn up the hill. When the Cronemire tugged again, these were joined by the leathery, boneless remains of the bog's oldest dead, which slithered up the hill, glistening slick in the moonslight, with their pinched and flattened faces turned accusingly upward. The island itself shuddered, and the stone bowl heaved. From beneath the earth rose a collection of enormous bleached bones far too large to be human.

When the shepherdess superior spoke of the Crone, I'd assumed she was speaking in allegory, like when Emerald had told me the tale of Regis and Ianna. Just as the star-crossed lovers personified the turning of the seasons, I had believed that the Crone personified justice or vengeance. That was before I'd seen the Fenguards' memories, however.

The Crone had been their original sacrifice. They'd buried her there, on her sacred island at the heart of the swamp. All that time, she'd been gathering her power. As the fragments of my diffused consciousness pulled together, the physical elements of the island tangled themselves into a single being, until at last, I lifted my head: the hollow skull of the Crone.

"You made me?" I was not the only one choosing the words. In fact, I was nothing more than the missing piece of a puzzle that the Cronemire had needed in order to fuel its vengeance. *"Am I not the one who made* you?"

A strangled sound behind me caught my attention, and the beast I'd helped create turned its ossified head to determine the source of the sound. Coirpre and the sisters had arrived, and all of them stared up at me with disbelieving eyes from their little boat at the edge of the island.

While my eyes were averted, Edur Fenguard made another attempt to control me. It failed, and the bare skull swiveled back to face him.

"Of course you didn't make us!" Edur blustered. "We made ourselves. All we bought with your life was time, and look at what we built with it! A city to rival any other on the island, a holdout against the Conjury, a place where people from all walks of life sit shoulder to shoulder. A port alive with art and opportunity and commerce. There is no other city in the world like it!"

The Crone shook her head. *"And yet the poorest of your citizens are still your most vulnerable."*

"It isn't perfect," Dionara agreed. "But no one starves. No one lives on the street. And we've given of ourselves, too—"

"Enough." The spirit of the Cronemire shuddered and shifted, and I moved with it, wrapping prehensile tendrils around the Fenguards' ankles.

"Stop it!" Edur commanded.

The Cronemire did not listen. The creepers wrapped higher and tighter.

"We only ever meant to serve the island," Dionara pleaded. "Every child born on the island was *our* child. We watched them grow and prosper, and their children, and their children's children—" She was cut off as one of the runners coiled around her throat.

"Excuses. You sought to save the land by poisoning it? You sought to benefit the people by killing them? The Bounder and its lands have been tainted by the same scourge for centuries. You."

Edur clawed at the vines around his neck and tried to speak, but no sound left his lips. The teeming bulk of the Cronemire shuddered again, and one skeletal hand emerged from its mossy hide. The cups of the hagmouths opened and closed, and everything with lungs and tongues that had joined forces began to wail, louder and louder until the sound became unbearable. With one last great effort, the Cronemire dragged the Fenguards down the slope and thrust them into the water. Vines pushed them from above, while the creased and puckered hands of the long-dead residents of the Cronemire dragged them down.

From my manifold locations within the great body, I began to struggle. I wasn't sure that the Fenguards deserved to be killed outright. That wouldn't restore balance any more than the other murders had. I tried to pull away, but the Cronemire wouldn't let me. The animus of the bog would not rest until its awful work was done.

The spirit of the Cronemire swayed and listed, growing weaker as its creators did the same. Two strings of tiny bubbles rose to the surface, growing smaller and farther apart. At last, the surface stilled.

The effect was instantaneous. The amalgamation of life around me collapsed, tumbling to pieces even as it released me. Birds flew upward, insects scattered, vines retreated, and the weathered bodies that had climbed up to join me tumbled back down the slope into the water. In a matter of seconds, I was left standing alone in the middle of the island, staring into the blank eye sockets of the Crone's bleached skull.

I knelt there stupidly, disoriented by the fact that I was now only one thing again. When I'd melded with the Cronemire, I had become powerful in a way I'd never been before. Shrinking back to my usual self, with only my usual set of skills, left me feeling very small indeed.

"Crimson!" Coirpre's voice jarred me back into the present moment. Even before I turned, I knew why he was calling me.

Emerald.

Kakura paddled in the water just off the shoreline, while Gemma and Linsee stood a little inland, staring open mouthed at the Crone's skull. Aster had left them behind to crouch next to Emerald. She and the bard had heaved my friend onto his side. A trickle of water ran from his mouth, but his eyes were still closed, and his limbs lay slack against the mossy bed of the island.

"Em?" I scrambled around the ruptured basin to the place where he lay.

"Will you please *breathe,* you stupid idiot?" Coirpre blubbered, striking my friend firmly on the back. Emerald shuddered, and a bit more of the water dribbled from his lips. I remembered the phial of water Aster had drawn from the dead sailor's lungs. It hadn't seemed like such a lot when I was looking at it.

I knelt beside him and let my hands hover over him. A more

wretched and useless creature than myself had surely never existed, not in the whole long history of Dregandresal.

"Lie him down," Aster said, and Coirpre lowered him onto his back with as much grace as my friend's bulk would allow. The sister pressed her palms against Emerald's chest and leaned her whole weight against him.

What will become of me if he never draws another breath? I wondered—but what did it matter? I couldn't imagine a world without him in it. I needed a chance to beg his forgiveness.

He had created me, just as the Fenguards had created the animus Cronemire. Emerald and I had even found ways to hurt each other, just as the two great powers in Upper Bound had lashed out at one another. I promised, then and there, that I would never turn on him again, if only he would stir.

While Aster redoubled her efforts, I knelt on the ground above my friend's head and pressed my hands to each temple. Instead of drawing memories out of his head, this time I tried to push them back. I started with the memories Tincrown had given me back in Dyrne.

[We need you,] I thought. I added the memories Coirpre had given me outside the inn, from his admiration to his blustering monologue: *He is the noble Emerald Flame, my only match in the art of illusion!*

[Please,] I begged, *[don't leave me.]* The memories I poured into became more jumbled and frantic: Kakura, with her legs trailing in the pool behind her, offering her guidance to a stranger; Aster, propping him up as she helped him stagger into the sacred walls of their convent and risking the secrets of their order to help him; Linsee, dragging the little barque behind her as she ran on her magical leg through the tussocks of marsh grass, urging the rest of us faster; Coirpre, his brow dripping with sweat, as he tried again and again to summon me because he knew something was not right; Tincrown, bidding me to keep watch over the wayward illusionist we both adored. All of them, like me, doing their best to protect someone we hoped would remain in the world.

Just as I began to fear that I had lost Emerald forever, a new memory fizzled in my mind, one that I had never seen before. *Tincrown sat on the edge of the bed and ran his slender fingers through Emerald's dark hair as he placed a kiss on the half-jotunn's temple. "No one could ever replace you, mir'ahai."*

The memory cut off as Emerald choked and coughed, rolling face down onto the spongy black peat of the hollow. He gasped for air.

"You absolute *troll*," Coirpre bellowed, although when he brought his hand down on my friend's back, it was in a caress rather than a blow. "You damned selfish, self-righteous *simpleton*. What were you *thinking?* Always have to play the hero, don't you?"

Emerald grumbled something incoherent.

Gemma joined us, but Linsee hobbled up the hill alone. She was still staring at the Crone's skull, and as I watched, she dragged her fingers over the smooth white dome.

"*She offered succor to anyone fleeing injustice or hardship*," the shepherdess superior murmured. She knelt down in the loam and pressed her forehead to the remains from all those years ago. "What might have been different if she lived? How many other lives would have been changed for the better?"

One dark act by the Fenguards had rippled outward over the centuries. I couldn't even begin to grasp how different the world might be if the steward of Upper Bound had made one choice in place of another.

It was too hard to imagine. I was exhausted, and for the first time in my life, I longed to be dispelled, just to put a little distance between me and the events of the night.

Emerald tried to lift himself to his knees as Coirpre and Aster steadied him. The fog that had surrounded the island for so long was gone, and both starlight and moonslight illuminated the water, so bright that the bog appeared to be lit from within.

"Come on," Gemma said gently. She took Linsee by the arm. Coirpre and Aster worked together to stand Emerald upright, and the five of them trooped down to the boat. Kakura waited in the water, and when the five of them were seated in the skiff, she took hold of the rope at the bow and began to drag them out into deeper waters. The little vessel sat so low that one good lurch would send its occupants tumbling into the drink, but as Aster took the oars and began to row, the rest of the passengers settled into a dreamlike trance.

I was left to follow them, wondering not only what would become of the Black Hollow now, but what would become of my friend. The Cronemire's wrath had proven that some wounds could not be healed.

I hoped that the rift between me and Emerald was not one such injury.

Chapter Twenty-Eight

I sat in the library of the Convent of the Crone, staring down at the book which Aster had laid in front of me. It was an illuminated text, and the image before me showed a square-jawed, wild-haired being with mismatched eyes. One foot was made of stone, one wreathed in fire; one arm commanded a geyser of water, while the other ended above the elbow. Its naked body was recognizably humanoid, and yet neither male nor female. It appeared to be dancing against a backdrop of stars.

"What is this?" I asked.

"This is one artist's vision of the Middling Godlet," Aster said. She leaned her elbows on the table and nodded to the text. "Ah've studied their koans for many years, since long before ah ever heard of the Sisterhood."

I pointed to her chest, where the red-and-gold emblem winked at me from amidst the black fold of her robes. "Is that their sigil?"

Aster smiled and dragged her fingers over the smooth surface of the brooch. "It is."

"And you kept it even after joining the Sisterhood?" I lifted my eyebrows in surprise.

"The Sisterhood has no rules about recognizing other spiritual powers." Aster smiled sadly. We hadn't discussed the implications of what we'd seen in the Black Hollow, or the effect that might have had on the faith of the sisters. According to their lore, I had brushed up against their goddess. Unlike Lady Fenguard, however, I felt no urge to claim any particular proximity to godhood.

"Besides," Aster added, "it is possible to believe in more than one thing. Ah've taken guidance from Aster and the teachings of the Middling Godlet, and both lead me here, tae the place ah now call home. Why would the Crone ask me tae turn my back on those who brought me tae her doorstep?"

"I suppose she wouldn't," I agreed. From what I'd felt in the Cronemire, the local goddess—or whatever she was—had a predilection for vengeance, but little appetite for jealousy. All she'd ever wanted was justice, and to be left in peace.

The nun shifted the book so that she could better view the passages. "*In the eye of Hharda, water is the purest source of power. In the hand of Nunket, land is the source of life. The Middling Godlet sees what both cannot: that without water, the land is barren, and without land, the sea will never end.*" She lifted her gray eyes to mine.

"You want me to take advice from the god of mud?" I asked wryly.

"The Middling Godlet rules o'er the in-between. Their power is strongest where things overlap. Where both things are true, and yet neither is entirely accurate." Aster drummed her fingers against the book significantly.

"Sounds like the godlet of riddles," I grumbled. "Why are you telling me this?"

"Crimson." Aster tapped the book more earnestly. "Ye were conceived on the equinox in brackish water when your creator hovered between life and death. Ye were born on the edge of the woods, in a place that was neither wild nor tamed. From what ye've told me about yer mind-cottage... a place which, by the way, is supposed to be *metaphorical* rather than *metaphysical*... the one time ye can interact with the world around ye unhindered is when ye are caught in a place that is both *nowhere* and *somewhere.* Are ye really going tae tell me that ye don't understand why ah think ye might want tae know about this particular deity?"

"I'm an illusion," I told her plainly. "Emerald made me. I wasn't brought into being by some god who took a special interest in me. That's the kind of thing that the Fenguards told themselves to excuse their selfish behavior. Thank you, but no thank you." I waved her away. "I've had enough to think about when it comes to the gods lately."

Aster sighed. "Do ye really think it's pure coincidence that after centuries of unrest, *ye* were the one who was able tae help the Cronemire settle her debts?"

I shrugged and twirled a curl of my bright red hair around my finger. Since we'd been staying on convent grounds, I'd gotten in the habit of being Simone, and I'd even gone so far as to wear black out of respect for our hostesses. "If it wasn't me, it would have been someone else eventually," I told her.

"Hm." Aster steepled her fingers before her. "Ah wonder if ye genuinely believe that, or if it's only the story ye're telling yourself because it feels safe."

"I really do," I insisted. "I know you mean well, Aster, but if Coirpre's ability to summon me proves anything, it's that I'm nothing more than a sentient illusion and not, I don't know, some sort of divine intervention."

"Why are ye so afraid of the alternative?"

Because it puts even more weight on my shoulders. If I'm Emerald's creation, all I have to do is take care of him, and I've proven that I'm rubbish at that. If I was something more, what would that mean for me? Who else would I be failing? What else might be expected of me?

"I'm not afraid of what you're telling me," I lied, "I just don't believe that even a minor god of mud and riddles would take a personal interest in me."

All the same, my eyes strayed back to the book. Coirpre had once told me that he knew I was real because I'd given myself buttons that Emerald wouldn't have imagined on his own. The image of the etched godlet, dancing across a field of glittering night, reminded me of the ceiling in the little room where I'd found myself when Emerald dispelled me: a blue background painted with golden stars. It was the first room I'd ever conjured that hadn't come from my memory.

Had I made it?

Or had someone else?

Emerald and I had been tiptoeing around each other in the days since I found him in the Black Hollow. At first, I'd fussed over him while he lay in bed, the victim of fitful dreams. Once he awoke, we'd sat in awkward silence while his strength returned. At last, he was able to get up and move around on his own, and we'd taken to avoiding one another. He'd spent long hours by the pond speaking to Kakura, and I'd given him his space. During their conversations, I never once intruded on his mind, either by prying at his thoughts or by speaking to him through our connection.

When I left Aster in the library, it was midmorning. Emerald was sitting in his usual place by the fishpond, and the pearl elf sat in the water before him, but a third figure had joined them. When she saw me, she waved merrily, and I lifted my hand to half-mast before I realized who it was.

"Amaya?" I approached the pond, surprised to see another visitor who didn't wear the Crone's black. "What are you doing here?"

The augur waved one hand at the berry bushes, which were still producing berries at a fantastic rate, even though the nights were growing so cool that the nuns could sometimes see their own breath. "I have a long history with the convent. I come by sometimes to make sure that the bushes are still healthy. A blight could wipe out the whole crop, you know." She crossed her hands over her belly and offered one of her uneven smiles. "I hear that you've been busy, Crimson."

I glanced automatically at Emerald. To my surprise, he didn't flinch away.

"Yes," he said softly. "Crimson's the one who put an end to all of it."

"It wasn't me," I protested. "It was the Cronemire. I only helped."

"I went out to the Black Hollow at sunrise," Amaya said. "I always wondered what it looked like, but I never thought I'd get a chance to see it for myself."

I squinted at her. I had never asked how she'd come to lose mobility in one side of her body, but it occurred to me that I'd already been told the answer.

"Amaya," I asked, "did you perhaps try to visit the Black Hollow once before?"

"I did." The augur nodded. "Without taking proper precautions, I must admit. I drifted too close to the island and nearly died. If it hadn't been for the king, I wouldn't have gotten off so lightly."

"Burp," I said sadly. "He told me he saved you." I sank down onto one of the stones at the waterside.

"I met the new king this morning." Amaya nodded her approval. "Hefty fellow. A bit less regal than his predecessor, but I think he'll mature into the role."

"It's hard for me to forgive him for killing my friend," I said bitterly, "even if he *was* only following the rules."

Amaya coughed in alarm. "Killed him?"

Emerald nodded. "We watched the battle. Squelch defeated him, and the poor lad was dragged off into the swamp."

Kakura made an indelicate sound, but when we looked at her, she shook her head. "Allergies," she said. I caught her smiling at the augur.

Amaya coughed again.

[Is there something I don't know about krubs?] Emerald asked me.

It was the first time he'd casually reached out to me since the Black Hollow. I hadn't anticipated how much of a relief it would be to open that line of communication again, in part because I'd feared we never would. *[Loads, probably. If you don't know something, it's doubtful I do, either.]*

Amaya hoisted herself off of the bench. Her wild black hair bobbed around her face, and this late in the season, her freckles stood stark against her fawn-gold skin. "You've solved a mystery that's troubled me for years," she said. "What will come of it remains to be seen." She tapped one finger against her chin. "And you know, I've heard new rumors on the streets that Maximilien discovered the secret of the Fenguards months ago. Folks about town are saying that the laird had him killed to keep him from going back to the Conjury with news that a brutal and ill-advised bit of magic was being practiced on the island."

"Are they?" Emerald asked. "That makes sense, I suppose. A man who was killing sailors every few days would go to great lengths to keep the Conjury from finding out. It might even jeopardize the port's relationship with the Trader's Guild."

"Which, gods forbid, might one day be reflected in the local coffers." Amaya grinned. "I think you're right, Emerald Flame. I'll be sure to encourage that rumor at every opportunity, seeing as how it's very likely to be the truth."

Kakura raised an eyebrow at me, and I shrugged. "Can you think of another explanation?" I asked the pearl elf.

"No," she said. "It sounds plausible to me."

"Then we're in agreement," Amaya said. "And I suspect that the Conjury will believe it, too."

❧

Once Amaya left, I thought that Emerald would ask me to leave, too. Instead, he got to his feet and straightened his clothes. He'd commissioned a new set, paying with his own coin rather than Laird Fenguard's emblem. The canvas trousers, cotton shirt, and double-breasted wool coat weren't flashy by any means, but they fit him neatly and would keep him warm as winter approached. The gold chain with its mounted emerald gemstone dangled about his throat, stark against the black material. Coirpre had given it back before he'd run off to... wherever he'd gone. I hadn't seen him since that awful night in the Hollow.

"I think we should walk up to the keep," Emerald said. "Don't you?"

"If you like," I said, hoping to hide my surprise.

"You aren't leaving yet, I hope?" Kakura asked. "I hope you'll say a proper goodbye before you do."

"No, we're not leaving," Emerald assured her. "I only want to check in on our acquaintances and see if they've heard the same rumor Amaya has."

[Ugh, not Dirkus and Benedite,] I complained.

[The very same. After all, the whole point of this misadventure was to protect Dyrne. If we weren't successful...]

[Your point is well made,] I assured him.

We made our way to the front door. In the privacy of the empty receiving room, I rearranged myself into Simon. Instead of my usual finery, I conjured myself a suit that complemented Emerald's. Yes, the collar and tails of my coat were a bit more flattering, the trousers more tightly fitted, and the boots more polished, but the similarities were undeniable.

"Have you *copied* me?" Emerald asked, askance.

"I've drawn inspiration from your wardrobe," I said primly. "You look rather dashing in it. I thought I'd try it for myself."

Emerald pretended to swoon. "The inimitable Crimson Smoke has judged my attire worthy. There can be no higher compliment."

"It is my fondest wish to see you in a silk jacquard coat one day," I sighed. "Dove-gray, I think, with a dark green underweave and perhaps a touch of gold? For the time being, however, I approve of your current style."

"Silk," Emerald muttered. "As if." He pushed the door open and waved me through.

In the weeks since the Fenguards' so-called disappearance, the dead hadn't risen once. The people of Upper Bound seemed to have taken the change in stride, although I wonder how many people were saddened to learn that their deceased loved ones would now go to the bog once and for all, never to return.

The tense silence between us returned, and I found myself dragging my heels, metaphorically speaking, as we strolled down the boardwalk. I was wondering what I could say to win Emerald's good humor back when the water below the boardwalk began to froth and foam. Two golden eyes appeared above the water.

"Master Crimson-Simon?" someone asked.

I stopped in my tracks and stared down at the smiling face below us. "*Burp?*"

Sure enough, my green friend waved up at us. Squelch's head appeared behind him a moment later, and the larger krub waved his bulbous hand in greeting, too.

"You're alive." Emerald returned to my side. He seemed more pleased than I would have expected.

"Very much so." Burp stood upright. "I was so nervous, but losing wasn't *nearly* as awful as I'd anticipated. In fact..." His face turned a darker shade of green, and he pressed his hands to his cheeks. "Well, I won't say too much."

"I'm glad we happened to see you," Squelch added. He wrapped one arm around Burp's waist, and my friend batted him away halfheartedly. "My wife was worried you'd leave before she was able to see you again."

Emerald's eye twitched. "Your *wife?*"

"Well, it's not official," Burp added hastily. "But we've been talking. And look, Master Crimson-Simon! I'm a *mother*!"

I was still trying to make sense of the fact that Burp was among the living. When he—she?—pointed down at the water, I looked without really thinking. The surface was rippled with the movement of small dark forms. Their round heads bobbed below the surface, and their stubby tails thrashed. A few of them even sported the beginnings of legs.

"Oh!" I said, and brought my hand to my forehead. "You had a *fight*!"

How many times had Burp seen me switch from Simon to

Simone and asked me if I was fighting with someone? I'd thought nothing of it until now, when the implications became clearer. He'd never once said outright what would happen if he lost the battle with Squelch, only that he'd be buried, and that he would never again be king. Apparently she was now the Queen of the Black Hollow instead.

"Burp," I asked slowly, "when two krubs fight, does the loser...?"

"The loser has to be the girl," Burp said. "And I thought it would be so shameful, but do you know something? I don't mind it at all. I'm surrounded by my krubibies, and I have a *very* handsome fellow at my side." She pinched Squelch's thigh, and he let out an involuntary ribbit. "I didn't realize how lonely I was before."

"I told her that next time, I'll throw the fight." Squelch winked at us. "It's only fair."

[Dear gods,] Emerald thought. *[Thank goodness it doesn't work that way for anyone else.]*

I glared at him. *[Don't be a prude. It's sweet.]* Aloud I said, "I'm so happy for you, Burp. It all worked out in the end."

"Thank you for being my friend when I didn't have anyone." Burp nuzzled her face against Squelch's neck. "I hope things go as well for you as they have for me." She turned to Emerald. "And I *do* hope you enjoyed your krub-bath."

A tiny tidbit of something Burp had once told me sprang to mind. "Out of curiosity, what effect does krub-spit have on the dry folk, Burp?"

My friend shook her head. "I'm not sure."

Squelch interjected. "*I* know. Makes 'em come over all funny. A few of the sailors went around barefoot after I swabbed the decks, and they started acting all peculiar. Brendan nearly toppled out of the crow's nest, and he said later he was trying to catch the stars."

[So krub-spit has hallucinogenic properties.] Emerald rubbed the back of his neck. *[No wonder I felt so strange that*

night. I told you one drink wasn't enough to make me act like that.]

[I'm sorry I didn't believe you. Although I reckon that'll be the last time you let anyone get their spit on you,] I thought.

For reasons I didn't understand, Emerald's cheeks flushed dark and he began to cough profusely.

"Come on, my darling," Squelch said. "Let's get the krubibies back to the burrow."

I lifted my hand in farewell. "Take care, you two!" We watched as the krubs marched back to the bog, hand-in-hand, with their cloud of krubibies in tow.

"Look," I told Emerald as I got to my feet. "You learn something new every day. No wonder Amaya and Kakura were laughing at us."

"I feel like I had more questions than I did before," Emerald muttered. "And yet, strangely, I don't want answers."

"I'm surprised that there's a whole *race* of creatures about which you don't appear to know the first thing."

"Yeah, well." Emerald glanced over his shoulder. "They're *weird,* aren't they?"

"Stop being krubbist," I told him. "You sound like Dirkus."

My companion shuddered. "Heaven forbid."

If only the rest of our stay in Upper Bound should be so satisfactory, I would be quite content with our work.

❦

We were halfway through the city when a small figure popped out of an alley to bar our way.

"You. Sir Snudge." Tala pointed a dirty finger in my direction. "The headmistress wants to see you. *Now.*"

"Oh, Aster's sake." Emerald turned to glare at me. "What now? Not another krub, I hope?"

"No," I sighed. "Unfortunately, I was rather rude to Marsha's... henchman? Paramore? To be honest, I'm not sure what he is, but at any rate, I *may* have given him a panic attack when last we spoke. At the very least, I ought to apologize to him. You can continue onto the keep without me, if you want."

"Not a chance." Emerald hooked his thumb at me. "If Marsha's going to box his ears, I want to be there to see it."

The small dwarf-girl pointed at Emerald's face while staring at me. "I like 'im better'n'you," she said before scurrying away.

We followed her into the depths of Midtown until the alleys started to look vaguely familiar. When we rounded a final corner, Tala pointed to a door I'd seen once before.

"Here you are," she said, and turned to go.

"Hold on," I said. "Emerald, would you be kind enough to pay our guide for her services?"

Emerald dug around some inner pocket of his coat— evidently, he had an affinity for hidden receptacles—and produced a single copper coin, which he dropped into the girl's outstretched hand.

"Hmph," Tala grunted. "I brought you here twice, Sir Snudge."

I stuck out my bottom lip, and Emerald produced a second coin. This time, Tala nodded, and the coins disappeared so quickly I wondered if she'd used magic on them.

"We're square," she announced. "'N' this time, you don't have to tell 'em you're a fribble or nuffink. Password is *I'm a truepenny.*" She nodded to us and then turned on her heel.

"What a strange child," Emerald murmured.

"Stranger than a krubibie?" I asked blithely as I approached the door. "Come on, let's get this over with."

Emerald slipped around me to knock three times on the door. This time, no one demanded our names. The door opened to reveal Boo's blunt and disapproving countenance.

"Oh." His brow lifted, and a shy smile stole over his features. "It's *you.*"

[I thought he hated you,] Emerald said.

[So did I. This is unexpected.]

Boo opened the door wider. "Marsha, he's here."

"Who is?" The Mistress of Midtown looked up from her books, adjusting a pair of wire-rimmed spectacles as she did so. "Oh! Crimson Smoke—and your strapping friend, to boot. Come in." She waved one graceful hand to the abundance of chairs and lounges that stood around the room.

Emerald followed me in, admiring the room as he did. "Quality assortment of bric-a-brac you've amassed," he said. "It's quite an extensive collection. Are those lamps from the Nomad Gamut?"

"They are. And aren't they just the babblebird's boots? I adore 'em." Marsha dropped down onto her usual seat and set her glasses aside. This time, instead of looming over her shoulder, Boo joined her.

"You two seem... happy." I perched on the edge of my chair, waiting for one of them to tackle us or hex us or whatever they had planned.

"We are." Marsha threw one arm around Boudreaux's shoulders. "And we have you to thank for it."

Emerald's head swiveled toward me. **[Quite the little matchmaker, aren't you?]**

[I can honestly say that I don't have the faintest notion of what they're talking about,] I replied.

Boo shifted closer to Marsha and settled one hand on her exposed knee. "Our conversation got me thinkin', Crimson. I don't like bein' just the muscle. There's more to me than tunin' up folks' faces or bustin' 'em in the knees."

"And I didn't know he was feeling so hedged-in." Marsha planted a kiss on Boo's cheek. "I know he's a decent guy, but I was putting him in a tough spot by treating him like the hired muscle. He's plum bricky, and I want the world to know *I* know it."

"Aw, baby." Boo leaned in for a kiss. "You're the jammiest bits of the jam."

Marsha tittered and pulled him down for a kiss.

[Did you walk around Upper Bound handing out love

potions?] Emerald demanded. ***[Really, Crimson, this is getting out of hand.]***

[And I am just as surprised as you are, I assure you.]

Marsha pulled away and grinned at us, but she left her arms around Boo's neck. "Anyway, we wanted to let you know what a nice turn you did us, even if it was by accident. If you ever need to call in a favor, you let Miss Marsha know, won't you?"

"Right." I forced a smile. "Perfect. For the time being, though, I think we'll just... go?"

"I'll show 'em out, kitten," Boo purred. Emerald shot to his feet so fast it was a wonder the chair stayed upright.

As we wove back through the alleys of Midtown, my friend didn't say a word. This time, I didn't think he was upset with me. More likely, he was thinking of his doctor and wondering if we'd be able to set out for Dyrne that very night.

❧

The laird was gone, but the courtyard of Fenguard Keep was just as busy as ever. Instead of bringing in cartloads of goods, however, the primary aim seemed to be to bear things away.

As we strode into the open door of the main hall, we encountered three figures, all of whom appeared to be dressed in garb raided from Laird Edur's clothes cupboard, bossing about a cadre of more modestly dressed sailors.

"Careful with that painting!" Hudson of Hardwick Home growled at a pair of dwarves, whose coats sported the Trader's Guild badge. The harbormaster wore a new silk suit in midnight blue, and a soft-crowned pleated hat made of black damask which sported a trio of white plumes. "That's an antique."

"What's going on?" I murmured.

"Simple." Emerald's mouth turned down in disgust. "The Fenguards are gone, and the Conjury is racing to liquidate their capital."

"*Emerald!*" Dirkus had been sitting on one of the tables and watching the sailors work, but when he saw us, he jumped down.

He was still wearing his purple-and-gold Conjury uniform, but he'd added Laird Fenguard's ermine-lined cape to the mix. It trailed on the floor behind him as he trotted over to us. "Haven't seen you in ages. I've got a letter for you somewhere. Oy, Benedite! Where'd we put the letter?"

"It's in your pocket," Benedite said. He was making notes of all the Fenguard property in his ledger, and he didn't bother to look up.

Dirkus stuck his tongue between his teeth and dug around in his pockets. His face lit up as he produced an envelope with Emerald's name written on the face. "Dunno why they set a letter and not a babblebird. Wildly inefficient. Anyone could have a peek." He held it out, and Emerald pocketed it without reading it.

"What happens now?" I asked.

Dirkus rolled his eyes. "Now that Laird Fenguard has been exposed as a lying murderer and gone on the lam, you mean? You won't *believe* the records we found." His eyes gleamed, and he leaned forward to throw one arm around Emerald's shoulder. In a hoarse whisper, he told us, "They were trying some ritual to become *gods*. Can you imagine that?"

Emerald and I exchanged a wary glance. "That's not possible, is it?" my friend asked.

"I suppose we'll find out," Dirkus said. "All the books and notes and things have been sent off to Venta Bulgarum. If it's possible, the Conjury will work it out soon enough."

I stifled a groan. ***[That seems like the last thing we want.]***

[The ritual doesn't work,] Emerald reminded me, but I could sense that he wasn't sure that would stop the Conjury from trying it out.

"Can you believe we sat at his table, drinking his wine, all while he was doing such awful things behind our backs?" Dirkus was still dangling off Emerald's shoulders, and he socked him in the arm for good measure. "Why didn't you sniff him out sooner? Were you too busy getting plastered in Midtown? Nice of you, though, to leave all the glory for us." The scout waved his hand in the air. "Maximilien's murder is solved, and the laird as good as handed rule over to the Conjury when he left. Benedite and I have been given commendations *and* a temporary posting until the new governor arrives."

With every world, Emerald's shoulders drooped a little more. *[Wonderful. We've managed to cover up Aindreas's crimes... and in the process, we opened a foothold for the Conjury just down the cliffside from Dyrne.]*

"Congratulations are in order, then," I told Dirkus. "I wonder how the locals will feel about the power shift."

"Oh, they'll come around soon enough. See, there's some rumor that this old god of theirs is the one who made this all possible. Don't know how these ideas get started, but I'm not complaining. All works out for us in the end!" He beamed at his own wit and thumped Emerald twice on the back before releasing him at last. "Lots to do. We've partnered with Hudson, who swears he can make a mint on all this old junk. If we don't sell it off before the new governor arrives, it'll have to be logged with the bursar, and we'll never see a single coin." He winked at us and waved once before striding back to Benedite.

Emerald and I left the hall in silence, dodging between the long line of movers who raided the keep.

[It's not the worst news we could have gotten,] I thought bracingly. *[Yes, the Conjury is taking over Fenguard Keep. Will the quality of life get worse for some people in Upper Bound? Possibly. Will the new rulers be absolute fribbles? Almost certainly. But we've bought Dyrne a little time, and stopped two murderers, and broken a centuries-old curse, so I expect that counts for something, doesn't it? And now we can go back and talk to Tincrown and Nechtan and make a whole new plan. Isn't that right, Em? Em?]*

I realized that he was no longer beside me. He'd stopped just outside the gates of the keep, with the letter that Dirkus had given him clutched in his hands.

[Em?] I asked again.

He lowered the paper he was holding, and I saw that his eyes were now red-rimmed.

"What's the matter?" I asked, hurrying back to his side.

"It's an official summons," he rasped. "From the Temple of Guise. I've been ordered home."

Chapter Twenty-Nine

Our return route through Midtown brought us close to
the inn where we'd stayed before Emerald's march to
the river.

"How official is an official summons?" I asked. "Is it the sort
of thing one can put off for a few weeks, so long as you get there
eventually? After all, the letter's been sitting in Dirkus's pocket
for gods-know-how-long. Could we just throw it in the swamp
and pretend we lost it?"

"If we do, there will be an inquiry." Emerald dragged his feet
along the alley. "Which could bring even *more* Conjury members
to the island. The sooner we leave, the better."

[But Tincrown—]

*[Is already in plenty of danger thanks to me. This case
went wrong at every turn.]* Emerald turned up the collar of his
coat to hide the lower half of his face from passersby. *[I'll ask
Amaya if she can find a way to warn Dyrne of what's
coming. I'm sure she'll help us.]*

[It's not your fault that things went wrong,] I assured
him.

Emerald narrowed his eyes and glared sidelong at me.

[Well, it **isn't**. *Even if you'd been sober the whole time*

and we'd confronted him from the outset, Laird Fenguard would have tried to kill you. And you'd have been in even more danger, because we wouldn't have made an ally of the Sisterhood yet. Coirpre wouldn't have been able to summon me without their help, even if he'd wanted to. You'd have ended up dead, or Laird Fenguard would be gone just the same, and either way, Tincrown wouldn't have been happy.]

[Have you really forgiven me for dispelling you?] he asked. *[Even when I promised I wouldn't?]*

[Only if you can forgive me for trying to possess you. That wasn't right. It's one thing if you ask me to, but to force it on you is no better than when you compel me against my will. I won't do it again, not unless I have your express permission.]

He nodded. *[Forgiven. Of course. And I won't drink again, so unless someone—oh.]* He drew up short and peered in the window of a tavern. *[Come on.]*

[Didn't you just say you wouldn't drink?] I asked as he opened the door.

[We're not here for the ale.] He nodded to the far corner of the room, where a man sat alone, picking at his lunch. *[We're here for him.]*

Coirpre looked up at us as we wove between the tables. He raised a hand in greeting, but he barely smiled as we took two seats on the bench across from him. He hadn't bothered to renew his illusion of youth.

"Still here?" he asked. "I'm surprised. I thought you'd have hightailed it back to your doctor by now."

Emerald pressed his lips together and cut his eyes away.

"We've heading back to the mainland soon," I said. "Conjury business. What about you?"

"I'm leaving, too." Coirpre waved vaguely out to sea. "Now that Laird Edur is gone, I've been released from my two-year contract. Figure I ought to ship out on the next tide before someone else decides I'm too talented to let go."

"An understandable concern," I replied archly. "Will you be restoring the bloom of youth to your cheeks *before* the ship ride, or after?"

The bard grunted and tossed a curl of hair back from his face. "People might be surprised to learn that the famous author of so many songs sports hair as silver as it is flaxen these days, but they'll have to get used to it."

"Mhmm." I mirrored his careless stance. "And I suppose this choice has nothing to do with what happened in the Black Hollow?"

"Of course not," Coirpre scoffed. "I've simply lost the taste for pretending to appear younger than I am. I'm hoping that my music will appeal to a more *mature* audience. Besides, staying young forever is overrated." He turned his attention to Emerald. "You're awfully quiet over there. Don't you have any promises you'd like to extract from me? Threats you'd like to issue?" He dropped his voice into a low growl and hunched his shoulders, jutting out his lower jaw in an unflattering yet uncanny impression of my friend. "*Watch out, Coirpre. The great Emerald Flame suffers no fools. I'll get you in the end! Blah blah, justice, morality, and so on!*" He wagged a finger in Emerald's direction.

My companion did not crack a smile. He sat at the table, picking at the wooden surface with one craggy fingernail.

"No," he murmured, "I'm not going to threaten you. Crimson showed me what you... gave him, I suppose. What you let her see when they touched you."

Coirpre glared at me. "Rude. That was given in confidence."

"It saved me," Emerald said bluntly. "Or at least, it helped."

Coirpre's glower lingered, but he drummed his knuckles on the table. "In that case, I suppose it was an acceptable breach of oath."

"I didn't show him everything," I added, "only what I thought would help him." Both men glanced at me in surprise. Coirpre met my eyes and held them for a moment, attempting— I suspected—a little soul-reading of his own. A fraction of the tension in his face relaxed, and he flicked the fingers of one hand at me dismissively. "Not that it matters."

"So what now?" Emerald asked. "I expect that you'll go to the mainland, where you'll write some tragic ballad about the sorry excuse for a half-jotunn who nearly drowned in the Cronemire *twice*."

Coirpre's head whipped around to face my friend. "*I'm* sorry, are you suggesting that I'd write a song about what you tried to do?"

"Isn't that your style?" Emerald retorted.

"Gods above *and* below, is that really what you think of me?" Coirpre put a hand to his chest and shook his head. As always, there was theatrical flair to his body language; above all else, he was a performer. All the same, a few small details gave him away, from the deepening of the wrinkles around his eyes to the pinch of his mouth. "I'm not a monster, Emerald. And I *certainly* don't write sad songs about other people. The common man loves a good romantic ballad full of mutual pining, and I would rather make my home in the miasma of the Black Hollow than write that sort of song about *you*. As for stories about sad men who sniffle into their cups? Those don't sell. It would be far too relatable to most of my audiences. Your affinity for drink and your compulsion toward self-harm are, quite frankly, your two least interesting qualities. And the combination? Unbearable. It's predictable and overdone."

A small smile appeared on Emerald's lips, the first real amusement I'd seen from him in some time. "Of course. I'll have to find a new interest, one that's more marketable in verse."

"I wish you would. Leave the wine behind." Coirpre leaned back on the bench and pretended to strum a lyre. "As for my next hit, I'll tell the story of how the Emerald Flame was nearly extinguished by a pair deathless murderers. In the finale, I'll recount how I swept in at the last second to coax a wild spirit from the bog to do my bidding, and thereby saved the day." Coirpre smirked. "It'll require a bit of artistic license, to be sure, but I think we can agree that I was instrumental in our shared victory?"

I leaned over to Emerald. "Did you hear that? He's going to put me in a song!"

Emerald snorted. "I should have expected nothing less from a cheap hack like you."

"And I predict that a tin-eared fellow such as yourself would hate *whatever* I come up with, so why should I care overmuch about your opinion?" Coirpre turned up his nose. "On that note, I have a ship to catch. Give me a head start at least before you begin making trouble for me, won't you?"

"Says the consummate troublemaker." A bit of the old rumble had returned to Emerald's voice. "Very well, take your leave."

"We won't even rat you out to what's-his-nose," I added.

"You're both too kind." Coirpre got to his feet and swept into a bow that managed to be both graceful and ironic at once. I wished that we had a bit more time together. Even with the ability to make myself appear however I pleased, I hadn't mastered the nuance of his body language.

He turned his back on us and began to strut away, but before he'd gone more than a few paces, Emerald grunted, "Coirpre?"

The bard looked back, and Emerald tugged on the cord that kept my gem secure around his neck so that the emerald that hung on it peeked out from the collar of his shirt. In a voice as deep as the boom of two boulders striking each other, he said, "Thank you."

"Of course." For a moment, I caught a glimpse of Coirpre as he was—not the bard, not the performer, not the mask, but the man beneath it all. I had *felt* the truth of him, but I had rarely seen it, and he had never once let his facade drop in our presence by choice. "It was my pleasure."

"May I ask you something?" I interjected.

Coirpre returned to the side of the table, although he didn't sit down.

"Why did you bother with all the..." I held out one hand as if something lay in my palm and wiggled the fingers of the other over it in a child's impression of his lightweaving technique. "You've made your stance quite clear: you can't help everyone. So why help us?"

Coirpre shrugged and gestured to Emerald. "I wasn't trying to save everyone. I was saving *him*. It's different."

"Because you know him?" I asked. "Because he's not a stranger? Is that it?"

There was one side effect of his life as a performer that Coirpre had not considered, and that was the fact that his theatrical emotions were so easy to read. I saw the moment that he opened his mouth, prepared to give some throwaway answer, and how his gaze slid toward Emerald's. He closed his lips again, teetering between dismissal and bare honesty. The latter, I knew, did not come easy to him. Our brief connection had revealed that Coirpre hated nothing more than being vulnerable.

In the end, he settled somewhere between the two, although not in the way I would have expected.

"He's irritating," Coirpre said in a flippant tone. "Both of you are, but my hero's journey doesn't work without you two. On top of that, I can't abide tedium, and the world would be a great deal more boring without this oaf in it." He leaned forward across the table to add, in a much softer voice, "And besides, there have been plenty of times in my life when I needed help and had nobody to offer it."

His eyes never left my face, and even without the kind of mental connection I shared with my creator, I knew exactly what he was thinking. He was remembering the fragments of his past that he'd shared with me, the ones that had nothing to do with Emerald: the boot, the floor, the insufferable smallness and the desire to shrink his way out of existence.

I wish you would tell him, I thought. *Not just for his sake, but for yours. You ought to talk about it with someone, and I know that Emerald would understand.*

The burning intensity of Coirpre's gaze lingered, and I realized he had. He might not have trusted Emerald with the most secret parts of himself...

...but he'd trusted me.

Without another word, Coirpre righted himself and turned to the door, walking with purpose this time. The heavy oak barrier slammed shut behind him, and he was gone again, heading on to some new adventure.

"Kenspeckle bastard," Emerald murmured fondly, but I knew better. Yes, Coirpre loved a dramatic exit, but his showmanship concealed a truth that I had only lately begun to suspect.

Coirpre was as lonely as Emerald had been before he met Tincrown.

Lonelier, in fact, because at least Emerald had me.

❧

Emerald moved about the little hut just outside the convent where the sisters had let us stay, gathering his few possessions and tucking them one after another into the backpack Tincrown had given him. I watched in silence as he put everything in order.

"I'll leave a few things out," he said aloud. "We've got a couple of things left to sort out. Amaya's got to send that babblebird message, we need to say goodbye to the sisters, and I need to book passage to Kinmore." He set everything on the desk by the window, which looked out over the harbor. "It'll be good to be on the move again. I wish we had time to go back up to the highlands, but there will be ice on the passes soon enough, and it'll be a relief not to have to stare out over the Bounder every day."

I nodded.

Emerald turned to me. "You're awfully quiet, Crim. Are we going to go back to not speaking to one another? Because I'd rather not. I've, ah... I've *missed* you."

"I've missed you, too." I perched on the edge of the bed. "But I still don't know how to talk to you about what happened.

About what you did. I'm angry, and I don't know how to stop being angry with you. And I hate it."

Emerald sighed and sank down next to me. "I deserve it. When we talked to Coirpre today, I wondered if you were going to ask me to give him the gem." He tapped his chest, where the shape of the emerald was just visible beneath his shirt. "I wondered if you'd rather travel with him than with me. Figured I'd give you the chance to propose it, anyway."

Truth be told, the thought had not occurred to me. Even after all of the ugly things I had thought about Emerald, even after bruising my knuckles on a likeness of him, I hadn't truly wanted to be rid of him.

"Do you think that would work?" I asked.

"I don't know. We could have at least given it a go." A little of his pain was evident in the twist of his mouth and the shimmer of his eyes, but even when I lowered the wall between us, he kept his emotions in check.

I traced a pattern on the rumpled sheets, using my fingertip to mirror what I remembered of the gestures I'd see in both men make when summoning an illusion. "Maybe we should try it, if we run into him again."

Emerald nodded.

When he didn't speak, I carried on. "I suspect we are a bit connected now, and not just because he summoned me. I've seen things about him that he would rather have kept private. Do you know why he showed me?"

"No."

"He wanted to prove to me that he was your friend."

Emerald started. "Not sure I'd call him a friend."

I gave him my most skeptical bardic glare. "You have a few enough friends as it is. Perhaps you better not discount any of them too quickly. How many times does someone have to save your life before you'll believe that they like you at least a little?"

Emerald winced as my words hit home. "Let it go for the moment," he told me. "I wasn't asking about Coirpre. I was asking about you."

"Traveling with Coirpre would be better than being *nowhere* again, but I'd rather be with you." I reached over and mimed patting Emerald's shoulder, although I was careful not to touch him directly. "After all, if Coirpre and I traveled together, we would be forced to one-up each other at every opportunity. It sounds exhausting."

"Are you sure about that?" He produced the letter from his pocket again. "This summons is going to lead me to a place I'd avoid if I could. Going home..." Emerald passed one hand over his eyes. "I don't want to do it. I'm afraid. Everything that Kakura and I have been talking about, every awful thing that I've believed about myself, it all comes from that place. I'm going to do my best to keep it together, but as you've seen, my best sometimes falls short." He flopped onto his back and smiled bitterly.

"I'll stay with you this time. Even if you slip again. I have two conditions, though." I held up one finger. "Don't lie to me."

"Easy," he said at once. "What's the other?"

"Don't dispel me again. If you have to, if there's a reason, if we agree to it... All right. But you don't get to unmake me just because you're angry at me or insecure about yourself. I know I agreed to forgive you for last time, but the fact that you have this power over me?" I folded my hands in my lap and knotted them together, just as Coirpre had on the day where he first let me see inside his head. "It terrifies me. And it *hurts*. I'm not some plaything, Emerald. You can't treat me like one."

"It doesn't make me any better than Laird Fenguard, does it?" Emerald stared up at the ceiling with his arms at his sides and his legs extended, just as he had been in the bog. "I should know better. I should know how it feels when people try to erase the parts of you that are inconvenient or uncomfortable or threatening."

I nodded. "You should, and that's what I don't understand. Why are you so quick to dismiss the best you have to offer? When you were with Tincrown, you were the happiest I've ever seen you, and the gentlest. Why is it so easy for you to forget that?"

Emerald licked his lips. "It's what they taught me back home. The rules of *right* and *wrong* were set in stone, and everything I am fell into the latter category."

"Then whoever raised you was a liar," I informed him. "Here, hold out your hand."

He did as I asked, letting one curled fist rest against the pillow beside his head. I let my fingers pass through his and showed him a little of what I'd shown him in the Black Hollow —but only a little. I held back this time, only letting snatches of memory flow between us. A glimpse of Coirpre's grudging admiration. A flash of Tincrown's selfless affection. A snippet of the fear and love I had felt when I found him at the riverside.

Emerald choked and squeezed his eyes shut.

"There," I told him. "*That*'s the truth."

He didn't answer me, and I let our connection linger, replaying those same isolated memories over and over and over again.

"Crimson? Will you do me a favor? I know I don't have any right to ask, but..."

"Stop saying that," I chided. "I'm giving you permission."

He smiled without opening his eyes. "Impertinent." He drew in a deep breath and let it out again, long and slow. "When I forget, will you remind me? Not all the time, but when I start to slip... Remind me." His hand flexed slightly.

"Of course."

Emerald sat up, breaking our connection, and swung his feet out of the bed. "Well, no sense in delaying the inevitable. It's time to start making preparations." He straightened his vest and stared out the little window over the bay, toward the bridge that had brought about the beginning of my life even as it almost ended his. "If Coirpre is setting out on today's ship, we should plan to be on the next one. Give him a head start, just like he asked. And after that—"

He turned to face me, flashing a smile so full of false bravado that he would have done the bard proud. "After that, it's time to go home."

❧

K.C. and I truly hope you enjoyed this Heavenfall novel. We love Crimson and Emerald as much as we hope you do.

Interested to read more in this world? We have a novella that takes place between this book and book three of the Crimson Smoke and the Emerald Flame series called the Tale of Upland Daughter. Find a link to it and many other Heavenfall titles on RileyRookhouse.com

Acknowledgments

From K.C. Norton: The first short story in the September/October 2003 issue of Cicada Magazine is Kim Culbertson's *Sunlight*. I read the story when it came out, and as I write this it is sitting beside me. *Sunlight* was released seven years before Culbertson's first novel. I have no idea where exactly Kim was in her writing journey in 2003, but I can tell you one thing: her short story saved my life. It has saved my life many times since. Reading it again now, it doesn't do much for me, but that doesn't matter. What matters is that this story came into my life precisely when I needed it and told me exactly what I needed to hear.

Emerald's relationship to his mental health, substance abuse, and depression is hard to write. I identify so closely with it. I was the one who suggested that Emerald might cope with his issues by drinking—in part because, at the time, I was doing the same thing.

Riley says that writing this series is just another form of therapy for me, and I'm not sure he's wrong. I want to explore things that I've both experienced and witnessed in ways I don't often see in fiction. If Emerald circles back to his bad habits one time too many... well, there's a reason for that. I hope people will see themselves in Em, and hear the love that the Crimsons of this world have for them. And more than anything else, I hope that this book reaches somebody at the exact right time, like Kim Culbertson's story reached me.

Some days, you have to stay alive so that you can solve a mystery and rescue the town from dark forces (you hope). Other times, you find smaller reasons, like Annie's white cheddar mac and cheese.

From Riley Rookhouse: I'd like to give thanks to all the usual suspects: Amy and Ami for our long bouts of plotting—I owe them so much; Diane Callahan, Story Garden's lead editor; and the Zanesville crew who inspired Heavenfall in the first place.

We have an amazing team over here at Story Garden. I couldn't ask for a more creative and reliable writer than K. C. Norton, who turned an idea I had decades ago into reality, creating characters with such depth that they have become living, breathing people in my mind. I often say that K.C. opened up an emotional vein and bled this story onto the page. You can see it in every word she crafted and every wound she exposed to make these characters more than the sum of their parts.

We're grateful for Angela Traficante's thorough copy editing. Our compliments also go out to the book cover illustrator Hannah Elizabeth who can finally add this cover to her portfolio. As well as letterer James T. Egan of Bookfly Design for his assistance on the cover.

We can't wait to share the rest of the stories in the Crimson Smoke and the Emerald Flame series. And thank you, dear reader, for reading until the very last line.